The Time of Man

ELIZABETH MADOX ROBERTS

THE TIME OF MAN

A Novel

With introductions by
WADE HALL and
ROBERT PENN WARREN
and illustrations by
CLARE LEIGHTON

THE UNIVERSITY PRESS OF KENTUCKY

Publication of this volume was made possible in part by a grant
from the National Endowment for the Humanities.

Scholarly publisher for the Commonwealth,
serving Bellarmine College, Berea College, Centre
College of Kentucky, Eastern Kentucky University,
The Filson Club Historical Society, Georgetown College,
Kentucky Historical Society, Kentucky State University,
Morehead State University, Murray State University,
Northern Kentucky University, Transylvania University,
University of Kentucky, University of Louisville,
and Western Kentucky University.

Editorial and Sales Offices: The University Press of Kentucky
663 South Limestone Street, Lexington, Kentucky 40508-4008

04 03 02 01 00   5 4 3 2 1

Library of Congress Cataloging-in-Publication Data

Roberts, Elizabeth Madox, 1881-1941.
    The time of man / Elizabeth Madox Roberts.
        p. cm.
    ISBN 0-8131-0981-7 (pbk: alk. paper)
    1. Children of migrant laborers—Kentucky—Fiction. 2. Poor
women—Kentucky—Fiction. 3. Kentucky—Fiction. I. Title.

PS3535.O172 T5 2000
813'.52—dc21   99-089766

To

J. L. L. *and* A. Y. W.

INTRODUCTION

by Wade Hall

In a lengthy essay in the March 2, 1963, issue of *The Saturday Review of Literature,* Robert Penn Warren "rediscovers" Elizabeth Madox Roberts's masterpiece, *The Time of Man,* a book that had been virtually forgotten for almost a quarter of a century. Indeed, at her early death of Hodgkin's Disease in 1941 (she was born in 1881 in Perryville, Kentucky, and lived most of her life in nearby Springfield), she had already outlived her popular and critical acclaim.

In addition to Warren, a number of other prominent critics have sought to revive her reputation, including Frederick McDowell, author of the Roberts volume in the Twayne series of American authors in 1963, and the editors of *The Southern Review,* who published a special issue dedicated to her in the fall of 1984. In October of 1981 a Roberts conference was held at Saint Catharine College in Springfield, with scholars, critics, and surviving friends of Roberts in attendance. Perhaps second only to Robert Penn Warren in literary achievement by a Kentuckian, Elizabeth Madox Roberts deserves to be read again in Kentucky and beyond.

The Time of Man was published in 1926 when Roberts was forty-five. Critics who admired her first novel included Joseph Wood Krutch, Mark Van Doren, Edward Wagenknecht, Ford

Madox Ford, and her friend, the novelist Glenway Wescott. It was also made a selection of the Book-of-the-Month Club. Within half a dozen years, she was considered one of the leading contemporary American writers, with five novels and two books of poems to her credit. Before her death she would publish two more novels, two collections of short stories, and another book of poems—all in all, a body of works that could support a significant reputation.

The Time of Man is the story of Ellen Chesser, the daughter of an itinerant Kentucky farm laborer, and her fitful journey toward fulfillment. Indeed, the opening of the novel states two of its major coinciding themes, Ellen's journey to knowledge and selfhood and the archetypal journey of the human family. "Ellen wrote her name in the air with her finger, *Ellen Chesser,* leaning forward and writing on the horizontal plane. Beside her in the wagon her mother huddled under an old shawl to keep herself from the damp, complaining, 'We ought to be a-goen on.'"

The remainder of the novel chronicles in a poetic folk prose Ellen's search for a good life, a modest good life. Her hard journey is littered with unfaithful lovers, unremitting work, painful childbearing, a near suicide, a child's death, and the whipping of her husband by night riders. At the book's end, however, she still has the strength and determination to go on. Her story is the epic story of human survival, with a cast of dozens, and a number of settings and subplots.

It is a Kentucky book to the core, centered in the Knobs country of Nelson, Spencer, and Washington counties, and filled with names familiar to anyone who reads mailboxes in the area—familes named Chesser, Bodine, Wakefield, Edelen, and Carico. The time is an indeterminate period near the turn of the twentieth century before the coming of automobiles. It is a story with its elements stripped to the bare kernel.

Ellen's family is the poorest of the poor. They have no home and few clothes. As the novel opens, Henry and Nellie Chesser and their daughter, Ellen, are stopped at a roadside blacksmith shop to have the broken tongue of their aged, patched-up wagon repaired. They intend to rejoin a wagon convoy of other farm workers. Ellen misses the friendship of Tessie West, a storyteller and folksinger who has four books in her wagon and a large romantic imagination. She longs to see her friend again and rehearses the story she will tell Tessie: "I saw you-all's wagon go on down the road till it got round and a sight littler and seemed like anybody's wagon a-goen anywheres. The country all around got little and narrow and I says to myself, 'The world's little and you just set still in it and that's all there is.'" Ellen is an observant and introspective fourteen-year-old.

While the family is waiting for their wagon to be repaired, a local farmer offers Henry a job setting out tobacco plants for three dollars a day and "a good tight house," with only a few leaks. Henry announces proudly that he is a traveling man, having lived in several Kentucky counties and taken trips down to Tennessee and Georgia, but now, he says, "We are a-looken for a good place to settle down." They move their scant belongings into the rank-smelling cabin and begin a new life, to which Ellen quickly adapts.

Soon she is glad to be rid of the vagrant life and the ridicule she suffered from settled people, who look upon the wagon travelers with suspicion and distrust, calling them "road rats" and "gypsies." Like her people, she has been ignored, scorned, and despised. Now, she, too, is settled and has her own room in the cabin loft and a cot to sleep on. Barefoot and dressed in a colorless, limp dress, she works in the garden and tobacco fields and explores the landlord's property. From a distance she admires his home: "In her mind the house touched something she almost knew. . . . something settled and comforting in her mind, something like a drink of water after an hour of thirst, like a little bridge over a stream that ran out of a thicket, like cool steps going up into a shaded doorway."

But Henry is still a wanderer, "not wanting to take root anywhere," and her family's traveling days are not over. They move to another farm and advance from laborers to sharecroppers, then once more to an abandoned toll house by the side of the road. Ellen is ever the dutiful daughter, moving with the family and doing yeoman's work in the fields and house, obeying her sluggish father and whining mother.

Ellen is, however, maturing physically and intellectually and will soon strike out on her own. Tessie has made her aware of the big world beyond her time and experience, and her consciousness begins to expand. Long familiar with poverty and ugliness, insensitivity and cruelty, she now begins to see the possibilities of joy and happiness. She doesn't want much. "If I only had things to put in drawers and drawers to put things in," she says wistfully. "That's all I'd ask for a time to come." Later, she wonders how fine it would be to sit "up in a buggy with a white plume on my hat and white slippers on my feet."

Sadly, her fantasies are far from becoming reality, and she must suffer the lover's pain and longing before she can begin to set up her own separate life. Living at a time when a woman's identity and meaning were connected to her husband, she is first courted by Joe Trent, a college boy and farmer's son who abandons her for a rich farmer's daughter. Then she meets the love of her life, Jonas Prather, a young farmer who also betrays her for someone else. Her grand passion for Prather, her desperate fight, her thwarted love, her loss, and her searingly real attempts to dislodge and root him from her memory—all are the ingredients of one of the most poignant love stories in

American literature. Finally, however, she meets Jasper Kent, a man she can have. He is friendly and caring and becomes the father of her children, but he has his flaws and betrays her with another woman.

Indeed, Roberts has a good story to tell; and, with a variety of techniques and devices, she tells it convincingly. She knows her Kentucky people and their locale inside out. No one has ever described the seasons and the natural world of Kentucky better, and no one has ever made them a more intricate part of her story. Roberts not only shows her characters in their settings, but she integrates them and shows their interrelationships. Here is how she describes the young Ellen working in the tobacco patch: "In the fields she wore the faded dresses of the summer before, and there, seen distantly, her figure blended evenly with the turned soil or sank into the corn rows, now waist high or more. . . . In the pale washed-out dress she drifted all morning up and down the lines of the tobacco, the tobacco flower come before its season, as the pale flower of the tobacco come to tend its young."

Roberts also uses her own version of the literary device known as the objective correlative to let nature reflect and intensify Ellen's moods. A happy time is described:

She liked to sit in the white clover by the road, away from the after-supper noises of the cabin, a white clover of thought playing over her mind and spreading a sweetness through her flesh, while another, less than thought, lapped folds of being around her. Gentle, inclusive folds of being lay across her shoulders, included her, covered her with vaporous arms, completed her and gathered her into an undefined sheath. She plucked a few clover blossoms and laid them on her skirt, placing them with care. Feeling could not take words, so melted in and merged it was with the flowers of the grass, but if words could have

become grass in Ellen's hand: "It's pretty stuff, clover a-growen. And in
myself I know I'm lovely. It's unknowen how beautiful I am. I'm Ellen
Chesser and I'm lovely."

On the other hand, there are the bad times, such as this one after she has been rebuffed by a boyfriend: "She heard a mockingbird singing in the bushes out toward the lane, singing a futile song which reiterated its uselessness and changed its hollow phrases from moment to moment. The sound fell flat upon a flat air. 'That old mock-bird. I wish he'd shut up,' she whispered."

Other examples of this interconnection of human life and natural life are easy to find. Jonas Prather says to Ellen, "It was in my mind corn-cutten time and after, all along through the hay, to want to ask you to marry." The narration also identifies human life with the seasons: "Life waited for spring and Ellen waited." Or: "The world was hard and impenetrable; the frost stood between herself and Jonas, the cold a barrier, and between herself and Dorine was the frost and the ice. . . ." Finally, Roberts celebrates the people who are naturally in tune with the eternal rhythms of the earth—like the enduring farmers and like the Dominican Brothers at the nearby Abbey of Saint Lucy—all accepting, after hard work, whatever comes, the good and the bad, the lean years and the fat years, the sorrowful as well as the joyful times.

Roberts also employs a number of traditional techniques in telling her story. Digressions in which men tell their life stories are common to the epic and to this novel. A young woman's mysterious suicide is recalled and expanded using incremental repetition, in which an event is retold several times and each time enlarged. Another kind of repetition is Roberts's use of parallel subplots that tell similar stories of love, obsession, and betrayal over and over. Interspersed with her narration and dialogue, Roberts has placed unidentified voices that serve as a kind of community chorus that comments and adds background information. Her close attention to detail is evident from the planting of tobacco to the description of a girl's dress that had "small sewing-machine stitches going in rows up the front and over the shoulder."

Perhaps Roberts's greatest achievement in *The Time of Man*, however, is her accurate and sensitive portrayal of the folklife of the Kentucky knobs, its speech, its songs, its etiquette, its health remedies for man and beast, its games and entertainments. Her people—like the characters of Harriette Arnow, James Still, and Bobbie Ann Mason, to name but a few of Kentucky's best authors—speak a genuine ancestral language which has been passed on by word of mouth for generations. It is filled with archaic words like "roystering" and remnants of earlier verb forms like "a-comen." "I'd as lief walk home" is a way a speaking that some old-timers still understand. It is a poetic folk speech that demands attention. The inverted syntax of such a statement as "Ask no favors, we will" requires that the reader slow down and hear all the words.

In *The Time of Man*, a tragic folk ballad fleshed out into an epic novel, Roberts takes us into an almost mythic folk world. Here are people who live close to the earth and are given to signs and portents. They read the stars and the moon, and springs by the roadside take on mystical meaning. Twenty-six-year-old Jasper Kent knew "the wonder of the light moon and how it drew the herbs and grains, and how the dark moon settled things back into the earth, and he knew the name of the morning star."

The novel has the texture and the aura of a timeless, placeless story—like a tale from the Old World. It is a story of fortune tellers, a woman who sells lovers' charms, a story filled with dreams, fantasies, winds "laden with faint phrases," portents and spells, mysterious walks through the woods, eccentric walkers along the roads and paths, a woman's heroic, futile journey to win her sweetheart, the grand passions of love, hatred, anger, jealousy, vengeance and violence, and hounds baying into the night—all woven seamlessly into a true Kentucky story.

One could call this story of the hardscrabble life of poor farm workers a veritable Kentucky folk pageant or opera, with dancing, storytelling, and singing, with passages that sound like arias, duets, and choruses. Moreover, its ceremonial, bardic style makes it an ageless, placeless story that could just as easily be located in ancient Greece or medieval England. This description of Ellen driving her cow and following the moving wagon suggests the rhythms of an ancient odyssey: "There were herself and the cow, passing forward toward a moving destiny, the wagon, all moving down the turning roads and crossing lanes, going by some genius forward and on. . . . the journey soon moved forward as before, the wagon far ahead and dimly seen up a long vista or lost around a curve, but still the forward-drawing force, and she walked quietly on, bound in the immediate certainty of herself alive and of the little cow moving evenly before her."

Echoes of the Bible are heard throughout the novel, but perhaps most notably when Ellen promises her husband that she will stay by his side all her life. "I'd go where you go and live where you live, all my enduren life," she says, repeating the words of Ruth in the Old Testament. People who pass along the road could have stepped out of a German or English tale: an ancient man known as Old Live-forever; a road gossip called Bell Carrier, who takes two eggs to the store each day to swap for "chewen wax"; a fruit tree salesman named Luke Wimble; and J.B. Tarbell, a carefree wanderer and sometime photographer who woos Ellen with his stories and his mouth harp.

One could hardly start life with more obstacles and fewer opportunities than Ellen Chesser. From the start, however, she affirms life. In the graveyard of a country church, the fourteen-year-old girl muses over the tombstone of a wealthy judge: "He's Judge Gowan in court, a-sitten big, but I'm better'n he is. I'm a-liven and he's dead. I'm better." Amidst sadness, suffering, and heartbreak she maintains her hold on life: "It's no knowen how lovely I am. I'm a-liven. My heart beats on and on and my skin laps around me and my blood runs up and it runs down, shut in me. It's unknowen how lovely."

A part of Ellen's awakening to life is her acceptance of the inevitability of death. Even as a young girl she learns her destiny: "You breathe and breathe, on and on, and then you do not breathe any more. For you forever. Forever. It goes out, everything goes, and you are nothing. The world is all there, on and on, but you are not there, you, Ellen. The world goes on, goes on without you."

It has not been an easy life for her, and Ellen eventually resigns herself to mere survival and the thin hope that life will be better for her children. Her son Dick speaks for the future: "But the wisdom of the world is the dearest thing in life, learnen, and it's my wish to get a hold onto some of that-there. It's found in books, is said, and that's what I know. I couldn't bear to settle down in life withouten I had it. It means as much as all the balance of life, seems like. Books is what I want. In books, it's said, you'd find the wisdom of all the ages." Indeed, this book contains its own large portion of wisdom. And finally you realize that "the time of man" is your own short span on earth, your brief part of the long journey.

Against the backdrop of the timeless earth, Ellen plays out her hour of "the time of man" with steadfastness and heroism. Just when she has the promise of a good life within reach, tragedy strikes. And so the book ends as it began—on the road, a family searching for a good place to live.

The Time of Man offers one of the great experiences in literature. If read slowly and patiently and savored like the many foods at a great feast, Roberts's novel will enrich your life and expand its possibilities.

ELIZABETH MADOX ROBERTS:
LIFE IS FROM WITHIN

by Robert Penn Warren

The Time of Man, a first novel by a spinster of forty-five, was published in 1926. It was received with almost universal acclaim. Edward Garnett flatly described the author as a genius. And such varied admirers as Joseph Wood Krutch, Ford Madox Ford, Robert Morss Lovett, T. S. Stribling, and Glenway Wescott were not much less guarded in their praise. Furthermore, the novel was a best-seller and an adoption of the Book-of-the-Month Club. The next year *My Heart and My Flesh* was, again, a success. By 1930, with the appearance of *The Great Meadow*, the fourth novel, it was impossible to discuss American fiction without reference to Elizabeth Madox Roberts.

By the time of her death in 1941, Elizabeth Madox Roberts had lived past her reputation and her popularity. Now she is remembered only by those who read her in their youth when she was new, and news. The youth of today do not even know her name. *

Elizabeth Madox Roberts was born on October 30, 1881, in the village of Perryville, Kentucky, where one of the

* There have been, in late years, several academic studies of the work of Elizabeth Madox Roberts, one of them quite good, but they have made little impact.

crucial and most bloody battles of the Civil War had been fought, and where her own father, as a raw volunteer of sixteen, had received his baptism of Federal fire. Both the father and mother were of old Kentucky families, now living, in the backwash of war, in what would euphemistically be called reduced circumstances but was, in brutal fact, poverty. Both the father and mother had been teachers, and were lovers of books and carriers of legend. The legends they carried reached back beyond the Civil War—and the grim tale of the cold-blooded murder, by Unionists, of the father's father because he would not join the National Guard—into the time of Boone and the Indian ambush and the opening of the settlements; and the imagination of the daughter Elizabeth was nourished on the long sweep of time from which the individual rises for his moment of effort and testing.

But to the sense of time was added a sense of place. Perryville and the little town of Springfield, to which the family removed when Elizabeth was three, lie in a fertile, well-watered country on the edge of the rich Blue Grass. It was then a quiet country of mixed farming and cattle-breeding, in sight of the Knobs, with the old ways of action, thought, and speech to be found up any lane off the Louisville pike, and sometimes on the pike. There were, too, the local gentry, whose ways were old, though different; and there were the colored people of the alleys and farms, whose ways were old and, again, different. In childhood, in young ladyhood, and later, as a lonely teacher in back-country schools, Elizabeth Madox Roberts learned those old ways. She knew the poetry of this pastoral quietness, but she knew, too, the violence and suffering beneath the quietness. Her stories grew out of the life of the place, and are told in a language firmly rooted in that place.

Stories grow out of place and time, but they also grow, if they are any good, out of the inner struggle of the writer; as Elizabeth Madox Roberts puts it: "Life is from within." So we think of the girl growing up isolated by poverty, dreams, and persistent bad health, trying to find a way for herself, but gradually learning, in what travail of spirit we cannot know except by inference, that hers would not be the ordinary, full-blooded way of the world. And how often in the novels do we find some vital, strong person, usually a man, described as "rich with blood"—and how much ambivalence may we detect behind the phrase?

Over and over again, the heroine of a novel is a young woman who must find a way. There is Ellen Chesser of *The Time of Man*, who struggles in the dire poverty of the poor white, in ignorance, in rejection by the world and by her first lover, toward her spiritual fulfillment. There is Theodosia Bell, of *My Heart and My Flesh*, who suffers in the ruin of her genteel family, in the discovery of the father's licentiousness and of her mulatto sisters and brother, in rejection in love, in frustrated ambition as a musician, in a physical and nervous collapse that draws her to the verge of suicide, but who finds a way back. There is Jocelle, of *He Sent Forth a Raven*, who is trapped in a house of death (as Theodosia is trapped in the house of her aunt), is deprived of her lover, is shocked and fouled by a random rape, but who finds a way.

To return to the life of Elizabeth Madox Roberts, she was thirty-six years old when, after the apparently aimless years of schoolteaching in Springfield and the country around, she took the decisive step that put her on her way, and registered at the University of Chicago. Or perhaps, somewhere in her secret being, during those apparently aimless years, she had already won her victory, and the going to Chicago was only the first fruits of it. In any case, a freshman old enough to be the mother of her classmates, she now found herself moving into the literary life of the university, associating before long with such young writers of talent as Glenway Wescott, Yvor Winters, Janet Lewis, and Monroe Wheeler. She had escaped from Springfield. But she had brought Springfield with her. And after her graduation she went back to Springfield.

She was forty years old. On the surface she had little enough to show for what Springfield must have regarded as her eccentric adventure, only a Phi Beta Kappa key and a handful of little poems; but beneath the surface she carried the confirmed faith in her vocation. In 1922, the year when the handful of poems was published as a volume called *Under the Tree*, she began work on *The Time of Man*. In it are the sweep of time, the depth and richness of place, and the echo of her own struggle to find identity and a way. These things were the gifts her experience had given. What she brought to the book was the deep awareness of the worth of these gifts, an awareness that, because it dramatizes the elements and fuses them in their inwardness, amounts to the moment of genius.

As she put it in her journal, Elizabeth Madox Roberts had originally thought of "the wandering tenant farmer of our region as offering a symbol for an Odyssy [*sic*] of man as a wanderer, buffetted about by the fates and weathers." But by the time she began to write, the main character was Ellen Chesser, the daughter of such a man, and we see her, in the opening sentence of the novel, aged fourteen, sitting in the broken-down wagon of their wanderings, writing her name on the empty air with her finger. This "Odyssy" is, essentially, a spiritual journey, the journey of the self toward the deep awareness of identity which means peace. As for the stages of the journey, again we may turn to the journal:

I. A Genesis. She comes into the land. But the land rejects her. She remembers Eden (Tessie).

II. She grows into the land, takes soil or root. Life tries her, lapses into loveliness—in the not-lover Trent.

III. Expands with all the land.

IV. The first blooming.

V. Withdrawal—and sinking back into the earth.

VI. Flowering out of stone.*

The numbering here refers not to chapters, but to the stages of the basic movements of the story; and the movements might, as I have earlier suggested, be taken as the form of the characteristic story in the other novels, a story which the author took to be, to adapt the phrasing of one of the reviewers, an emblem of the common lot, of the time of man. Rather, what is common to all men is the basic problem from which this story springs; the solution of the problem, as we find it here, gives the story only of those who have the strength to survive the shocks of the world and have the fortitude to take the inner journey by which one may learn to convert the wound into wisdom.

The abstract pattern given in the journal is, in the novel

* The references to the journal are drawn from *Herald to Chaos*, by Earl H. Rovit.

itself, fleshed out in the story of Ellen Chesser. In the life of shiftless wandering she yearns for a red wagon that won't break down. Later, as she passes by the solid farmhouses set amid maples and sees the farmers on sleek horses or encounters their wives with suspicion in their glance, and learns that she is outcast and alienated, she yearns for things by which to identify herself. "If I only had things to put in drawers and drawers to put things in," she says, remembering herself begging old clothes at the door of a rich house. And later still, when she has found her man, she dreams of "good land lying out smooth, a little clump of woodland, just enough to shade the cows at noon, a house fixed, the roof mended, a porch to sit on when the labor was done"—all this a dream never to come quite true.

What does come true in the end—after the betrayal by her first love, after the struggle against the impulse to violence and suicide, after love and childbearing, after unremitting work and the sight of reward tantalizingly just out of reach, after betrayal by the husband and reconciliation over the body of a dead child, after the whipping of her husband, by night riders, as a suspected barn-burner—is the discovery of the strength to deal with life. "I'll go somewhere far out of hearen of this place," her husband says, nursing his stripes. "I've done little that's amiss here, but still I'd have to go. . . . I aim to go far, so far that word from this place can't come there or not likely. . . ." And she says: "I'd go where you go and live where you live, all my enduren life." So they take to the road again: "They went a long way while the moon was still high above the trees, stopping only at some creek to water the beasts. They asked no questions of the way but took their own turnings."

Thus the abstract pattern is fleshed out with the story of

Ellen, but the story itself is fleshed out by her consciousness. What lies at the center of the consciousness is a sense of wonder. It is, in the beginning, the wonder of youth and unlettered ignorance, simple wonder at the objects of the world, at the strange thing to be seen at the next turn of the road or over the next hill, at the wideness of the world, sometimes an "awe of all places," and a "fear of trees and stones," sometimes a wonder at the secret processes of the world, as when her father tells her that rocks "grow," that some have "shells printed on the side and some have little snails worked on their edges," and that once he "found a spider with a dragon beast in a picture on its back." But all the wonder at the wideness and age and ways of the world passes over into wonder at the fact of self set in the midst of the world, as when in a lonely field Ellen cries out against the wind, "I'm Ellen Chesser! I'm here!" Or as when, standing in a cemetery by the grave of a judge long dead, she bursts out: "I'm a-liven."

Beyond naïve wonder and the deeper wonder at the growth of selfhood, there is a sense of life as ceremony, as ritual even in the common duties, as an enactment that numinously embodies the relation of the self to its setting in nature, in the human community, and in time. Take, for example, the scene where Ellen is engaged in the daily task of feeding the flock of turkeys—turkeys, by the way, not her own:

She would take the turkey bread in her hand and go, bonnetless, up the gentle hill across the pasture in the light of sundown, calling the hens as she went. She was keenly aware of the ceremony and aware of her figure rising out of the fluttering birds, of all moving together about her. She would hear the mules crunching their fodder

*as she went past the first barn, and she would hear the swish of
the falling hay, the thud of a mule hoof on a board, a man's
voice ordering or whistling a tune. . . . She would crumble down
the bread for each brood near its coop and she would make the count
and see to the drinking pans. Then she would go back through the
gate, only a wire fence dividing her from the milking group, and
walk down the pasture in the dusk. That was all; the office would
be over.*

This sense of ritual, here explicit for the only time but
suffusing the book, is related to the notion of "telling."
Ritual makes for the understanding of experience in relation to the community of the living and the dead; so does
"telling." Ellen, when the family first drops aside from the
life of the road, yearns to see her friend Tessie, one of the
wanderers, for in "telling" Tessie of the new life she would
truly grasp it. Or the father sits by the fire and tells his life:
"That's the story of my life, and you wanted to know it."
Or Jonas, the lover who is later to jilt Ellen, makes his
courtship by a "telling" of his sin. And later on, Jasper
"would come that night and tell her the story of his life
and then, if she was of a mind to have him, they would get
married."

The novel is not Ellen's own "telling," but it is a shadow
of her telling. The language, that is, is an index of her
consciousness, and as such is the primary exposition of her
character and sensibility. But it is also the language of her
people, of her place and class, with all the weight of history
and experience in it. We can isolate turns and phrases that
belong to this world: "She let him take all she's got and
when he's gone she pukes up a pile of hard words after him
for a spell." Or: ". . . if he comes again and takes off the

property he'll maybe have trouble and a lavish of it too." Or: "I got no call to be a-carryen water for big healthy trollops. Have you had bad luck with your sweethearten?" But it is not the color of the isolated turn that counts most. It is, rather, the rhythm and tone of the whole; and not merely in dialogue, but in the subtle way the language of the outer world is absorbed into the shadowy paraphrase of Ellen's awareness, and discreetly informs the general style. For instance, as she sits late by the fire with her first love, Jonas, with her father snoring away in the bed across the room:

The mouse came back and ate the crumbs near the chairs. Ellen's eyes fell on the little oblong gray ball as it rolled nearer and nearer. Jonas was sitting up with her, tarrying. It was a token. She looked at his hand where it lay over her hand in her lap, the same gaze holding the quiet of the mouse and the quiet of his hand that moved, when it stirred, with the sudden soft motions of the little beast. The roosters crowed from farm to farm in token of midnight and Henry turned in his sleep once again.

It is, all in all, a dangerous game to play. In a hundred novels for a hundred years we have seen it go sour, either by condescension or by the strain to exhibit quaint and colorful locutions—which is, in fact, a symptom of condescension. But in *The Time of Man* it is different. For one thing, the writer's ear is true, as true as, for example, that of Eudora Welty, Caroline Gordon, Andrew Lytle, Erskine Caldwell (at times), William Faulkner, or George W. Harris, the creator of Sut Lovingood. Like all these writers, who differ so much among themselves, Elizabeth Madox Roberts is able to relate, selectively, the special language to her own special vision. For another thing, the language is not a façade over nothingness, like the false front of a nonexistent second story of the general store on the main street of a country town. It is, rather, the language of a person, and a society, which is realized in the novel with a sober actuality.

If *The Time of Man*—or *My Heart and My Flesh* for that matter—is as good as I think it is, how did it happen to disappear so soon, almost without a bubble to mark the spot? We may remember, however, that this is not the first good book, or writer, to go underground. There is, for one thing, what we may call the natural history of literary reputation. When a writer dies we find, immediately after the respectful obsequies, the ritual of "reassessment"—which is another word for "cutting-down-to-size." In the case of Elizabeth Madox Roberts the ordinary situation was aggravated by the fact that her later work had declined in critical and popular esteem. The firm grip on social and individual actualities which undergirded the poetry of sensibility in the first two novels had, in the later work, been progressively relaxed. More and more we find a dependence on allegory and arbitrary symbolism; and with the natural base cut away, the poetry degenerates into prettification and preciosity.

Furthermore, this situation—which, we may hazard, had some relation to the writer's gradual withdrawal into illness —was in a setting which would, in any case, have made for the rejection of even her earlier work. It was the period when a critic as informed as David Daiches could reject Conrad because, at least as Daiches believed, he "does not concern himself at all with the economic and social background underlying human relationships." Or when Herbert Muller could reject Flaubert as irrelevant to the age. Or when Maxwell Geismar could reject Faulkner as a "dissipated talent" and the victim of a "cultural psychosis," explaining that in him "the heritage of American negation reaches its final emphasis." So we can see why *The Time of Man* fell out of fashion: the novel presents Ellen Chesser, not in active protest against the deprivation and alienation of the life of the sharecropper, but in the process of coming to terms, in a personal sense, with the tragic aspect of life.

The agenda of the 1930s carried many items bearing on the urgent need to change the social and economic environment but none bearing on the need to explore the soul's relation to fate. Any literary work that was concerned with an inward victory was, in certain influential quarters, taken as subtle propaganda against any effort directed toward outward victory. It was as though one had to choose between the "inner" and the "outer."

What was true in the world of literature was more vindictively true in the world of actuality. There, even when the awareness of the desperate need for changing the economic and social arrangements was coupled with an awareness of the worth of the individual who was a victim of the existing order, the tendency was to accept the graph, the statistic, the report of a commission, the mystique of "collectivism," as the final reality. The result was that, in that then fashionable form of either-or thinking, the inner world of individual experience was as brutally ignored as by an overseer on a Delta cotton farm.

It is now possible that we are growing out of this vicious either-or thinking. We may now see that we do not need to choose, and that if we do choose, in anything more than a provisional, limited sense, we are denying reality and are quite literally verging toward lunacy. And verging, in fact, toward a repetition of the bloodiest crimes of this century.

Elizabeth Madox Roberts says that "Life is from within," and her typical story is, to repeat, the story of an inner victory. In dealing with the dispossessed of the South she has, like Eudora Welty or Faulkner or Katherine Anne Porter or James Agee (to refer to a document of the 1930s, *Let Us Now Praise Famous Men*), recognized the dignity of the lowliest creature. But she knew that to recognize fully the dignity of any creature demands that we recognize the anguish of the collision with actuality. So in the story of Ellen Chesser we find no scanting of the grimness of fact, of the pinch of hunger, of the contempt in the eyes met on the road, of the pain of the lash laid on the bare back.

She was aiming, she wrote in her journal, at a fusion of the inner and the outer, at what she called "poetic realism":

Somewhere there is a connection between the world of the mind and the outer order—it is the secret of the contact that we are after, the point, the moment of union. We faintly sense the one and we know as faintly the other, but there is a point where they come together, and we can never know the whole of reality until we have these two completely.

This is as good a description as any of what, in *The Time of Man*, Elizabeth Madox Roberts was trying to make of Ellen Chesser's story, a story of the moments of contact between the self and the world. The novel is, in a sense, a pastoral, but only a false reading would attribute to it the condescension, the ambiguous humility on the part of writer and reader, and the sentimentally melancholy acceptance of the *status quo*, which often characterize the pastoral. No, it is the inner reality of Ellen and of her people in the contact with the world that, in the end, makes social protest significant, makes social justice "just."

Perhaps now, after the distortions of the 1930s and the sicknesses of the 1940s and '50s, we can recover *The Time of Man*. Perhaps we can even find in it some small medicine against the special sickness and dehumanizing distortions of the 1960s. Perhaps we can profit from the fact that Elizabeth Madox Roberts came, to adapt the lines by Yeats on John Synge,

> *Towards nightfall upon a race*
> *Passionate and simple like* her *heart.*

The Time of Man

I

ELLEN wrote her name in the air with her finger, *Ellen Chesser*, leaning forward and writing on the horizontal plane. Beside her in the wagon her mother huddled under an old shawl to keep herself from the damp, complaining, "We ought to be a-goen on."

"If I had all the money there is in the world," Ellen said, slowly, "I'd go along in a big red wagon and I wouldn't care if it taken twenty horses to pull it along. Such a wagon as would never break down." She wrote her name again in the horizontal of the air.

"Here's a gypsy wagon broke down!" Some little boys ran up to the blacksmith shop, coming out of the field across the road. "Oh, Alvin, come on, here's horse-swappers broke down," one called.

Ellen's father was talking with a farmer, and the boys

were staring, while the blacksmith pecked from time to time with his tools, the sounds muffled in the wet air. A voice complained, "We ought to be a-goen on."

The farmer said that he would pay three dollars a day for work that week. Henry Chesser stood with one foot on the hub of the wagon, thinking over the offer, drifting, his slow speech a little different from the farmer's slow speech.

"I look for rain again tonight," the farmer said, "and tomorrow will be a season. This is likely the last season we'll have, and so, as I say, I'll pay for help and I'll pay right. But the man I hire has got to work. Three dollars a day you can have. You can take it or leave it. As I say you can have three dollars and that-there house over in the place to stay in. It's a good tight house. Leaks a little, hardly to speak of."

Ellen and her mother sat still on the wagon while Henry decided. Later they drove up the wet road, following the farmer, who rode a sleek horse.

As night came they brought the bedding in from the wagon and prepared to sleep on the floor. Henry tied his two horses to a locust tree off by the creek and these began at once to eat the grass about their feet, biting hurriedly. Ellen was told to lie beside her mother on the quilts, her father lying beyond. The strangeness of the house troubled her, the smell of rats and soot. When she lay on the floor in the dark beside her snoring parents, she thought of Tessie, gone on in the wagon with Jock, sleeping she could not think where that night but not far off, on the road to Rush-field, in some open space by a bridge, perhaps, with the Stikes wagon near, and Screw Brook and Connie a little way on down the pike, the horses grazing about wherever they could. She would have something to tell Tessie when her father's wagon overtook the others. She recited in her mind the story of the adventure as she would tell it. Her thin, almost emaciated body fitted flat against the cabin floor, lying flatter and thinner than the tall bent woman stretched out beside her.

"After you-all went the blacksmith worked on our wagon tongue a long spell before he got it fixed. A farmer came up alongside the wagon and talked to Pappy about work in his patch. You could smell the iron when it went in the tub red hot and you could smell horse hoof. I saw you-all's wagon go on down the road till it got round and a sight littler and seemed like anybody's wagon a-goen anywheres. The country all around got little and narrow and I says to myself, 'The world's little and you just set still in it and that's all there is. There ain't e'er ocean,' I says, 'nor e'er city nor e'er river nor e'er North Pole. There's just the little edge of a wheat field and a little edge of a blacksmith shop with nails on the ground, and there's a road a-goen off a little piece with puddles of water a-standen, and there's mud,' I says. When it rained Mammy pulled up the storm sheet. The farmer kept a-walken up and down and a-looken at the sky. 'I need a hand tomorrow and I'm a-goen to pay well,' he says. He'd put his hands inside his pockets and say, 'You can take it or leave it.' And then he climbed up on his big black critter and made like he was gone. 'If that-there gal's any good a-worken she can have twenty-five cents a hour, and the woman too.' Pappy said, 'I don't allow to work my old woman. The youngone can. She can do a sight in a day.' Then towards dark we went down the pike and off up a little dirt road to the house the farmer said we could have all night, and we dragged our bed in on the

11

floor. It was a poor trash house. There was water a-runnen down the wall by the chimney flue and a puddle on the floor off on the yon side of the fireplace, but we kept dry. You could hear the rain all night a-fallen on the roof and a-drippen on the floor, and it was a fair sound. The house was a one-room house, an o'nary place, but before night I saw a cubbyhole against the chimney and a cubbyhole is good to put away in. The chimney was made outen rocks and it had soot smells a-comen outen it, and there was Negro smells a-comen out from back in the corners. When it came on to rain Pappy went out and put the critters under a shed."

The next morning a mist was spreading over the farm, but the rain was over. As soon as he had eaten from the supply of food in the wagon, Henry went off without a word. Ellen watched him cross the creek at the watergap and go up the fencerow toward the farmhouse. Her mother sat in the door of the cabin and waited.

" If you're a mind to drap you better be a-goen up there," she said. "You better leave your shoes behind you. Baccer setten is a muddy time."

Ellen hid her shoes in the wagon. She took off her outer skirt, a dark blue garment, and folded it neatly over the shoes, for Tessie had given her the skirt. The garment removed, she stood clothed in a drab-green waist and a short gray cotton petticoat. She went up the fencerow, the way her father had gone, shy at being between fences, at being penned in a field, a little uncomfortable for the beans and bacon she had eaten, uncertain as to which way to go and as to what was expected of her.

At the top of the field she found the laborers assembled. The farmer had drawn plants out of the bed earlier in the

12

morning, and he gave a basket of these to Ellen, showing her how to drop them along the rows, how to space them by an accurate guess. The men who set the plants into the ground followed her. They made a hole in the soft earth with a round stick and pushed the plant into the hole, squeezing the mud about it with the left hand, bending along the rows, almost never straightening from row end to row end. Ellen walked ahead of the men, dropping a plant first to right and then to left, completing the farmer's field and leading a procession over a rolling hill, her bare feet, red from the sun and the dew, sinking into the mud where the field lay lowest. Her father and a grown boy named Ezra were those who worked behind her. In the mid-morning her mother came slowly, aimlessly, up the fencerow. The farmer offered her twenty-five cents an hour to take his place at the plant bed. "You could sit here on this board and be right comfortable and be earnen a little pin money besides. There won't be more'n a hour or two of it and then a rest."

"I might work for a spell," she said.

At noon they sat under a tree by a fence and waited until food was brought from the farmhouse. The farmer himself came with a basket, his wife following with a coffeepot and some cups. The farmer displayed his offering, bread and pieces of ham dripping hot. There was milk to go in the cups after the coffee and there were fried potatoes and stewed peas. The farmer's wife stayed only a moment, mopping her face, and the farmer said, pointing to the basket, "Here's a pie when you-all are ready for it, and if anybody wants any more helpens all he has to do is to ask. I always feed my hands well." Then he too went back up to the house.

Their fingers were brown on the white bread. They ate

13

shyly, making at first as if they hardly cared to eat at all, picking meagerly at the bread, letting the peas stand untasted in the tin pail. Ezra said:

"I allow you-all are foreigners."

"We are on our way a-travelen. We are a-looken for a good place to settle down," Henry said.

"Is the place where you-all come from a far piece from here?"

"A right far piece."

"I allow you-all been all the way maybe to Green County, or maybe to Hardin or Larue."

"Larue! I been all the way to Tennessee and then on to Georgia."

An expression of wonder.

"I been all the way to Tennessee and then on to Georgia and back once and on to Tennessee once again. Me and my old woman and that-there gal there, all three of us. Say, old woman, I'm plum a fool about peas. Let's have some outen that bucket there."

"But before that I lived in Taylor County," Henry said after the peas had been eaten.

After the hour spent by the tree the work went forward again. Ellen caught the rhythm of her task and rested upon it, gaining thus a chance to look about her a little. The farmhouse stood off among tall trees, a yellow shape with points here and there, two red chimneys budding out of the roof. In her mind the house touched something she almost knew. The treetops above the roof, the mist in the trees, the points of the roof, dull color, all belonging to the farmer, the yellow wall, the distance lying off across a rolling cornfield that was mottled with the wet and traced with lines of low corn —all these touched something settled and comforting in

14

her mind, something like a drink of water after an hour of thirst, like a little bridge over a stream that ran out of a thicket, like cool steps going up into a shaded doorway. That night she lay again on the quilts on the cabin floor beside her mother. Her shoulders ached from carrying the basket all day and her feet were sore from the sun and the mud. Until two weeks before, when her father had bought her shoes at a country store, she had gone barefoot for many months, and her feet were tough and hard, but the mud had eaten into the flesh. When she had returned from the field at sundown she had found that someone had stolen her shoes from the wagon. Her folded skirt had been thrown aside and the shoes were gone, but nothing else had been taken. Lying on the quilts she thought again of Tessie. Her closed eyes saw again the objects of the day in the field, the near mud over which she bent, her feet pulling in and out of it, little grains of soil swimming past her tired eyes. The farmer was there with his stiff legs and square butt, bending over the plant bed, urging everyone forward, trying to be both familiar and commanding. Across the mud and the swimming grains of soil ran his yellow house, off past trees, ran mist, roof-shapes, bobolinks over a meadow, blackbirds in locust trees, bumblebees dragging their bodies over red clover.

"Nine hours I worked and made two dollars and a quarter, but shoes cost two dollars. I'll have a heap to tell Tessie."

A faint sinking came to her breast. What if her father couldn't catch up with Jock after he left Rushfield? She knew that Jock did not care whether he caught up or not, that Henry was but a meek hanger-on of the cavalcade, unbelonging. Her father's voice came back, floating under the spell of the farmer, "Monday is a court day in Rushfield and

I can't very well see my way clear to work that day. I got a right smart to do in town a Monday. I got to meet my partner . . ." Henry's voice, wavering. Then the farmer, "Now see here. I'm afeared the season can't last over to Tuesday. I can't work my hands on a Sunday. Some men can but by golly I'm placed so's I can't. I'll give you four dollars to stay and set for me Monday and the gal thirty cents a hour . . ."

The grains of dust floated before her weary eyes, under the lids, and flecks of mud caked into heavy lumps, impeding and clodding. Ants walked over the warm mud and worms lay dead in the sun or turned crawling back into the soil.

It was not until Sunday that Henry Chesser brought the grub box in from the wagon. Nellie, his wife, set out the things on the mantel over the fireplace, and she and Ellen built a fire and cooked over it, frying bacon and making a corn pone. Henry turned his two horses into the pasture at the farmer's suggestion. After he had eaten of the bacon and the pone, Henry lay on the ground in the shade of the house and Nellie sat in the doorway watching the yellow lane down which a few people passed during the morning. She began to smoke a cob pipe, wheedling the tobacco from her husband. When they were quiet, Ellen went off through the underbrush along the creek and waded across the stream behind a screen of willows. She saw her work of yesterday, ragged and new, the plants set where she had dropped them. Today it would rain again and tomorrow there would be the rest of the field to plant. She could hear the loud cackling of the hens over toward the barn and the farmer's house, a high fluted sound spreading over the farm. She saw Mr. Hep Bodine—the farmer—stroll down the fencerow beside the tobacco, looking at his field, stopping to look, walking jerkily on. He wore a pale shirt that stuck out of his vest stiffly—his Sunday clothes. She hid in a thick clump of brush until he went back up the hill, for she was afraid he might ask her what she was doing, or he might order her back to the cabin. Sometimes men cursed her when she walked on their land—"You damned little road rat, get out of here." Mr. Hep might not; he was going to pay her thirty cents an hour tomorrow to drop plants for his men, but she felt safer in the brush.

"If only some o'nary trash hadn't stole my shoes," she said when a thorn drove into her heel and sent cold quivers of pain to the very roots of her hair. She bit hard at her cheeks and lips and waited until the tremors passed out of her flesh. "It's o'nary to steal," she said. "It's right low down, now, right wrong. You dasn't steal from your own set. That-there would be awful wrong, and I reckon it's wrong nohow. It's wrong to the folks that lose the stuff and that makes it come around wrong to the body that takes it. Only if a man's got so much he never misses what you take, why then it seems like it might maybe not be wrong, only you can't tell whe'r a man is a-goen to miss it or not and so it's wrong, I reckon, no matter."

A deeper whisper came in her mind suddenly, so sharp as to have the force of another speaker: "What about the times you took things yourself? Eggs sometimes, more'n often. What about the chicken? Wood, if you call that-there stealen?"

"Pappy don't steal, not a lick, nor Joe and Jock. If they did they'd get put in jail and it takes a sight of money to get

17

outen jail. The Stikes youngones are always a-finden things. If they see a thing it's lost for sure and they find it right off." She liked to dwell on this last idea to deny the hard voice any interval for speech.

"Sometimes you been a-finden things," it rolled out, unbidden. Her brain felt very cold and hard. Cold spread back to the base of her head. She had found things. Tessie knew, or maybe Tessie knew. But sometimes it was so cold they must have a fire, her mind argued with its knowledge. Oh, bitter burning in fingers that were like sticks, shivering body and no underwear. Cold, even in Tennessee, but warm when one got under the covers, other bodies lying close. But the eggs and the chicken, that was more. You had to go out of your way to get them. That was just plain stealing any way you looked at it.

"But you have to eat. Your belly makes you do it," her lips said.

The land lay rolling in large plates, some of them green with high wheat, some faintly crisscrossed with corn rows, some in pasture. She kept among the bushes as long as she could, going toward the house by indirect ways. She found some wild strawberries in an upper pasture on a hillside and many of these she ate as she passed. Higher up a fenceline she came to a wild apple tree with little knotty green apples hanging, and she ate two of these, wishing for salt. The yellow house allured her but she dared not approach it directly. She wondered if the farmer knew about the dull roof, now sharp in the sun, and if he knew how the yellow gables came out of the tree boughs, all set and still, fixed behind boughs, gables fitting into each other, snug and firm. Going up and down roads she had seen many houses, the angles turning with the turning of roads. Up the fence

18

tangle, creeping and worming, she went now, to lie at last among tall weeds just beyond the vegetable garden. A horse, hitched to a two-seated buggy, was tied to a post beside the house. At the side doorstep a shepherd dog lay in the sun, but once he lifted his head and growled lazily. After a little the farmer and two women came from the house and climbed into the buggy, calling impatiently to someone. Then a grown girl hurried out and climbed into the buggy beside the man. There was a brief dispute and an argument with gestures, and then the girl got down from her seat and went crossly into the house.

"No use to lock the front door," she called back.

"Every last one," the farmer said, making his voice sharp and loud. "It pays not to take chances with people like that on the place."

The girl came out of the side door, locking it after her. She hid the key under the doorstep, brushing aside the old dog to tilt the step a little. Then she drew on long gloves and climbed into the buggy again, and the farmer pulled the lines tight and drove away. They were going to church; they had little black Bibles in their hands.

Ellen pushed her brown bare feet through the tall grass and snaked her way down the fence to the front of the garden. She could see the front wall of the house now as well as the side, and the trees that had belonged to the gables when she had seen the house from the field now stood off along a fence to the rear. They no longer attached themselves to the house, but rather they grew in a row along a barnlot enclosure and held a wire fence. There was no avenue reaching up from the highroad and no shrubs grew near the stark yellow walls. The paint was hard and sharp in the sun. She remembered sweeping avenues outlined with

19

trees, reaching back from roads she had traveled in the wagon. She remembered vines on walls and high shrubs and rose arbors, peeped at through fences or snatched in quick visions from over palings or hedges.

"Hep Bodine's got a poor trash sort of house," she said. She stuck out her tongue at the yellow wall and made three ugly faces at the bare prim lawn. She laughed a long laugh at Hep Bodine, and when she had finished she laughed another long ugly laugh at Hep Bodine's wife. Then she turned away from their premises, singing a jargon of many phrases that were remembered for the pictures they preserved or the tones they carried.

> Hounds on my track,
> Chicken on my back.
> Oh, Brother Andrew have you got a G fiddle string?'
> Oh, Brother Andrew, have you got a G string?

She was walking down the upper pasture, bending back and stepping high, her feet cringing at the hot stones but her body setting them down without heed or mercy. She played a short while with one of the colts in the enclosure, making friends with him easily, for she knew the ways of horses. She knew why he kicked up his heels and ran a little way, and she knew what his soft muzzle meant in her hand and what his soft biting lips and his tossing forelock. She kissed his forehead with her forehead, pushing hard. She ran with him down the pasture, screaming and jeering a wild man-animal talk, forgetting her fear of fences which enclosed land. When she remembered and went back to the brush, the colt followed her there. She knew little of the cows that grazed about in the pasture, knew only horses and dogs, the animals of roads.

A pain lay in her chest, under her breath, tokening something impending. There was something to do, something to happen. She thought that if she only had some bread or an egg she would not go to the cabin at all during the day, for she knew what there was to eat, beans and bread and fat bacon—old bread. If only she had an egg, cool and juicy. You could slip in your hand and take an egg. The creek came out of a steep valley that was grown with bushes and trees, making a ravine which wound back into the hills. She saw into the curves of the ravine and went slowly over the creek sand, thinking: your hand would slip into the straw and there would be the egg. Blackbirds were chiming in the trees at the edge of the tobacco field and the bobolinks of yesterday were still busy over the meadow. Up in the narrow ravine she sat with her feet in the water, as still as stone, waiting for the life which her coming had disturbed to return. Presently a snake came out from under a white rock, making a sigh in a tuft of water grass. It went off down stream, flowing more quickly than the water. Your hand would glide in over the straw and you would hardly know when it happened, she thought, and then the egg would be running down your throat. She watched the gray waterbugs walking in the sandy mud under the still pool. They floated more than they walked and they made faint trails in the slime. Where the water ran over a stone it had a low purring sound like children talking far off, little children saying,

> *I found one.*
> *I found one too.*
> *Look at mine!*

Her mind lay back among the people she had left two days before; the people made a certainty which spread back of her strange new sensations that were derived from the fields. Scraps of talk, lodged in mind, loomed out now in unprepared moments.

"Eleven. They've got eleven youngones, eleven brats now."

"What they think they are? White rats? Belgium hares?"

This was Screw and Connie and their talk. Screw and Connie in a fight Tuesday, talking loud and throwing things. Screw whipped Connie and knocked her down often, and then she would hide her razor in her dress and swear she would kill him when he came back, but, next day, she would be washing his dirty shirt in the creek and singing a song:

And I fancied I could trace
Just a tear on her dear face. . . .

She was thinking about Connie and Screw when she climbed over a watergap and went higher up the creek. A hunger pulled at her inner part in spite of the strawberries and the two green apples, and this hunger she could separate from the pain that lay under her breath, but she did not wish to go back to the cabin and see her father and mother, the one lying leg-weary in the shade, the other sitting listlessly in the door, smoking the pipe. When her father waked they would talk a little:

"Wonder where Jock and Joe is by today?"

"On the road down below Rushfield a piece. I could catch up in three hours or a little more if I was of a mind to."

"And Eva Stikes as like as not has got on her red head rag and is a-tellen fortunes to the Briartown niggers."

"And her hoop earbobs on, maybe."

"And Tessie is a-palaveren, wherever she is. I never see such a vigrous woman to palaver."

Her mother and father whipped her for running off to

22

Tessie's wagon. Now she sat by the water of a pool, stirring the mud with a stick and thinking of Tessie. Tessie was always ready to take notice. "Hear that-there redbird!" she'd say, and she would walk like a street parade when she told about a circus. Her eyes would round big when she would say, "Oh, Grannie, what makes your ears so big? To hear you the better, my child." She was all for tree-shaded avenues and stone gateposts and people walking down to sundials to tell the time of day, and even for horses they bought and sold every week. "I don't know what you see in that-there old carcass," Jock would say, and Tessie would be rubbing the critter's nose and looking into his eyes. She was married to Jock, Jock West; some said she was only taken-up with him, like Screw and Connie. The cathedral at Nashville, a great church, came into her mind. Once Tessie slipped her away and took her there to see—it was twittering candles and great music running down suddenly into little music and people swaying all together until there was a river running through the church, up and down, and her heart surged in her breast. She and Tessie sat on a back seat watching. Another time they had stood beyond a paling when a white-robed man called in a voice rich with music, "Oh, Brother Andrew, have you got a G string?" Some nights sitting around the fire Tessie was so shiny you could hardly take your eyes off her. . . . Hanging her clothes up on a wire fence to dry, stepping quick, no shoes and stockings on. "Tessie is our kind of folks," she said.

She stirred the mud with a forked stick, thinking of Tessie's voice, hard and tight in a curse, pushing the curse down at all four corners and holding it steady, coming not often—Tessie was full of ways and plans and she did not have to curse much. But sometimes when a wagon stuck

23

in the mud and they could never budge it for a whole day, then she did, and once when Connie said she was sweet on Screw. "God-almighty for God's sake! A damn little I think of Screw. Thick neck! Always a-knocken down. Connie can have Screw. Damn Screw!"

Ellen went further up the creek, jumping from white stone to white stone, feeling safe in the narrow ravine hidden among the willow bushes. She heard quails calling over in the fields, and farm sounds came into the hollow, a calf or a mule crying out. After a little she knew that the farmer had come back from church; sounds heard less than felt told her this, echoes in the hillside, screen doors slamming in the right-hand bushes and rocks. She found a dead snake still bloody from his wounds and this made her think of the man Screw had killed—blood and the breath gone out. She turned the snake over and over to see it writhe, pity and wonder and cruelty in her mind. Screw had killed a man. Haldeen Stikes said he had killed two, but you never dared speak of it even if you called it one. Her father had whipped her once for asking, "Did Screw kill a man?"

The day clouded over and rain gathered in the sky. Ellen lay on a large rocky shelf, tired from wandering. Her thin flanks sank against the white stone and her stringy legs quivered with their exhaustion. Her closed eyes saw the book out of which Eva Stikes had learned to tell the fortunes, a little green book, rolled at the corners and dirty, smelling of snuff-dip. Eva had sent ten cents for it; it had come from Batavia, Illinois. "Gives lucky and unlucky days, interprets dreams, tells fortunes by all methods, cards, palmistry, tea-cup zodialogy," was printed on the paper cover. The picture on the back of the fortune book looked very much like Eva herself, for Eva's mouth sank together

24

where her teeth were gone. Tessie knew all about Eva's youngones; she had six dead, but four were living. A high thin voice and a low deep voice took turns in memory:

"Mammy, I want to eat."

"Well, go to the grub box."

"There ain't e'er bite there, I been."

"Well, ask Joe Stikes to feed you, he's your daddy."

HENRY CHESSER drove the mower up and down the clover field, cutting the hay for Mr. Bodine. Ellen lay on a bed of the cut grass under a cloudy sky and rested her tired muscles, her mind at ease, her body glad for the day of rest before the long jolting of the wagon should begin again. She looked at the clover narrowly, minutely, trying to see it as ants see, as bees. She piled cool clover on her face and felt the smell come and go until sense was drugged and there was no odor left in the blossoms. Henry was singing as he drove the clinking instrument up and down the field, his song coming when the machine ran easily along the clear sweeps of hay and checking itself when the horses turned and the blades must be matched to the uncut corners. She was amused to hear her father singing loud and rolling out long high "ohs" to keep the song a little longer in his mouth.

> *As I went up the new-cut road,*
> *Tired team and a heavy load—oh . . .*
> *Cracked my whip and the leader sprung,*
> *Bid farewell to the wagon tongue—oh. . . .*

She would be telling Tessie about the hay field, perhaps tomorrow, at any rate by the day after. "Warm smells a-steamen up and a lark a-singen when he hopped up on a snag tree, and Pappy a-whistlen when the team goes down the field. A hay field is a good singen place now. But a baccer patch, who wants to be a-singen in baccer! I just wish you could 'a' seen Pappy a-sitten up big on that-there rake and a-whistlen to fair split his sides. I didn't say e'er a word or let on like I hear. If I'd taken notice he would 'a' shut right up. I never in life hear Pap sing so hard before."

The day went slowly, warmth, idleness, weariness that passed with the turning of the shadows until, when the chimney birds came darting about the cabin ridge, the world lay clearly seen through clear eyes, lay heavy with color, lying back outstretched upon its own color and way. The leaves hung still on the locust tree, or they moved a little. The lane ran down to the highroad, clear to see, easy to go. Ellen stood about the stone step, without a care, without a wish, or she walked into the cabin past the cooking fire, ready for something more and passive for the next happening. In the early dusk Mr. Bodine and Henry came talking beside the cabin door.

"I'll give you twenty dollars a month in cash money and the house rent free to live in and I'll furnish you-all with your lard and side meat and wheat for flour, all at a cost figure. I'll keep your horses till you can sell to suit you. They can run on pasture for a spell, till the end of July, nohow. You can have all the wood you-all need to burn. Twenty dollars in cash money." Henry was being offered the tenant's place on the farm.

"You can have a garden patch here by the creek. Time enough to plant some truck, and I'll give a day off from farm work to let you put it in. That-there gal can keep it hoed and keep the weeds out."

Inside the cabin Ellen stood listening while her immediate future was being arranged, little darts of pain shooting out from the inner recesses of abdomen and chest, anger making a fever in her blood.

"I'm not a-goen to stay here. I want to go with Tessie. I'm a-goen where Tessie is." She murmured it out of her catching breath, growing bolder as her fear grew. "I'm a-goen where Tessie goes. We can't stay here." She caught her mother's arm to insist. "We can't stay. I have to go."

"You think you're the boss of this-here place? The boss of your pappy? I'll skin you alive if I hear e'er word more outen you." There was a dark quarrel and Ellen was shaken and slapped.

"I want to go . . ."

"I'll skin the hide offen you . . ."

"We can't stay. We have to go. I have to be where Tessie . . ."

Nellie leaned over the fire, turning the frying meat, her broken hair hanging in oily strings around her forehead. Ellen wanted to plunge the knife she held in her hand into the bent head, and the recognition of her want tore her mind in two. She began to scream. The cries brought her father, who slapped her with his hands and sent her up the ladder to the loft room above. She had slept there the night before and her old quilt lay on the floor where she had left it.

In the morning she came down the ladder hungry and whipped, degraded, grateful for any companionship. She cried softly when her mother gave her food, a pone of bread and a piece of bacon, and these she ate sitting in the doorway near her mother, who was smoking tranquilly, words edging their way out from her mouth between the lips and the pipestem from time to time.

27

"Your pappy went to work soon after sunup. . . . It'll be right good to settle down for a spell. . . . You'll like liven here right well after you get used to the ways of the place." Ellen knew that she could not stay. She had no thought of staying, no picture of herself as keeping there, in the doorstep, going the paths. But she dared make no answer. She ate her bread, her hunger eager for it, her head turned aside. "Your pappy and mammy don't belong to that-there parcel of road trash, nohow," Nellie would say. . . . "Your pappy is a farmen man. . . . Don't you recollect how we was a-moven to Nelson County when he caught up with Jock? . . . Travelen the road is one o'nary life. You'll like right well after you get broke to the ways of the place, right well."

A day for planting the garden was allowed Henry before the week was over, and he prepared the soil for beans and corn. Ellen stood by, subdued, obeying readily, even watching his hands to anticipate his want. She dropped the corn into the hills, three grains to the place, her mind full of pity for the corn, pity for her father.

"Now get the hoe," Henry said.

She brought the hoe, handing it gently across the cornhill. She waited abjectly for her father's next wish, her eyes on the clods or on her father's feet where they sank into the cloddy soil.

"If you water your garden and keep the weeds down you'll have a right sharp parcel of truck here in no time," Henry said. "You'll be right proud of your garden after a spell. Look at that-there toad-frog. . . ." He had brought some tomato plants down from the farmhouse garden and these he planted beyond the corn, watering their roots with the water Ellen carried from the creek in a large tin pail. "When these-here grow a spell you set a stake alongside.

28

Now fetch more water." Ellen watched all his processes and obeyed his directions, thinking nothing, feeling nothing but the great out-reaching pity into which she was spread, pity for the water sinking into the dust, pity for the soil that turned unwillingly and sprawled abjectly apart, for Henry's hands leaping with the hoe, for his voice, "Look at that-there old toad-frog. . . ."

AT the end of June Henry had gone to town to buy things for his family, driving his team hitched to the wagon. He came back with some iron cooking utensils, a kitchen table, and a cot bed for Ellen. The farmer had sold him an old wooden bed for himself and Nellie and this now stood in the cabin room opposite the fireplace. Ellen's bed was placed in the loft room above, a sloping chamber of one window which was closed by a rough wooden shutter during storms but left open at all other times. Ellen went up the ladder to her bedroom on light arms and legs, first a hand up and then a foot, wheeling over and over. The new bed filled her with a pleasurable excitement whenever she thought of it, even in mid-morning when she chopped the wood for the dinner fire, even when she hoed lightly about the cornhills to cut the grass and weeds, but this pleasure but strength-ened her pity for the farm and her renewed need to see Tessie and to tell her of the bed. The beans, the tomatoes, and the corn, these were all the vegetables planted. From the woodpile and the garden she could see the rolling lines of the surrounding farms, curve cutting curve, and some-times she traced the lines in the air with her finger. Pictures of the old life grew sharper in her mind although they appeared less often, and the misty details faded out. For a little while she dreamed of the people of the road when she slept, but after a few weeks she was dreaming of the tobacco field, herself turning over the green leaves looking for tobacco worms, of the cabin room where the food was cooked over the open fire. She would remember the weary rumbling of the wagon bed, her sore body, tired from driving, from walking to relieve the load on the up-grade. There were the infected sores on her feet, great sores that would never quite heal and were always cut by the road dust, but were now fading. She would see the pageant of them going down the road, one of the Stikes youngones in front driving a lean filly hitched to a buckboard, either Haldeen or Irene it would be. Then the Stikes wagon with Eva driving and Joe Stikes asleep inside and Lige and Esther on the seat beside the mother. Then Screw and Connie, perhaps, or Tessie and Jock in their new wagon. Jock would be on the seat driving with Tessie beside him, her deep eyes burning in sunburnt skin, her quick mouth with little sharp corners. Then Henry's wagon, a rough old thing mended everywhere, her mother inside on the bedding, herself driving the team, her father out bringing up the horses. Or maybe they would be cooking something beside a little bridge, then she would be by Tessie's fire hearing Tessie talk about a house. Tessie was always wanting a house, a house with vines up on the chimney, a brick house with a gallery, a stone house with a fountain, a little brown house with white on the windows and doors, a house by a seaside, a house on a street. Tessie was always talking.

"And I would have, if I could, a slated roof, red up there in the sun . . . steps a-goen down to a grass place where would be a sundial in the other end. Me a-comen down in

30

the morning dew with a flower basket on my arm. Me a-cooken breakfast and a-setten out the pretties. . . . I'd have a room in my house for Ellen . . ."

"Or I would have"—this would be another day—"a little house on a high bank above a river—let it be the Ohio or maybe the Tennessee—and me a-washen windows in a great hurry because company is a-comen." Or another day she would say, "I'd have a parlor to sit back in, cool and fine." "Me a-comen down marble stairs . . ." "Me a-washen up things after dinner at a white sink like the one in the house where I worked for a spell in Bowling Green."

The corn came through the soil in little green tubes, closely curled. Ellen had been carrying water past the hills when she saw the green pointing out of the clods, and she stopped in her act, surprised. In a few days the corn had slim grass-like leaves that bent in the sun and waved lightly, and she thought that she could see how much the plants grew from one day to the next. She ran to the garden eagerly each day to watch for the changes, and her pleasure in the growth of the corn was very real. The beans in their rows seemed to be a creature, one, brooding in stillness in all hours of the day and growing rank and full and lush in a few weeks. They said: "I'll be you; you wait and see. . . ." The tomato vines with their strong sour odors coming from leaves and stem cut into her skin. She felt them before she came near them for they were strong and piercing. They laughed, big bold rank things, ugly and jeering and strong. She strutted and jeered when she came into the tomato patch, her head jerking to one side: "You sting my skin. You think I'm trash. You lied, you lied, you lied!"

She liked to sit in the corn after it grew waist-high or more. In the soft clods of the bright days or in the soft loam of the days after showers she would sit, looking about, feeling herself moving with the corn. A voice would come to her mind:

"Or even suppose it was the poorest sort of shanty made outen boards set on end and only one room, or two; and suppose the people that lived there last used to be a dirty set and left their filth behind them when they went; and even suppose there'd be fleas under the house where the hogs had been a-sleepen. . . . I'd set about maken it fitten to live in, you'd see. I'd scrub that-there floor . . ." Or then:

"They'd be a fair sight to see when the roses came in bloom next summer and when the grapes got up over that-there arbor—big bunches of grapes a-hangen down all summer and a-turnen purple in the fall and the bees a-comen to get sweet outen some. That would be a sight to see now."

She remembered Tessie pushing her book under the quilts to hide it out of the wet. A deep-set fact that was as one with her breath lay back of all her thought, a fact gathered into an unspoken phrase, "I couldn't stay here, I'd have to go where she is." Tessie had four books now. She used to have five but the story book was gone. "Jock a-haulen around Tessie's trash. I'd dump them books in the first ditch . . ." a noise like a snarl out of another wagon.

ELLEN carried water to the house from the spring that gathered in a scooped-out pool above the creek on the south side of the ravine. She would hold her left hand far out from her body to balance the load, her head bent toward the right. When she could slip away she explored the ravine to its head in the tree-grown hills lying beyond Bodine land. One day in July she saw three women walking on the dirt road that ran past the house, one of them leading a small child. She had caught glimpses of a woman on the yellow road before. These people, seen clearly, wore faded limp clothes, long and drab and weary from many washings. One wore a black sunbonnet but the other two had small hats. They carried no bundles and for this Ellen thought they must live near.

"They're our kind of people; they look like us. We might, maybe, get to know them. They live in a little house or a cabin or a shack, or maybe even a wagon."

When she saw them returning in the late afternoon she went down near the fence and waited, looking at them. They passed without speaking but they did not cease to watch her, sending back diffused good humor and well-wishing. The next day one of the women passed again, and Ellen ran down to the fence when she saw her coming out of the curve of the road. The woman had been seen now a half-dozen times and had become a mass of characteristic motions and friendly staring eyes. Ellen longed to fix her into a thought, to know what she would say now that she knew how she would look saying it. She longed to find her out, to like her or to hate her. This day when she passed Ellen she spoke.

"Howdy do!"

"Good evening!" Ellen said.

"I allow you-all are the new people that moved in here."

"We moved in."

"Do you like?"

"We like well enough."

"Hit's a good place, Hep Bodine's."

"You might stop to see us sometime when you happen to be a-goen down the road."

"I'd like to get acquainted right well. My name is Mrs. Pinkston, Artie Pinkston."

"My name's Ellen Chesser. Mammy's in the house."

"How many you-all got in family?"

"Just Mammy and Pappy and me."

"Well I do know. I got myself and Hez—I married Hez Pinkston—and three youngones."

"But we got six dead before I came, when we used to be a-liven in Taylor County and in Green. One was right puny and died three years old, and two taken fever and died. Then Mammy had Harp and Corie and they died. I don't recollect what they died with, and Davie died when he was three months old."

A wave of pity for Davie swept through her body, a froth of motion flowing from her sides and spreading through her chest, pulling back at her throat, a wave running out upon the air.

"If Davie was here he'd be sixteen now."

"Well I do know!"

The woman was gone now and the talk was over, and Ellen watched her receding, a large woman, her long skirt kicking out in little points at the hem as she walked. Ellen lay on the ground near the laneside under a thorn tree, but there was no coolness in the grass, which was hot like her own tingling skin, and the heat rolled down in waves from the sun. She heard something crying far off, some undetermined crying, sharp and full of pain, but too far away to touch pity, the mere outline of a cry duplicated without feeling on the hot air. Then her closed eyes began to see people walking quickly up stone steps, some of them turning out of a paved way with little skipping motions, and the scene tilted, wavered and grew dim and then came back larger

34

and clearer in color before it went into nothingness. Then out of nothing she came into a quick and complete knowledge of the end. You breathe and breathe, on and on, and then you do not breathe any more. For you forever. Forever. It goes out, everything goes, and you are nothing. The world is all there, on and on, but you are not there, you, Ellen. The world goes on, goes on without you. Ellen Chesser. Ellen. Not somebody heard about and said with your mouth, but you yourself, dead. It will be. You cannot help it.

She rose to a sitting position with a cry and sat looking out upon the thorn tree and the hot wilted weeds of the lane where insects clicked as they passed about. This was the world and she was in it, glad with a great rush of passion. Her hand reached out and touched a plantain leaf and her eyes recognized the dog-fennel and the wire fence beyond the dust of the road. She was still there and everything was secure, her body rising tall above the narrowdock and the dandelions. The sky came down behind the locust trees, in place, and everything was real, reaching up and outward, blue where it should be blue, gray haze, heat rising out of the dust, limp dock leaves falling away toward the dusty grass. She walked back to the cabin, moving slowly to feel the security of the path, touching a tree with her fingers, trailing her hand along the stone of the doorstep.

The farm was beautiful and secure, running up over a hill and lapping into a ravine, spreading flat over the lower pasture. It was there, in place, reaching about into hollows and over uplands, theirs to live in and to know and to work. The locust tree beside the woodpile and the tall bushes along the creek, as they always were. She was there, there yet, her body walking up through the pasture with a tin bucket

35

swinging and making a high thin brushing noise as it touched her moving skirt. The farm was secure and the land was placed, all beautiful and near. She began to gather the hot blackberries from the briars of the wasted hill pasture. A few berries made a low tinkling as they fell into her pail, and then the brown colt came from the other side of the enclosure, nibbling offhandishly at the wilted grass and edging always a little nearer. She left her berrying and they played a short while together, she pitting her arms against his neck and pushing hard. He let her throw one leg over his back and ride a little way, or she would pull his long forelock and twist his mane, or feed him choice bits of grass which she gathered from under the briars. While she held out a tuft of clover to the colt's quivering out-reaching muzzle, the hillside was clear to see and to have, hers, and who cared if there was an end. Let it look out for itself. The colt's lips came down upon the white clover blossoms which went into the long cavern of his mouth, turning as they went. The large straw hat which her father had bought for her would catch in the light breeze and flash off over the briars to hang on a cluster of twigs or glide off over the waste stone grass. Just as she recovered the hat from under a rose briar and gathered a last mouthful for the colt a sharp voice cut through the heat, coming from the path that lay through the high bushes. It was the voice of the farmer's wife.

"What you want in here?"

Ellen was too much frightened to run away. She stood staring at Mrs. Bodine, holding her hat in her hand, and her hands being engaged, the one with the hat and the other with the pail, a feeling of utter defenselessness overcame her. The question was repeated several times before she spoke.

"Mr. Bodine told Pappy," she trembled.

36

"Nobody said you could have them berries. I need every one for myself."

"Mr. Bodine told Pappy we could . . ."

Ellen felt herself to be hanging in the air, cut off from the ground, while she waited in the long stillness that followed. The farmer's wife wore a crisp dress, the waist and skirt alike, both blue, both starched, both washed at the same time. Ellen's skirt was blue and her waist was greenish-drab, faded and limp and old. Washings no longer made them new. A fear of dogs and men came into her terror, and she felt as if her shoulders were tied to a post or a tree, lifted high. The farmer's wife was a sharp crisp shape, standing tall out of the blackberry bushes. It pushed against her body and filled her mouth with a bitter taste. Little prickling needles stuck in and out of the skin of her face.

"Mr. Bodine told Pappy . . ."

"Well, maybe he did, but he's got no call to be a-tellen any such. I need every berry I got to make my own jam. I need every last one for my own self. Don't come up this way a-picken any more. You keep down along the branch nohow. I got no berries or anything else to spare."

Ellen went down the field feeling her dress pushed against her skin, shoving her along, the look of the woman and the voice of the woman shoving at her clothing, her clothing shoving at her skin and making her bones articulate stiffly. Her mind stood blank and motionless while nerves and limbs came stiffly down the hill. "Oh, Brother Andrew, have you got a G-string," stood in her throat, contending to be said, but against this arose and fought other sayings. Her bare feet walked on stunted wild clover and struggling crab grass, and the little stones were hot like cinders on her skin. She passed the last blackberry bush saying, "Weep, weep,

37

weep no more. Only ten cents more and I'll read the other palm for you, Lady, only ten cents, one dime, ten cents." A nausea spread up from the pit of her stomach and died in her mouth, diffused. "And you'll live a long and happy life. Only ten cents more, one dime. A long life, a happy life, a long life. Happy happy long long. Long and happy life." She was walking on cooler grass near the foot of the hill, and the grasshoppers splattered away from her feet. The woman stood crisp on the top of the pasture, gathering her berries, still pushing with her look and with her shape, up in the sun. At the clump of thorn bushes beyond the last rise Ellen dropped quickly to her knees and crawled quickly out of the sight of the woman on the hilltop. Sitting under the leaves of the thorn bush she felt little prickers tingling along her skin. Lice, she thought it must be, her lice crawling, stirred up and going about. She drew her legs under her skirt and sat, the thorns of the bush worrying her neck and her moving hands. She was pushed up from the thorny grass, but she peered out at the hill from which she had been driven and saw with a quick sob that she was well concealed. Then she crawled down to the branch and went secretly over the watergap, intent on being unseen. The ground was rough and hot, scraping meanly at her as she clung to it.

"She thought I lied to her," she said, sitting by the water of the creek. "She thought I was a-stealen her berries. I could steal all she's got and she'd never know, if I was of a mind to. I could get all she's got some night if I'd set my mind that way. I'm not afeared of her old shepherd dog. He'd come up and rub his neck on my leg and I'd scratch his head for him a little. I know about everything she does, in and out of her big ugly house, a-planten her late cabbage one day and a-putten up jam the next, with Pappy to cut

38

her stovewood. I got no lice on me. A-goen off in her buggy and a-comen back with big bundles. I could take all the blackberries she's got and she'd never know when."

Her skirt was the one Tessie had given her, now plucked from briars and worn limp from many washings. Her waist had come out of a bundle of rags some people in Marion County had given her mother, the color now gone, but traces of it lingered in the seams. The farmer's wife had made her feel lice crawling, and she turned to the inner seams of her garments, searching for a moment. She counted the berries in the bottom of the pail, twenty-one, and then turned back to the inner surfaces of her clothes again, laying her fingers on the seams to pry them out.

"I got no lice. She lied that-there woman. I got no more lice 'n she's got. Pappy can have twenty-one berries in his blackberry pie." Then she ate the berries.

Except when she helped her father sucker and worm the tobacco, Ellen never again went up the rise toward the farm-house and she saw no more of the colt in the pasture. Her ways closed in around her and the hills drew nearer. She dragged home the brush which her father cut in the ravine, making her way slowly to the cabin with it or cutting it into fagots where it lay, and she carried this into the house when her mother called out, "I ain't no firewood." She would run down the lane to the turnpike and watch up and down. When a passer went along the road in a buggy or wagon or on horseback, she experienced intense tremors of excitement at seeing a figure, a face or a conveyance, at seeing wheels or the stepping feet of horses. There would be fat ladies with pink plump daughters, or there would be thin ladies with little children in straw hats or starched bonnets. Little girls with curls filled her with happiness, as did gay colored ribbons flying off from hatbrims or white flying veils blowing out from ladies' hair. The people usually looked straight forward because there was a turn in the road ahead, but if they looked at her she suffered great shame. Then she would try to shrink under her skimp dress and she would feel her skin trying to shrink into her sinews, drawing inward toward her very marrow. But when the gazers were passed, as the carriage receded along the road and the noise of the wheels funneled down into fainter clatters of sound, she would be her former self again, and she would keep afterward a renewed sense of people pointing with their fingers, of people carrying things in their hands, of voices rising and sinking away.

She would often chatter a little with Artie Pinkston in the lane. This woman was carrying a child and Ellen appraised her coldly, listening to her speech with the knowledge in her mind. The woman breathed shortly, suffocatedly, her lips parted.

" It's a hot spell of weather."

"July is a hot time."

The great ugly figure stood up in the lane, the lips open to take breath, the face red and coarse. Why did she let herself be like that? Ellen would ask herself with an inner contempt, for she knew all the externals of child-getting. She had pitied her father and mother for their futile efforts toward secrecy; "Ellen is asleep," or "Is Ellen asleep?" Life turned back upon itself and looked upon itself coldly. Night, dark, filth, sweat, great bodies, what for? She pitied them with a great pity, the pity of a child for adults.

40

"I might sit down on this-here bank for a spell and rest myself," Artie said.

"You might maybe like a cup of water to drink if I'd bring it out to you."

"I'd be right obliged."

Ellen hated the woman for the pain she was going to have. The hills gathered closer in and Artie Pinkston helped to wind them tight and twist them close. "I had enough Mrs. Pinkstons in my time. I'll wait a spell," Nellie said, and she kept indoors when Artie stopped in the lane. After a while the hills would open up and send out great cries. Ellen knew. She would go a little way up the lane, past the first rise and around the curve and up again between two fields, until the top of a boarded cabin came in sight, but she dared no further, listening, ready to run back. The hills stood shoulder to shoulder. She would go to the garden in the early morning to gather the beans for dinner, thinking of soft sweet beans cooked in grease, or she would carry water down from the spring to drink, or water from the creek to wet the newly planted cabbage. She would sit under the tree by the wood-pile and gaze at the chips, at the black earth, at her own brown legs and white thighs. A sudden voice would call out in her ear, Haldeen Stikes saying a lewd word. Haldeen had pursued her with his words, shaping words with his lips when he could not say them aloud, Haldeen with downy hair on his lip. Haldeen's word would cry out at her and something in her laughed at it while something else stood back, meek and futile, and she laughed down upon her hard sun-darkened legs and her slim white loins.

Running up and down her ways she made beaten paths, down to the bank above the lane, down the laneside to the highroad, back to the bank, back to the house through low summer weeds, to the woodpile, through the garden along the side of the bean row, and out of the garden toward the creek, up the creek to the mouth of the ravine. Her paths grew hard and smooth. Ten times, twenty times a day she ran through her confines, pounding the ground with bare feet.

"Jingle at the window, tidy-o," she sang. "Somebody a-jinglen on a thump-thump guitar, that is. If I had a guitar I'd be a-jinglen on it to a fare-you-well." She was coming in from the farthest part of the yard in the dusk, walking about in the warm languorous air. The stars were out, very low and very near, pushing down, falling of humid weight. The air scarcely moved at all, but now and then a warmer motion spread down from the higher places, pushing through skin and lying along the inner threads of nerves, fiddling on delicate quick with familiar searching hands. She walked into a tree before she was aware of it. Its great trunk spread against her breast like a broad chest upon her. A quick memory of Screw, of the time he caught her behind a wagon and hugged her close, came with the touch of the tree. She had been afraid of him for he was drunk. Whisky smells came out of him, and man smells, sweat and dirt, different from woman dirt. She had felt the buttons on his coat dig into her thin old dress and his great broad chest spread out before her slim body and his drunk arms trying to catch her closer. She had hated him and despised him, despised his whisky and dirt smells, but a slim thread like a thin silver serpent had rushed through her flesh, straight through her trunk, when Screw held her.

She knew the walls òf the house in all their swaying lines and all their mossy softness. The roof pole bowed slightly, drooping into a curve. The roof was the color of weather,

42

white with the sun, gray with the rain, deep gray with the moon, rosed with the sunset. The wall leaned back from the rock doorsteps, and the shingles on the sunny slope of the roof were curled like autumn leaves fallen in wavering lines. In the ground around the house were imbedded bits of trash, relics of former tenants, such as wisps of paper, cut hairs, iron nails, pipestems, coffee grounds, threads, and pulps of rags. Dull mouldy smells that were faintly sickening came out of the earth here when she scratched it with her finger. She knew the ground around the house intimately. Once she scratched up a bit of a broken mirror, once a human tooth, once a rotted glove with a bright metal fastener. The soil was black and stiff like felt.

Sitting on the bank above the lane she watched for Artie Pinkston's coming for the reward of a few words exchanged. She drew her legs under her skirt and tucked the edges of the garment under her knees and her feet. She drew herself together, her slim body scarcely needing a foot of ground, shrinking from the ground, while Artie Pinkston stopped for her brief say—the heat, the price of eggs, the scarcity of wild berries. Ellen watched the woman until she passed out of sight and then she drew herself together even closer, shrinking and gathering in upon herself. Memory played up a monstrous picture in her mind although she shook back her head and tried to efface it. Eva Stikes in labor with Esther. Irene scared, running out of the shanty. The two of them, she and Irene, scared, standing about the door. Her mother calling to Tessie:

"Eva Stikes is a-bawlen. Get the water hot whilst I see what's to do."

"Oh, people are ugly and everything is ugly," Ellen muttered, remembering. "Brown ground ugly and yesterday

43

ugly and all the things people do—eaten and a-walken and a-haven things to keep. Terrible, it is. Ugly. Hard to do. Everything ugly. Eva Stikes a-screamen and a-pullen on the bedpost and Mammy a-sayen do this and do that. Irene a-screamen and a-holden onto me and a-getten sick enough to throw up, and Eva a-sayen, 'Kill me, somebody, knock me in the head with the axe, oh, for the love of God somebody kill me!' and it goes on all day in the shanty. Yesterday ugly and everything ugly, all the way back to the first, as far as you can recollect, ground, sun, things to eat, cooken, things to keep, wanten things, backward as far as you can recollect. And then a little cryen, a thin cryen, and Tessie is a-washen a baby by the cookstove, and everybody is a-smilen, glad it's all over and glad about the little new baby that's so pink and clean, little hands and little feet.''

THE creek was almost dry in the August drouth. A green scum stood on the stagnant pools of water in the small basins among the fluted rocks. Ellen traced images in the smooth green surface with her vaulting pole and watched them twist away into grotesques or take other meanings. With the pole, a long broomstick she had found among the rubbish in the shed, she could easily swing herself over the pools. The lower pasture was burned brown except where the shade of the trees had saved a little moisture, but the tobacco was spreading wide fronds that crowded for room, and these were a brilliant green with waves of heat vibrating over them. The green scum made a curtain over the water holes, but when she tore the curtain away she saw the reflections in the water, the sky, blue and dry, the hills and trees. In a little

44

while the scum gathered back and there was left only black water. To push the film aside with great zigzag strokes and make the world come into the pool quickly, the world big and clear and deep with a sky under it, this was her intent.

"People a-dyen in ships at midnight and people a-goen to a foreign country with pots made outen gold and skillets made outen silver on the pack-horse, and gold cups. People a-goen to London-town—Is this the way to London-town? —and an old, old queen. And a story about a horse could talk."

She was sitting on a great flat fluted stone of the creek bottom, beside a water hole, sitting in the middle of the dry creek bed. "And a story about a horse could talk and one about Fair Elender. 'O Mother, O Mother, come riddle my sport, come riddle it all as one. Must I go marry Fair Elender?' Elender, that's me. And people a-dyen for grief and people a-dyen for sorrow.

"And there was the book with the poetry pieces to say. A brown book, it was. I can see as plain as day and I can see the words inside, pieces to say in school of a Friday. 'O Sailor Boy woe to thy dream of delight'—a piece about a shipwreck. And then, 'Come back, come back, he cried in grief across the stormy water.' I could say all that-there if I was of a mind that way. I know a right smart of pieces now, for a fact. And the Sands o' Dee.

> O Mary go and call the cattle home,
>   And call the cattle home,
>   And call the cattle home,
> Across the sands o' Dee.

Water a-rushen up the almost dry creek all of a sudden, a flood a-comen in on Mary!"

She jumped from her seat and ran up the bank of the

ravine, terrified, clutching at the brush, dry stones rattling back in her path. At the top she turned to look at the wall of water that might be coming up the valley through Bodine's lower pasture. She sat on the brow among the bushes and snags, laughing at her fear, and after a little her pulses calmed.

"I'm a-thinken about the geography book, Tessie's other book, an old one all torn at the corners and spotted where somebody left it out in the rain some time long ago. London Bridge across the Thames. The Cathedral and Plaza, Mexico City. You could see yourself a-liven in the brown house, a-walken up big stairs and a-looken out that-there tower window, a-sitten down in a tower to look out all day, a-sitten back cool. Or you could flip the page over and there—Elephant a-drawen a load of coconuts in Ceylon. High palm trees, black men with white hippens on, wagon made outen sticks. . . . Town Hall, Leeds. Wide stairs, flat-topped roof and a tower with a clock to tell the time of day. A fountain a-drippen out in front. You could see yourself live in that-there house, a-looken out the window at sunup to see if the fountain is a-goen yet. . . . City Hall, Brussels. Slant roof with a tall steeple up high. Yourself a-walken down long halls inside. Yourself a-walken up stairs with a gold pitcher in your hand, a-goen down a long room with a checkered floor like the one in the Ewington post office.

"It was a good book, a learned book. I read it a heap here and yon and I looked a heap at the pictures. . . . I remember Tessie. . . . And I didn't forget one time we saw who could sing the most songs, first one and then the other a-singen one. . . . I recall the Carolina dove. Little-headed, he is, and a-walken on the ground, and once a boy down by Cherry Creek in Tennessee told me every dove has got one drop

46

of human blood in his body somewheres. For sure, he said, one drop.

"One of the books mine. Tessie gave me one to keep, but it's safer with the balance, I said, along under the quilts. . . . It would be the dearest thing in life if I could find my book someday and have it in my hands or in my room hid under the bed to get out when we'd have a rainy spell of weather."

BEFORE autumn Ellen was fifteen. During the summer there had always been food and she had grown less thin. Her bones had withdrawn under the flesh and her eyes were no longer hollow. Signs of woman began to appear on her meager body; woman took possession of her although she was hard like spines and sharp like flint. She looked at herself in the mirror of the creek, for she dared not unrobe herself in the house before the eyes of her mother. She thought that with the change of one or two externals everything might change—a room to sleep in where there would be pink and blue, herself reading a book by the window. Things to put in drawers and drawers to put things in, she would like, and people to say things to. Her mother would sit in a gay chair on a gallery sewing a seam, the little stitches falling up and down, her mother saying gentle things. Or even suppose they were poor, then she would be sitting with her hair clean and combed, and she would call out, "Ellen, come see the sparks, they're in the chimney a-flyen like geese here and yon," or "Come look at the cherry tree; it's like a little girl dressed up for summer."

She wanted to sit beside Tessie and talk about a house. She wanted to talk about a desert where camels walk in long lines, or about glaciers where men explore for poles, or about

47

men walking into mines with little lights on their hats—
about the wonders of the world.

"If I only had things to put in drawers and drawers to put
things in. That's all I'd ask for a time to come." She could
feel herself stooping to pull out a drawer, taking out a garment, at first vague and soft and fine, lace and ribbon and
sweet smells, but she let it turn to coarse cotton in her hands,
for when it took shape and grew definite there was no other
way. She remembered a place where she and Irene had
begged. "Could you give us some old clothes, Lady?" And
then a tall dark lady before a chest, bending to open a
drawer with a faint stooping gesture, bending a little forward, a woman like slow water, a slim fine lady with dark
hair and flowing hands.

More wood was needed for the supper fire now, for the
nights were chilly and Henry liked to sit a little while by the
blaze before going to bed. Ellen was pecking at the sticks
by the woodpile with the sharp new axe her father had
bought for her, making burning pieces. Nellie was sitting
beside the cabin door. The pipe had hung in her listless hand
until it had fallen to the ground, spilling its dead ash, but
now and then quick hands turned up a garment or opened
a vent and searched along the inner seams, eyes bent close.
The blackbirds were assembled in great flocks now. They
were gathering in the high trees on the hill above the ravine
and their cries made a continuous chattering broken into
chimes and waved to the flutterings of winged bodies. The
twilights were falling earlier day by day, and strange
shadows, different from the summer-cast shadows, slanted
under the locust trees. The cry of the axe struck out against
the cabin wall and against the bare tree branches, spreading
wide, and the light came into the yard in unaccustomed

ways. The cabin showed itself more, out in the hard light. Winter would come soon now. Nellie stooped quickly and rummaged at her garments, annoyed by the fleas, searching with her nearsighted eyes. They, Nellie and herself, were out before the cabin and out before the hard light, the leaves almost all fallen from the locust, an early falling. She stacked the cut wood in her arms and felt the rough surfaces and the rounded limbs and smelt the odors of green sap. Stooping to gather the wood, with her face close to the vapor of the sap, a great motion of tenderness for her mother swept through her nerves. "Get Ellen the shoes. I can wait a spell. My old ones will do me," she heard the words again. Minnie and Edd and Lue and Harp and Corie and Davie, before she came. "Mammy, what made your teeth go snaggly and all come outen your head?" she had asked once. "Do you reckon you could have seven brats inside twelve year and have e'er a tooth left to your name?" Now her face was close to the vapors of the wood and her lips brushed against the bark.

"She's my mammy, mine," she whispered. How could she ever live without her mother? Suppose. The yard without Nellie, the cabin without, supper without. A great terror went over her, followed by renewed tenderness. She could hardly walk past the cabin door, so great was her emotion. She went past her mother very gently and walked up the steps on light bare feet. The wood fell softly from her arms to the hearthstone making scarcely a whisper and settled down upon itself mutely under her hushing hands.

ELLEN lay in her bed up in the loft in the cool of a late September evening, two old quilts pulled over her. Brown

49

shocks of corn were dotted about in her mind pictures, and between the dun splotches of the corn there were large yellow pumpkins lying, naked, the vines withered down by the frost. From the cabin door she could see the hill where the tents stood up against the sky, the tents of the corn, and her thought sat down in the doorway to hear the blackbirds chattering and to see the plowed field of the summer, the tobacco field now plowed again for rye. Great hawks made wide shadows soar among the clods. Little turnips came into her mind, little pink things growing now where the beans had been, crowding together. The cornblades were brown and hard. They would crumble and break if she bent them in her fingers. Jock would be going down the road toward Tennessee, taking his drove of horses down, going the old road. He might come through Rushfield next court day on his way down from the Bluegrass. He would be sure to come that way.

She sat up in bed, jerked from her back by the force of the thought. She stared out the open window into the hillside which was lit by a full moon.

"He might be there, now, might, a-campen down some road."

She would go there, walking in the night. By morning she would be in the town; eight miles would not be far to go in a long night. She would see Tessie once more. If only for a day or a half day, she would see Tessie. She would walk into town and ask over and over on the street, "Do you-all know whe'r there's any gypsies a-campen down the roads or not? Any horse-swappers? Any movers?" She would come straight out with the question. "Any travelers?" Somebody would be sure to know. "I see a parcel of wagons out that-there road this very day." Then she would walk out to the place and there would be the wagons, the tongues pulled up against a fence. Tessie would be behind the best wagon cooking something on a little fire, or maybe she would be just at that moment starting to town with a little something to peddle under her arm.

Her father would whip her when she came walking back the next night. She could feel the switch on her back and the blows cut in with little sharp stabs of joy. Nellie's voice:

"Say you won't do that-there no more!"

"Triflen brat, to traipse the road and to run away! I'll skin the hide offen you. . . ."

Her face drew together with pain too keenly remembered, but she laughed. The switch would cut into her legs like fire and she would roll on Nellie's bed and scream. But she would go. She would see Tessie again and after that she would be glad enough to come back. She would slip out Sunday night soon after bedtime.

The thought that she really would see Tessie again thrilled her senses and caught at her breath all day Saturday, whenever she dwelt upon it. On Sunday evening soon after the early bedtime of the cabin she took her shoes in her hand and her cloak upon her arm and slipped quietly down the ladder, past her mother's side of the bed, and out the door. The moon was shining hazily, hanging a little west of the top of the sky. She found it necessary to put on the old cloak, a garment left from the winter before, used in summer for bedding. It smelt of musty straw as she drew it on her arms. Having put on the shoes at the top of the bank above the lane, she walked down to the highroad and turned south, crossing the creek where it came out of the Bodine farm. The large yellow house was very still, on fire with moonlight. She had not been to Rushfield along this way, but she knew that the road would take her there without any turnings. The roadbed was rough and stony with deep uneven ruts, but since she could hear her footfalls echoing against the hill on the right she decided to take off her shoes and carry them so that her footsteps would fall noiselessly. Soon the Bodine land lay behind her and she passed into a strange country, the road winding unevenly among the hills. When she heard a buggy approaching she ran to the fence-row and lay in the shadow of the roadside growth. A feel of last year was in the road and in the moonlight. All the wagons of last year's travel might be just around some curve, her father's wagon in a fence corner or in some roadside waste place. She might be out searching for firewood for the supper fire or out looking for a stray colt. She noted pieces of wood, good burning pieces, as she passed, and she felt a sharp impulse to gather them. An owl sang in a tree by a farm gate, his notes coming in a slow trill. After she left the owl she heard some boys approaching, playing along the road and throwing walnuts about. She grew weary waiting for them to pass, for they moved forward very slowly. They sang out in unharmonious chords and one mimicked the owl in derision.

"Shut up there, Edd. You'll wake up Old Man Brother Hep Bodine. He needs his rest," another said.

Finally they were gone and she crawled out of her hiding-place and went slowly on. She could hear the boys screaming higher up around the curve and she knew that they were screaming at the echoes. She remembered running sounds like singing, like tinkling water rippling over creek stones, like pretty bells ringing brightly in little towns on Sunday morning, and she walked faster, for she remembered Tessie. Up in the Bluegrass of the state all summer, she had been, but now she would be going back down again. Where had Tessie been? She pushed her mind hard into the shadows, into the dark of what she did not know. Where had Tessie been? Tessie! Where had she been the day the cabin floor caught fire? Now she sat on a stone to think of that. A carriage full of voices was approaching, men and women singing, the parts sweetly blended. When she heard them coming near she climbed a wire fence and hid among low weeds in a pasture.

"It makes a fair sound," she said.

There was a smell of pigs about in the weeds where she lay. A little pig-house stood out sharply in the moonlight on the upper slope of the enclosure and from somewhere off in the weeds came the sound of a sow's deep breath. Sweet voices, men and women, sang in the night, with the irregular beat of the horses' hoofs walking through the rhythms:

Through the sycamores the candle lights are gleaming. . . .

The sound went on up the hill, four voices blended, or five perhaps, the horses taking their time at the road. "Sycamores" kept in her thought, tone at first, spreading out two ways and gathering back into unison. "Men and women have pretty singing," she thought. "I wish I could sing like that." She tried to sing a chord but only her own voice came, a weak voice after the chorus lately there. Far up the hill she heard the carriage stop and she knew that the voices were singing to the echo. The night brought sublimated tones across the interlying space, thin planes of sound spreading through trees and rocks. She stood beside a white stone, a large white stone lying blank in the moonlight, and tried again to make a chord with her throat, but only a dull small tone came. Why could not she sing a full wide singing,

53

she thought as she tried the word "sycamores" over and over.

After that the road swept upward and outward to the west, running unmarked and white between bald fields and then dipping down suddenly to a small runlet, now dry. The dip and the culvert at the bottom, and the upward curve beyond, lost their moonlight and lay dim in a white noon sun, hot beetles ticking in the weeds and the wilted July grass, down below the Knobs in the cave country. A buggy came by in the noon sunlight, a man and a woman in it, the woman's white summer dress almost like a mirror in the sun. The woman was weeping when they passed. "Not once but ten times," the man said. "Not once but ten times," a man's voice was saying, roughly, accusingly. "Not once but ten times." Now a mist was spreading up in the hollow, glowing in the moonlight, lying out in a layer of dull silver. "Not once but ten times"—her feet marched to the uneven rhythm of the saying as she climbed the rough road in shadow.

"It's a long way down to that-there place, and the Knobs are a jolty way to go," she said. "Not once but ten times! I wish I had a blue hat with a big white ostrich plume a-flyen for myself. Me a-sitten up in a buggy with a big white plume on my hat and white slippers on my feet." She was marching steadily ahead now on a long level stretch. "A dog barks curious," she said again, "curious now. He can go two ways at once, a yelp out and a growl down under. A growl goes on down under the bark. A dog knows as soon as a body sets a foot on the road. But I can tell whe'r it's a big dog or a little by the sort of bark he lets out. A house back in a bunch of trees is a pretty sight now, for certain."

54

A little church was set back among beech trees, the red bricks holding their color in the spaces where the moonlight spread through the open boughs. Behind the church a gay little graveyard twinkled in the light, its gay white stones and blossoming flowers as happy as a flower bed out in the sun. The windows of the church were dark and there was no house near, and Ellen decided to rest awhile in the recess of the doorway. She lay on the floor of the vestibule where a smell of dusty boots arose from the boards. She put on her shoes and stockings to warm her feet, and presently she knew that she had been sleeping long, for the moon had set and the land seemed very dark. The road was gray-brown in the shadows and dull gray in the open; beyond lay blackness in the fields. A short distance from the church she hid close to a gate while two horsemen passed. They stopped to drink from a bottle and one of the horses knew of her hiding for it nickered uneasily.

"Glory to God, I feel like hell!" one of the men declaimed slowly, gesturing in a deep passion of joy and sorrow undefined.

They whipped their horses and rode away quickly. Ellen walked fast after that, giving her attention to her journey and fearing that she had wasted time. But when the hills unfolded, curve on curve, up and down, past black nothingness, past white-fenced yards, past white barns, past black nothingness again, her steps lagged and she grew tired. Two miles or more beyond the church she came to an iron bridge over a little river. The road lay along a high curving embankment, and so she saw the bridge before she reached it. The iron frame hung between the banks of trees, a black spiderweb crisscrossing in the air. It was somehow beautiful, the dark bridge hanging between the dark trees, and she

55

walked around the curve of the road and entered the bridge with awe in her mind, her mind so heavy with wonder that her feet dragged and little prickers of pain pushed in upon her face and chest. The water lay below, a dull silver black, and there were stars in it. "Oh, I didn't know this-here would be!" she said.

She stood on the bridge high above the water and watched the stars above and below. There were frogs and crickets singing, and katydids crying their flat notes. The black shadows of the black trees pushed into the water, over-lapping. She stood very still at the rail of the bridge, scarcely breathing, leaning lightly on the wooden structure. Her own want was undefined, lying out among the dark trees and their dark images, and she reached for it with a great wish that shook her small body. After a while she whispered a little, brokenly, almost without breath, but the words were Tessie's words, borrowed now because her own words were stricken.

"Such a leetle house is all I want, no matter how leetle. . . . I'd make it fair some way or how with things set about proper, or with vines and trees and flowerpots."

She sat on the floor of the bridge, looking north down the stream, wondering why the town did not begin to appear against the sky and fearing, presently, that she had missed her way. It seemed a very long while since she had lain on the floor of the church, which now seemed far back on the road; it seemed far to the moonlight and far to the place where the dog had barked. The drinking men were far back in time. She lay on the floor of the bridge, close to the edge, and it seemed that she lay in an endless night between two sets of stars. Then she cried a little for her limbs were very cold, and after a while she forgot even the cold. There were streaks of dawn in the sky when she awakened and a twilight had come to take the place of the black nothingness and the dimly outlined shadows. A large white house stood on the tree-shaded hill before the bridge. A man walking beside the house peered down at her and she jumped up quickly and started off along the road, skipping with light steps, for the way curved up under dense trees. The people of the morning began to appear; a man came out of a farm gate riding a harnessed horse and leading another. When she was exhausted from skipping, she sat by the side of the road to catch her breath, and while she sat a Negro woman in an old buggy came up from the way of the bridge and a ride was offered. The woman was going to town to wash clothes all day, she said. When Ellen left the buggy at a gate, she came to a little whitewashed cabin that sat on the roadside and here she had a drink of water at a pump in the yard.

"Help yourself. Take all you want!" the man said. He was milking a cow by the house door.

Down in the town she sat a long while on a curb by a church, resting and trying to feel out the ways of the place. Negro women came there with bundles of clothes tied up in sheets. They would say to each other in a way of greeting:

"Powerful big county court today!"

Ellen felt estranged to all the people about and even to herself. An unutterable awe of all places swept through her, a fear of trees and stones, and she shrank even from the roadway of the street which lay out dusty before her. Familiar itself became unfamiliar, and a glance down at her own hands where she saw accustomed lines and folds of skin brought bewilderment. She sat for an hour. She tried to seem unconscious of the glances which the Negro women cast upon her. She tried to think of some place in which she would prefer to be, but all places were alike abhorred. She stared down at a tuft of sourgrass growing in the gutter at her feet. Suddenly out of the chaos in her being there came a hunger, a quick craving for food to eat. Food. Her mouth wanted it. Bread. Bacon fried and laid on bread. Bread sweetened in grease. If she had a pone she would not even be looking at her hands, would not even be seeing the stones of the road or the gutter, not in such a place as this. Suddenly it came to her that she was going to walk away from the curb before the church, that she had risen and was walking off past a yellow Negress and past three white bundles of clothes. She went up the street down which she had come, and after a little she knew that she was going to ask for food at some door. She went far up the street looking at house after house before she decided upon a place to ask, a white house with vines on the porch set back among elm trees. A tinkle of piano playing came out of the house, curves of music running through the air. When she walked up onto the porch a fear of doorways, of wide sills and glass panes and doorbell fixtures, came upon her. A rug on the porch filled her with terror under which lay a joy. She scarcely dared knock on the smooth doorframe, and her knock fell faint and meek. She asked her wish in a voice that was low and full of anguish. The woman was kind and she asked again.

"Do you-all know any gypsies a-campen out any the roads?"

"No. Are you lost from your folks?"

Ellen thought a moment, putting ideas together and separating them in her mind.

"I'm a-looken for somebody I know," she said. "Just a-looken."

The woman gave her buttered bread and meat and these she hid under her coat until she was sitting again on the curb before the church when she ate them with all the reserve she could control. After that she walked down the street toward the center of the town and there she found many people who looked like the people of her world. No one minded her or noticed her old dress or the coat now hanging on her arm. Many of the people must be richer than herself, she thought, for they had things to sell in baskets and things in buckets—eggs, butter, sorghum molasses. A few of them, she supposed, must be very rich, those riding high-stepping horses or driving in high traps. These went along the roadway with puckered brows, holding tight bits, and they seemed to be worried for fear they might drive over some of the other kind, but those with this worry were a very few. A man began to sell cattle in the square, crying in a loud jargon. The people walked about in the street, ignoring the pavements and the crossings; the order of the town fell down before the way of the country. Ellen stood by the fence that surrounded the courthouse, laying her finger along the wrought-iron spikes and looking at the mouldy walls where the red bricks sank away into shadows. The white stone wall of the jail showed at one side, and in this wall there were little long windows with one iron bar dividing them up and down. A man was standing under one of the windows talking to a voice that came through the iron bar. The courthouse bell rang almost merrily, and lawyers with papers came out of stairways. A man carrying a banner was ringing a bell, and the sheep were crying. "Vote for John

Moran for Sheriff" were the words on the banner, but later there came another banner saying, "Burley Growers Join the Pool." Act fitted into act and turned upon a word; the whole was a drama already well rehearsed; a man leaned out from an upper window just as a cow bawled sharply, and a little boy ran across the square just as an old Negro man led a mule away from the watering tub. A man stood in the door of the courthouse and chanted in a loud voice a chant which came to Ellen thus:

> *O yes! O yes!*
> *The Honorable Judge*
>
> .   .   .
>
> *Is now sitting*
>
> .   .   .
>
> *Come all ye . . .*
> *And you* shall *be heard!*

By mid-morning vehicles could scarcely pass through the throng in the street. Ellen asked her question often. An old man dropped a bag of apples and one rolled down at her feet. She took it up and handed it to him gravely, eager to take part in the play.

"It rolled outen the poke," she said.

"You can keep it, sis."

"Do you know of any campers out any the roads?"

"Not out my way."

Once through an opening in the crowd she saw Mr. Hep Bodine in his Sunday clothes, and she turned around quickly and went another way. Up by a feed store she met a woman dressed much as she was dressed. She carried bunches of coarse lace under her arm.

"Do you-all know any folks about a-swappen critters?" Ellen asked.

60

"*He* is a-traden some. Go down that a way."

Ellen found the place where the men were selling horses, in an alley behind an old hotel. She looked into the crowd eagerly for Jock, but he was not there. Men were riding the horses up and down, tired hacks, bony underfed nags, the kind Ellen knew best. Farmers and traders were bargaining, betting, cursing, laughing.

"Even swap and I'll give you a drink to boot."

"I'll give you nine dollars and seventy-five cents for that-there old mare and that's all I'll give, every dum cent."

Ellen touched a man's arm and asked, holding his coat sleeve: "Do you know a man by the name of Jock West? Do you know Jock West?"

The man shook his head and walked away. The woman with the lace came to the alley and held a short conference with the man. When they had finished speaking and she had turned aside, Ellen stood in her way.

"Are you lost from your folks?" the woman asked.

"Yes ma'am. Tessie is my folks." A pain pushed at her breath and made it quick in her mouth mingling with her words. The woman was smiling with the flesh beside her nose and that across her cheeks, and her nose sniffed at the air. Her lip drew up from her teeth and took a feeble part in the smile.

"Well I do know, lost now!"

"Do you know a woman named Tessie that goes the roads with a man named Jock West? Tessie West, married to Jock West? As you go along the road you might maybe see a sight of Tessie sometime. Jock, he's a great one to swap the critters. Spick span wagon as good as new. Would you tell Tessie for me where I am? Maybe she could write me a letter. Tessie can write. He would be a-goen south by now."

"We are a-maken hit towards Parksville where we aim to stay a spell. But we might . . ."

"If you did happen to run across . . ."

"Well I do know! Lost!" The woman was faintly excited under her dreariness and faintly pleased.

"If you did happen to run across Tessie would you tell her?"

"I'd be right glad to favor you," she said. "We might run onto your folks now. For a fact we might."

"Tell her Ellen is at a farm out a piece from Rushfield, on Mr. Hep Bodine's place, if you see Tessie."

"I couldn't gorrentee to remember hit unlessen you write hit down. Dave, there, he can read hit."

They borrowed a pencil from a man and Ellen wrote on a piece of paper they picked up from the ground:

Ellen Chesser
Rushfield, Ky.
Mr. Hep Bodine's mail box

Ellen stood staring after the woman when she walked away from the alley, seeing her shoulders rise and fall unevenly, stiff, green-drab shoulders that sank into the crowd of the men. The paper was in the pocket of the waist; Ellen had seen fingers push it in beside a little dull pocketbook and a piece of orange peel and a bit of a bright rag. It was gone now, down the long alley past the men and the horses. One sob shook her throat and then peace came after the hours of strain. She had sent a message to Tessie. She had sent word. Turning partly about she saw her father waiting for her, beckoning with a stiff, quick finger, "You come here!"

They rode home on the rear seat of Mr. Bodine's buggy.

II

IT WAS another year. Late May sounds and smells spread over the plowed field, the tobacco field of the season before, ready again for plants. A cool rain had fallen and dense clouds obscured the blue of the sky. Ellen stopped in the row and wound her braid more securely around her head, the blunt end of it just reaching to the nape of her neck. When she had pinned the encircling crown flat with a wire hairpin she drew on the wide straw hat, which fitted snugly over the braid and kept its place. She must wear the hat and keep her skin bleached; her mother said so and Artie Pinkston confirmed the suggestion. "A gal is a long sight prettier if she bleaches." Now an uneasiness troubled her, dragging at her elbows as she adjusted the hair and the hat. Henry was in a quarrel with Mr. Bodine. Her father's voice of yesterday called out sharply in her mind. Usually meek and afraid he had been driven by his anger. "If you don't like the way and how of my farmen you can get somebody else." She walked slowly over the field, dropping the little plants along the rows, with Henry and a man named Goodin following. She felt impatient at the slow progress and kept ahead of the men, her tall slim body moving evenly down row and row, flashing ahead and waiting. Her bare feet were gleaming white in the mud and her skirt hung near her ankles. Her mother's voice came back to her from the fireside talk of the night before, a wailing voice, troubled and angry. "Twenty-four dollars is no sight of money when it's all you got and when there's three in family. . . ." They no longer had the wagon and they could not ride away. Her uneasiness beset her while she waited at the row ends. Mr. Bodine was bringing the plants to the field in baskets, riding his large fine horse to the distant plant bed. He spoke little to Henry and not at all to her, but set each basket down with a brisk attention to the matter. She knew the thought that lay back in his mind. If Henry Chesser left him he could hire Goodin.

In the mid-morning a tall young man came along the fencerow, passing up from the creek. He stood under the locust tree and watched the labor or he talked with Mr. Bodine. "Finished yesterday," he said. "Only a patch this time." Ellen knew the young man's name.

"Joe Trent, he is," Artie Pinkston had said, standing in the lane, "Old Man Sam Trent's boy. He goes off somewheres to study now and then, but his pap brought him home here a while back to help put in the crops. They say he does a sight of work when he sets to. They say he's a fine young man, friendly and easy to know, easy to get acquainted with a body. Just like his pappy before him.

They say his pap come to this country withouten a cent, a cropper. And now look, he owns a right good farm. Some can make whilst some they don't seem to get on so well. Old Man Trent has got a heap to be proud on. They say Joe's got not one lazy bone in his body. He's a worker, they say."

He had come to the creek one April day when Ellen had gone there to get brush. He had seemed very delicate in his suit of clothes and his brown shoes that were narrow and thin, sometimes even gay and pleading. The first day he had talked to her about spring, about the wood, about anything, and his eyes had been bright. She had felt a new kind of smile come to her mouth and a new look come to her eyes. He had come there another day, asking absent-minded questions. She had felt very sad that day. Now when a shower came she stood with her father and Goodin under a thorn tree on the side of the field opposite the locust. The fine mist fell with a whispered sound and the robins set up their songs afresh. Joe Trent went at the first lapse in the rain, going toward the Bodine house, walking carefully to keep his brown shoes out of the wet grass. Ellen watched him go, feeling strange before her altered self. She rubbed the mud from her bare feet, dragging her ankles against the wet herbs. She bent her hat low against her cheeks to hide her strange eyes, and she heard fearfully her father's words spoken to Goodin.

"Hep Bodine thinks he knows all there is about farmen. Well, it's his farm. . . ."

That night she went to bed soon after supper, afraid of the talk below and dreading morning.

"You'll have us set out on the pike, that's what you will, with your eternal faulten."

"Hep Bodine thinks he owns a man that works on his place. I won't stand none of his jaw. . . ."

"You keep your mouth shut or he'll hear you. You're not so bold as you talk. I'm a-tellen you. . . ."

"If Hep Bodine thinks . . ."

"Where'd you go if you got set out on the road?"

The voices fell away and Ellen sank lower into sleep, her thought running back into the day, into the tobacco field, up the fencerow and under the locust tree, across the field in quickly stolen looks. "He likes me even if I wear an o'nary kind of old dress and my old hat that's all I've got," thought spread itself wide with words. "He might maybe be somebody I'd know all my life. The next time he might talk about cities with doors set in close by doors and people walken quick in streets. Or he might tell about some of the wonders of the world."

She would remember his shining eyes all day, and the accompaniment of the memory spread a gentleness over the ugly doorway, over the ladder, over the rough floors. She often felt the smile come to her mouth, always when she remembered any of his phrases. She felt it while she carried the water or while she hoed in the garden, and it came back to her from under the clods. The tobacco field was planted now and the rainy season was over. She had planted beans in the garden and she hoed the patch of corn again and again when her father told her she must. It was toward evening when she went to the ravine for the firewood. One day in June Joe Trent came there again, passing up from the farmhouse with a sharpened scythe in his hand. He stood before her, looking at her, looking at her dark dress and at her stockings and shoes.

"And so you say this is your axe," he said.

66

"Yes sir, it's mine. Pappy made it for me."

"And so your pappy made the axe." He rubbed his hand over the smooth steel. "He's a wonder, your pap. What out of?"

"He never made the blade. He made the handle outen hickory and wedged it in."

"Oh, I see. He didn't make the axe. He made the handle and wedged it in." He held the axe in his hand turning it over and over. Suddenly she wanted to play. She had not played except with herself or with the colt in the pasture for more than a year. She dared not snatch the young man's cap from his head; it was very new and clean, and sweet smells came out of it, new-cap smells. His soft collar was open at the throat, lying easily back, the blue faded a little, the shoulders of the shirt faded even more in the sun. She could have put her finger on the faintly blue threads, but she snatched the axe and ran across the creek, laughing.

"I won't run after you. What I want with you, Louse Patch!" A strange voice ran over the creek stones, coming from the young man's mouth.

"Did you ever see in your time a fountain a-goen? They say that's a pretty sight now." She felt diverted from her play but could not relinquish the curious hour at the point where it touched upon the world. "Have you ever been to London-town? Or to Mexico City or to the Tropic of Cancer? Do men really get sponges outen the sea, do you know? Did you ever go a-washen in the ocean?"

"I saw you in the field with your white stockings on."

"How far would a body have to go now to get to the place in the world where it's dark all winter?"

"What would you say to taking a walk with me up to the thicket in the head of the valley?"

69

"What's 'take a walk?' "

"Any day you say, we'll go."

Sometimes his clothes were made of thin brown stuff with little flecks of amber hidden in the mesh, soft and cool. Another time the threads of blue lapped over each other in the fresh blue necktie, neatly and firmly set, or there were little blue dots set over and over on the white surface of his shirt, unfaded and fair, small as blue dust sprinkled evenly over braided snow. Today the intimacy of the opened throat and of the gray clothes that were frayed at the trouser hem, of the fading blue, came to her as something she shared. He made his voice very low, "Any day you say."

She dragged her bit of brush back to the woodpile and chopped it into fagots. She saw Mr. Bodine stalking through the lower pasture, going up from the way of the cabin, and she carried the wood to the hearth in apprehension, looking fearfully at her mother's face.

"Mr. Hep is a-looken for a heifer that's astray. Did you see e'er one?" Nellie asked.

"Ne'er one did I see."

Mr. Bodine spying about in the dusk and losing a yearling, suspicious of them, it was an evil token. But Joe Trent's eyes were bright, gathering brightness as she set out the plates for supper, as she wondered what would become of herself and her mother if Mr. Bodine told them to go. She did not know how to dispossess them of their goods. She could carry the bedding but what would she do with the bed and how would they move the table and the kitchen safe, acquired after much labor and much waiting? The little bed in the loft became very dear to her, partaking of her self-love and anxiety and standing in need of defense. Joe Trent's eyes were full of gentle looks, but they could

70

draw down into little tubes of looks that went into her dress, under her skin, into her blood. They looked at her blood running under her skin. His bright gentle looks spread through the cabin, lying over all things she saw as she laid the bare table and drew the chairs in place. She could not separate three diffused images, the probing look that went into her flesh, that came flowing from narrowed eyes, the uneasy feel of the house when her mother dished up the food with quick, apprehensive gestures or thumped down a cup with hostile and awkward elbow movements, and the warmth of a smile bent upon her face and running with kindness in her blood. Her mind gave equal and diffused values to the voices within and without.

"He must like me, even if my dress is old-styled and o'nary. He might be somebody I'd know all my whole en-duren life."

A quick flare of words. "What I want with you, Louse Patch?" but she could not define the saying or set it apart from its tones and it fell back unheeded into nothingness.

She thought of a room where there would be fair colors and she felt herself to be stepping down hard white stairs, walking on wide stairs, a low wind fluttering her sleeve. An angry burst of tone came from near the fireplace.

"Your pappy ought to come on now and eat his victuals while they're hot."

"He might be a friend I'd know all my days. 'We'll take a walk,' he says. 'Any day you say.' " She saw little flecks of amber on brown threads of cloth, minutely seen.

"Your pappy ought to come. What's he a-loiteren for? In trouble I reckon. . . ."

"And so this is your axe." The sinking fire made a pink glow on the cups, three cups standing together on the table.

71

"I don't want you, Lousy Brat. I wouldn't tech your lousy rags."

Nellie lit the lamp with a small splint of wood which she held to the dying fire. "We might as well get ready to move out. I'd lay my last quarter on it. A-stirren up Hep Bodine. Your pappy ought to come on."

The outside became deeply blue after the lamp was lit, blue air seen through the glass of the window. "Somebody I'd know all my enduren life."

"And now he's lost a yearlen calf . . ." Nellie returned the supper to the hearth with angry comments. "We might as well move out now."

The trees spread upward into the blue air and were lost, and far away some geese, disturbed, were crying, the tones coming as high thin music flaring upward into the dark. She would have something pink to wear, or fair blue, a bow or a ribbon somewhere on her body. Blue cloth could go trailing over wide stairs, down white steps . . . herself spreading and trailing through blue cloth, gentle and sweet-scented . . . all her enduring life. . . .

Henry came, sullen and tired, bent from his week in the fields. They ate the food in silence, the only noise that of clicking knives and sweeping spoons.

THE grass was high and full with seeds and the white clover was in bloom—late June. Ellen sat by the mouth of the lane watching in the dusk. In a little while she would go to bed, pulling her body lightly up the ladder with her arms. She liked to sit in the white clover by the road, away from the after-supper noises of the cabin, a white clover of thought playing over her mind and spreading a sweetness through her flesh, while another, less than thought, lapped folds of being around her. Gentle, inclusive folds of being lay across her shoulders, included her, covered her with vaporous arms, completed her and gathered her into an undefined sheath. She plucked a few clover blossoms and laid them on her skirt, placing them with care. Feeling could not take words, so melted in and merged it was with the flowers of the grass, but if words could have become grass in Ellen's hand: "It's pretty stuff, clover a-growen. And in myself I know I'm lovely. It's unknowen how beautiful I am. I'm Ellen Chesser and I'm lovely."

She heard wheels coming and she sprang to her feet, caught in a sudden whorl of nervousness. Joe Trent was coming in a buggy with Emphira Bodine, the farmer's daughter, the horse ambling along under loosened reins. Ellen stood ready to speak, her head lifted, but Joe Trent looked back without a sign. He touched the horse lightly with the whip and said something further to Emphira:

"Now I'll tell you how it is. You take those business colleges . . ."

The buggy went on along the road, jolting easily over the stones, the sounds of the wheels growing each instant more flat and remote. Ellen could no longer hear the loose spoke rattle, and then the noises became one running sound that thinned away into the twilight as the vehicle rounded the curve of the road and was lost. She walked back to the cabin, her arms folded under her breast. She passed up the ladder lightly, as her custom was, and retired to her bed in the last faint glow of the dusk. Little shivers of cold passed over her as she took off her clothing in the summer evening, and her hands were stiff and awkward as she pushed off her

73

shoes. She heard a mockingbird singing in the bushes out toward the lane, singing a futile song which reiterated its uselessness and changed its hollow phrases from moment to moment. The sound fell flat upon a flat air.

"That old mock-bird. I wish he'd shut up," she whispered.

If the song had sorrow or wistfulness in it, or any lightness or joy or form, these took place in some other medium than the world of that dusk. The shallow jargon beat upon her pained ears and made no tone. Behind the hard vibrations of this singing the evening seemed very still and very long. She heard the cattle come down to the creek to drink, heard them slopping in the water and pulling at the locust sprouts beyond the fence. The warmth of the bed shut around her and after a while the sounds of the night became remote in their setting of stillness. The well-being of sleep stole over her limbs and she could see white clovers in a pattern, designed against dark threads of cloth. "I'm lovely now," this well-being said. "It's unknowen how lovely I am. It runs up through my sides and into my shoulders, warm, and ne'er thing else is any matter. I saw some mountains standen up in a dream, a dream that went down Tennessee. I will tell somebody what I saw, everything I saw. It's unknowen how lovely I am, unknowen."

SHE was in the ravine, far up past the third pool, to gather brush. Some men were working on a high slope, dragging out walnut stumps, their axes leaving the sound behind at each stroke. Their voices came down to her strange and thin. Mr. Bodine was slowly clearing out the hillside, a little

74

now and a little then, and after a while it would be a steep tobacco field. She saw someone moving among the brush on the slope opposite that on which the men were working, she saw clothing gleaming an instant in the sun and a form slipping back into the brush. It was Joe Trent keeping behind the redbud glade, and when he saw that she looked up he beckoned to her. He signaled many times but he was careful to keep behind the redbud clumps.

He would have on his Saturday clothes, she reflected, the blue shirt washed smooth and fine, spreading out in fair ways over his shoulders and wrinkling down to sweet smooth wrinkles by the sleeves. His straw hat would smell sweet, like varnish and like sweet chalk. His hands had little marks like tiny wells set close together behind the thumbs. His eyes would be bright and they would look at her and grow brighter. A voice said quickly, coming up as one motion from her deeper mind: "I saw your white all-overs the day you went washing in the creek."

She could see the blue necktie as clearly as if it lay on the ground under her hand when she gathered the sticks. The threads of the silk lapped over and over like a woven basket, only infinitely fine, growing finer as she gazed. Perhaps he would not have his stockings on, and then there would be the skin of his ankles, or perhaps he would have on the blue overalls. The skin of his ankles was under her hands and under her eyes as she reached for the twigs, and his brown hair with its whorl at the crown, so lovely and uneven that she had wanted once to touch it with her fingers and smooth it down. She shrank back from the lovely thought of his cheek and a quick voice spread across her confusion, "Lousy Brat! I'd be afraid to touch your lousy rags."

Then she gave back the whole thought to her mind to play

75

over. She shrank from nothing. Why not go? Soft white skin. Hands that were stronger than her own and softer to touch. Why not? Why was she always there? Nobody to see but Artie Pinkston and her youngones. Her blood leaped before her up the canyon.

But her feet kept among the littered grass and weeds and her hand outstretched for the cut fagots. The sticks were very clear and plain to see in the afternoon light. She gathered the last of the armful and went down stream slowly, the axe in her right hand, the wood piled on her left arm and shoulder.

When the walnut stumps were gone, hauled away to town in a wagon, the men no longer worked on the hillside. Ellen avoided going to the creek ravine although her mother demanded wood. She searched for burning pieces about the yard and the lower pasture, or, if none could be found here, she hid in the tall weeds beyond the garden patch and gave no heed to her mother's calls.

"That lazy triflen brat! I got no firewood!"

She would sit among the high growth, covered with shame, shame drawing downward in her face and weighing down her head. Joe Trent beckoning to her, hiding in the brush, waiting up in the ravine, passing up from Bodine's with a tool; she never saw him closer. Nor did she ever speak of him to either of her parents. Her mind tossed up its sayings even while it denied her the solace of thought. "Where'd you go if you got set out on the pike? . . . Somebody to know all my enduren life. . . ." She pictured them out on the pike, herself and Henry and Nellie. They would walk away down the road, far, on and on, or they would sit by a creek to rest. They would sleep in the quilts and there would be something, perhaps, to eat. In two days they could be gone far, and she would be glad. But she was sitting in the tall weeds and they were there as before; Goodin was gone from the country and Hep Bodine, his stiff legs walking unevenly up and down his hills, could not farm without Henry. . . . "Somebody to know all my enduren life. . . . There's no knowen how lovely I am. . . . How lovely . . . Lousy rags . . . I'd be afraid to touch . . . Take a walk . . . Any day you say . . ."

She discovered a way to bring down the wood and avoid the angers of her parents. She would go to the mouth of the land and watch the road in the direction of the Bodine house, her body well hidden in the summer growth beside the fence. When she saw Trent go out in the buggy with Emphira she would run to the ravine and drag down wood all afternoon, and she contrived to keep the pile under the locust tree replenished in this way. The plan succeeded very well, and she followed it all summer, but she lost the shaded ravine and the upper creek as a pleasant place to go, and she bathed no more in the water. The white stones and the moss stones of the farthest creek became beautiful in memory. The name, Joe Trent, went out of her being slowly. For weeks the mention of it brought a first flush of warmth to her mind and a gentle flow of momentary joy to all her members. "Friend" lay in thought with the word, "Somebody I might know all my life. A body to tell things to." But finally the chord was cut. By the time the tobacco was ripe the name no longer caught at her nerves when Artie Pinkston called it in her gossip.

"Well, Joe Trent he's gone back to his college. I see Emphira a-driven him to the train today."

77

THE first of January came with mild thawing weather after a season of freezing and snow. A sense of expectancy and tension lay over the cabin, a tension met by apathy. Henry was going to a new place, to the Al Wakefield farm in another end of the county. Ellen pushed into the new life that was coming to try to make pictures of it, but it was but vaguely seen as drawing back from her tense nerves. A man from Wakefield's would come for them and their furniture, but the necessity of stirring, of going to a new place by physical efforts, stifled her. She glanced from time to time at her mother's drawn face as they sat by the log fire during the winter morning. No one made any preparation for the departure; instead they sat close to the fireplace answering each other nervously.

"It's a sight richer farm," Henry said. "And croppen on the shares is a sight better contract and I'll tell you for why . . ."

"Well, put some wood on. I'm plumb cold," Ellen wailed, drawing closer to the hearth.

"Move over, Henry, and let Ellen in. Quit a-spreaden so. . . ."

There would be a stairway up to Ellen's room and there would be a kitchen with a stove, all set up and ready. They would be furnished with a cow. Henry told and retold the details of his contract, wanting praise.

"But old Mrs. Bodine was a right good neighbor-woman," Nellie said, "a-senden down a bundle of clothes every now and then." At her mother's words Ellen looked down at her skirt, Emphira's skirt, dark gray wool, torn a little at the hem. The man came for them when they had sat half the morning staring wretchedly into the flames. He turned the team about briskly and backed the wagon near the door.

"I reckon you-all are ready," he said.

They hurried excitedly, tumbling the things out of the house into the wagon. Ellen cried softly as she rolled up her quilts and lapped her clothes into the bundle. She was acutely aware of the little loft room at the moment of leaving it, and she looked about at the brown splintered floor. She knew the knots and marks on the ladder, the shelf in the cubby-hole, the stones of the hearth. She wanted to go; she had talked much of going, of the stairway and the kitchen, of the cow she would milk, of the cream they would have. She wanted to go but her mind clung to its familiar objects. The roll of her things seemed very futile as she laid it on the door-sill, shapeless and burdensome and ugly, herself somehow so identified with it, with what she had, that she wept.

"Oh, what for?" she cried softly when she sat among the household goods at the back of the wagon. She saw the last of the yellow lane crying, "What for, anyway?"

Nellie and Henry rode on the front seat with the driver and as they rolled away from the lane Ellen watched them sitting huddled and restrained, their heads showing above the upturned chairs. The horses jogged gaily along the road, careless of their light burden, and presently Ellen was aware of the pleasant feel of the sun's warmth on her shoulders. After a little she noticed the lilt of the horses and she found words on her lips that fitted in with the rhythms they made. Some little birds hopped about on the stone fences dropping little beads of winter song. The few white clouds stood back from the sun and runlets trinkled out of every field, out of every ledge. The green winter mosses along the road were full of life. The horses slopped merrily through the pools that stood along the low-lying bits of road. Something about the wagon jingled, as a loose chain or tire, and this made a

79

gay accompaniment to the clatter of the hoofs and her lips repeated merrier phrases, merry nonsense jargons out of old remembered songs. They went by a little schoolhouse where heads bobbed up at windows to see them pass. She could see her mother and father more plainly now, for something had settled down out of the line of vision. Nellie had the brown scarf drawn about her head and Henry wore a tight old coat pulled up to the chin. Their bodies quivered with the quivering of the wagon-seat and they were talking eagerly, included in a chat with the driver. White and roan shorthorn cattle grazed in an upland field off to the right as the wagon came swaying lightly down a slope and thundered briefly across a little bridge. When Ellen glanced forward again her mother and father had been looking back at her. They caught her glance and looked again, smiling. Nellie nodded her head comradely and said with her lips, "How you a-maken it?" and Henry touched his hat in salute. "How nice we-all are. I didn't ever know us to be so nice," Ellen said when she looked back at the merry hills. A warmth of being beat in her blood and in her breast it spread to a great size. Beyond her chair rose the safe and beyond that her own cot bed, up on end, familiar and gay, all there together, whatever happened, and the sun came down warm and lush. Her roll of bedding lay behind her chair; she could touch it with her hand, the blue cover sticking out from under the brown one and her clothing sticking out a little from the inner part.

They avoided the town, taking turnings and crossroads, and at noon they stopped at a store set in front of valley fields where the roads went off in a Y. The driver and the storekeeper lifted two bales of fence wire into the wagon and tucked them snugly in a little beyond Ellen's feet.

"That'll ride all right, Sissy. No trouble to you a tall," the storekeeper said. "Hit looks like a boey constrictor, but hit's only fence wire." When the old man talked his skin quivered and showed the tobacco stains running in the wrinkles about his mouth.

After they started on again the way was even gayer, for every little while someone was met and there were greetings and salutes exchanged with the driver. "The new tenants for Wakefield's." Ellen would catch a phrase now and then from a vehicle passed. She felt herself and all of them become what they were said to be—new and tenants, something for Wakefield, something along with the big quick-stepping horses, along with her mother smiling and Henry waving his hand as if she were somebody else. They were ten miles west of the county seat now; she read the numbers on the mileposts. The road curved· gently down among valley farms and crossed a wide creek. They were in a richer and better country, Ellen knew. The driver stopped at a white gate and pulled a long pole that hung out toward the road, and when the gate swung open the horses trotted through, hardly giving Henry time to pull the pole on the other side to close the gate. The Wakefield house stood above on a gentle slope, a large old house of blue-gray weatherboards with tall trees gathered about. The wagon kept in the valley, rounded a hill, put the house on the right, and thus came to a small whitewashed cabin set in a little yard of its own. The rear wall of the large house stood now divided from Ellen by cattle-lots and large white barns and was faint behind tall, close-standing trees.

THE tenant house had three rooms, two below stairs and one above—the latter would be Ellen's bedroom. A narrow staircase passed up from one of the lower rooms, the main room of the house. The other room, the kitchen, stood back a few feet and in the L was a little porch from which wooden steps went down into the yard. Ellen looked at the kitchen stove, walking around it, comprehending its doors and grate. Something like it but different came up in her mind, another smooth dark surface with doors that would open. The house seemed hollow and damp while she stood there, full of silences and voices suddenly speaking out. A broken flatiron lay behind one of the doors, but the room was swept clean. There was a shelf above the stove and another shelf in a corner. She could walk through the door and be standing at once in the larger room beside the fireplace where Henry was fanning a blaze under wood and chips. She could walk back through the door and there was the kitchen again, the front door going out onto the little porch, the back door going down tall steps into a hollow place behind the house where some out-buildings stood. It was very lovely and very strange. The rooms were full of hollowness and sharp sudden noises when anyone spoke. It was something she remembered. She had been there before, only there was, the other time, a brick floor and there was a tall white cat. A tall white cat came out from under the stove and on the stove a teakettle was boiling. She had been six years old then and she had lived in a house under some nut trees. One day a man went by with his back full of tinware to sell and she could hear all the little cups crying and chiming together when he passed on. "What I want with any more tin? I got no money to buy tin," a voice said. "Take care your fingers, I'm a-goen to shut the door. . . ." She could remember the strange smell that hung about the nut trees.

Ellen went up the staircase to the room above which was filled with the late afternoon sun and was quite warm. Henry set up her bed in the middle of the floor, telling her she could push it anywhere it best pleased her. Her first night there was strange and sleepless, for a high wind blew. She heard mules running overhead in the wind. Other mules were crying out somewhere over toward the barns and farther off a jack was braying. It was far back to Bodine's. She had slept there only the night before and she had risen there that morning, but the loft room seemed far, beyond the moss on the road, beyond the bale of wire, beyond the white cat and the tinman, beyond men fishing in a river, wading with long naked legs and drawing in a seine full of fishes with little horns. There were hounds in the air before morning, rushing down through trees full upon the cabin. She could hear the beating of their feet above the pleading of their voices as they passed the door on the trail of the hunted thing.

Ellen milked her cow by the little gate which led from the dooryard to the pasture. In three days she had learned to make the milk flow easily, stroking the animal flesh with deft fingers. The cow was a slim tan Jersey with a bright face and quick horns. Her body was bony and full of knots—bone joints, and her sides were unsymmetrically balanced. She had slender short legs and small sharp feet. She seemed to Ellen to be all paunch, a frame skeleton supporting a subtended belly with buds of milk, a machine to produce milk hung under a bony frame. Ellen looked at her each milking time; she knew the wrinkles on her skin around the eyes and her wrinkled neck, her loud breathing, her corrugated tongue and lips, her moist muzzle, and her pathetic mouth with its drooping lower lip. The tight eyelids seemed scarcely large enough to fit over the large round eyes and the hair spread out from a center on her forehead, making a star. Her horns were like dark rough pearl and they slanted up over the big skeleton of her face. She moved about very slowly, turning away from the milking place when she had been drained dry, always humble and enslaved, or she walked off across the pastures joining many others at the feeding rick near the stock barns. Ellen saw the men milking in the barnlot, or three or four men and a woman, doing one thing and another, seeming very earnest about the opening of a gate or the hitching of a team. The land rolled out in all directions from Ellen's milking place. There were rolling hills laid out in fields reaching north and east into a long distance but standing closer and higher in the other points. Through the pasture a farm road ran, unfenced, passing into fields through gates and finally out into Mac-Murtrie land and then over the west hill. The February white frost lay over the farm in these first mornings and the gentle north hills rolled away like low waves. Day after day Ellen saw the men moving about the farm yards and pens, a Negro man—Ben—three white men and one or two women. Some day she might get to know them. They went briskly up and down in the February cold or they stood by gates and called to one another. They might some day call to her; they might be saying quick things to her some day, upward-bending words. For her the people were all folded into one mass which passed and turned, now quick and now slow. The silo tower stood up against the sky. Sound fitted upon sound, never returning, the pageant always flowing.

Henry was pleased with his new place. He went to work early each morning, building fence, clearing new ground on a hillside, making ready his plant bed. He grubbed away roots and chopped out brush, and by the middle of February the smoke went up from his clearing, for he piled brush onto the ground and burnt it for the good of the soil. On other hills near and far away other fires were burning; from the hillside Ellen would see the great flames leap into the air and then smoulder down to a smoke that arose all day. She helped her father clear the plant bed of its stones, and working on this hillside she could see MacMurtrie's house where it stood toward the south, a dull wall of dark bricks seen through old cedar trees, and she would hear over and over the echoes of Henry's satisfaction with the new place and of Nellie's relief, "I'm right glad we got shed of Hep Bodine." The excitement of the new life kept her aware of all her acts. Each time she passed from door to door on the little porch she saw the low hillrim to the east, a part of the north valley, the white walls of the barns, and the upper planes of the house, gray in the sun but blue in the shade. It was a larger house than Bodine's, more reserved and more remote.

The farm road lying through the pasture did not come near the cabin but ran in a curve up from the gate at the turnpike, past the pond, and made off toward the upper fields. Men sometimes went along this road on horseback, neighbors from the small farms toward the river. Ellen chopped the wood at the woodpile in the yard and she carried water from an old well in the rear of the pasture. She was afraid to pass beyond the ways allotted to her by her labors, and so the region beyond the pond stood off as a picture, unexplored. The cow would turn away from the other cows and linger down toward the osage shrubs beside the pond, humble, not sure she was wanted, ready to come when Ellen made a little detour to drive her in. Ellen looked forward to the time when the turkeys would be hatched at the barnyard, for she was to have charge of them during the day and see that they came safely home at evening. These duties would take her nearer the barns and the people working there. She might get to know Ben the Negro, and John Bradshaw the hand who looked after the mules and horses; she might get to know Josie the yellow girl, even Mr. Al Wakefield, or even Miss Tod, his wife. Wonder colored every act with a haunting sense of its past or its relation to something. In the cabin she would look at the doorways, the knobs, and the latches, at the closet under the stair. She felt a great rush of well-being as she mounted the stairs, a sense of pageantry, and she tried different methods of descent, walking demurely, gliding down stiffly, or tripping down with dancing steps.

WHEN Henry had burned his plant bed he plowed and hoed the ashes into the soil and made a frame of logs about the whole, a light frame to hold the canvas that would be stretched over the bed when the seeds were sown. There were more stones to gather after the plowing and these Ellen piled outside the bed. The rocks were dark with mould and moss, for this was a virgin hill. It was a mild March day, cool and clear, with winds worrying the hillside brush and leaping off across the farms in a great rush or beating gently now and then at Ellen's garments. Henry nailed at the frame while she worked with the stones.

"No plow iron ever cut this-here hill afore, not in the whole time of man," Henry said.

"The time of man," as a saying, fell over and over in Ellen's mind. The strange men that lived here before our men, a strange race doing things in strange ways, and other men before them, and before again. Strange feet walking on a hillside for some purpose she could never think. Wondering and wondering she laid stones on her altar.

"Pappy, where do rocks come from?"

"Why, don't you know? Rocks grow."

"I never see any grow. I never see one a-growen."

"I never see one a-growen neither, but they grow all the same. You pick up all the rocks offen this-here hill and in a year there's as many out again. I lay there'll be a stack to pick up right here again next year."

"I can't seem to think it! Rocks a-growen now! They don't seem alive. They seem dead-like. Maybe they've got another kind of way to be alive."

"Maybe they have. All I know is they grow."

"Rocks have got shells printed on the sides and some have little snails worked on their edges and some have got little worms-like worked on. But once I found a spider with a dragon beast in a picture on its back. Some rocks, now, are shaped like little silos and some are all marked with little snails and waterbugs and some are open fans and some have little scallops on the edges. Rocks grow in ways that are right pretty now. It's a wonder, really."

"I wish I could see a rock grow," she said again. "I can't think how it is. You could watch a rock for a whole year and you'd never see any sign of it growen. The rock doorstep over at Bodine's didn't grow e'er bit all the time we lived there."

"Maybe it did and you couldn't see."

"It might maybe be they don't grow if you watch, like fish don't bite if you make a noise."

"I don't expect, now I come to study about it, I don't expect rocks out like that grow. It's rocks in fields that grow, if you ever noticed."

"Maybe they take soil, like everything else, but it's a strange wonder nohow. Like ants now, and like where wind comes from, like horsehairs that turn to snakes, or like warts that go away and you never know when."

"I heared a man say once that the sun was made outen fish oil. He said when fishes die they float on the top of the water and the air dries up the oil and it draws up to the sun. Up in the sun it burns and that's what makes the heat and light. I heared a man say that. I don't know whe'r he was a learned man or not."

"Well," Ellen said. And again, "Well, some people sleep on beds but some sleep on the ground and some sleep on the floor and some sleep in wagons. I've heared it said sailors sleep in hammocks. The people on the other side of the world might, maybe, sleep some other way we can't think. It might be that way with the sun for all we know. It might be fish oil like that man said and again it might be some other kind. I wish I knowed for sure."

She was working alone on the hillside. Henry had gone for the seeds and was long in returning. She gathered stones from the plowed soil and piled them in her neat mound, and the wind continued to blow off the hilltop. She found spotted ladybugs hidden under the leaves and the twigs; they shone out like jewels in the brown and black of the earth. Far away toward MacMurtrie's cedar trees doves were crying, and over the plowed field plovers went circling, sing-

88

ing on the wing. To the northeast the hills rolled away so far that sight gave out, and still they went, fading into blue hazes and myths of faint trees; delicate trees stood finer than hair lines on a far mythical hill. She piled stone after stone on the mound, carrying each across crumbled earth that the plow and the hoe had harried. The rocks fell where she laid them with a faint flat sound, and the afternoon seemed very still back of the dove calls and the cries of the plovers, back of a faint dying phrase, "in the time of man." The wind lapped through the sky, swirling lightly now, and again dashing straight down from the sun. She was leaning over the clods to gather a stone, her shadow making an arched shape on the ground. All at once she lifted her body and flung up her head to the great sky that reached over the hills and shouted:

"Here I am!"

She waited listening.

"I'm Ellen Chesser! I'm here!"

Her voice went up in the wind out of the plowed land. For a moment she searched the air with her senses and then she turned back to the stones again.

"You didn't hear e'er a thing," she said under her breath. "Did you think you heared something a-callen?"

ELLEN's room had been papered with a yellow print at some time long past, but in the meanwhile the roof had leaked and the water had run down the walls, which were now stained with brown marks that changed with each rain. When she first gazed at them as she lay in her bed they were monsters depicted in shadows and running lines of brown and clouds of amber. They became demons impaled on trees, on walls, crucified on bars of black and dying lewdly, not decently agonized on their crosses. One spouted a jet of water from a snout that protruded from its armless trunk, laughing with a great jaw. After the next rain a woman in a long shawl came walking through the crosses and a slim hand held up a flower. Another time hands were sinking under tawny water, calling-out hands, but the rains of April smudged all out and began a new story with large bears running after little beings of some sort. Ellen stood turning about in the little room. She had hung her wardrobe on the nails of the east wall, her skirt of black wool, her dark waists, and her nightdress. The cot stood by the south window, through which came the April sun to make a long warm rectangle on the bare floor, and the morning with its hard light searched out every meagerness of the apartment. The window panes were marked with smudges left by the painter's careless hands long ago, and Ellen had not been able to wash the glass clean and clear. The floor tilted a little toward the south wall. Ellen turned about in the morning glare, bending her neck to look at herself, stepping about to search out the ways of her movements.

"I'm ugly," she said, "and I might as well know it and remember. My hands are big and coarse and my skin is browned and redded in the wind. My eyes are slow and big, always a-looken at everything in the world and always expecten to see something more. My face looks like the ground and my back looks like ground with my old cloak pulled over it. I'm ugly. My hands, they're ugly and my feet have got on big old shoes. My feet are like roots of trees. I look like a board and I look like a rough old pond in a pig pasture. I'll remember. I'm ugly. Ugly. I'm ugly in the way I walk; sometimes a-goen fast and sometimes slow, scared-like. I might as well remember. No need for you to think about something pink to wear or something blue or yellow. No use to think about soft colors. You might as well wear one kind as another. Drab. Brown. Faded dark old shrunk-up anything is good enough. Why don't you just give up and be ugly? That's what you are. Ugly. That's all.''

She went down the stairs slowly, beaten back upon herself. Out in the pasture she cut dandelions and wild mustard for greens for dinner, searching over the ground and cutting a bit here and there, wild lettuce and lamb's-quarter and a bit of narrow dock. A great load was gone from her body. She went lightly from place to place to search out the green herbs as they grew among the grass. No matter about her hands or her searching eyes or her heavy-shod feet. They did not have to be any other way. It was pleasant to bound lightly from place to place in cool green stuff and find out tender young green bits to cook for dinner. The sun and the ground and the herbs to eat, the herbs cut and dropped into her basket, to spring from one tuft to another on light-going arms and feet—that was a good way to be.

THE turkeys had been hatched several days when Ben came to the tenant house door one morning with a sack of coarse corn meal and a bunch of red peppers. The flocks had been turned into the pasture that day and Ellen would make bread for them out of the ground corn and a little of the pepper and feed them at noon near the pond. Ben told her that Miss Tod expected her to watch after them from time to time during the day and to bring them to the barnlot just before dark and close them into their coops. All day Ellen remembered, scarcely able to wait until evening when she should become a part of the movement about the large barns and pens, when she would go, she hardly knew where, and do things she could scarcely foretell behind the small red gate. The two barnlots made right angles with each other and in the extreme end of each stood a large barn, one for the cows and one, that on the left, for the horses and mules. As Ellen approached the enclosures from the cabin she passed near the mule barn while the cow barn lay off to the right, and in the corner where the two lots came near together there was a gate leading into a third lot which was used for the calves and turkeys. This was the small red gate through which she would go. The first day the turkey hens were shy of her and it was Ben who enticed them through the gate, the chicks running uneasily after, slinking under their strange crumpled shoulders. Ellen fed them the pepper bread and the corn, lingering near them to cure them of their fright of her. Ben pumped water into the trough for a short while but when Josie came from the house with pails jangling he left this and went to help with the milking. Mr. Al came to give an order to John Bradshaw, and then the milk began to flow into the pails with a high thin crying sound that became low and dull as the liquid beat upon the foam, but other high thin cries overtook the low ones as John Bradshaw filled his pail and started another. Mr. Dick was working in the horse barns feeding the mules and horses. He would pass across the runway with a great fork of straw on his shoulder. He was large and tall, like Mr. Al, his brother, but younger and more neat. "Wakefield Brothers, Stock Farm" was printed on paper. A piece of it had come fluttering down across the pasture one March day and lodged in the cherry brush. Now the hens were afraid of Ellen and she left them to their corn. She stood off by the gate, feeling useless and incompetent and, when no one was looking, she slipped through the gate and went quickly down the hill.

In a week, however, the strangeness was gone, and when she crumbled pepper bread by the pond at noon the hens came with their speckled broods that cried "pee pee pee." There were five or six hens, each with fifteen or twenty chicks. Ellen's orders came from Ben who conveyed messages from Miss Tod. "Was the old bronze hen a good mother?" She must be sure to keep the drinking pans clean. Going about her labors Ellen carried pepper bread in her apron pocket and she would give some of this to the chicks whenever she met them. They would flow about her feet like strange water when she walked across the pasture toward the tobacco field.

Mr. Al was large and gentle, moving slowly through his farm, speaking to his stock in a firm gentle voice, deep-sounding out of his broad back and full sides. He spoke gently to Ellen:

"See't you shut that-there gate always. Them calves mustn't get out."

Ellen could hear the deep echoes of his words flowing through the barns, flattened against the hay, hollowed-out in the corridors, and rolled out in a sheet before the high outer wall. Mr. Dick had the same voice, gentle among the mules, firm and wide-flowing.

"Stand up there Buck. Woah there! Get in there Ike!"

The two voices flowed around her as she crumbed the pepper bread for the little turkeys. The voices were full of deep, gentle, abrupt undercurrents; they went stepping

93

down notes with long steps, as men's voices go in singing, walking through a tune, walking down a tune to the very bottom of song. Ben's voice came upon her too, an old voice, full of cracked words that were jointed in the middle, each fragment full of harmonies.

"Take yo' turn, now, you li'l' devil, an' suck yo' mammy. Dis-here calf's big 'nough to wean, I'm a-thinken. Get outen dat bucket, Ol' Black! Always got yo' nose in somewheres!"

Once in a while Miss Tod came to the lot. She was a large woman with plump hands that were often full of rings. Sometimes there were stains around the corners of her mouth from the snuff she had taken. "I'm right proud of my turkeys this year," she said. "If you take care the best you can I'll give you one for a present for your Thanksgiving dinner, besides the pay."

Ellen would milk the cow before sundown and carry the milk to the little porch before the cabin and strain it there. Then she would bathe her face in the wash pan and brush her hair smooth before the kitchen mirror, winding her long braid around her head. In the glass she would see her own clear eyes and brown lashes and she would look at the little pits in the corners of her eyes. If she strained her face upward she could see her neck where there were a few brown freckles, and she could see the little hollow in her throat between two white bones. Sometimes she looked long at her teeth and her lips, searching them out, trying to know all their ways, or she would search out her dimpled smile or stand back to see her smooth cheeks or draw down her dress at the throat to see her white breast and shoulder.

"I'm a-goen now, Mammy," she would say. "Is it time?"

"I expect it is. You better."

She would take the turkey bread in her hand and go,

94

bonnetless, up the gentle hill across the pasture in the light of sundown, calling the hens as she went. She was keenly aware of the ceremony and aware of her figure rising out of the fluttering birds, of all moving together about her. She would hear the mules crunching their fodder as she went past the first barn, and she would hear the swish of falling hay, the thud of a mule hoof on a board, a man's voice ordering or whistling a tune. She would take the flocks in at the gate, careful not to let any of the calves out, and she would know that John Bradshaw knew that she was there although he said nothing and looked nothing. She would crumble down the bread for each brood near its coop and she would make the count and see to the drinking pans. Then she would go back through the gate, only a wire fence dividing her from the milking group, and walk down the pasture in the dusk. That was all; the office would be over.

A dim smoky light would shine out from the kitchen where Nellie had placed a supper on the table. Henry was always very tired after his day in the fields, walking slowly and stiffly. Sometimes Nellie was angry because they came in late, but often she was full of talk. She had seen this one or that go by along the farm road, one of the Townleys or O'Shays, people living on the small farms along the river. A wagon had broken down by the pond and spilled a load of hay, everybody running from all sides. The beans were right good seasoned with a scrap of jowl meat. Ellen must make fast that hole in the fence or else the cow would be in with the calf before morning. She was out of soda and salt, and there was not a dusten of meal in the house, and if they expected any more victuals they could fetch her some. Sometimes there was no oil for the lamp, and the gloom would settle over their spirits and over the food. They would fumble their way to bed, dreary sequel to a day spent in the sun and the wind, in the rain or gray mists. But neither the unlit house nor the stumbling on the stairs, nor tired muscles, nor the cruel evenings when there was no salt in the bread and Nellie angry, cruel evenings when the rain crept on the yellowed wall, could take the eagerness out of Ellen's day or the memory of it out of her night. People knowing her, having her in their thoughts, saying things to her, coupling her acts with their acts—"Take the calves in as soon as Ellen gets through." The days ran by quickly, mounting higher and higher; she felt herself spreading over the farm. Evening after evening she would go lightly up the stairs with the coming of dark, a little impatient with the night for its interruptions and impatient with her tired body. Or one evening in June when a soft breeze full of earthy freshness spread through the cabin, coming from the south hill where a little marsh lay under willows, tears came to her breast and a strong hand was laid on her vitals. She sat on her cot, too wretched to unrobe herself. The perpetual sadness of youth had flowed upward to engulf her. She was unable to gather her sense of it into a thought.

"Oh, why am I here and what is it all for anyway? What is it is a-beaten down on my breath? I'm a-fallen through the world and there's no end to the top and no end to the bottom. Mammy a-getten up and a-cooken and a-goen to bed and Pappy works all day, and we have to eat and we have to wear and we have to have fire, and there's no end to anything."

Twilight settled down into the room with diffused shadows and the walls sank out of sight. The nightjars were crying in the sky and a bleat of sheep would come now and then across the half-dark, sadder than she could bear.

"I'm old. I'm so old I'm about done with liven. I can feel how old I am. I'm old and old and old. I've been in life a long, long time. Oh, how old I am."

A sob stood, a bar, before her flowing mind. She was pushed and shoved up against the barrier. She let her body fall to the bed and lay curled there, too sad to make further preparations to sleep. On and on, without end, she felt herself and all other things going, day and night and day and rain and windy weather, and sun and then rain again, wanting things and then having things and then wanting. Eating and then wanting to eat again, and never any end, and it goes on and on. On and on. And then you're old. And what did you ever have that was enough? And what was it for anyway? You could never see any end to anything and it goes on and on. Night comes and then it gets to be day, and sheep cry and then they're still and then they cry again. Voices beat on her memory but they made hollow meaningless noises. Something that came to nothing went on and on. "Open the gate, Ellen!" It was nothing but sound running up and down. What for? What for? On and on. Thus until sleep, the comforter spoke, running gentle hands down her tired nerves and sad thought. "It's no knowen how lovely I am. I'm a-liven. My heart beats on and on and my skin laps around me and my blood runs up and it runs down, shut in me. It's unknowen how lovely."

ONE evening in August one of the turkey hens failed to bring her brood back to the pasture, and Ellen searched the near-lying fields all through the dusk crying "pee, pee, pee," and looking into the fence corners. She thought the hen would

97

be sitting with her chickens huddled about her. "Some varment will get you-all for certain if you stay out all night," she whispered over and over.

The next morning the hen had not come and Ellen went off across the fields as soon as she had milked the cow and cut the wood for the dinner fire. She looked anxiously through the oat stubble and down the tobacco rows. Beyond the tobacco field lay a stretch of lightly wooded hillside sloping down toward the north, and when this had been searched she came to strange fences and other fields belonging to neighboring farms. She retraced her way to the tobacco field again, climbing on fences to peer out over the land, but later she went down the wooded hill again, drawn by the strange vistas seen through the trees, framed by the trees, and climbed a stone wall which ran up one side of a cut grain field. It was a clear day with blue sky and wind and a hot sun shining. The wind and the sun were one. The sun flowed in waves over her and throbbed in the mesh of her cotton dress. The sun quivered in waves over the stubble and over the moist pasture. She walked through crab grass and timothy and wild barley, the way leading down a creek toward the north, a little creek that lay against the side of the hill and was crossed at each fencerow by a watergap. She broke a long withe and with this she switched at her ankles as she walked quickly down the creekside. The angles of the hills turned in strange ways and the white stones of a strange creek lay wide in the sun. She began to sing a song she had heard Ben mumbling.

> *Oh, little Blue Wing is a pretty thing,*
> *All dressed out so fine.*
> *Her hair comes a-tribblen down her back*
> *And the boys can't beat her time.*

She went over a watergap where a little willow grew, swaying down into the heart of the willow tree with a sweep of bent branches. Emerged from that she walked on gravel and rank creek grass and frightened the snake doctors away from a still pool as she pranced quickly by.

"Not a-goen anywheres, just a-goen . . ." She crossed the creek on a sandy bar, murmuring a little to herself as she went. "You're spiderwort. You're tansy. I know you. I'm as good as you. I'm no trash. I got no lice on me."

A path lay under her feet, a path cattle took to go to the deeper water holes and she saw the little steps of cattle in the pale soil. The beaten ground made walking easy, and when the way swerved away from the creek she followed although it drifted into an upland, an undulation of pasture where strange cattle grazed, black and white beasts lividly spotted. They made vivid color against the green of the hill and they drifted in the quivering air, raising a head now and then to see her as she passed. She sang loud in the face of the cattle as they stood on their up-sloping pasture.

> Liddy Marget died like it might be today,
> Like it might be today, like it might be today,
> And he saw the bones of a thousand men.

"Saw the bones of a thousand men. Saw with his eyes, that is. I thought till just now when I studied about it he sawed the bones with a saw. Sawed the bones of a thousand men. I saw that-there man there a-sawen with a big saw and bone saw-dust a-siften down. I'm a fool for sure."

In the enclosure beyond the pasture of the black-and-white cows she came to a tobacco field, a struggling crop unevenly growing on worn-out soil. She sat on the fence and marveled at the ill-conditioned plants, jeering at them.

99

"Gosh, what a crop! Durned if I ever see such runty trash a-growen in a field. What you call yourself nohow? Sallet?"

She inspected the tobacco for worms, a habitual action, as she passed down a row. Struggling clover grew between the drills and wild grass inched out from the fencerow.

Beyond the tobacco field she saw that there was a grave-yard set beside an old church. She came upon it from the rear, walking down a path through brush tangles, and when she had climbed a high rail fence she stood among the aban-doned graves. She parted the growth and twisted her body through the brush snarls until she came to the part that was grassy and well kept, some of the mounds adorned with blossoming flowers. There were no trees and thus the graves and the gravestones were open to the sun and were blown over by the wind. The sun came down more freely here than in the fields for it had the stones to play over, white and shining marble. The wind swayed the grass and the sun vibrated over the white monuments. "Erected to the Memory of," she read. "To the Memory of," or some held simply the legend of a family name, as Wakefield, in large stiff letters blocked out of the stone. On one a high winged creature stood holding a lily and a book.

"How would you buy a tombstone, now?" her mind chattered within itself. "Would you go to the store and say . . . But it would have to be some other kind of store beside Kelly's at the road corners. Say it's a tombstone store some-wheres, and say he has a sign out, 'Tombstones cheap today.' You go inside the store and there the tombstones are all up and down the big counters, counters made big on purpose, and on the big shelves. You say to the man, ' I want to buy a tombstone' and he says, 'Would you like one that says "To the memory of" or would you rather have

"Erected to?" Here's one that you can have cheap if you taken it offen my hands today. It's nicked a little at the corner and it says "Pray for the soul of" and that's not the latest style. But if you don't care so much about style and if you want something that'll wear you long, you'll never be sorry for a-buyen this-here one.'"

She laughed a little at the thought and walked about in the swaying grass and felt the hot waves of air as they rolled back off the large marbles. She came to a tall stone marked Gowan. It glittered in the sun where the small flecks like fine silver lay under the surface that shone in some places like glass. She read the legend slowly:

JAMES BARTHOLOMEW GOWAN

Born August 3, 1839

Departed this life May 17, 1906

An honored citizen, a faithful husband, a loving father, a true Christian. . . . Five times elected judge of the County Court. . . . Fulfilling all trusts with . . .

"That's Judge Gowan," she whispered, awed by the personality erected by the legend against the tall stone. "He owned the Gowan farm and the Gowan horses and the Gowan peacocks . . . across the road from Mr. Al's place . . . and he left Miss Anne, his wife, all he had when he died, and people a-goen to law about it big in court. And when he died there was marchen and white plumes on hats and a band a-playen, and his picture is a-hangen up in the court-house, life-size, they say. . . . And when he was a-liven he used to ride up to town in a high buggy with a big shiny horse, a-steppen up the road and him a-sitten big, and always had a plenty to eat and a suit of clothes to wear and

101

a nigger to shine his shoes for him of a weekday even. Ben told me. And he was a-willen money big to his wife when he died and always a-sitten judge in court. A big man, he was. That's you." Her voice was whispering the words. And then after a long pause she added. "He's Judge Gowan in court, a-sitten big, but I'm better'n he is. I'm a-liven and he's dead. I'm better. I'm Ellen Chesser and I'm a-liven and you're Judge James Bartholomew Gowan, but all the same I'm better. I'm a-liven."

The sun came down white on the gravestones and beat back upon the hot air. The wind blew down from the west field and bent the grass. Ellen's eyes shone brighter when a new memory came to her mind. She lifted her head suddenly and her sunbonnet fell back, swept off by the breeze. She was calling aloud now, her shout growing into a song.

"Up in town on court day, it is, and a mighty big crowd is a-comen in the roads and horses are a-rampen up the street, and such a gang you can't stir withouten you watch where you go. And sheep a-bawlen and cows, and a man says loud and fast . . .

> *Fifteen fifteen who'll make it twenty*
> *Fifteen now come on with the twenty*
> *Who'll make it twenty*
> *Who'll make it twenty*
> *Fifteen now come on with the eighteen*
> *Fifteen fifteen*
> *Come on with the eighteen. . . .*

And bells a-ringen and banners go by and people with things in pokes to sell and apples a-rollen out on the ground and butter in buckets and lard to sell and pumpkins in a wagon, and sheep a-cryen and the calves a-cryen for their mammies, and little mules a-cryen for their horse mammies,

and a big man comes to the courthouse door and sings out
the loudest of all:

> *O yes! O yes!*
> *The honorable judge*
> *James Bartholomew Gowan*
> *(It must 'a' been)*
> *Is now a-sitten. . . .*

That's just what he said, that man in the door of the courthouse that time.

> *O yes! O yes!*
> *The honorable judge*
> *James Bartholomew Gowan*
> *Is now a-sitten . . .*
> *Come all ye . . .*
> *And you shall be heared.*

"Powerful big county court today, they said. But I'm
better'n he is. I'm better'n you. I'm a-liven and you ain't!
I'm a-liven and you're dead! I'm better! I'm a-liven! I'm
a-liven!"

III

BY AUTUMN the turkeys had grown almost to maturity and they filled the lot with their dark, bronze-brown waves of motion. Ellen fattened them with corn which she and Ben shelled by hand, a labor which required half the afternoon. They worked sitting on a rough bench not far from the watering trough where the mules came to drink, a wire fence dividing them from the runway leading down to the trough. Inside the barn a great drove of mules stood all day before the high feeding platforms, and sitting outside on the bench Ellen could hear the grinding of teeth, for the mules could never have done with eating from the tables which were never empty. Mr. Dick scattered more and more fodder before them, working all day, and they daily grew more sleek and round. Later he would take them away to the south and sell them to the sugar plantations. Ellen felt the mild sting of the dry autumn air on her face as she sat with Ben over the shelling of the corn. Not far off was a flaming sugar tree. In a little while the mules would go south to plow the cane lands. She remembered cotton fields where men and women and children were bending over white flowers that puffed out raggedly into down, in a great ragged field of white down. A white field went off a long way over a flat country, and the road went sandy and wet under wheels, all almost forgotten now.

"Them-there mules is a-haven a good time if they only knowed it," Ben said.

"There is a place on a road down past somewheres in Tennessee where a little house stands off in bushes and trees, a lamp a-shinen out one the windows, after sundown. A youngone is a-cryen little tired cries. You cross a bridge, a rocky road and a little up-hill way to go, I recollect, and then the house and a tired little child a-cryen for to be put to bed. It's a sweet sound, now. You want to take it up in arms and put it in its little place."

"They'll go a long piece past Tennessee, them mules, and they'll never see another such a time, a-eaten their fill and a-doen not one God's thing all day."

"Or you hear music come down the road and you run as fast as your long legs can take you to catch up with it, and there he is, a foreigner, dark almost like a—like a black man, but straight hair and a different smell. And a-hangen on the front of him is a music box and down in the road is a little monkey with a coat and a cap on, a-looken for all the world like a man, long fingernails and all, a-scratchen his head and his leg, just like a man, his little old nose and his big mouth. And his forehead a-frownen down on the people and a-looken up at the sky like he was a-searchen it out for something, looken out from under his eyes to try to see."

Ragged hens went about the barnyard to pluck at the scattered corn. The despoiled cock walked unevenly down the yard, his tail feathers gone, plucking aside the hens he had fed in the spring. An odor of drying tobacco came across the pasture. Henry had cut the last of the crop and had hauled it on a slide to the tobacco barn over in the farm where the cut plants hung yellowing now, filling the entire building. Ellen had seen the plants hanging from the sticks, great inverted yellow waves, for she had been to the barn the day before. "Not very good quality," Mr. Al said, turning away from the barn door. She felt the sting of the grains of corn through the rough glove she had made to protect her right hand and she saw Ben's bony old hand reaching for another ear. Ben was dark yellow fading away to brown. His little beard grew in knots of spiral hairs. He had a dirty rag tied around his throat and his shoulders seemed strangely knotted as he bent over the corn. Out of his wavering, double-jointed voice came a scurry of words:

"And he says 'Who's that-there fine looken gal you see out after the turkeys?'"

"Who said?"

"A white man said it, a nice fine fellow. He says, 'Who's that-there fine looken gal over at Wakefield's?'"

"Quit a-foolen, Uncle Ben. I don't believe e'er word of it."

Mr. Al called the hounds in from the fields and fed them sparingly of coarse bread, keeping them lean for hunting. Sometimes he and MacMurtrie would ride away at sundown with twenty hounds around their horses' feet, but now the dogs were fastened in a room off the barn. Mr. Al was gone away somewhere now, gone to buy stock. He would come

106

back with a great brown Jersey bull and a new cow or two. They would have blue ribbons on their horns.

"A nice fine fellow said it, I swear 'fore God he did. He says 'Who's that-there fine looker?' "

The cows waiting about the gates spoke to each other with low mutterings, rumbling into deep notes that sank off into mere vibrations and shook coarsely on the air. The thought of Mr. Dick lay formless in Ellen's mind, gathering back of all the pictures of the farm, a remote voice accompanying quiet unseeing eyes. He rode away somewhere almost every day at sundown; his shining brown horse made little steps on the gravel of the drive, but he was always back among the mules in the morning. The mules crunched their fodder all day and all night, trotting down to the watering place to drink, rolling back to the high tables down which someone often went with more food. The grinding of the great jaw could be heard halfway down the pasture. Sitting on the bench outside Ellen could feel them crowd at the feedings and make the barn tremble—fifty or sixty great animals tearing at corn. In a few days the mules would be fat for the market, and then Mr. Dick would go away with them, and she thought faintly of the many things he must know in his quietness, of his going away at sundown.

"And he says 'Who's that-there good-looker you see over in Wakefield's place?' " Ben was droning on.

She stared down at the dry ground where the surface was broken in uneven cracks. The ants were gone; they were never seen running in and out of the soil. The little wisps of fodder that lay about changed places now and then in the sudden breeze that swept the lot floor. She was pushing grains of corn off the cob with her thumbs, two or three grains at a time, feeling the spring of the grain react to her wrist, feeling the grains yield and fall. The autumn cries of the peacocks came, wild screams from across two hills. She had found a shed peacock feather in the pasture, blue and gold and green, bold design lying in the frail mesh of feather. All day she had worn it in the bosom of her dress and at night she had pinned it on the wall of the room below stairs over the fireplace. Nellie had looked at it wonderingly, turning it over and over. Blue and black and green and gold and peacock blue, brass and pale purple. . . . Suddenly it seemed that there was a baby in her hands, a little baby in the crook of her arm. Her baby, it was, and a great wave of power went over her. She was strong at once with a great strength. A wave of tenderness ran up her face and sank deeply into her eyes that closed to hold it. Her back felt its power to curve protectingly over a defenseless little thing and her breast reached out to it. Her shoulders were large and strong and her breast was deep. . . . It was nothing. It was gone and forgotten in the moment of going, and there was the ear of corn in her hands. A jointed voice was mumbling words close at hand, "The time of they lives if they only knowed so."

Two young men came one morning in late autumn to help Ben drive the turkeys away to town. The air was full of frost. Ellen threw the turkeys great handfuls of corn and their feathers made a low thunder as they swept down upon it. The flocks still kept together in general, five groups flowing in and out of one another. One of the men beat his hands together in the November cold and called out, "Let 'em come on. They'll drive just like hogs against they get out on the pike." Ellen stood back with Miss Tod and watched the fowls go, five groups to the last, never entirely lost, the pattern of the flock still printed upon them, the mark of the nest. Her bonnet blew down into her eyes and the cold of the morning stung her throat. The flocks went down the front pasture following Ben who dropped corn before them, flowing in and out and creeping forward over the ground, their ways of keeping together went, the little hurt one, now grown large and strong, all went. Ellen bent her bonnet down over her face and brushed off tears. Why, she wondered, should she be liking a flock of anything, flocks, things nobody ever could have forever? She turned away from the fence slowly and walked back through the lot where a few fowls stood about. "You can have one of them that's left," Miss Tod said.

After the turkeys were gone Ellen was asked to help with the milking at the barn while Josie was kept in the house. Often she went to the tobacco barn to help Henry strip the tobacco where they worked in a little room which was heated on cold days by a small stove. The dust of the tobacco would hang in the air and make long beams before the small window. Henry would stoop over his task, muttering from time to time, telling himself things he had long known, working very slowly. One day a girl and a child came passing through the farm by the road which led over the hill toward the river. Ellen heard strange voices outside and her breath leaped with joy. Some hand opened the door of the stripping room and a girl pushed a crying child before her saying:

"Could we come in and warm? This-here chap is a-cryen."

Henry stuffed more wood into the little stove and presently the boy took down his small hands which he had been holding up to the warmth and looked about with drowsy eyes. The girl stayed by the door, refusing a seat on a wooden box by the stove. She said her name was Effie Turpin. She answered the questions asked her with meager half-phrases, eyeing Henry and Ellen minutely. She lived down the river, a long way to go. She had been to see if Miss Tod wanted any weaving. She did not come often. The boy was seven. She must go. Yes, it was cold. She had told Sam it would be cold. He had grown out of his overcoat. Ellen looked at her from time to time as she stood by the door, swaying as she stood, wavering against the brown wood. Her flesh was dull and life crept slowly under her sunburnt skin, but it was there, moving her eyes and staring in her face that searched out the ways of the stripping room, probing Henry and Ellen for ways. The girl said she must go but she lingered on. Ellen saw herself in Effie Turpin's body as it stood by the door wavering. She saw herself standing there, half of her afraid, unable to go when she knew she must, held by the other persons until she was unable to reach up her hand to the latch string, the other half of her bold, jerking out brief bold answers. The flesh under Effie Turpin's eyes was her own flesh and Effie Turpin's rough cold hands were her own as they shrank from the latch and lay over each other jerkily before the brown coat that was pulled tightly across the girl's chest. Ellen tore off the leaves carefully and laid them in their piles, a joy in her being because someone had come, another, almost herself but separate in body, a girl her own age. Wanting the girl to stay, she asked her a question now and then to keep her. Finally the girl went uneasily out at the door, jerking through the partly opened doorway quickly, and the child ran in fright after her.

Or Ellen sat in the house by the open fire drying her wet shoes. Around the house outside was mud, wet, and dripping eaves. Inside clothes were drying by the fire and the cabin was filled with soapy steam in which floated the odor of human bodies. Up the stairs, and the walls were wet from the leaking roof and the figures on the wall sank away into darker brown as in a fog, the procession endlessly going— trees, women, letters, women, crosses, unfeathered birds, swords, demons. Out of doors there was slop and mud to the ankles, cow dung and slush, deeper in the low places by the pond and deeper again in the cowpens. In the morning she would go up the hill in the dripping wet and her feet would sop in and out of the slow mire. She would help milk the cows under the shed and another day would be upon her, more mud, more wet, days endlessly going alike to every other, each one. Suddenly out of the still air of the dusk she felt a kiss on her face and arms gathered close her shoulders.

The apparition was gone, forgotten in the warmth of the fire. She held her damp feet to the blaze and felt the drowsy heat on her face, watching the sycamore log that burned with a soft liquid light. She was hearing pleasantly the re-membered tones of a voice she had heard many days back, a shout that had come to her from the pasture road. "No use to plant beans till you hear a whippoorwill!" She had been digging potatoes in the garden, turning up the half-frozen soil to the deep warm inner part where they were buried safe from the frost. A voice had cried out to her from the pasture, "Not safe to plant beans. Have you heared e'er whippoorwill?" A boy was teasing her across the winter pasture, calling out from the road. He had been riding a plow horse, a great sack of something across before the sad-dle. She would not even know him if she should see him again, for he had been too far away to be seen clearly. Now a smile straightened her lips and quivered in and out of her eyes as she looked at the sycamore flame.

"A-teasen and a-foolen. Beans and whippoorwills in a winter time. 'Have you heared e'er whippoorwill?' December it is, right at Christmas, and he says to me, 'Not safe to plant beans till you hear a whippoorwill.' "

In January came a dry frozen time, hard and cold. Each cow made a long white breath in the morning air. Henry worked all day at fencing and Ellen was never done finding wood and bringing it to the cabin to keep the fire on the hearth. In the night sometimes lonely horsehoofs went galloping along the beaten mold of the pasture road, thumping on the frozen dirt. The sound would waken her with a thrill of pleasure, a joy at being awakened for any purpose, at feeling herself suddenly alive again. Into the joy would come a sadness for the lonely throb of the horse's feet that were going, the unspeakable loneliness that settled down on the road and the yard, on the cabin, on her own body, as the pulse of the hoofs beat dimmer on her ears and faded farther and farther away. Her mother's words would call out in the lonely stillness of her mind. "Where's the fellows that ought to be a-comen?" She had been brushing her hair before the kitchen mirror, looking into her own clear eyes. "What fellows?" she had said, dreaming over her hair. "A big grown girl, nigh to eighteen and no fellows a-comen!" She had been lifting a lock of her hair, making it lie in different ways, searching out the ways of hair. The taunt had come upon her unprepared and now the words would probe the still dark after the passer was gone. A hard cry snarled into the dark. "Where's the fellows that ought to be a-comen?"

She had not been thinking of them as fellows, fellows that should come. The house had grown very flat and still afterward, and objects had sunk into each other. All the rest of the day she had spoken in a stifled voice, scarcely heard. It was expected of her, something undefined and expected, she would think, abashed, something stated boldly through the words of a hard voice. "A big girl eighteen and no fellows. . . ." All day, all week a great still cry had gone out of her. Unjust become just become unjust, confusion and hard hands laid on her throat. She came timidly into the house and went silently about her labors. Henry was loading his crop onto the wagon frame, preparing for the market, and Ellen helped arrange the hands of it in the mounds, working in the cold with quick arms. The crop had been short for Henry was but a slow worker, but it would pay for the food they had eaten and the clothes they had worn, and perhaps there would be a little over. On the dry open days Henry worked at the new plant bed, grubbing out more space on the virgin hill, and soon the light was set to the fagots and Ellen grew bolder again with the spring. One night not long after the coming of the first signs of the new season, into sleep came a beautiful tonk tonk tonk a-tonk of guitar strings out on the pasture road, some man that lived in the glen behind the hills going home. Strong rhythms came beating in the rich harmonies, coming out of the pasture that all day had been sopping mud—tonk tonk a-tonk tonk; quick notes danced under the firm beat of the chords and other quick notes ran lightly down while the mellow chord waited. The tones came very beautifully over her waking body, but they were scarcely recognized until they began to recede into the night, growing less vividly present as consciousness came. They rounded the osage

113

shrubs and moved lightly away toward the west, changing rhythms with inter-playing chords and transitional notes that scurried down flights of tune. Ellen had not known that such a thing could be—full-throated chords falling quick and strong, beautiful, breaking in upon dreams, rising out of the muddy pasture. In the end a voice jerked into song, leaping into the middle of the sweet string tones,

> *Oh . . .*
> *Say darlin' say,*
> *When I'm far away. . . .*

It was gone and sleep came back over her languorous mind that was haunted now by the people who moved and lived just beyond her knowledge and acquaintance, apparitions from beyond the hill and from the river glen.

Effie Turpin came to see her during the summer, staring in understanding and good will. She told the names of all the people who lived up and down the roads and who owned land and who rented. Sebe Townley was a nice fellow and Mr. Jim, his uncle, played on a guitar and was a master musicianer. She herself lived in the torn-downdest place you'd ever see, just a plumb shanty. She talked often of Miss Cassie MacMurtrie who was, she said, free-hearted and kind, would give anything she had to a body that needed it. She could ride a horse like a man, out on the hills of a night with Scott and the men. The next day you would see her busy with the hens, managing the little chickens, cooking the dinner sometimes, and milking if the hands were gone. A pretty woman, a beauty with big quick eyes and a heavy suit of hair. When she herself had had lung fever one winter Miss Cassie had come every day for a while and had brought a warm comforter and something hot to rub on her chest to drive the frost out of her lungs. Miss Cassie owned the land herself for she had heired it from her father, but Scott MacMurtrie, her husband, worked it and made a heap of money off his fine horses and his crops until he was as rich as cream. Effie would leave slowly, reluctantly, hardly able to go at all, and long after her departure Ellen would keep a rich sense of the land, all the land about, as filled with an ever-increasing people, gathering into her knowledge incessantly. People were coming into the land, filling the country all about, and her life ran more quickly, leaping from day to day, as her knowledge spread beyond the farm and took in MacMurtrie's, spread even farther and caught at the farms in the glen where names and faces were now known a little.

One day in autumn when Ellen came down from the hill with a few hickory nuts in her apron, another girl came up MacMurtrie's path just beyond the wire fence. The tractor in the distant barnlot, where the silo was being filled, made a low throb run through the farm while she stopped to talk, and this pulse beat into her sense of the girl, whose hair was pale brown and whose fingers tapped lightly on the wires of the fence, slim fingers with wild grape stains about their tips. She had never seen this girl before and they told each other their names. The richness of the autumn came into the air, the throb of the engine, the abundance of the farm, the hickory nuts which she offered to the girl and which her thin hands took. She was Dorine Wheatley.

"We moved into MacMurtrie's tenant house a while back," she said. "Are there any parties around here? Any fellows to have a good time with?"

THE broods of turkeys were white instead of brown for Miss Tod was trying a white breed, and the waves of their undulating bodies as they flowed about Ellen up and down the pasture were white and dusty yellow. Miss Amanda Cain, who lived with the MacMurtries, a cousin to Miss Cassie, raised bronze fowls and Miss Tod had changed to the white sort to save confusion. All summer Ellen had heard a cry over toward the marsh, a woman calling " Pee-o-wee-wee-wee-wee." It came like a high thin whistle out of the land, but later Ellen knew that it was Miss Amanda calling home her turkeys. Miss Amanda was some cousin of Miss Cassie's who had no land, no property, and had lately come to live at the farm. Effie Turpin brought news of her when she came and later had news of her enterprise, the turkeys, and of her finery. Sometimes Miss Amanda rode over the farm on horseback, her slim feet dangling in little shoes, or at other times she would go away along the pike with Miss Cassie, riding in the high buggy Miss Cassie used. Then she would wear a large black hat with a plume or a stiff little hat with a feather, and her lips would break into easy smiles. Hearing the high thin cries in the autumn Ellen would remember the one time when she had met Miss Amanda on a path. Her bright cotton dress had come flashing in the way and she had walked quickly by, without a greeting, her mouth lifted into a bent smile and her eyes slanting away as if she said, "I don't care!" Even in her denial she added to the increasing richness of the farms.

The yield of the autumn was abundant that year, the crops fair, the corn plentiful in the shocks, the pumpkins many in number and great in size. Ellen helped Henry to gather the apples in the bright fresh cold of an October day, and she saved the largest apple for the new girl, Dorine, whose name came often to her mind as holding much generous grace and much music. She intended to go to see the girl some day and to carry the apple for a little gift. Dorine was easy to know, for by the time Ellen had found the largest apple she had seen her ride along the pike with one of the young men from beyond the hill. She had already brought something to the farms, something facile and free, mingled with the abundance of the season and the secure hope for the winter, whatever its weather. The days flowed swiftly around the tasks of garnering, the burying of the apples under their straw, the burying of the potatoes, the plucking of the corn. Apples had been dried in the sun and beans were shelled and laid by. The pumpkins were brought from the field in wagon-loads and a choice few were set in Miss Tod's cellar for winter food. Then Henry began to plow his tobacco field for its stand of rye and the season was done.

Too eager to wait for supper, Ellen brushed back her hair before the kitchen mirror, put on her cloak, and ran away toward Dorine Wheatley's home where there was to be a party. Her head was bare in the frosty night and her hair caught the vigor of the air and crisped richly over her forehead. Her dark skirt had been brushed that afternoon and her waist inspected for holes and loose buttons. Her shoes had been viewed in several moods, critically, hopelessly, hopefully, carelessly, mournfully, but in all moods they were old and worn. When she drew near the small white house that stood close beside the road, half a mile from her home, noises were bursting from its walls, voices and footfalls. A

thin flat music came merrily over the other sounds, over
the quick feet pursuing other quick feet, a slow foot settling
back upon itself leisurely, little steps of women and long
heavy steps of men. Ellen did not think to knock at the door.
She lifted the latch with her thumb and went headlong into
the room where many people were standing about or sitting,
strange people. She closed the door behind her back and
stood leaning against the doorframe, her body trembling.
A voice was saying, "Did the prize come?"

"Came yesterday evening," Dorine's voice called out
from some other room.

It had seemed a little house when Ellen had come to
bring the apple. Now it seemed large to be holding many
people. All were laughing and talking very loud but
Dorine's voice came again out of the jargon of words and
laughter and shuffling feet.

"It's Ellen Chesser. Here's a chair."

The other people seemed to have come much earlier and
all the first awkwardness was worn away. The party was
congratulatory, for Dorine had won a three-piece combing
set in a satin-lined box, had won it by selling eight boxes of
some salve. Now that all the guests had arrived the prize
was brought to the table and displayed. It was a brush and
a comb and a hand mirror, all of a hard white stuff. The
articles were fastened by little clasps onto a ground of pink
satin.

"Ain't that something pretty now!" voices cried out.

"Eight boxes! That was a heap to sell!"

"It wasn't so easy to do, either," Dorine said. She wore
a pink dress and her cheeks were pink and warm.

"Name who bought," her mother said.

"Eli bought one and Elmer Ware, and then Ras O'Shay

and Mammy. That's four. And then Sallie Lou and Mrs. Al Wakefield and Jonas Prather and Mr. Jim. Eight boxes of Lily-bud salve I sold." Ellen wished that she had bought one. But then she had not known about it and besides she had no money.

"I bought it to grease my old buggy with," a young man said.

"I bought mine to see if hit might cure my hens outen their roup." A half-dozen unflattering reasons were offered.

Dorine made faces at the speakers. The combing set was passed around and dark rough hands took out the white pieces and passed them to other dark hands. Splintered fingers caught on the soft spines of the satin. Someone discovered that the lining would come out of the box, for it was a crust of cloth glued onto wooden pegs. The three pieces of the set, the two linings of the box, and the box, six articles, were passed through the room. The prize was put together and taken apart several times for joy in the wonder of its mechanism. Ellen sat in her chair, out from the wall, conspicuous, miserable, her feet crossed under her dress, her eyes looking everywhere. She did not want to be sitting on the best chair out in the middle of the room, the chair nobody else would take because it was the best. Scarcely anyone knew her and she longed to be in a corner, but she dared not move. At the same time she longed to be known and to be liked. If the boy with the little beady eyes had said something to her she should have been most happy, or if the girl with the white stockings had, although that last was far too much to hope for. Effie Turpin stood over by the fireplace and presently Ellen knew that the girl called Maggie was a Turpin also although she was prettier than Effie. She wished that someone would ask her to move back into a corner, or she wished that she could say something pleasing and quick and that one or two would look at her and know what she meant. She wanted everyone to like her, to take her into the dance, into the game, into the jokes, or even into the crowd that went into the other room to be out of the way of the dancers.

"Maybe this lady would be good enough to move back." Someone had said it and she was sitting in a corner. She sat, eager, ashamed, embarrassed, the joy of people near making her breath flutter. She heard names called and soon she had a flow of names confused in her mind, blended with running currents of action, looks and words. The fat girl was always slapping at the boy with the beady eyes and these two were always coming back to Tim McNeal and the girl with the white stockings. The graphophone was wound for the dance and then the music came from a large blue and pink metal morning-glory. In another room Mr. Jim Townley strummed a guitar and now and then he sang a line. Once his voice jerked into the middle of his tonk tonk a-tonk of guitar strings with

> *Oh . . .*
> *Say darlin' say*
> *When I'm far away. . . .*

The dance ended and there was a romp. Ellen rose from her chair and went into the other room where she stopped at the door to look about her. Mr. Jim finished a stave with a tender arpeggio on the instrument and then muted the strings with a gesture and a little upward flash of his eyes which was directed toward her as she stood just before him. Suddenly she went out of her regret for her torn shoes, out of her memory of herself, out of her lonely nights, out of her presence sitting strangely in the corner at a party.

"I can sing a song," she said.

The people close around grew still. Ellen was standing by the door, terrified at what her lips were saying, her body leaning a little forward from the hips.

"Well, sing it," Mr. Townley said. "Hush, everybody, hush you-all. Ellen Chesser is a-goen to sing a song."

"I can sing 'Lady Nancy Belle'—that's a story one Mammy taught me a long time ago, one she learned offen her grannie, or I can sing 'Lucy Is a Mighty Generous Lady,' whichever you'd rather."

"Sing both."

"Sing the story one."

"Aw, let her sing the Lucy one."

"Sing both."

Nervous movements came over her mouth and strained at her eyes and her throat, but she took a deep breath, caught her breath twice, and began in a shy voice, smiling a little, looking at Mr. Townley, or casting down her eyes. After she was well started Mr. Townley caught her tune and began to touch the chords on his instrument, and this pleased her very much. She sang:

> Lord Lovel he stood by his castle wall
> A-comben his milk-white steed;
> Down came the Lady Nancy Belle
> A-wishen her lover good-speed.
> A-wishen her lover good-speed.
>
> "Oh, where are you goen, Lord Lovel?" she cried,
> "Oh, where are you goen?" cried she;
> "I'm a-goen, my dear Lady Nancy Belle,
> Strange countries for to see. . . ."

She sang of the departing lover and of his promise to return in a year or two or at most in three. But when he had been gone but a year and a day a languishing thought of Nancy Belle came over his mind and he returned only to find the bells of St. Pancras tolling and all the people mourning for Nancy Belle who was dead.

> He ordered the grave to be opened wide,
> The shroud to be turned down;
> He kissed and kissed those clay cold lips,
> And the tears came a-trinklen down.

Ellen sang with bright eyes, her low voice going to the end of the room, settling down over the hushed feet and the listening faces. She had forgotten herself in her pleasure. All had crowded into this room from the other rooms and the guitar was beating a-tonk-a a-tonk-a a-tonk a-tonk, true to every measure.

> Lady Nancy died like it might be today;
> Lord Lovel like it might be tomorrow;
> Lady Nancy died for pure pure grief;
> Lord Lovel he died for sorrow.

> Lady Nancy was laid in St. Pancras church,
> Lord Lovel was laid in the choir;
> And out of her breast there grew a red rose,
> And out of his a briar.

> They grew and they grew to the old church top,
> And when they could grow no higher;
> There they tied in a true lovers' knot
> For all true lovers to admire.

There was a great laugh and a clapping of hands and a stamping of feet when she had finished. Mr. Townley made a great bow for her.

"Hit's a story about a couple of sweethearts, that's what hit is," one said.

"Hit's like a book to read."

122

"Miss Nancy, she died like it would be one day, and this man, her sweetheart, like it might be the next."

"Yes, but all he could grow outen his grave was a briar, and that's something to chop down and grub out."

"Hit means a briar rose, you durn fool you."

"It's like a story book to read. Get her to sing it again."

"Let her sing 'Lucy a Generous Lady.'"

Ellen said she would not sing again. "Lady Nancy" was a long song, long enough, she said. She felt confused, wrecked, when her voice ran off the song, ran off the last word of the song. She had moved a long way from herself sitting neglected in the corner and she could not know where her place would now be. She thought the party would break in two, but Dorine came forward proudly and took her by the arm and introduced her to everybody present.

"Let me make you acquainted with Jonas Prather," she said.

"Howdy do. I'm right glad to know you."

"Let me make you acquainted with Eli Prather."

They shook her hand. After she had been introduced to everyone Jonas asked her to dance and then she stood in the long line with the others singing,

> Susie says she loves him
> A long summer day. . . .

When their turn came with Jonas she went down the lines, she turning all the men while he turned the girls. After a while names became permanently attached to figures and faces. The boy with the little beady eyes was Eli Prather, cousin to Jonas, and the fat girl was Rosie O'Shay.

"Eli *talks* to Rosie," Jonas said to her in a low tone. *Talks* to Rosie, *talks*—she knew what he meant.

123

The lovers would slap each other on the back, going out onto the porch in a romp every little while. "Say, you can stay in here and kiss. You don't have to be a-goen out in the cold. Might as well," some voice called out.

The girl with the white stockings was Sallie Lou Brown and her fellow was Tim McNeal. Sallie Lou was very quick with her white stockings that twinkled in and out of her dress as she danced, and her green flowered dress made her look very slim up and down. Rosie's dress was dark and her shoes were old and scabbed, but she had a good time, and Ellen minded her own broken shoes much less. The Turpin girls had on dim cotton dresses of no color at all, and some of the young men had no neckties. A feeling of intimacy with the place had come to Ellen and this helped her to move lightly in the dance-games. She knew the fireplace with the broken dogiron and she knew the knot-holes in the floor by the door and the window where the water bucket stood. Mr. Wheatley, Dorine's father, took off his shoes and walked about the house in his stockings. They were of gray wool and they wrinkled about the ankles just as Ellen knew. Voices grew familiar as recognized from the other room, and gestures and looks came back again and again to this one and that. All were weary of dancing, and they gathered about the fire in the larger room, jostling one another on the wide stone hearth, their voices flowing fast, running out from the high warmth of their blood.

"Durned if here ain't a louse," one said.

"Oh, shut up!"

"Keep hit to yourself, hit's your'n."

"Well it is one, now."

"Well kill hit then."

124

"Hit's a tater bug."

"Hit's a gnat or a flea, maybe."

"Flea your hind leg! Hit's a body louse."

"Step on it with your foot."

"What was it, Dorine?"

"It was a spider, Mammy."

"Call hit a spider for manners!"

They were sitting on chairs and benches and on the floor, drinking a hot drink made of eggs and milk, a custard, from cups and mugs. There were small round cakes. "There's plenty of spoons for everybody to have one," Mrs. Wheatley said. She was eager for everyone to like the custard. They romped over the food, pulling at arms and legs, pinching flesh. They did like the custard and each one tried to say how much he liked it until Eli outspoke all the rest.

"Gee durn! I wish I had a stream of this-here stuff a-runnen through me all the time."

Eli closed his eyes to feel the stream he had pictured and everybody laughed, feeling it likewise. Elmer slapped Ellen on the back in his happiness and she was glad again that she was there. Mr. Wheatley sang a bit of a verse:

> The Mammoth Cave, oh, what a spot!
> In summer cold, in winter hot!

"Eli and Rosie, now that's a match," Erastus said. "I seen the minute they commenced to spark each other."

"Eli and Rosie, they already promised to name their first after me," Tim said.

"You go on!" Rosie said. She was taking her cup for more custard.

"Already promised. Sure. Tim T. Prather. I can see him now."

"A lousy brat, hit'll be. No help to hit. Tim T. Prather! God knows!"

"A-squallen and a-puken. I can see hit myself. Timothy T. Prather. Look at Rosie blush."

"You go on!" Rosie said.

Mr. Wheatley sang again, his refrain "Black cat kicked out the yellow cat's eye. . . ."

"That-there yeller cat was a tom cat. I see two cats once out behind the barn," Ras said.

"Shut up, Ras," Elmer said. "Where you been brought up?"

"Well, I know cats, now. That-there black cat, she was a puss cat and that-there yeller he was a tom. Black, he lost an eye."

Tim McNeal held a mug of custard over Eli Prather's head, spilling a little.

"I baptize you in the name of the Father, Son, and Holy Ghost."

"Quit, I already been bapsoused, soused, I say."

"I saw you when you was pulled up outen the water. You looked like a drownded rat."

"Washed your sins away, didn't you, Eli? The creek was muddied all that next day. I went by and I seen what was left back in Dover Creek."

"Preacher said baptizen wouldn't do me e'er bit of good. Said they'd have to take a scrub brush."

"Saw old Sallie Lou a-cryen the night she joined."

> Whoop law, Lizie poor gal,
> Whoop law, Lizie Jane,
> Whoop law, Lizie poor li'l gal,
> She died carryen that ball and chain.

"Saw old Sallie Lou a-cryen."

"Old Sallie Lou was a-mournen for her sins. I see her on the mourners' bench that night."

"Home! Who said home? Home's a fool beside this-here place. Strike her up again with a tune, Mr. Jim, and let's dance another round."

They were going home, everyone leaving at one time, with loud goodbyes for Dorine and her mother and father flung back from the road. There were many goodbyes and parting messages.

"Go through Wakefield's, Jim, you and Maggie and Ras, and take Ellen home," Mrs. Wheatley called from the house door.

Tim McNeal and Sallie Lou rode away together, driving a wild little half-broken horse that went jumping off in the crisp air. Mr. Jim had a lantern to peer out the ruts of the road, and near him walked Erastus and Maggie and Jonas. Effie Turpin walked behind him to borrow of his light, and Ellen moved along among them but she thought nothing of herself. They were five shapes lying beyond herself, herself forgotten, five shapes, one of them carrying a light, a deep voice, a high voice, and muffled words, now reached up and now bent down in sweet arcs, in high bridges suddenly flung across chasms of thought, in little down-drooping sayings, low and final. All of them were beautiful to her in their closeness, their offered friendship. She walked home in silence, forgetting to speak. They were tired after the long merry evening, and their weariness made them speak gently.

"Hit's a mild winter for sure," a voice said.

"It sure is."

"I look for a heap of sickness along February."

"And the old a-dyen off."

"Oh, that's what I'm a-thinken."

127

"I tell you what I've seen in my time. I've seen a winter so mild the grass was a-growen and the birds a-singen right along from sunup to sundown."

"It's a dove though really tells when spring's come."

They walked quietly on, their feet making uneven rhythms on the road. "It's a dove though really tells when spring's come" lingered on as tone refalling on Ellen's ears, "It's a dove though really tells," a phrase from some playing instrument. They passed under low trees for a space and then came out onto an open stretch of road.

"I vow there's a heap of stars out tonight."

"And them that's out is a long way off."

"How far is it to a star? How far now do you reckon it is to that yon one in the row off north there?"

"Hit's a far piece, a right far piece."

"It's a million times as far as from here to the North Pole and back, they say."

'Now, no!"

"You can't think hit. You can't get your mind on hit, someways you can't."

"You can't get your mind to think on it."

"Ah, gee! ain't there a heap of 'em!"

"There's more every way you look. There might maybe be a million and I'd never know hit."

"And they're up there night in and night out, year in and year out, and how many times do we ever take notice to it?"

"I heared tell about a man once that followed studyen the stars all his life."

"That's something to do now, if a man had time."

"That's hit, if a man had time."

Five shapes were thumping the dry road with their feet, stumbling a little, five abreast now and now drifting into forms like those the stars made in the sky. It was here that she felt them become six, herself making part of the forms, herself merged richly with the design.

"I studied a heap about the stars, since you named it, in my own mind I have. Now I wonder what they're made outen."

"And what they're for, nohow."

"Ah, God-almighty, ain't we little things a-goen around."

"Ah, God-almighty, we are now and that's a fact."

"But of a morning, when you go out to feed and water, how often do you ever remember the stars you saw last night?"

"I studied about that once before in my time. I was watchen a fish trap all night down on the river."

"And once I got to looken at the moon. That's something worth studyen now."

"God knows!"

"It is and that's a fact!"

"I heared about a man once that followed nothing else but to study the stars his whole enduren life."

They stopped at a small white gate beyond a leafless cherry thicket.

"Goodnight, Ellen."

"Goodnight, Jonas."

"Goodnight, Mr. Jim."

"Goodnight."

"Goodnight."

"Goodnight."

IV

THE bright-faced little cow bore her calf in March, at the end of a damp snowy week. The heifer was pale brown with darker shadings about the feet and muzzle. The two beasts stood by the gate one morning when Ellen looked out from the upper window onto the dull brown hills that were spotted over with clumps of soft snow. The muddy road and the sop near the pond seemed very black beside the dots of white and splotches of creamy foam on the landscape, and the color of the cow and the calf stood out brightly. The cow cried now and then with a low rumble or a questioning bleat, very soft and very patient. Ellen put on her clothes quickly, watching the calf and the cow from the window and smiling because the calf was little and tender and appealing. The cow was asking for food and Ellen knew that it was herself that was being petitioned, and the thought, meeting her at the stair, filled her with a slow misery, that a being depended on her, begging for life with slow patience and a low rumbled cry that ran along the ground. She felt very tall and useless, thin and tall and help-less, as she walked across the lower room.

"I might be the cow's mother, or more, for the way she asks," she said. She poured meal and bran into a large pail and made water ready for the mash. "I might be like what the farmers keep a-wanten in long dry spells when they say, 'If it would only rain! . . .' Or like what we mean in a cold time when we say, 'Oh, if it would only get a little warmer, or nohow if the wind would only lay!'"

After she had fed the mash she took the cow and calf to the barn and asked Ben for a stall to stable them for the day. Five other calves were born to the herd that month. The wheat fields were green and they caught yellow lights out of the March sun when it shone. Winds blew cold from the west. New lambs ran about in MacMurtrie's pasture, little shapes of fleece on dark legs, Miss Cassie MacMurtrie's flock. In the Wakefield pens eleven pigs were littered, and then five more, all fresh and clean, lying against the great brown wrinkled mothers. Ellen helped Ben make a hot slop for the sows, carrying pails of it up the pasture hill to the pens behind the mule barn. Her head was tied in an old black head shawl and her feet were in large high overshoes. A faded brown coat, marked by sun and rain and wind, flapped loosely about her. Blown by the wind, the color of the earth standing on the rails of the pigpen high above the great sows—the dispensing spirit of the swine had risen out of the brown wallow.

"A hog is one thing, just one, like I said a Sunday to Elmer," she said when she turned back from the pen, "and that one thing it points out at his nose. His back points. His nose points at the air, a-waiten to hear something and to smell and to see."

Nellie had told her that she might have a new light colored dress, "You must have a light colored dress for summer." Ellen came down from the pens smiling, for Jonas had laughed when he had heard her tell Elmer about a hog. Sundays were bright days. Then the whole troop of them, Dorine, Rosie, Elmer, Jonas, Sebe, Eli, all would come stamping into the little porch, all talking at once and laughing. "We came to get Ellen. We aim to go a-walken to the top of MacMurtrie's old hill." She could have a pink dress or blue, whichever she pleased.

She piled more stones on the plant-bed hill and dragged brush to the new clearing. The wild plum thickets burst into white flowers and the cherry boughs shook on the cherry tree, twisted in the late March gales. The peach orchard on Gowan's hill came into blossom. Horse colts and mule colts stood stiffly about the barns, long legged and innocent, conceited and suspicious. Three more calves came to the herd. Ellen found one of the fine Jersey cows strayed into the hill field, a little premature calf lying under her side. The calf was too weak to stand on its feet and Ellen held it up so that it could nurse milk from the mother. Then she carried it to the barn in her arms and made it a bed of fresh straw to lie in. Several times during the day she went to the barn and held the calf to the mother until it was able to stand on its feet. The story of the little calf went over the farm, for the cow mother had come to the herd with blue ribbons on her horns.

She could have a pink dress, or a blue one, or white, and perhaps she would have a hat with flowers, and these pleasures, anticipated, gave grace to all her thought. The egg money would buy for her. She turned away from the milk can where she had poured her pail, turning back to another set of udders. Mr. Al was coming down the cowpen smiling at her.

"You could have that-there heifer down at your house for your own cow when she grows up. I give her to you."

"You give her to me for good, to keep?" She was in a tremble.

"Sure. She's your cow. Your'n. You saved me my little thoroughbred. That-there heifer down in your yard, she's your'n. Your cow."

Ellen was out much in the changing weather—sun, rain, wind, sleet, sun, wind. The gales whipped her garments and bent her skirts in changing curves and lines. Clean, quick weathers, friendly and hearty and bold, swept over the farm hills, following her down into hollows and up onto slopes, along the fencerows and up into wooded crests. The weather, with its winds, snatched at her hair and tore at her garments; it wet her face with its rain and laid wet fingers on her arms and shoulders, or warm amorous hands on her back and loins. Dorine brought flowers into the house and set them in jars of water before the windows, brought dogwood blossoms or lilacs or violets gathered from the rise above the marsh. Flowers on the hillside and then flowers in the house; Ellen was glad that she knew of this; she had never seen flowers in the house before. A redbud tree came into deep red blossoms back of the old abandoned stable, fading slowly day by day to pink, and MacMurtrie's bees were humming over it. The wind was new albeit it was the same that had blown before the time of man came to the hillside. From MacMurtrie's pasture would come the baaing

133

of lambs, and all about from farm to farm were the soft young litters of pigs, the stiff colts, the calves brown or white, the whimsical adult males, aloof and apart, despising the young, and the animal mothers of beasts, meek and unconscious out in the weather, offering suck. Ellen brought a branch of thorn blossom into the house and put it in a glass jar on the shelf above the fireplace, smiling a little for she was remembering Dorine's words, Dorine's laugh, Rosie's words, Rosie's quick smiles and little skipping steps, Jonas's words, and Elmer's, and Mr. Townley's quick music. Rosie was always giving things, bringing presents. "Here's a little mess of teacakes for your mammy," or "I brought a little example of the sugar bread I made," and she would hand forward a little package as she said it. Sometimes when Jonas or Elmer passed along the farm road they would shout to her as she worked in the garden or mended the fence or cut the stovewood for the dinner fire, "Hi there, Elleen!" or "Think hit'll snow, Elleen?" They had made her name like Dorine's, gathering her in with Dorine in the sounding of the name. Sebe Townley often came, leaning on the fence in the dusk while she milked the cow.

"Plowed all day, a-pushen that-there durned mule of old man Beam's along. I vum, I'd soon put harness on myself as worry along with that lazy mule, always a-looken for a place to stop and rest in. I bet I cussed that-there blamed mule five hundred times if I cussed once today." He would lean against the gatepost to retell his grudge.

Ellen milked, training the stream into her cup with a proud free hand, her head high and free. She withdrew from Sebe even while she smiled at his story of the indolent mule, hating his way and his look. She felt homely and degraded when she was with him for he enkindled nothing within her and thus gave her no beauty. From moment to moment she rejected him. "His ears are a sight too big," she was thinking, she always thought. "If I had ears like his'n I'd tie a rag around my head at night, just to train my ears in." Then her pity would begin, "But he's right nice though, all tired out and nobody to talk to all day. Fellows like to tell about their troubles. He's right nice." Her thought would float away from him to herself and sink under her pleasure in her own being, in her hand running free with the stream of milk.

"I allow to take a farm next year, to rent a place," he said. "I can get some of the Gowan land or maybe I'd rather have a patch of the Dorsey bottom. If prices hold up I think I might maybe be ready to pay on a place year after next. I allow to have a place of my own."

"Don't you think that's as pretty a calf as ever you see in all your time?" Ellen turned her heifer into the pasture to let it have its turn at the milk. "Mammy says I let her have more'n her share. She's a caution to eat. Ain't she plump now! Feel how soft her hide is. She's no hide-bound starved-out white-trash heifer. Ain't she got pretty ears now! Look how soft they are, a-reachen out in the air and a-turnen this way and that and up and down, trembly. Feel her horns down under the skin, feel. She don't know what horns are, and there they are, a-comen on her. I could lift her up at first but I can't now. Look at her back, how straight it is, and look at her plump little round sides. Feel how soft she is all over, feel."

"Huh? What I want to be a-feelen of a calf for? Dum, I seen a calf afore in my time. What I want to be a-feelen of a old calf for? Yes, you're right, you're right. Hit's soft enough. Hit's a fine calf for sure. Hit's a premium calf at the fair, I'll lay a dollar hit is. Which you think'd be better land, the Dorsey bottom or some of the Gowan farm? Which you'd rather have? Which you'd rather live on?"

By that time it was May.

ALL the girls had bright summer dresses and presently there were summer hats, some of them trimmed with flowers and some with ribbons. Ellen's hat had daisies about the crown, and she could feel the flowers softly moving when she walked, making a dry rumbling clatter in her ears, or tossing in a storm when she ran, beating against the hatbrim. She saw them in a storm when Jonas or Elmer jerked the hat away and held it high overhead, fending himself from her clamor with feet and arms. The girls liked to try on one another's hats, borrowing graces from one another for the moment or testing, each, her own charms under the scrutiny of alien ribbons and hatbrims. All together they walked along the road toward Gowan's gate in the Sunday afternoons, or they walked the long way to Fairhope churchyard and rested awhile among the stones, reading the stones. All together, Jonas, Rosie, Eli, Dorine, Sebe, Maggie, Erastus, and Ellen, they would join hands and run down MacMurtrie's hill, and once Ellen read the fortunes in their palms, giving the boys riches in the form of farms and crops and fine horses, or making this one a lawyer or a doctor as a supreme behest, and giving each boy or girl a long and happy life as his natural desert. Then Dorine brought back her hand, greedy for more, "See if you can find out who I am a-goen to marry." And Ellen, "Ten cents more and I'll read the other palm for you, Lady, only one dime, ten

136

cents," and ran hand in hand with Elmer down the pasture singing, "A-walken, a-talken, a-walken goes I," and all the troop came after. Sundays were fragrant days, filled from morning until sundown with the bright dress and the flowered hat.

Ellen went up to the tobacco field, a new field this year, behind the pasture and lying out toward the west and the north, and there she dropped the plants for Henry and John Bradshaw, or hoed the young crop, her mind reaching out over the hills and hollows with a new knowledge of the land, out over the farms and woods and creek bottoms, Squire Dorsey's and Gowan's and MacMurtrie's and those lying further, until she pushed her task quickly and smiled to herself or sang, or lifted her back from its bow over the clods to look at the crows or the plovers or the bees as they flew over, for to them there were no farm lines, and all the land reached out and away as one portion, hills and hollows and sparse woodlands. Elmer and Eli were shearing the sheep in MacMurtrie's barnlot with Uncle Ben to help and Scott MacMurtrie tying up the fleeces in bundles or crowding them into great hempen sacks. Elmer and Eli would catch the great padded bucks and ewes in their arms and slit the fleece away with great shears and peel back the rich fat wool, turning into the pasture the gaunt fleeced ewes and bucks that wobbled unsteadily on their feet and stared curiously at their own ugly shadows. Then Elmer and Jonas and Sebe and Eli were plowing the corn, Elmer in the high field on Gowan's hill and Eli on the rolling slope that edged away from the marsh and spread back in dark undulations to the foot of the wooded hill where the MacMurtries hunted foxes, and Jonas was driving the plowshare up and down Marion's corn rows in the far lonely field behind

137

Gulliver's creek, singing loud as he turned the plow at the corners, hearing his echoes as they called down from the rock-cliff in hollow, farther-going blurs of flattened song. Or Dorine gathered berries from the pasture briars and pressed them into a red juice that flowed over her fingers and fell in great red globules into the bowl.

Erastus found a bee-gum tree and robbed the wild bees of their fruit, carrying home their dark yellow-brown honey, wild smoke-colored drips, to share it with the rest, a pail of it for Ellen and a pail for Dorine. Maggie and Effie were taking turns with their mother at the loom, weaving the strips of carpet, sitting now one and now another at the great rude loom on the entry porch of the cabin, beating and treading, crossing the warp into its shed and passing the great bobbin from hand to hand, hurrying against the coming of winter to buy for themselves lard and meal. Or Jonas and Elmer were harvesting Wakefield's wheat, Elmer driving the great red reaper across the field and cutting wide ribbons of grain which fell under the knives and flowed in a stream through the trough to fall in bundles behind in the stubble. Then Jonas would gather the sheaves and stack them in even shocks, with Henry and John Bradshaw helping, and Ellen herself lending a hand one hot afternoon when sullen clouds gathered in the west. Then they raced with the coming storm, making each shock secure but building it with swift skill, Ellen carrying the bundles up for Jonas to stack. He took them from her with merry words and quick hands, his eyes on her laughing eyes and on her moist face, and once, behind two upheld sheaves, he kissed her as they met in the stubble. He laid one hand behind her neck and drew her forward quickly to kiss her mouth.

Or on Sunday, two and two together, they walked to

Fairhope churchyard, waiting there for the service to begin. Men would stand about among the carriages, a foot on a hub or on a wheel spoke, spitting the juice from their quids and talking in low offhandish voices, careless seemingly of whether they were heard or not, uncommitted. The women would sit in the semi-dark of the church talking, they too in low tones. Their voices came to the doorway mingled with the strange odors of the pews and the echoes that lay over each sound—crooning voices, falling into rumblings and dying away, brooding voices. They would sit in clusters waiting, and their words, "Joce is expecten another." . . . "So soon?" . . . Quiet voices like the low crooning of birds, such as pigeons in flocks. . . . "So soon?" . . . "This makes six, don't it?" . . . "Five only . . . but five, that's a houseful . . . And two dead.". . . Pigeons in flocks crooning. "Two dead. . . . So soon!" . . . "Dell is expecten . . ." "Dell?" . . . "They say. . . . She put off a right smart while but I knowed her time'd come." . . . "I'm right glad. She's no different from the rest." . . . "No, let her have her hard time like the balance." . . . "So soon!" . . . "Poor Dell, she was taken bad, they say. . . . Miss Min was sent for finally. . . . They say Tom was up all night a-doen for her. . . . But what does a man know?" . . . "Poor Dell, she'll see sights afore she's done. . . . Afore she's done." . . . Their voices would stop at the doorway. After a while the preacher would come and then those outside would pass within, Elmer, Dorine, Jonas, Maggie, Ellen, and Sebe, sitting in a long line near the rear of the church. They heard the voice of the preacher as it broke and parted among the corners of the room and flattened against the ceiling—Rehoboam and Jeroboam, kings, and the kingdom divided, never again to unite, Rehoboam and Jeroboam, great words striking the wall, great words with jagged fringes of echoes hanging from each syllable, and the lonely kingdoms, divided and apart forever, the great sadness of the lonely kingdoms settling upon them as they sat, Elmer, Dorine, Ellen, Maggie, and even Sebe. Dorine's dress was of new sweet cloth, bright threads like hair lines running evenly through the white. Her own dress was fresh and new, her dress, Ellen's, folded away all week in the box across from her bed, now lying out under her hands, the blue flowers repeating each other over and over on the field of white, small blue flowers, so small that only she and no other knew the curve and thread of each design and every faint shading of color. And as she sat in the church a shy thought came halfway into her mind and she wondered if Jonas knew the flower of her dress a little as she knew it, and if he would know it for hers if he saw it far away from her.

Dorine was pretty with her thin skin and her damp mouth, and Rosie with her big cheeks and round lips and bright round eyes. Maggie had slim hands with little broken nails and one of her front teeth was smaller than the others. She was pretty, always slow and tired, wanting to rest. Elmer had a gray lock in his black hair and his head cocked on one side when he smoked his cigarette. Sometimes he lisped his words a little; everybody liked him. Eli was big and heavy-necked, deep-chested; swelling sometimes when he talked until he looked like Squire Dorsey. He would lift his head quickly and say, "It is not anything of the sort," or "I do not anything of the kind, now." Eyes like little beads swam in his head and he would talk with all the rest while he waited for Rosie, calling out, "Come on, Rosie, it's time we's off." All of them liked Eli. She thought of herself as somebody Jonas liked, as filled with an inner sweetness, thought thus as she went about her tasks and ways, the thought mounting with her as she mounted the stairs and bursting upon her anew as she passed through a door. She would take the turkeys through the small gate and as she passed within the enclosure Jonas's words gathered into a nucleus and spread wide with the opening out of the grass lot and the dispersing flocks. She heard the work mules crunching their fodder and the deep voice of the mule barn rising firmly among the noises, sharp and firm, gentle, and with it came Jonas's voice, related to it by its unlikeness and remoteness, close following.

Moonlight nights and there was church at Fairhope every night with quick singing to stir the breath and make the heart beat faster. All together, Jonas, Elmer, Eli, Rosie, Dorine, Ellen, Sebe, Maggie, they would walk each night along the road, falling into pairs or flowing together, and they would sit together in the church. Once the preacher told of hell and the damned. Then Dorine was frightened and she clung to Ellen's hand, and when the last song was singing she whispered that she would go up to join if Ellen would, and Ellen, remembering hell, was frightened too, and with Effie and Sebe they went to the front of the church where the crowd was gathered. They walked homeward in pairs and Ellen, remembering hell, was very gentle in her way to Jonas.

Elmer lisped his words when his speech was approaching laughter and his tongue kissed his upper teeth sweetly in the confusion of his words. He liked Dorine, and he would tell Ellen of his liking, holding back from his wish, curious of it and reticent, swearing Ellen to keep secret all his confidences. In the telling he would live again his scenes with Dorine, wondering over her, over her likes, her ways, her speeches, dwelling on every least inflection of her voice in recounting her sallies. For him, Ellen's kiss in the game was easy and light, intimate and light, the reflector of summer and of herself in moods of play. It was the frivolous quirk of her dress in the dance, the fleeting pose of a body in momentary attitudes. Her laughter with Elmer was carried from one meeting to the next, always near the surface of their being, and for his leading she stepped wantonly in the quadrille and beat the rhythms with her head and shoulders. Or for Mr. Townley, who was identified with his music, her manner was an extension of the ripple of her dress, and when she went dancing down his guitar notes between their eyes passed the flash of all laughter, music and dancing made one in the moment, each chord a thread or a ribbon on which she walked with light feet as she twinkled down the dancing floor. His wife with their many children would be standing along the wall. Dorine on her side would tell the confidences of her liking for Elmer, dwelling on each to relive its significance, so that their two likings and wishes, Elmer's reticent and unformed, Dorine's eager, unshy, realized, flowed over her and around her as if she were its musical core. With Elmer she made laughter, each complementing the other, each playing a little with the fountain of his own need. In their kiss the froth of the high tide of summer arose and frayed. It was as if they sang a come-hither-come-hither to all the summer and all the countryside.

AFTER the first broods were turned away the hens would often wander off to stolen nests for their second settings. Ellen would search for these among the high weeds at the

144

back of the garden or in the old abandoned barn where a quantity of mouldering straw sometimes concealed sly nests. Hens would brood there even though the rats would devour their young as soon as they were out of the nest. If she went near the barn at nightfall Ellen would hear the bats slipping through the air and often she had heard the whippoorwills cry out their songs from the yawning rafters, songs more mournful than all sorrow, as of beings blighted by all loss, repeating with monotonous cry a loss incurred over and over as often as some mocking or futile hand restored, of the endless futility of nests and litters fathered and mothered to be the prey of some other as futile kind. Ellen would go half fearfully into the barn when the sun was bright on the south front. Once in the midsummer as she came softly out of the old corn room, she met Amanda Cain suddenly in the wide corridor, walking quickly from some inner place. Her hair lay over her forehead in large tumbled curls and was gathered high on her head in a knot, and her mouth twisted from moment to moment in a proud smile, the corners of her mouth, unlike each other, bent, one downward, and then her thin lips shut together closely into a fine thin line. Her bright dress flared quickly in the sunny doorway above the dry dusty floor, and then out into the shade of the locust thicket. A little later Ellen heard her over beyond the fence in the other farm calling pee-o-wee-wee-wee, at first low and broken and then high and insistent. Standing in the barn door, looking down into the half obscurity of the thicket, for a moment Ellen felt the feeling of the other farm and what it would be to be a part of the land beyond the fence. She would be "that girl that works on Wakefield's place," and "that white girl over at Wakefield's." Her coarse blue cotton dress hung skimply against her body, a strong body, sturdier

145

than Amanda Cain's, round breasted and strong shouldered. She saw herself as a creature in a coarse dress and broken shoes that went up and down the farm lifting heavy clods and cutting wood. Amanda Cain's dress was bright and fine every day and her slippers had bows on the instep.

She went cautiously into the inner parts of the barn, searching again for hens, "that girl on Wakefield's place." She saw her strong hand feel into the dark straw, reaching for eggs. Once when she had come here in the early evening, a bright moon shining, come to look for her straying calf, she had seen Scott MacMurtrie going into the doorway and later she had heard low words from within, Amanda Cain's voice, "You took your time to come. You must 'a' come around by town." Now she went slowly from manger to manger, gathering an egg or two, looking half fearfully, for once a snake had fallen from some timber above and had writhed away through the dust at her feet. At the rear of the hallway that gave into the stalls an old feeding frame was raised a few feet from the ground and in this was strewn a bed of straw, hollowed in the middle like a great nest, and drawing toward it cautiously and peering in she knew that it was Amanda Cain's bed, for the sash from Amanda Cain's bright dress was strewn across the straw.

She came away quickly, bringing four eggs in her apron and hurrying through her tasks, going up to the milking pens with Amanda Cain in her mind, and Scott Mac-Murtrie and Miss Cassie, thinking how Scott and Amanda came to the mouldering old barn, a den of rats and snakes, and how they flirted with the horror of the place and with disclosure to make their evil more sweet. Then Scott would go to the hills with the hounds and Amanda would slip back into the house to sit through the evening with Miss Cassie,

146

sewing a sly seam or reading a page. She walked through the cattle pens knowing this, herself the only one knowing, "that girl on Wakefield's," or she glanced down at her strong body and remembered Amanda Cain's slippers with their little bows at the latch. In the milking pen she heard Ben's croaking words, "Miss Cassie, she bought her a mare today, I see Miss Cassie a-riden a new hoss," and only the week before Mr. Al, standing in the gate, calling back to Mr. Dick, "Scott and Cass will sign the note," or another voice from Miss Tod's yard, heard over the hedge, "Scott and Cassie are a handsome married couple, as handsome as any ever you'll see. Did you ever see Cassie out a-fox-hunten with Scott? Both the same height on a horse and Cassie not afraid of the devil himself."

Coming down from the pens Ellen stared so intently at the herbs along the path that they swam and floated near her eyes. Amanda Cain was a shape lying back in her mind, a sour pain that cut swiftly through her flesh, a sweet evil that lay snugly nested deep in body somewhere, that turned in its secret nest and drew back into a deeper cradle and laughed, bending one corner of its mouth downward. She was a lightning that went crookedly across the sky and lay down to rest in some secret place. She herself, Ellen, was the only one who knew, she thought, and she would never tell any of the farms. All evening her mind would return to Amanda Cain and to the swift step in the barn, and into her secret knowledge came the thought of Amanda Cain bearing a child in the straw of the mouldering feeding frame and hiding the child away there while it lived and grew. Its image would arise unbidden, a phantom, a naked child of no sex, having a slim long face and a mouth that shut into a thin line and hair in a tumble of curls on its forehead.

Holding their knowledge, she lay between them, intensely sensible of their way, seeing herself vividly reflected in their common knowing, "that girl on Wakefield's place," until she shuddered to see herself passing among the fields and pens. The image that haunted the barn would arise unbidden, a child of no sort, running over the decayed floor. It would catch the lizards if they ventured into the doorway and eat away their lank sides, and in the evening after the lamp was lit, hearing the whippoorwill's call, the lonely quiver and lash of the notes was like a thong, and she would think, "Mandy Cain's brat is a-cryen."

A DROUTH came, hard and brittle in the soil and in the sturdy little pasture herbs, but soft and pliant in the hazes that gathered over the far hills. A hot wind blew out of the southwest and the raincrow would cry his cl-uck, cl-uck, cow, cow, cow, cow. All the people of the farms knew the state of the air and the weather, knew just how the growing things met or resisted the drouth, of the swiftly ripening corn and the blight appearing on the tobacco. They would feel the deep satisfaction of the rain, yearning for it before it came and accepting it afterward as their due—rain at last, it was time. During the dry season Jonas passed often through the farm road, intent upon some errands, for the work on the land was delayed. Sometimes he would stop at Ellen's gate or linger a little on the porch before the cabin. Then he would offer bits of news about the farms, sitting negligently on the edge of the step or leaning on the fence beside the gate, faintly smiling. Or his voice would

fall away after each saying and they would sit quietly together, watching the little brown horse he had ridden paw
the turf beside the gate. Sometimes Ellen would bring the
horse a stalk of green corn from the garden. In those days
she delighted in her own sweetness and kindness, and a
smile lay always close behind her eyes, long after Jonas had
gone. "It's no matter," she said, when Nellie told her she
had taken all her money from the teacup to buy a skillet
from the peddler, "It's no matter, Mammy."

Or when Jonas leaned forward and she saw that a button
was gone from his overalls and that he had fastened the
suspender to the garment with a nail, then a pang of
amused compassion flowed over her mind. She knew that
he had forgotten the nail and her cruel eyes would keep
wandering back to it. Then she would listen to his slow,
half-dreaming speech and look out across the pasture and
remember his eyes and their smile, and remember his look
when he caught her eyes and that he had singled her out to
walk beside her or to sit beside her on the stone wall. Or
sometimes when he leaned over his cigarette she would look
at his shoulders hanging loosely under his coat and a
momentary pang would arise within her, a pity for his
thin back and his flat-boned shoulders. But he would arise
again, lifting his hands from his tobacco, and sit with his
wrists crossed between his knees, his head thrown lightly
back, and she would know a joy in the fall of his hands,
in the droning of his voice, in the quiet of his careless words,
in his nearness. With the coming of the rain the work in the
field was resumed. The pasture was quickly green again
and the tobacco put out new vigor. The labor multiplied,
teeming toward the harvest, and Jonas was busy from one

week's close to another, but on Sunday when he found her in the crowd as they walked down the river lane and kept beside her she knew that he had not forgotten her.

Sebe would often stop as he passed going to the grist mill with the corn, or sometimes he would come in his buggy, stopping casually, warily keeping his seat in the vehicle, gathering up the lines from time to time as if he meant to be off at once. He had bought the buggy from a farmer beyond the river.

"Hit's a right pretty turnout," Ellen said, teasing the buggy with a willow switch, twiddling the spokes of the wheels, twiddling Sebe's pronoun before his eyes. "Hit is now. You look like you was fatched up in town."

"You could ride along with me if you are of a mind to, maybe, if you happen to be a-goen my way."

"Which way you aim to go?"

"I aim towards Fairhope church and back around by Fox Creek. Or some other way if you'd rather."

Sometimes Ellen would climb in beside him and ride down the pike. Then he would talk about his corn crop and his tobacco. In another year he expected to be able to rent a place. He knew a good strip of bottom over beyond the creek, fine corn land. A body could make the store bill off the ducks and geese alone. It was a prime place for ducks, right on the water before the door. He knew a man used to live there and his wife made the store bill every year off the ducks and chickens. He knew a fine breed of ducks, Indian Runners. He could get a setting of eggs for little or nothing and in a year, look how many you would have. A body could do a sight with ducks, a good thrifty woman could. And look what you could do with chickens. Take a good breed like the Rhode Island Reds and say you had

150

twenty hens to start, you could raise two hundred or three hundred frying-sizes in no time, and even say corn kept to eighty cents, you could make. He knew a man had a wife made enough to buy a disc plow, just off the egg money alone. And there would still be the geese to pay the store bill.

Ellen saw in her mind the little farm beyond the creek with ducks floating out in a stately procession on the water holes and the hens cackling their high barbed songs in the bright mornings, and a quick woman, herself perhaps, gathering in the eggs and selling them for coins, gathering in the coins and spending them for a disc plow or a binder or a horse rake, and the wind blew brightly, sprightly in clear mornings, cool bright mornings, and the little house would stand off in the bottom among cornfields, crisp cornfields. She thought of the woman as always gathering in eggs and trading them for coins and spending the coins for bright new machines that would go clickerty-click across the sparkling meadows.

"How much is a setten of duck eggs worth now?" she asked.

"I know a man would give me two settens for a dollar."

She saw the woman hurrying in and out across the yard with a pan of corn mush in her hand to feed the little ducks, hurrying in and out of henhouses, her apron full of eggs and her pocket full of coins, in and out of coops, in and out of barn sheds, hurrying, all easy and light and free-going on oily wheels. Or, to make the picture more real, let there be a sick chick, sick with gaps or the roup. Then she would— say it had gaps—twist a bit of bluegrass top down into its throat and swab out the worms, drawing them up clinging to the grass brush; or if it were sick with the roup perhaps,

151

drooping about and getting no better, its head swelled up and its tongue hard, eyes all bunged up, then knock its head against the henhouse door, one sharp blow, and bury it out behind the barn. All the chicks were well again, laying eggs and hatching young, eating, crowing, growing up to frying-sizes, fattening in the coops and sold to the peddler, the money jingling in her pocket and the bright new disc plow, red and gilt, would go clicking all the while across the bottom field. One day Sebe slipped his arm around her as she rode beside him and then she drew herself up into a stiff spear and said, "Mr. Sebe Townley, do you want me to jump outen this-here buggy and walk home? I'd as lief walk as not and a little rather."

The pictures Sebe made stayed in her mind and grew brightly definite, neat farms lying beside running creeks where ducks spread out in thrifty processions, brightly whitewashed henyards where fowls snapped up nourishing corn and turned it into profits even when it sold for eighty cents a bushel, neat tenant houses with bright dooryards full of hollyhocks whose culture took nothing from the care bestowed upon the chicks. She seldom went inside the house, her life moving outside among the poultry and the shifting coins, viewing the clock-work of the barnyards and the plenty of the cribs. If she went inside the house it was Jonas who came there. Sebe kept remote in the picture as the mere organizer and mover of the pageant, for she could not endure the sight of his ears, and if they came within the scope of her vision she looked away quickly or dropped her eyes in half-amused disgust; or if they persisted in holding a place, then she smote the pageant with light words, tore away hencoops and barns with gusts of laughter, desecrated the bright disc plow with derision, and sent the geese and ducks scurrying with her hard scorn. But most often Sebe's offending members kept out of the picture or retreated humbly, having been caught overstepping, and then she helped build back the barnyard she had demolished by asking the price of ducks or the annual yield of feathers.

ALL the signs of the autumn came, the heavy plush-like asters, buckberries and frostflowers, everlasting and chicory—all the last tokens of the living year. The mockingbird would sing a few notes, reminiscent of spring after the quiet of the late summer, and on moonlight nights the cocks would crow all night long. Ellen bought a fresh ribbon for her dress and a bit of lace for her throat and blossomed anew with the frostweeds and the last of the chicory that lingered far into October. The abundance of autumn was again in the air, the summary of the growing season. Elmer had ceased to tell her of Dorine or to recount Dorine's sayings, but his ways toward her were ways of gentle friendliness, sometimes unmindful and detached. She stood in a third place, no longer a medium between them, no longer a current flowing with them, and, alone, she grew into greater strength when the flow turned back upon herself and pooled deeply within. They brought her gifts, a great basket of nuts, a bucket of fresh cider from MacMurtrie's press, but they went away together. Leaving her, while she stood alone in the doorway, already forgotten, they would merge as one in the confusion of her thought and share her momentary hate.

In the time of the great autumn moon the people of the glen met to fish on the river one Saturday afternoon, the

Townleys, O'Shays, Prathers, with others to share the feast; for the catches were cooked over open fires, the women cooking while the men tended the lines. After supper a place was scraped clear in the sand and there was dancing in the twilight and later under the risen moon. The older men would sit in groups talking about the corn or about their fattening hogs, or they told boasting stories of other years. The young men scurried the dust here and yon with their measures, and Mr. Townley sang the dance figures, beating time with his guitar strings, his voice small and flat before the out-spread river.

> Cage the bird and three arms around,
> Bird hop out and hoot owl in,
> Three arms around and hooten agin,
> Right and left and shoo-fly wing. . . .

Sometimes between dances the young people would walk away along the road in the moonlight or stop under the dark trees to hear the hunters and the hounds off among the hill fields. The women sat by the smouldering fire, indulgent, too heavy in body and mind for dancing but glad enough for the girls to have their day. Old Dan O'Shay told a long story that droned endlessly among the men as they sat beside their fire. When the young people had wandered away to the lane or to one of the fires, Mr. Townley would presently call them back with his sudden strumming. Dorine danced with Elmer and Rosie with Eli, Maggie with Erastus or Sebe, Ellen with Erastus or Sebe. The moon was a small white disc in the sky accompanied by an incredibly vast light, widely spread. As she danced Ellen's thought went widely with the moonlight, but deeply underneath in the roots of sense it drew toward the secret shadows. Jonas would pair the couples for the sets, giving Ellen to Sebe or to some of the O'Shays, but never taking her himself. The sky was clear like glass and their faces were clear, clearly discerned, each one telling its like with the candor of the moonlight. Dorine was quick and slender, her back daintily curved in the dance, and Ellen put flowers in her hair and hung her own chain about her neck, a chain Maggie had made by threading bright red haws, wanting to reward Dorine and endow her grace and her quick laughter. Then Jonas kissed Maggie and gave her to Erastus for a partner and went to sit among the men while the dance went forward. Some of the older men joined the revel. They would stare at the girls and then contend with the young men for places, dancing languidly as if but to fulfil the obligation of the dance pattern, as if they held the dance but lightly beside the matters of their days, the hogs and their slop, the tobacco and the corn. Jonas would continue to pair the couples for the sets or he would stand beside Mr. Townley and call the forms or sit beside the elder O'Shay, smoking quietly.

Then Ellen left the dance and went to sit among the women about the dying fire, but she came upon them from the shadowed side and they were unaware of her. One or two smoked quiet pipes and others chewed dip sticks. Their voices arose out of their meditations, arising aimlessly, gathering into a saying or falling away into drowsy quiet. A hard voice from a thin withered throat:

"If the girls only knowed what they wanted they'd take the fellow that could make, that had property."

Another voice, high-pitched: "And easy-goen, not stingy."

"When I was a gal they was six horses tied to Pappy's fence of a Sunday. But I set my head on Joe and looked like I never see any the rest."

"If gals only knowed one is as good as another, but you couldn't tell a gal e'er a word."

"A good provider is what you want."

"When I was a gal they was six horses tied to Pappy's fence and one of them was Sol Beemen's. He lives over in Nelson now and look, he owns a fine farm. His wife gets ten dozen eggs a day, they say. Sol Beemen."

"Over and above that, one man is as good as another, and all about alike, if gals only knowed."

"But lands sake! I must have Joe. I never see Sol when Joe is by."

"I ain't never been sorry I took Dan, though. I never see the day I'd take anybody else."

"Hear Lute O'Shay talk!"

"When they say, 'Come see the bride,' I always say, 'I'd rather see her in ten year. I'll wait my time,' I say."

"Yes, teeth all gone. Back crooked."

"I say I'd rather see her in ten year from now."

The dance went hurrying over the sand and the voices of Mr. Jim and Jonas rolled forward the measures. Ellen sat by the fire of the women, unmissed, hearing their speech.

"I saw Lenie May over in Nelson a while back, this summer it was. You remember Lenie May?"

"Pretty as a picture, I remember. Shiny eyes and round cheeks. Ne'er other girl could hold a candle to Lenie. I remember one time . . ."

"I see Lenie May last summer. Three a-cryen around her feet and the least one in arms, hardly got hit's eyes open. And Lenie dragged out as thin as a fence rail, her cheeks hollow and her eyes, oh, my Lord!"

"That's what the gals want, fast as they can. Can't wait to get in Lenie's shoes."

156

"For all Lenie's got one man's as good as the next one."

"Under their shirts they're all just alike, as I see."

"In the dark you couldn't tell one from e'er other one."

"But the gals, they can't wait to get in Lenie's fix, fast as they can. Three a-cryen under foot and one in arms. And Lenie dragged out till she looks like a buzzard. Up by sunup to cook for Tom and up till midnight with the youngones, off and on, one and another always sick, teeth and bad colds and the least one colicky from the first."

"And not much to do with, Lenie May. Tom is right poor shucks at maken money."

"That's hit. Tom can't make no sight of money. Barely gets on."

"A good provider is what a body wants first and last. A man that's got it in head to own a place and some property."

"Tom was a master hand at sweethearten though. That's what caught Lenie May's fancy. A regular bantum rooster. Tom could 'a' had his pick of all the gals. Sweetheartenest man I ever see."

"Sallie Minervy wanted him. Remember?"

"And Maudie Beam and Josie. Josie, oh, my Lord! She called Maudie a sight of hard names over hit. I recall how upset Josie was. Ready to gouge and fight that-there time over at Bethel Church."

"A man that's got it in head to own a place . . . got get-up in his hide. . . . Beyond that under their shirts they're all just alike. In the dark you couldn't know one from the next."

Mr. Tom was calling for a new dance, "Swing your partners!" and couples were standing in place. Ellen was missed from the group and voices called to her, her name leaping from the huddled throng, and then the throng broke

157

and swept toward her, Dorine, Eli, Sebe and Elmer dragging her back across the shards to the moonlit space of the dance. But when Jonas did not come to dance with her but lingered back of Mr. Townley, leaning against a tree, she gave herself to Sebe and danced the set with him. The new dance caught up all the vigor of every former one and raced with wild frolic over the loamy sand which had been packed to a hard floor. The dance ran away from the music and interposed steps of its own, and now and then Mr. Townley would add a line or a refrain and make a rhyme.

> *Kiss the gal that's on your arm.*
> *Forward and back and home you go,*
> *Kiss her Sebe don't be so slow.*

In the dance Ellen turned her cheek to the men unless they fought roughly and gained her mouth, and then her whole being rushed upward to her lips, but above, far above, her lonely anger flashed for she wanted only Jonas.

A wind began to blow, arising among the hills to the west, beyond the river. The dance swept forward more wantonly, the men circling around the girls, scraping a foot as cocks woo. Sebe kissed Ellen over and over, but she hardly knew who held her or who released, or who carried her around the circle in arms. Jonas stood against his tree. She would not care if the dance had her or if it carried her away into the dark of the woods or over the river. She gave herself up to the dance not caring if the end of it never came. It swirled around her confusion and plucked it into greater chaos. She let the dance do what it would, and if it asked for her mouth she gave that, now careless and willing, or if it wanted her laugh or her smile or her arms. The wind blew and she felt as if she turned about in the center of a great wind, the other persons of the dance being but arms of the wind or limbs or the wind's ribbons or clothing. Her own mouth was in the wind, blown with its currents, ready for any gale, curving to any kiss that came to it. Then the wind was fraying the beach sand and blinding her eyes. It blew out the lantern that hung on the tree beside the fire of the men, leaving Jonas in the dark. The women were gathering up the utensils and calling, were stamping out the fire, and some of the men ran toward the horses. A great cloud rolled over the sky and the moon went out. Dust and dead leaves poured across the air. The dance had melted away into the certainty of the wind. Mr. Jim slipped his guitar into its sack and ran for his horses. Then Jonas's horse took fright at the deep bolts of thunder and pulled back upon its bridle until the leather snapped and it was free to run, but Elmer caught it before it was away. Ellen was taken into the wagon with Dorine and several others, and the horses set swiftly off up the hill lane, the wagon jolting over the stones. There were few goodbyes and these were lost in the crackling of broken twigs and the pelting of dust and the rolling of the thunder. A cooler wind came with the storm and the girls shivered in their thin dresses. Ellen scarcely saw the others depart for the dust was heavy in her eyes, but she knew when Jonas swung on his wild little horse and went leaping off under the swaying trees.

THE bright cold of November was crisp over the winter herbs and the fallen leaves, making shaggy the hides of the beasts when the hairs snarled and pied to exclude the frost of the night. A great wind had blown all the night of the dance, the out-reachings of a cyclone which had passed over the farms to the south. Rumors had come of trees uprooted, and a small elm on MacMurtrie's high ridge had been twisted out of the earth by the storm. Ellen had passed her hands over the roots of the tree and knew how they had once sprangled through the solid earth, wondering at the deep hole plowed out by the tree as it twisted itself free in the gale. Now the knotted roots stood up in the air and she could pass her hand along the disordered snags. She could perceive that there had been a great force in the storm but she could never know it or feel it with her fingers or taste it or see it now that it was gone. She had run to MacMurtrie's hill in the early morning after the dance, summoned by Henry's words, "A tree tore up plumb by the roots." Jonas was plowing now for the autumn wheat on Dorsey's land, going up and down the furrows in the bright hazy air. Ellen knew the day he began the field and she knew the dark even spread of color and light as the plowed rectangles grew day by day and consumed the areas of withered stubble, although Dorsey's farm was several miles away, for she knew what field he overturned and the nature of the plowing.

All day her mind clung about his furrows or she hovered over his team and his plow in her thought, her hand on the plow handle or on the plow line, not merged with his but accompanying. At the dance he had sat among the men, and in the days that followed he had stayed apart. "Jonas has got religion," Elmer had said, "Jonas has settled down." Dorine said that he must be sick. "He looks dauncy," she said, but Ellen knew this was not true for she knew how steadily his plow went through the stubble, having reports from this one and that. Or once, riding to the store at the crossing of the roads she met Jonas as he brought his team through a gate. Then he looked at her, biting at his lips, but after a moment he was glad that he saw her again. He would have something to tell her, he said. He would come when he had time; he would come the first chance he had. He closed the gate and climbed onto one of the horses to ride over the field to his furrow, but once, before she went beyond the road's turning, he waved his hand in the old salute. He would come. He would tell her whatever it was that troubled him. She went forward through the week placidly, slowly, watching for Saturday when she thought that he might be expected. It was Monday when he had spoken to her at the gate. She would wait. It would be some small thing that he had to tell. Then they would walk to Rosie's and get black walnuts for the winter, or they would plan a surprise party for Dorine. She thought that he had changed in his nature and perhaps he would not want to go to parties hereafter. He had become matured and settled, then. She would do as he liked to do, sit quietly apart with him if he so desired.

But he came one afternoon in the midst of the week, Thursday, and sat with her on the cabin porch while his plow was being mended at the shop. One of the plow horses was tied to the gatepost for more than an hour while he sat in the falling cold.

"That-there feisty bay mare jumped straight upwards and broke the tongue outen the plow. But Sandy says he can fix it against work time tomorrow. That-there bay fixed it so I wouldn't have to work after two o'clock today. She fixed me a holiday when she jumped. I've been a no-account cuss, nowhow. You don't know, Elleen, how triflen I been," he said, "in my time. Throwen my wages here and yon. I could 'a' owned a small-sized farm if I had 'a' saved up. I'm satisfied I could. Not had the sense of a pecker-wood."

"Yes, I reckon you been right o'nary," she mocked at him.

"I want to tell you all about me." She saw him glance at her sidewise, uneasily. "I ain't never told you about Jule Nestor."

"You don't need to tell me if it's a trouble to you."

"I ain't never told you about Jule Nestor. Down on the river away on past the reach. Wife of a man named Bill Nestor. Lived with some people named Jones, dirty trash, stinken house. I ain't never told you about Jule."

"It likely ain't anything harmful."

"I used to go there last winter," he said.

"Was it so wrong to go there, Jonas?"

"I been a sinful man, Elleen, low-down. My own mammy would cry if she knowed."

His elbows were on his knees, his face in his hands now. Irregular tremors passed over his limbs and shook unevenly at his fingers that beat upon his temples. She turned away from him and looked off toward the barns and the west hills, unprepared for grief, looking over the barns toward the sky and the spreading haze, wondering why he was so distraught that he could scarcely speak. His trouble followed her, however, coming out of his shaking voice, the words low-spoken and tight as if they were set into his throat with a hard will.

"I used to go there last winter and winter afore last, away in the night, knocken on the door. The Jones old woman, she'd say, 'Jule's up the steps. You can go up for yourself.'"

She was still looking toward the barns and the cattle pens, but pain had gathered within her, gathered from his pain. The fact that he valued what he told highly as an evil and shuddered from the telling, and that he felt it concerned her and that she must know, this troubled and pleased her in

162

one confused pang. He was quiet for a while, but when he spoke his voice crumbled away, insufficient, falling to a hard whisper.

"I reckon you don't know what Jule was, what kind she was."

Her pain had spread over her now, knocking at her breast and drawing at her throat. Her eyes left the sky and turned to the ground, to the withered grass of the yard and the hard earth of the path.

"I know," she said.

"Every time I went I taken a dollar."

"Yes, I know."

"Sometimes old Jones, he'd say, 'Jule's got company. I reckon you can't go up tonight.'"

The sun slanted long rays through the air, rays which cut through the hard bare trees and printed dim shadows of boughs on the ground, the light lying widely dispersed over the spent bushes and debased grass, over the burnt chicory, frost-eaten and done. She had thought that Jonas was for her and that he was something to her, and Dorine had so thought, and Elmer and Rosie. She had been too bold within herself, she reflected. She was remembering slowly, the memory lying in a cumbersome, shapeless mass under her pain and under her abashed need. She was remembering Dorine's first party. He had told her the names of all the people there and had told her that she would like them when she knew them. Her wish for Jonas was crowded back into a minute point and under this plodded or spread the matter of a vast shapeless memory which turned about in a movement to a summary but came to nothing, confused and blurred anew by the fact that he now wanted her to know, that he felt that his story concerned her.

163

"Not but twice have I been there since I knowed you, Elleen, and them times I came out and sat alongside the creek all night and I says to myself, 'Jonas Prather, you're a stinken, o'nary fool, a low-down damned-to-the-devil white-trash.' I wouldn't name all I called myself as I sit out alongside the creek all night."

"Was that a long spell ago, Jonas?"

" 'Twas last summer, the last time I see Jule. After plowen time in the corn, I recollect now, after wheat harvest."

Ellen pulled her coat around her and drew her thinly dressed knees under its folds. The chill was spreading up from the hollow with the approach of evening. The cows were waiting at the barn and after a little she would have to go to shell the corn for the fattening turkeys. He was speaking again, asking her if she would hear the rest, for there was more to tell. After they had walked up Dorsey's hill, she reflected, and after he had kissed her in the wheat harvest. She stared at the ground beyond the steps, but his side, blue work clothes and crooked plow shoes, reached into the edge of her vision, one long broad hand laid out restlessly on his knee, a twitching hand that moved in and out of her sight. He wanted to tell her and the rest was harder to tell, harder to bear, and suddenly she wanted him to find relief and ease. She herself or what she felt about the wheat harvest did not matter if he found ease.

She turned toward him a little and glanced at his face, and he began to speak again, quietly, approaching cautiously to some point he held in his mind, circling widely about his story as if to remove himself from it for a little space. Jule Nestor's husband was Bill Nestor, a low-down tramp, gone awhile and then back, a sort of low gambler

164

who worked with loaded dice and hung around the Negroes on their pay days. You might see him any court day in town. He did not care what Jule did if she made a little money and gave him his share, even helped her. They were gone away now, over toward the Knobs, had cleared out when the law was after Bill for some meanness. They were a dirty set, white-trash if ever there was any such on the earth. Jule was dirty, inside and out, worse inside, he thought. A dirty talker. But they were gone now, over toward the Knobs, cleared out overnight one time during the summer. It was said Bill robbed a man on the road, held up a man traveling along the pike, an old man, feeble and sick. Bill handled him rough and hurt the old man and left him almost dead on the side of the road. Then the law got on Bill's track and he cleared out overnight.

Jonas told his story sparingly, deferring its point. Eli had been over into the knobs beyond the river looking for work for next year, not that there would be any farm work in the Knobs, but his errand to see a man took him there. He had run on the Nestors, had found them in a shanty by the side of a sawmill. Bill and Jule were hanging around the sawmill hands, Bill with his dice. Eli had seen them, Bill and Jule both, had even stopped to get a piece of string to mend his bridle.

"His mare shied at the sawmill and broke her bridle, split her throat latch."

His voice was dry and husky as he told of the broken throat latch, drawing near his story which now could no longer wait. Eli had thought he would stop in the shanty and borrow a piece of twine from the people that lived there, and there were Bill and Jule inside eating a sup of something. Jule was as dirty as ever and dirtier, offering

165

dirty talk. There was a baby, just born a few days back, a girl baby. Eli said it was his child, Jonas's; it looked like him; it had the same eyes and the same kind of face and the same dark hair.

"Eli said it looked like Mammy, my mammy."

They looked at the thought, sitting together in quiet, or they turned the thought about with a few brief words or a question. Jonas was still now, his hands holding his bowed head or folded together in a strong calm grasp. He had told no one but her, he said, and Eli would not tell.

Over and over Ellen's mind reverted to the little baby in Jule Nestor's house, a child that looked like Jonas, nursing Jule Nestor's dirty milk and lying in Jule Nestor's foul bed. The baby, a month old now, would be lying, little and weak, crying for food, being fed, crying for Jule, pushing its head into Jule's breast, closing its eyes to sleep.

"I been in torment ever since I knowed," he said. "I can't think it out. Seems like it oughtn't to be. My little gal that looks like my own mammy. And Eli, he's my cousin, our own kin."

The child that lay in Jule Nestor's bed could not be denied a place in her thought now. A great emptiness spread over the farm and over her past, as if life itself had emptied its inner portion and had given birth to some remote matter. Jonas was troubled and his thought went far from her and had another center, gathering around his hurt. He wanted to be beside her but he wanted her there to share his pain, and she hated his pain for a moment. A part of him was gone and in the loss she was confused in a crossing of demands, denials, and finalities. Something was lost to her. She thought continually of the child in Jule's bed, its mouth pushed into Jule's breast.

166

"I been in torment," Jonas said.

"You knowed two weeks back?"

"Yes. Eli, he told me two weeks ago. I thought I'd tell you, Elleen. I was in torment a week and then I says I'd tell Elleen. I reckon you think I'm right o'nary."

"I think it's a . . . pity," she said.

"I thought you might want me to go away far off, outen your sight."

"No."

"I thought you might so want."

"Do you want to go off, outen my sight?"

"God knows I do not. I want to stay close by if it ain't a trouble to you."

"You don't need to go."

"I'd like to see you every day. I'd like to be beside you a little every day. For a while. I'd like to now, if it ain't a trouble to you."

"You could come if you're of a mind to."

"It was in my mind corn-cutten time and after, all along through the hay, to want to ask you to marry."

The sun slanted its last long rays through the farm, falling away weakly to its early setting, and the air grew more chilly. Her loss lay as a pain along her empty arms, but beside her Jonas still sat, speaking half haltingly from time to time, recalling her to the trend of his troubled thought.

"I been in torment," he said. "Maybe you could tell me what to do."

"I'd have to study it out. I can't now see there's e'er thing to do."

"Whatever you say I'll do, no matter what 'tis."

"I can't see e'er thing to do now. Maybe when I study it over a spell."

167

"But nohow if you don't tell me to go outen your sight."

"I wouldn't tell you to go outen my sight."

"But we wouldn't be the same together as we used to be."

"Not everybit the same, Jonas, dances and parties and so much to laugh at."

"Seems as if I couldn't dance any more. Seems like I'd turn to something hard like iron if I tried."

"Maybe we wouldn't dance. Not for a spell nohow."

"I been in torment, downright hell. At night afore I could sleep. Then I says, 'I'll tell Elleen nohow. Maybe she'll tell me to go off, but nohow I'll tell her.'"

"No matter how much I study it over I can't see e'er thing to do."

"But if I could be beside you a little spell tomorrow and day after."

"At sundown you could come."

She arose from the step and went down to the path where she stood until he came to stand beside her. She asked him if he would like to go with her to feed the great white turkeys, for they were a sight to see, like great birds, all their feathers in a flutter. At the pens he kept beside her, even following her closely when she went into the barn on some errand. There was a moment when he leaned over the drinking pans to pour the water out, when she hated his pain and his shame, and her hate spread to his limbs and his back, his bent head and reaching hands. She talked about the white turkeys and about the price they would bring Miss Tod, or she had him lift one to guess its weight. Or standing at the bars beside the milking lot, when he came forward down the calf pen, when the turkeys were housed in the barn and the hush of their feathers was settling over the dusk, she gathered Jonas with her eyes and pitied him, and pitied herself and all men and women, and took his hand and walked back across the pasture.

There was nothing they could do, they decided, and they would wait. The winter would come. In the next day her thought of him was hushed and tender, muffled under her emotion, her ways were gentle and her voice low. Another day she was strong and cool; she would ask Jonas to give her a lasting promise, but when she spoke of it he was so full of lowly grief, saying that he would pledge her anything she asked with his right hand as forfeit, that she did not name any demands. He came every day until the cold fell. They would sit a little apart and they would talk of common things.

V

THE cold settled down over the farms in November, freezing the turf, so that the cows lingered about the feeding racks all day and were seldom seen off on the barren pasture. Ellen helped strip the tobacco, working in the dim stripping room where Henry kept a fitful fire in the little stove. The December cold was bitter with snow and sleet lying over the ground. Chill air gathered in the shady places and was never dispelled, and no green thing was left growing in the bare spots from which the snow had blown in its drifting. Cold came into the upper room where Ellen slept, a room which was now a mere place where her cot bed stood. The box where her clothing lay seemed very far from the bed; the distances in the little room were magnified by the crystal of the cold. The summer dress with its blue flowers was withered and blighted, crumbled flat, lying shriveled and faded in the box under the petticoats. When she told Nellie how the dress had withered, she was assured that she might have another when warm weather came, "And anyhow it'll freshen up a right smart against spring comes and you wash and iron it." The flowered dress with its sweet odors, then, would blossom again with the spring. Jonas stripped tobacco at Squire Dorsey's place, four miles away, but he sometimes came on Sunday afternoon, or Ellen would meet him at Dorine's home and they would walk back through the cold of the twilight, hurrying to be out of the frost, their thin coats buttoned close and their fingers numb. Ellen cut a strip from her shawl to make a muffler for him, winding it about his throat that had been bare to the wind and making him say that he would wear it whenever he went out.

But often the storm raged, sleet or wind or heavy snow, and Jonas did not come for several weeks at a time. The coldest winter in years, men said, the coldest in the time of man. An epidemic spread through the valley and over the hill farms, and the Turpins, ill of it, were scarcely seen all through the winter. Dorine coughed and grew wistful and thin and all the O'Shays, the Townleys, and the Prathers were afflicted, one after another, and Henry sat by the fire in misery for many days. Life waited for spring and Ellen waited. If Jonas came on Sunday afternoon he would take his horse to the barn and ask Ben for a stall or a bit of room, but often he walked the three miles from Dorsey's and left his little mare in the barn all day to save her from the heavy roads. Ellen slept long, drugged by the cold, and in the moonlight the frost glittered on the window and the frost of her breath gathered on the outer quilt. The world was hard and impenetrable; the frost stood between herself and

Jonas, the cold a barrier, and between herself and Dorine was the frost and the ice; between them also was Elmer. Between herself and Elmer was Dorine and also the frost, the latter barrier magnifying the first to a great and permanent size. She housed her yearling in one of the barns and saw that its food was ample. The tobacco, now neatly rolled into hands, was piled onto a wagon in a smooth high four-cornered mass and covered with an old carpet. Henry and John Bradshaw left at four in the morning on the day the crop was marketed, the wheels of the laden wagon crying out in a thin high tinkle on the frozen road. There were no gatherings in the cabins for fuel was scarce. When Erastus O'Shay went to see Maggie Turpin he carried a sack of wood to keep the fire all evening in the front room of the cabin.

The hens moped all day in their coops if the day were stormy and the yard wind-driven, or some of them, frightened by the unknown cold, crept under the house where their feet were frozen. The work on the farm was halted after the tobacco was sold. Ellen did not go to the milking pens now for Mr. Wakefield had told her she need not come until the cold weather passed. She helped Nellie to thaw the frozen foods and to prepare the cabin against the inroads of the frost. They found heavy sacks to lay against the crevices under the doors and at night they hung thick comforters over the ill-fitted windows. They clung close to the hearth when each task was done, returning again and again to warm their numb fingers. A visitor was doubly welcome because there was little news by the fireside. Life waited. If Jonas came he sat close to the fire, drowsed by the warmth after the long walk in the cold. He would sometimes whisper a little with Ellen when she sat beside him. He had left

Dorsey's in January and was staying at his father's house. He whispered news of his mother and his little sisters; his little sister, the least one, was better of the misery she had had in her ear; his mother was making him a thick warm quilt for his bed. He would sit beside Ellen for a while and then leave to be well set upon the cold way before night fell.

In February the bitterness went out of the cold, the sweet acrid sting, and a hard steady frost was left which still held the ground in a firm crust. The milder weather was even yet the cold of any other winter, bitter to endure. People passed along the pike now with their teams, but none ever went along the pasture road but those of the farm, for near the end of February Scott MacMurtrie closed the road which ran across his land, building a high strong fence across the way at the top of the lane that gave into the glen. Nellie was lonely for the sight of the passing horses and wagons and fretted often at the stillness of the farm.

One Sunday in February Ellen went to the O'Shay cabin with Jonas, walking by the footpath that avoided Mac-Murtrie's land, a path that had been broken through the snow after the old road was forbidden. Eli was working now beyond the river, making fence; he would marry Rosie soon and take her beyond the river to live. In the large cabin room a half-dozen men of the river glen were sitting or standing, among them old Dan O'Shay and Nannie, his wife. Jonas joined this group but Ellen went to the inner room where Rosie was helping her mother put the dishes away. Rosie talked of going beyond the river to live. Her mother had given her some feathers and had bought her a carpet from Mrs. Turpin's loom. "Try on my new hat," Rosie said, and Ellen went to the larger room and put on the hat before the glass that hung above the chest of drawers.

The hat was bright and new, a token of spring in its warmth and brightness. The men about the fire talked with low muttering, complaining at the closing of the road. The hat was fresh and fragrant, a promise of Rosie's wedding, but the low muttering of the men came into her pleasure in the hat, a faint menace that lay under the air, so that her joy in the hat was magnified as it stood out brightly before their threatenings.

From the kitchen came the sounds of heavy china disposed hastily, dull clacks of plates and cups. In the mirror she saw her face under the new hat and she wondered at the fresh new shape it brought to her chin and to her mouth. Mac-Murtrie must open the road, the men said; he would have to let them out, and there was an argument as to the law. "Go up to him and say, by God, open up that road," a voice broke in a low snarl. "Say open up, by God, or we'll open for you. Go as a mob and say . . ." Nannie's voice spoke then, deeply admonishing, asking for peace, for time, bidding them wait, and then an impatient cry from some younger O'Shay, deep and demanding. Ellen took off the hat and looked at it closely, at its little bits of red velvet twilled into a strange flower, pleasant odors coming out of the velvet and out of the new clean felt. A flower stood on the turned-up brim close to her hair. When she put the hat on again Jonas across smiled toward her from his seat by the chimney but the mutterings went on, now low and complaining, now breaking into angry snarls and threats and after a little growing low and cunning. Jonas had seen her in the hat and he had smiled to see her bright skin under the red bits of the winter flower. She remembered such a flower from some summer, but not in Miss Tod's garden. Such a flower grew beside a path somewhere, among blue flowers and yellow ones, a low flower, not a pansy and not a marigold. She thought that the flower she remembered was not red perhaps, but alike to this in shape while this had the red of some deep red pansy in Miss Tod's border.

Jonas smiled across at her in the way of the summer that was past and her need for him grew with the deep glow of the flower and with the soft rich mesh of the velvet petals. "Let Cassie MacMurtrie do hit," a voice was muttering. "Let Cassie." It came to her then, looking into the heart of the blossom as she held the hat in her hand, that it could only be a short while now until Miss Cassie would know the thing she herself knew, for everybody now seemed to know of Scott and Amanda Cain. "Let Cassie." They had only to wait, a voice said. "Bide your time and don't say e'er word more about that-there road. I give Scott a week now and that's all." Another voice, high-pitched and angered, foretelling, "I know Cassie Beal. I went to school along with her down on the creek." Another, low and more final, "I'd like to see Scott when Cassie gets done. There won't be enough of Scott MacMurtrie left to wad a gun with. . . . Like throwen a lame rabbit in amongst a pack of fifty starved hound dogs." "Bide your time. Old Scott, if there's e'er rag of him left, will clear out from here in less time than a week now." "Let Cass MacMurtrie do hit for us. I know Cassie Beal. She's made outen fire and hell. Bide your time."

Presently Rosie came and tried on the hat to show Ellen how it became herself, her generous round face beaming with its yielding, "It's prettier on Ellen, now, for a fact it is." Bye and bye Jonas came away from the men to talk with them, the glow of the flower lingering in Ellen's breast, and Rosie took them to the kitchen and gave them each a dish of sweetened cherries she had preserved the spring before and gave them cake.

Later, going home, they climbed the steps onto the little porch and longed audibly for spring. "It looks like winter just can't break," Jonas said, and hand in hand they went in to the hearth fire. Then Nellie asked Jonas to stay and eat his supper and this pleased Ellen very much. When she went up to the cowpens to help milk the cows he went too, carrying her pail and milking one of her cows while she milked the other. He chatted a little with John Bradshaw and Ben, who accepted his presence without comment, and all was sweetly familiar and casual. The lowing of the cows came to Ellen as something familiar and beseeching, and it met a willingness and tender pity in her being. In willingness and tender pity she poured the last of the milk into the great can and passed with Jonas through the gate and across the pasture, his free hand reaching for her hand and she, consenting, walked beside him but neither spoke on the way. The cows were quiet, but their remembered lowing continued, beseeching. The thumping of their feet on the hard turf merged with her rising tenderness, and the latching of the gate was a renewed token of it and their steps on the porch, their long caress in the dark—small fulfilment of her infinite affirmation.

They sat by the fire during the evening eating the sugar bread that Nellie had baked and talking of all the incidents of the farms, of the closed fence. They sat, Ellen at the corner in the little chair, then Nellie in her accustomed place and then Henry, looking at the flame, dazed by the flame. Jonas sat at the other end of the hearth, his feet on the stones, or he pounded hickory nuts on the dogiron with a loose stone,

176

breaking away the shell with careless hands and tossing the largest kernels across to Ellen or giving an entire cracked nut to Henry or Nellie. There was no lamp but the light of the freshly built fire was yellow and bright, or when the fire fell away the pink glow survived and colored their faces and their persons but left the back of the room darkened. When they had sat their fill in the warm glow and when they fell into reminiscent sadness or speculation, Ellen or Henry would toss on more wood from the pile and after the fire had died away more dully as it searched the new wood, it leaped into blaze again, and once with the leaping Henry sang a song, shuffling his feet on the boards of the floor.

At one sinking of the fire Nellie withdrew and moved about in the back of the room or in the kitchen. Then she took off a little of her clothing and lay down in the bed, falling asleep as the pink light faded from her forehead. Ellen moved into Nellie's chair and thus they sat, Henry reminiscent and outward-flowing, warming to his own past as he searched his mind for it.

"And so you been plumb to Tennessee and back," Jonas said. "Well I vum!"

"But my pap he never went out of sight or hearen of Luckett's Branch, never in his whole lifetime."

"You was a rover, for a fact now."

"My pap, he said his pap was named Edd Chesser and said the name was by rights Cheshire away back, afore his time. My grandpap was a master hand for honey bees. I'll tell you what he could do. He could walk right into a swarm and never get a sign of a sting. Twenty stands he had if he had one. I recollect once when I was a tad how I got stung. I recollect as well as if it was today. We used to take bread and honey to school to eat at big recess for our school dinner.

177

I recollect once when I opened up my dinner bucket the whole place was lined with these-here little brown ants, all gaumed into the dinner."

"What did you do?" Ellen asked. "How'd you get shed of them?"

"I reckon I didn't eat my dinner that-there day. I never could abide to have ants in my victuals. A man over by Coulter's sawmill said once, 'Law, ants is such clean little things, I never take notice to an ant.' A woman over at grandpap's said once she never ate blackberry jam because it was made in flytime. Said if you ever took notice to it blackberry jam was about half flies cooked up and most people never knowed the difference. The taste was about the same, she said. She said she never ate jam on that account."

"What did she say peach jam was half? Wasps, I reckon, yellow jackets," Jonas said.

"I recollect when I was a youngone," Henry resumed his memory. "We used to live in a house over against a knob and once the chimbley smoked all one winter so bad we looked black as buzzards and Mammy was drove half outen her mind a-tryen to tidy things. That spring when Pap was plowen he turned up a skull bone. Sure thing, he did, a small-like skull as if it was a woman or a child. Out in the middle of a field. He brought it to the house but Mammy she wouldn't let it rest till she got it outen the house, but my brother Newt, he stood it agin the door to make a door prop. Then Pap threw it out to please Mammy and it laid out behind the henhouse all summer upside down, and once when it rained I see the chickens drink water outen it. Then Mammy she told Pap he better bury it and Newt buried it when he went to dig a post hole one time. It was a small-like skull and might be a woman or a youngone half growed up, and then after a spell we heared that a man killed his boy in the house away back, man drunk and killed his own boy about twelve year old and they buried him out in the field. War time, it was. Said there was blood on the floor up in the loft room where the boy died, and sure enough there was, when you looked sharp, a brown spot on the floor but you couldn't say on oath it was blood."

"Why don't you go on to bed," Nellie said, waking out of her first sleep. "Nobody wants to listen to your long-winded blab all night. Can't you-all get shed of him, Ellen?"

"I recollect I was ten year old and next year they all put at Preacher Wilder to teach a school and he gave in. I recollect the first day. Preacher Wilder's shoes hurt and he taught all day in his sock feet and I recollect the holes in the heels of his socks. No new sight to anybody but it made the big gals laugh to see Preacher Wilder's naked hide shine outen his sock holes. Next year Preacher Wilder's wife died and he married Farney O'Bryan and went off, but he was in nobody's debt though. Then we didn't have a school for a right smart while and when we did I never went. Stayed at home to help Pap. It was when I was sixteen that Tom Begley stabbed Shine Mather, stabbed him clean through the guts and laid him out as bloody as a hog. Then the mob came and hung Tom to a white oak down by the creek along past our house and me and Pappy and Joe Deats, we took Tom down and laid him out for the funeral. Quarrel over a shotgun, I recollect."

"Did Shine Mather think it was his shotgun?" Ellen asked. Henry's words burst loud on her ears, reverberating

179

against her sense, but she attended to nothing he said and leaned dejectedly in her small stiff chair, her shoulders back. "Did Shine claim the shotgun?"

"It was a trade between a shotgun and a filly, but I disremember how it was. Tom, he owned the shotgun, I reckon, and he traded for the filly. Seems like it was the filly that was lied about, but I disremember. Seems like the filly had a lame shoulder and seems like Shine knowed it but traded when the filly was all rested up and the lame didn't show. That's how it seems. Nohow Shine greened Tom outen a good shotgun."

"Why don't you go to bed," Nellie said, waking again, "and quit your eternal blab? Nobody wants to listen to blabber all night."

"Next year or year after old Uncle Billy Rudd went insane and used to carry all the dinner pots outen the house when his old woman was cooken dinner and set everything over against the hencoops. Once he carried the cookstove out and set it out behind the ash hopper, fire in it, they said, the whole enduren time. Poor old Aunt Plez had a sight of trouble outen her husband. They had, a long while afore that, a couple of brats that died just about the time they was up any size and could 'a' been any help. One died with lockjaw and the least one died with fits. They never seemed bright, their children never did. Billy and Plez took a right smart risk when they married, folks always said. Said the day they was wedded the floor to the house where they stood up fell in and let the whole party down amongst the timbers, floor fell plumb in. Folks said it was a bad token and advised against it but the preacher was already there and the couple wouldn't hear to any let-up in the ceremony. Said the preacher was halfway through when the floor fell, splintered, and everybody tilted into the rubbish under the house. Well, they hauled out the bride and groom and advised against any further hitch-up, but Aunt Plez and Uncle Billy had set their heads to it and the folks went out in the yard and finished up under a tree, some of the women so shook up they cried like a funeral and hardly knowed what was up. It was a token I reckon. Everybody always said it was a token. People take a heap of risks, from first to last, in a lifetime. I knowed Uncle Billy in his old age an he was queer in his ways, even before he went plumb outen his head and commenced to torment Aunt Plez about the dinner pots and skillets. But that wasn't what I set out to tell. Once Uncle Billy . . ."

"For God's sake!" Nellie said, waking a little.

"Once Uncle Billy took it into his mind to roof the house, but the house had a good tight roof all the time, but Uncle Billy took it into his mind he'd put on a new roof. Took it in head to take the roof offen the henhouse and put it on the house and swap back the roof offen the house onto the henhouse. Well, he set to early one Tuesday afore day to rip the shingles offen the house. I recollect Pap sent me over there to borrow a whet rock offen Aunt Plez and there was Uncle Billy on top the house and the shingles a-fallen like rain and Uncle Billy gay as a songbird. I recollect his red face to this day. Aunt Plez was worried half outen her own mind and said what would they do if it come on to rain afore night, which it did, and worried about Uncle Billy up on the roof, his legs wobbly ever since he got insane in his mind. Aunt Plez said to me she was beside herself with worry and asked would I go get somebody to try to get Uncle Billy down offen the roof afore he fell down and in a manner killed himself. I studied out that it would take five men at least and so I went and got Pappy and some more and we got four plow lines to hoist Uncle Billy down. He took half the roof offen the house afore we got everything ready, and a heap of trouble it was in the end because Uncle Billy didn't come gentle at first and Wilks Sanders had to ease him down on the roof and tie his hands and feet. Did you ever hear tell of how strong Wilks Sanders was in his time?"

"I never heared of him," Jonas said. "He was a strong man, I reckon."

"Strongest man I ever see and I've traveled a right smart," Henry said. "I see him lift four plowshares at once and never lose his wind either. He took a right smart risk too when he married Josie Tinnie. Josie, it was said, hated him afore a year was out and tried to put spite in his victuals, parisgreen it was said, but they lived on together off and on in quarrel and had ten youngones. Well, Wilks he tied Uncle Billy's hands and tied his feet and made fast a rope around his middle, tried not to hurt old Billy no more'n he could help and he and two more hoisted Uncle Billy down as easy as if he'd been a bale of shingles. Then we all set to and rerooked the house for Aunt Plez, poor old Aunt Plez, and Uncle Billy got so bad they had to send for two doctors and finally the county took him over and he was sent on some-wheres, but I see him just afore he went and he was all foam at the mouth and wild in his eyes. That was the last anybody ever see of Uncle Billy in our parts because he died pretty soon arter they took him, and Aunt Plez sold out and went to live with her sister. She seen a sight of trouble with her youngones not bright and Uncle Billy the way he was. That was when I was seventeen, I reckon, when Uncle Billy died and Aunt Plez sold out."

"For God's sake!" Nellie said, turning again in her bed.

"Can't you get shed of him in no way or how, Ellen? To blab the enduren night long!"

"A body takes a heap of risks in a lifetime, from first to last," Henry said. "Next year I was eighteen and then I was nineteen, I recollect. I recollect that was the year Newt got horse-throwed and got his shoulder busted. Saturday it was. A wild critter he traded for, bay I recollect, a critter nobody could gentle, as it turned out. I recall how Newt was throwed a Saturday. Then come Sunday. I recall as well as 'twas yester. Then a Monday. Tuesday. I recollect Wednesday Doc Marks set Newt's arm bone and Newt he suffered a right smart with a misery in his side. Thursday I recollect, then Friday Newt was up and about and come Sunday he was about near all over it but except his arm and that took a pretty considerable time to knit. Newt said he'd vow he'd ride that critter inside a month but I don't recollect he had any luck with that-there nag. He traded finally for a light bay colt. That was fall. Then I recollect spring. Yes I recall. Then come fall and warm politics on. I recollect the barbecue on the creek and old man Hardin on the stump for office. Spring then I recall. I went off that spring and lived with old Mr. John Lucas that next year. I recollect what heavy crops there was. Prices down to the bottom. Six cents for fair good burley or even four. Bad that was. Then I lived over on Tick Creek a spell. Then I went down in Taylor County and I recollect Minnie, a right puny child, sickly from the start. Then we had Edd and Lue. Bright youngones enough. Then Harp and Corey. I thought I was a Taylor County man for good. All the youngones died. Bad luck Nellie had with her youngones. I recollect Harp. Bright as a new dollar. But I recollect plainest the time Newt was horse-throwed. It comes back in head somehow. I don't

183

know when I ever think of Newt since a right smart while. I don't know for sure where Newt lives now. He may be in Taylor and again he may be somewheres else. That's the story of my life now, and you wanted to hear it. A body takes a heap of risks from first to last. I recollect how mad Newt was when that-there bay busted his shoulder. I recall how Newt cussed when we fetched him home and how he said he'd break that-there critter or he'd be busted wide open. But I don't recollect he had any luck outen that nag after all. I recall Sunday. Then a Monday. Then a Tuesday and Doc Marks come and set Newt's arm over. Or was that Wednesday? Seems like it was Tuesday. Again seems like it was maybe a Wednesday. I recollect how Newt groaned and yelled when Doc Marks set his arm over. It must 'a' been a Monday after all. Seems like Doc Marks wouldn't let it go till Tuesday. I recollect he didn't get over to set it right away after Newt was horse-throwed because he was busy with Sookie Harmon and Newt had to wait his turn, but I don't recollect whe'r he had to wait till Tuesday or a Monday. Some ways it seems like it was Monday and again it seems Tuesday. I'd have to study that out. Seems right enough to call it Monday, and yet I can't satisfy myself it wasn't a Tuesday. Monday though I reckon it was. Maybe Newt was throwed a Sunday. Someways that seems correct. Then come a Monday. I don't know. Tuesday it seems nohow. I ain't satisfied in my mind it was Tuesday more than Monday. . . ."

Henry suddenly became full of sleep and he arose abruptly and left the fire. The blaze had fallen away long since and now one hard ember glowed in the midst of the fallen red ashes yielding a faint pink glow. Ellen let the fire

184

lie untended while she gazed sadly at the iridescent ember, and Henry moved about in the dark of the region beyond the bed, making slow sounds of slipping into the bed with the low sigh of the quilts and the creak of the settling slats. Then Jonas moved Henry's chair back and hitched his own nearer to Ellen's chair, looking at her with amused eyes, and she arose and laid two sticks on the fire, an ash piece and a piece of sycamore, and they lay darkly together for a few moments to enkindle, which assured Jonas that he would stay longer, answering his questioning movements. The sticks lay together in the bed of the fire for a little and then sprang into first flames, bright, unheated, and new, uncertain, leaping higher and sinking away, but leaping brightly again. Ellen sat in her chair and Jonas drew his chair nearer, and sitting thus they talked a little, caring nothing for what they said but bridging the space Henry had made with his long rememberings.

"Eli thinks he'll work for old Man Bagby beyond the creek. I see Eli for a talk last night," Jonas said.

Ellen asked something but she did not know how the reply came for she heard only the assurance of a voice that brought her pleasure now whatever it said. The low monotony of the words trailed across the music and spread it widely at the end, and pleasure gathered in her body and in her mind. Now and then the voice flowed forward and her pleasure flowed upon its monotony or its falling away, taking it but not heeding its words unless a question appealed to her for a reply, and then she heard and gave the answer. Then Jonas moved his chair until it stood against hers and he began to touch her face with his fingers and to kiss her and to look at her throat. He put his arm

185

about her shoulder and thus they sat for a long while. A mouse came out of a little round hole beside the chimney and ran over the floor toward the bed, but after a little it ventured toward the fireplace and ate the crumbs of the nut kernels that were dropped, or it rolled as a little oblong ball beside the chairs or stopped beside Ellen's shoe. It moved slowly about, unafraid, a faint sound of diminutive feet as it came and went. The fire burned brightly now, the sycamore log and the ash, their flames blended into one flame and one light. Far away the hounds bayed, fixed voices, crying at no fox but rather at the night. A sound of hoofs on the road, far away and hollow, the sounds growing uncertain and un- rhythmical as the horse came through the pasture gate and then muffled but swift again on the driveway. Mr. Dick coming home. Then the barn door swung shut with a heavy hollow clatter and the footsteps were still. Jonas settled his shoulder a little nearer and whispered:

"We'll get married," he said.

The mouse had run away to hide in the dark beyond the bed, and the fire sank from its brilliance and grew more warmly red as the wood turned to rich embers. Henry breathed noisily in his sleep and Nellie waked no more, her face now turned toward the shadows. Jonas trailed his hand over the outlines of her arm, over her shoulder and over her breast, looking at her with his fingers and with his eyes.

"We'll get married," he said. And then he added, "I look for winter to break."

"I look for spring," Ellen said.

"Soon now. Afore you know."

"The spring birds up in the thicket."

"But the ground is froze deep."

"But it'll come, spring will," she said, her hands on his

throat and on his shoulder. "Thawen time and then spring."

The mouse came back and ate the crumbs near the chairs. Ellen's eyes fell on the little oblong gray ball as it rolled nearer and nearer. Jonas was sitting up with her, tarrying. It was a token. She looked at his hand where it lay over her hand in her lap, the same gaze holding the quiet of the mouse and the quiet of his hand that moved, when it stirred, with the sudden soft motions of the little beast. The roosters crowed from farm to farm in token of midnight and Henry turned in his sleep once again. The fire sank slowly from the hearth but Ellen tended it, adding the last of the wood, a few small sticks of sycamore and ash that had been designed for the morning. She settled them together and they came quickly to life among the rich embers of the former fire, renewing the old fire that had not died. Then the mouse came back from the dark beyond the bed and lingered among the nut shells on the stones.

"I aim to go to town this week," Jonas said. "What you want me to fetch you from town?"

"What would you fetch me?" she whispered.

"I'd fetch out anything you took a fancy for if I had to shoot the judge hisself. Anything you fancy."

By the renewed light of the fire he looked at her anew. She felt his gaze and his hands searching her for her beauty and she felt her beauty grow more full and rich when he called to it, and it became something which they held and owned together. The last light from the burning sticks shed warmly over her and she shed a rich warmth in her turn, and Jonas buried his face in the glow of her throat, whispering, covering her with his soft words.

"We'll get married. Some day afore summer. Spring it

187

will be. The thaw is bound to come now."

"I'll know when spring comes. The first token. I'll know," she said.

"We'll get married."

Jonas's horse was stabled in the great barn, snug from the cold. Ben had thrown it a feeding of hay when he passed, and now it was asleep among the other horses, but it would be shy of the strange place and glad when it was in its own stable again. She murmured a few words about the little horse and Jonas replied. Then a wind arose after midnight and rattled the insecure windows and worried the boards of the porch roof, and Jonas drew her nearer and murmured about the wind. The fire faded slowly and the room dimmed. The mouse came back for a long season with the crumbs and the shadows that had lingered beyond the bed drew nearer. It was long past midnight and Jonas whispered that he would go. Three times he arose from their reverie and whispered that he must not stay, that it was time to go, and Ellen acquiesced. He would go.

"A night is short," he whispered, "Sunup would soon come."

He would go. He drew away from her and arose, gathering his hat from where it lay on the floor by the door. Ellen moved to the space beyond the hearth and stood in the dim light of the last ember, and he returned once to her there. Then he put on his hat and went swiftly out at the door. She lingered for a little on the stones, kneeling there, forgetting the night, looking into the heart of the coal that throbbed among the hot ashes. Then she covered the fire, using the shovel noiselessly so that Nellie need not be awakened, shoveling the dry gray ashes from the wings of the fireplace and banking them over the living ember that it might be preserved. When she had covered the fire securely she went softly up the stair.

THE cold lingered through the first days of the week, thawing a little in the midday but freezing again at night. Ellen moved through these days in a hush of expectancy, finding small tasks, mending a garment or searching out a ribbon, preparing for the thaw and tending the flame of her own beauty. Jonas would go to town at the end of the week and after that he would come again. Once she awakened from her reverie and remembered the words of the men who had sat beside Dan O'Shay's fire and remembered their threat. All the people of all the farms knew, then, of Scott Mac-Murtrie's secret, she reflected, and her knowledge of it was no longer a furtive knowledge hidden deeply in her own mind although her mouth was closed dumbly upon it. She thought of all the farms as waiting to see what Miss Cassie would do, watching the house among the cedars, all the other houses turned that way to see, Gowan's and Wakefield's and Dorsey's and Fairhope church. Miss Cassie would know soon and when she knew there would be a different feel in the air and another way of thinking in the farms. Her own reverie closed about her and she left Miss Cassie out, centering about her ribbon and her bit of lace, her hems and buttons made neat, and, as her reverie grew and became real, the air grew mild and the hold of the frost, at first loosened, became lax and then fell away. The ice would rot away altogether and the earth become pliable, and her reverie grew intense, remembering each moment of the night when Jonas had stayed long with her, distilling each moment of its sweeter fruit. Jonas would come again; there would be another night; it would be as if they had not spent the interval apart.

Thursday she made new nests for the hens, using fresh straw, and leaning over the drinking pans where the last of the ice was delaying in a pan-shaped mass which she threw out to the sun, she thought of Miss Cassie, quick among her hens. She thought of Miss Cassie's wide brow and her heavy hair and her eyes, and with the thought a stillness seemed to settle over the air. The chickens came out into the sun and ate their corn, moving quickly as if the winter were forgotten, and later one cackled noisily in the henhouse doorway. It was already spring. Any day she might find the blue flowers and the white ones on the hillside. Within a week perhaps the yellow March lilies would be showing spears of green above the ground in Miss Tod's garden. She would see them if she looked over the fence from the calf lot. Her bright dress would freshen and Jonas would remember that he had said that it became her well, and his arm about her would lie along the flowers and they would be gathered into her flesh and pressed back into her being. Sitting by the slow afternoon fire her emotion gathered again into a reflection. She had taken his shame and had taken his pang as in part hers to trouble, and she had felt her loss, but it was time now to put it by, to make no matter of it. Jonas would come and they would be as if no interval had ever stood between them, as they had been during their last hour.

On that night it was that Miss Cassie MacMurtrie hanged herself. Ellen, when she had been asleep but a little while, heard the MacMurtrie farm bell ringing an alarm and in a moment the Gowan hounds began to bay. Henry said that he had better go, that MacMurtrie's house was probably burning, and Ellen dressed quickly and started away with him, leaving him behind before they reached the sheep pasture beyond the marsh. The bell continued to ring out some terror from the house which stood dark among the dark trees without flame or light except for the one lamp which stood on the doorsill. When Ellen ran up to the door an old Negress who had been ringing the bell dropped the rope and limped across the yard, wringing her hands. She told her broken, fearful story, the words gathered into her cries. Miss Cassie was hanging dead up in the upper hall. She had wondered why Miss Cassie did not come to eat her supper and she had warmed the food over and over and once she had called up the back stair. Amanda Cain and Scott MacMurtrie were gone. Then one of the hounds had begun to moan, had gone wandering through the house whimpering and the other hounds in the stable had taken up the cries. Then she had set a light in the hall.

The night seemed very long to Ellen. The spacious house widely set and high roofed, after her cabin homes, seemed to float in a mythical air. From the moment when she first mounted the great mythical stair, carrying the lamp for Mr. Al, all through the time that was spent in trying to revive Miss Cassie, through the warmer rainy dawn when the chilled rooms were colder than the outside air, she had moved through great spaces, going up and down for Miss Tod, who came at daybreak and set the house in order, or she carried messages from the lame Negress to the upper floors or sat stiffly in a chair to answer the questions of the coroner. "Hold up your right hand and take the oath," he had said, and the large room quivered and the walls receded, the great black bed rolling back into ultra spaces. On the wall there was a picture of Scott MacMurtrie, a young likeness, a stiff coat on his shoulders, a smooth roundness on his cheeks. Scott's collar and tie hung over the back of a chair. Squire Dorsey came into the room and sat in a chair beside Henry. The coroner was a large blond man with little red lines on his cheeks, a troubled man. "Do you solemnly swear that the evidence you are about to give shall be the truth, the whole truth and nothing but the truth, so help you God?" he said to her, and she trembled before the solemn words and before the kindness of the voice that uttered them. "You can sit down," he said, "no need to stand." She could see Miss Cassie's dress hanging in the opened closet; Miss Cassie still lay as Henry and Mr. Al had first placed her in the hall, covered now with a sheet. "Tell all you know of this," said the coroner. She had heard the bell, she had run through the dark, running ahead of Henry. The old lame woman had met her in the yard, had limped away from the bell post, Aunt Julie was her name. Aunt Julie had stood outside the house door on the stones before the steps while she went a little way into the hall. She was herself the first one of those outside the household to enter the house, the coroner said, and she acquiesced. When did Henry Chesser and Al Wakefield come? They were just behind her when she stood in the hallway and they went ahead of her up the stair. Did she know anything of the whereabouts of Scott MacMurtrie? When did she see him last? Did she know any reason Cassie MacMurtrie might have for hanging herself?

She tried to go into the stillness of Miss Cassie for reasons, to probe for reasons, Miss Cassie being everywhere present in the room, in the closet, in the air, in the furniture, everywhere about but still now. Miss Cassie had seen Amanda Cain walking before her with bright looks and a bent mouth, looking backward for two years she had seen, all in one look perhaps. Deceiving Miss Cassie before her eyes for two years, but would that, she asked herself, be the reason for the end of a life? Jonas enveloped her mind stirring in the farthest corners of her being and she could not think why one would quit life. A great will to live surged up in her, including the entire assembly—the coroner, Squire Dorsey, Henry, Miss Tod, Mr. Al, all of them. They would all live. She was living. Only life was comprehensible and actual, present. She was herself life. It went with her wherever she went, holding its abode in her being. She was alive, she was alive. The coroner waited for her answer.

"Miss Cassie didn't say e'er word to me about her trouble," she answered. "I knowed Miss Cassie only when I see her go by on the pike or see her off on her land. I couldn't say e'er word for sure about Miss Cassie."

THE morning too was strange and long, for Ellen waked several times to see the sun dimly shining at her window. The pictures of the night stood back and far away, hardly troubling her sleep. Her body was tired and heavy and dull, for a night of watching was strange to her experience. She slept heavily from hour to hour and awakened in the afternoon to sit by the fire in a dazed silence. Henry had told Nellie of the night and now he slept on the bed. After she had milked the cows Ellen looked for her own heifer in the great pasture, for she had not seen the yearling for many days, and now she wanted to see the beast, to rub her neck and claim her again as her own, to enjoy the simple sheen of her rich fur and the pleasure of possession, to touch her warm impersonal being. She thought that there would be rain and her mind clung about the fact of the rain. It would settle down by nightfall and all the frost would go out of the ground. She looked away toward the north country, ignoring the south, willfully forgetting the cedar trees and the doves and the marsh. The clouds shut out the far hills and many white vapors hung near the earth, dull over the pasture. It was spring.

Overhead the clouds ran near the earth, shutting together with deeper seams of leaden silver. A great change had come in a day for it was spring. On the pasture's brow, just where the hill rolled up to a smooth faint crest, Jonas came, leading his horse. She let her little cow drift away down toward the feeding ricks and met Jonas as he walked on the slope. He had come to tell her that he was going away.

"A man named Cornish wants me to put in his crops. It's away over toward Cornishville, near twenty mile or more maybe. A man came up to me on the street in town today and he says, 'Want a good job?'"

Jonas was full of the new enterprise, eager to tell of it, proud of it. "It'll be a job now, to look after everything on a big place. A small parcel of cows and a few sheep. All the crops."

His going, elevated to managing an entire farm, filled her with a rich pride. He would make a journey to a new country, she thought with fervor, and she herself expanded to take in the adventure and the new world and the new way between them.

"I aim to leave right now," he said. "I promised to be there afore sunup."

She hardly realized that she was not going herself. They stood together under the leaden twilight on the brow of the low bare pasture with the land reaching far about them, the cows gliding slowly before the feeding ricks and Ben going from barn to barn. Some crows were flocking over Gowan's field, stretching in a long mass across the sky's edge, and now and again came their slow deliberate laughter, ha . . . ha . . . ha, hollow and high-pitched; ha . . . ha . . . ha.

"I was a-standen on the street corner when a man says, 'Want a good job? Out past Cornishville. Good pay. Man crippled a Saturday that owns the land. Good clever man. Treat you fair and pay all that's right.' Thinks I, I can do it if any man can. Just you watch Jonas." His head was high in his pleasure and pride.

It would rain all night, a slow dripping wet, and in the morning the road would be spotted with standing puddles. Jonas would be riding far into the night, wet with the rain, leaping ahead on the little horse. "Which way is Cornishville now?" she asked.

"You couldn't see. It's a far piece off."

The ground was dull and colorless, and there was no green anywhere but in the few low cedar bushes off at the pasture's edge. The lead of the sky settled down over the earth and another leadenness arose out of the earth seams and hollows.

"Is it that country I can see in a fair time from the hill maybe?" she asked.

"You couldn't see. It's a long piece that way," he pointed.

"I'll come back," Jonas said, looking at her for parting. She felt his look penetrate her face and reach her need of

195

him just as a few drops of rain began to fall. "I aim to be off now. I'll ride Jake here." They were two leaden figures rising out of the earth, walking down the brow of the gentle crest. Ellen saw their feet rising and falling darkly into the dark of the ground, themselves the living part of all the dull spring. Their figures were mingled with the darkness of the horse that came down, head bowed, close behind them. Then Jonas took her into his arms and kissed her for leaving, pressing her against the shoulder of the horse and gathering her to himself.

"God blast me to perdition if ever I forget you, Elleen. When I come back we'll get married," he said.

"Elmer and Dorine. . . . Do you know it?" he said again.

"I knowed a right smart while."

"I'll come back afore long. Then me and you."

She separated them in her mind while she clung to him, knowing for the first time that she was not going, realizing that when he went she would be there, herself, Jonas gone, the two divided. Then she flung back the shawl from her head and buried her face against his face, pressing her bosom into his bosom, crying, "Jonas, don't go, Jonas, Jonas, take me," until he trembled under the impact of her pleading, and they stood together weeping, she with tears and he with wrenching sobs.

"God-almighty blast me to perdition, I'd as soon give up life itself as you, Elleen," he said. His words mingled with their weeping, falling between their cries and their caresses. "God-almighty damn me for a fool if ever I forget. If ever I forget e'er look of your face or the feel of you. God blast me. . . ." The crows had cried their last laughter and went away into the dark, and Ben's voice came over the pasture calling some straying hog, "Ho-eee, peeg, peeg, peeg, peeg," over and over. "Blast me if ever I forget or don't come back like I say," Jonas bound tight his oath. He put her shawl over her head and folded it about her breast. "I got to go tonight. It's a fine job, the best I could get anywheres, and I already given my word I'd be there by sunup. I'll come back afore long. And I'll write you a letter." Then he climbed on the horse and rode away in the falling rain.

THE house among the cedar trees stood empty and presently the shutters were falling, making of it a fearful place to see, the great blank windows staring. Someone took MacMurtrie's hounds away and the cows went somehow from the pasture. Ellen never heard again the high eerie cry, pee-o-wee-wee, going out over the marsh or over the sheep pasture. The absence of the cry came over her mind as a power holding the land and touching herself, and when she climbed Wakefield's wooded hill or stole a little way into the thicket lying around the marsh her ears were half-alert for it although she had a deep knowledge that it would never come. With the thought of the cry or of the stilled cry there would be the thought of Jonas, or if she stooped over a bank his hand reached with her hand to gather violets. His hand reached with her hand when she dropped the beans in their rows or when she placed chosen eggs under a brooding hen. His fingers curved with her fingers and his foot set itself in the path with her foot. In the early morning, going up to the tobacco field, looking up into the blue of the sky that was finely granulated and delicately moted with dissolving cycles flowing outward and forming forever under her gaze, something to breathe and to have, plovers in it, his gaze went up with her gaze and his happiness parted her lips while his hand on her back steadied her shoulders.

Eli and Rosie were married and went away to another country to live, and Ellen saw no more of Rosie, for the way was long and hard to go and Eli could spare no time for journeys. When Jonas had been gone two weeks or more he wrote Ellen a letter which she read many times, following each phrase to its last degree of meaning and searching out each connoted thought. The letter: "Friend Ellen, I came up here and I am working for old Mr. Bee Cornish. He got his arm ripped wide open in a sawmill. Last week I plowed for corn and this I am planting. I hope it holds off raining until I get done. Then the patch is to set out, about three acres in all, not much tobacco. Dear, dear Elleen. I think of you every day. I will kiss the letters of your name. Mr. Cornish is a fine man and the pay is good. I hope the weather stays pretty until after next week. Then let it rain. I will be back sometime. Goodbye dear Elleen." It was signed "Jonas W. Prather."

Ellen wrote a reply in which she told of the newly worked highway and of the opened road through MacMurtrie's land, of the geese Miss Tod was growing, silly things always thinking someone was about to pester them. The dogwood tree was a fair sight to see this time, she said, and she told of Rosie's wedding. When he came back the cherries would be ripe and she would bake him a pie. She wanted to tell him something more, but pore over the words as she would and empty her mind of its phrases, she could not find the adequate sayings. On the paper the words seemed hard and dumb, or given freedom they were sugared and easy and light. She tore these away and began anew, leaving in the news of the farm and of the dogwood, of Rosie, and the promise of the cherries. In the end she wrote that when he came she would have much to tell, trusting that she would then find a way.

Elmer and Dorine went to town one day and returned married. The Wheatleys moved away from MacMurtrie's tenant house and in a little while the dock and the fennel overgrew the yard and tall sprouts obliterated the windows. Ellen never knew whether Jonas had her letter or not, and when no reply came with the passing days she felt sure that it had gone astray. The cherries ripened and went, but then they were earlier than usual that year, and there would be the blackberries coming and these were in plenty.

VI

DORINE and Elmer lived on Gowan land, back in the farm, far from the large house, their place approached by a different pike. The cabin stood under a great poplar tree, strange and distantly removed as Ellen came toward it along its fenceline, as if it held its occupants but temporarily, and she always felt that presently she should go there no more. She went to see Dorine several times in June, whenever she could get away from the tobacco and when she could find a work horse idle in the pasture. Dorine would be glad to see her and eager to display herself as mistress of a house, but she was changed, and Elmer was changed. If Ellen went on Sunday she would find Elmer sitting around the house door, and he would talk a little. He seemed secure and satisfied, even drowsy and unalert. If a man he knew came along the road, stopping to talk, they would spend the hour droning. One day Dorine talked much of Sallie Lou Brown and her pretty dress, her new stitches, her pink petticoat and her bracelet. Sallie Lou had no home; she lived about among relatives, and now she had come to stay a while with the Seays, three miles away. She had been to see Dorine the week before and she was coming again soon. When Ellen went again Dorine said:

"Sallie Lou was here Sunday with Jonas. I reckon you know he's back and a-worken for Barnet down the river a long piece."

Ellen felt with her hand for Jonas's letter where it lay pinned to an inner garment and crushed warm against her breast. She had not known that he had come back.

"They drove up in Barnet's buggy hitched to Jonas's horse and they looked all spruced up fitten to kill."

"I reckon Sallie Lou is a right pretty girl by now," Ellen hardly knew what her mouth was saying. She had not known he had come.

"You know Jonas was a-worken, while he was gone, right in the Brown neighborhood, amongst Sallie Lou's kin."

"I reckon Sallie Lou is right pretty."

"Sallie Lou is pretty enough. She and Jonas went together a right smart while he was over there, from all they have to talk about."

Ellen went home long before sundown to be ready for the turkeys and the milking hour. She was penetrating deeply into her memory to try to reconstruct Sallie Lou, whom she had seen but once, on the night of Dorine's first party. She saw again the lamplight with the dust floating through it. Voices were singing together and feet were tramping to measures. A girl was stepping about in the dance, a girl with white stockings on her slim ankles. She had on a green flowered dress that made her look very slender up and down. Her hand was lifted to catch the hand of her partner and she had a gold ring on her finger, a slim gold ring. Ellen saw her again, this time in the kitchen by the little mirror. Her hair this time was yellow and brown; it had fallen down and she was pinning it up before the glass. A boy—his name was Tim—was beside her, handing her the hairpins and teasing. He dropped a hairpin down her back. When she laughed her mouth became square at the corners and a little mark came under one eye. She was nearly always in the dance with Tim. Her dress had small sewing-machine stitches going in rows up the front and over the shoulder.

"Tim talks to Sallie Lou. That's a case for sure." Jonas's voice.

"She's a pretty girl." Ellen heard her own words again.

"Who? That! Naw, not much! I know one that's prettier."

They were sitting on the floor eating the custard and cake. "Saw old Sallie Lou a-cryen the night she joined," one said.

Ellen still kept the note against her body. It was folded into a little square of clean white cloth. While she walked slowly up and down the tobacco rows she could feel it push against her flesh, could feel it anew each time she bent over the hoe. One afternoon Dorine came; they sat on the porch just outside the kitchen, Nellie, Dorine and Ellen. Ellen had put on a colorless dress, the dress of the summer before washed clean and sweet, crisply ironed, and she had tied a small blue ribbon about her throat as the other girls were using. Dorine talked about her turkeys which she was raising with a chicken hen. She was afraid to stay alone in the house and sometimes she went to the field where Elmer was at work and sat in a fence corner or under a tree, but she became lonesome doing that. She had canned some cherries. She came back again and again to the turkeys and their hen mother, to the cherries, to what Elmer liked to eat. She seemed very well contented although her hair was not so glossy as it had formerly been, as if it were untended. Ellen went away to get some corn to shell for the hens and while she was gone Dorine and Nellie talked, their voices running into low confidences and they seemed both to be talking at once, but when she came back they were still until Dorine asked some idle question about the corn. She had some bit of news of Rosie, and then came back to the cherries again. Ellen shelled the corn and went away to feed the hens, and while she was gone she heard the low eager purring of voices. "Ellen don't know," she heard Dorine say when she came near the porch again.

She sat in her chair, her pale dress crumpled about her body, her back straight and strong, her shoulders high and easily moving. The blue ribbon under her chin adorned her, even her mind, and she felt it upon her as a mark of daintiness, and she drew herself together, feeling the lightness of her body while the gossip flowed uneagerly about this thing and that. Dorine liked to talk with Nellie better than with herself, her friend, Dorine. She went indoors and began to rearrange her hair, going above to her room and letting the confidences flow unhindered. She had learned to pile her hair on her head in low even rolls and she had learned to brush a sheen into the brown strands. Dorine liked to talk with Nellie better than with herself. They had more things to talk of together than they had with her. Her hair rolled into soft pliant coils that lay one beside another and there was the blue line at her throat. She lingered over the hair, preparing it lovingly, thinking of Jonas as she rolled the loops and settled the mass. Jonas had wandered away a little, but when he came back he would weep again at her breast, for he would come, any other way being impossible to think, and when he came he would like this new way of her hair. She went back to sit again on the chair with her pale dress crumpled over her knees, her body straight and light, and she could feel the hair, like a crest on her head, and feel herself apart from the other two. Presently Dorine went and Ellen went to her evening tasks, milking the cow by the yard gate and gathering home the turkeys. Her hair still kept its graceful poise and the ribbon at her throat set a beauty upon her thinking and upon herself. Dorine was gone. It was not the same between them. Rosie was gone. Elmer was gone; he would never come back. They had all been around her, but now they were gone. She had bound a blue ribbon about her throat, about herself. She had thought it would last forever but it was gone from them, whatever it was, but not from her.

All the outer part of her made itself more beautiful, her hair, her dress, her light body. She walked among the cows with a still grace, light and high and free, standing above the cows. John Bradshaw looked at her, and Mr. Al looked, even Ben, but no one spoke except on the business of getting the milk. She turned away the cows, one by one, as she milked them, opening the gate, holding herself aside, milking another, moving slowly but lightly, never hurrying, never changing, every beautiful part functioning. The old way was gone. They had been around her, friends, and she had thought that it would be forever, but they were changed and gone. Perhaps Jonas, even Jonas was gone.

She came down from the pens knowing that all her beauties, assembled, standing around her, serene and proud, were standing about a great hollow inner space. In her body, in her breast, there was gathering a void, and it was spreading past her power to hold it. She knew this while she walked along the summer path beside the stepping stones, and she knew it again and more completely as she moved up the gentle slope from the pond.

DORINE held her in slight contempt because she had not been able to keep Jonas, or so it seemed to her, and she strove to hide her disgrace from Maggie and the others. She thought that she would go to see Sallie Lou. There were eggs to take to the store and she would come back through Robinson's place and stop at Seay's house. For a day or two she thought of this plan, and then one afternoon she put on her new dark cotton dress, her newest garment, planning the journey. She argued between the blue sunbonnet and the hat, for if she wore the hat the call would seem formal, almost as if she had come on purpose, dressed up. If she wore the bonnet it would seem more as if she had been somewhere else and had merely dropped in on the way. The bonnet would be best, she thought.

Then the space about the corners of her lips drew tight. She would wear the hat. Her eyes were hard and waves of strength passed along her spine. She would go on purpose to look at Sallie Lou, to look at her close and find out her way and find out where she was pretty. She would look at her. She would stare her in the face and the look would ask, "Let's see your beauty, then, where is it?"

But no, she thought, the bonnet would be better. It would be that she had just happened to come on her way

205

from the store; then she could look at Sallie Lou without her knowing. She would throw off the bonnet carelessly and say, "Kelly is a-given only fourteen cents for eggs. Did you ever hear tell of such! I taken a dozen and eight over for Mammy."

She went to the barns and asked Ben for a horse to ride and he fitted a side-saddle onto one of the unused work horses. Down at the gate her mother waited with the eggs in a basket.

"Trade for anything you think we need," Nellie said, "or get yourself a ribbon or a pretty. Anything you please."

She found it difficult to make her journey seem casual, for the Seay house was three miles from Wakefield's place. It was not easy to make it seem casual even to herself as she rode across the farms and came to the small yellow house in the midst of fields. Sallie Lou came out of the house to make her welcome, and then Mrs. Seay came, Sallie Lou's aunt. Ellen had once met the aunt at Dorine's.

"Invite Ellen in," she kept saying.

"I'll just sit out here," Ellen contended. "I got but a minute to stay. I dropped in a-comen from Kelly's where I taken a little mess of eggs for Mammy."

"I'd a heap rather you'd come in the house," Mrs. Seay fretted. "It seems more as if you'd come to see a body if you come in and set awhile."

"I'll stay out here. I only dropped in."

Ellen felt very cool and unafraid. The presence of others set her passion a long way off behind cool banks of intercourse, cool reserves of decision. Sallie Lou was sewing on a new dress for herself, a flowered muslin, and she brought her seams out into the yard and sewed while she talked with her guest. A little boy brought chairs from the house, a fair

206

little boy of about seven years. He was called Hank. Ellen watched Sallie Lou's hands as they pushed slowly across the flowered print stuff, the right hand beating a rhythm up and down with the needle, the left hand holding the cloth firm and making the rhythm of the cloth meet that of the other hand. The hands were short and puffed at the knuckles but the skin was moist and white, and there was a small gold ring on one finger, the same ring Ellen remembered. Sallie Lou talked quickly, changing from one thing to another as anyone led her, letting a matter go without caring, because she was happy. As well talk of one thing as another, whatever you like. Her eyes would take on quick lights that were like little stars in their corners. There were so many places to go in summer, she said, that she was glad to have another organdie dress, even if the season were late. Jonas was going to get a new buggy. He needed it. A boy could hardly get along without a buggy; there were so many places to go.

"We aim to go to the Glen to the picnic Saturday. He said he'd aim to go."

"Yes, but he won't take you," Hank said. He tickled her ear with grass.

"He will. He'd better." Her eyes turned in upon some inner memory and her face became hard. The next moment she laughed and her mouth was square at the corners and her lips peeled back until there showed the soft inner lining of red moist skin. Then she talked again of the new dress and of how it was to be made.

"You could have one too," Sallie Lou said. "They have a plenty more at the store, some in pink and some in green. A pink would become Ellen, now, wouldn't it? The same flower, only pink. It's a-sellen out cheap this week. I'll give you a little sample and you can get one offen it, or some other color, if you like.

Ellen tucked the sample of Sallie Lou's dress in her bosom. Then she said:

"There used to be a boy named Tim around. Where's he gone nohow? I haven't laid eyes on him for a long spell."

"Tim McNeal? I don't know. He went off. He went off last year."

Hank began to tease again. "Aye, Jonas! Mrs. Jonas Prather, that-there is. Mrs. Jonas is to have a new flowered dress to wear to a shin-dig a Saturday over to the glen. It'd tickle me plumb stiff if he forgot to take you and went off by his own self."

Sallie Lou would look up quickly and her face would change from hard anger that gathered in the eyes to the half-smile of the squared mouth where the inner softness of flesh quivered in and out of view. Ellen looked at her un-hindered, watching through all Hank's teasing. She saw Sallie Lou's anger and how it ran out toward Jonas, holding him, offering, taking, tightening. Tim had gone off. "Don't you dare go," her anger said. Ellen could feel this force run in upon herself. She felt Sallie Lou winding through her body and calling to her. In another moment she knew what it would be to kiss Sallie Lou's mouth and what it would be to want to kiss there. She felt near to Jonas on the instant, nearer than she had been for many months. She felt herself merge with Jonas. It was somehow true and necessary that Sallie Lou should hold Jonas for the moment, and she her-self was forgotten. A long time passed while she sat in-visible, her breath scarcely moving in her throat. But finally she remembered, conscious of her own confusion again.

"I must be a-goen," she said. "I'm right obliged to you-

208

all. I was right glad to drop down to rest a spell. It was hot a-riden up the branch. I thought this-here way would be a little nearer, but I believe it's every bit as far as the pike. You come."

She played a moment with Hank, who had been shy of her at first. Then Mrs. Seay told the child to ride down to the pike with Ellen so that she would not have to dismount to open the gates, and this proposal pleased him very much. A hush had come to Ellen's breast. On the horse they talked eagerly as they went down across the stubble field, and at the last gate the child had not finished singing his song.

> *If I had a needle and a thread,*
> *I'll tell you what I'd do,*
> *I'd sew my truelove to my side,*
> *And down the river I'd go, dog-gone!*

Ellen waited while he climbed out on the gate to finish it. His eyes were clear and his way had the frankness of a bird singing, so that he merged with every other beautiful object she had ever known, and she almost wept to see him.

"Could you sing me a song, Ellen Chesser?" he called from the gate.

"Sometime I will, Hank Seay."

"Could you sing now, Ellen Chesser?"

"Sometime, Hank Seay."

She rode away down the highroad, leaving the child sitting on the gate. At every few paces of her progress he would shout a goodbye and she would answer, sometimes waving her hand.

"Goodbye, Ellen Chesser!"

"Goodbye, Hank Seay!"

"Come back again, Ellen Chesser."

"I will, Hank Seay."

She passed over a little rise in the road and then down beyond his sight, answering his last calls.

"I like you, Ellen Chesser."

"So do I like you, Hank Seay."

After that the old horse continued to take the road in his own way and the midsummer roadside growth swam slowly before Ellen's eyes. She began to weep. She took the sample of flowered cloth from her bosom and, without looking at it, let it drift from her fingers and fall wherever it would. With a passionless gesture she put it away from her. A dull nausea spread through her body and a sense of impending duty, a sorrow not yet realized. The fireflies made dull streaks of light beyond the water of her tears, scarcely seen. The cows would not be milked, her cows, until she came, unless Ben milked them for her, but when she thought of this, dwelling upon it, she was sure that Ben would milk for her, and Nellie would take home the turkeys. She passed the empty house where Dorine once had lived; the yard was now grown with weeds and the fences falling. Her eyes slid from one white stone to another as she passed on the road, and she found that she had been searching for the difference between Sallie Lou and herself, had been feeling the difference, whatever it was, feeling it in a mass and trying to resolve it into some clear statement. She looked at the difference with deeply penetrating thought, probing the mass and trying to bring it to some precise maxim, to resolve it to angles or edges, but it turned about, elusive and undefined. Sallie Lou held life lightly and held herself lightly, letting any winds blow over her, but over this came a picture of a cavern surrounded by quivering blood and moving flesh that peeled back until one saw its red inner part, Sallie Lou's mouth. But these ideas faded and she was left again with the fog to penetrate. Sallie

Lou was insolent and careless because she was happy, she thought, and then an image of her in a bright muslin dress, in numberless successions of bright dresses, Sallie Lou moving up and down in the dance, but she herself had moved lightly in dancing before Jonas had said he could not dance again; and she had been able to draw great tenderness to Jonas's face with one appealing glance, asking for it. Jonas liked Sallie Lou because she had not seen him in the first hours of his suffering, she summarized at last. She seemed paralyzed, incompetent to assume her grief in its whole. As she turned into the pasture at the gate she knew that she would be going here and there with Sebe until Jonas came back. She would ask Nellie to let her have another bright dress, she decided, and her mind set itself to contrive the dress, deciding, even while it busied itself elsewhere. All evening her voice trailed away, breaking its sentences and leaving the last of them unsaid, so great was her preoccupation with her confusion. She would somehow find a way to bring back the old relation, she thought for comfort; this was a shadow. It was a sickness, a great pain, but it would surely go. Jonas would remember.

RIDING with Sebe along the roads she would but half listen with dull ears to his speculations and plans, his farm wisdom, or she would awake from her reverie and offer lively oppositions to his scheme for feeding hens or his ideas of crop rotation. At the Turpin house she had a gay laugh.

Maggie had scarcely ever been seen speaking to Erastus, but together they carried an unspoken understanding, and one morning she went to live with the O'Shays, having married Erastus in Squire Dorsey's sitting-room. She gathered a few things into her arms and walked up the lane with him one morning toward noon, hurrying to be in time to help old Nannie cook the dinner. Ellen let Effie teach her to run the loom and she spent many of her free hours weaving the great coarse cloth, rag woof and heavy cotton warp, making a carpet for Mrs. Turpin to sell. It would bring twenty cents a yard; some farmer would buy it to lay on his family-room floor, and heavy boots would walk over it and spurs, perhaps, catch in the mesh. Children would crawl over it and spit their excrements on it, or creeping over it they would trace out the fine red line that now and then appeared in its pattern, running their little white forefingers along the thread and looking at the bright line with solemn, curious eyes. She would wonder if Jonas would ever walk on the carpet, if his eyes would ever happen to see the blue strip she was even then drawing through the shed, and she would weave strand after strand lost in contemplation and pain. One morning as the web grew the conviction grew in her mind that she would not give up Jonas. It would be in the end that she had not meekly acquiesced. She would find a way to search him out; and let Sallie Lou look out for herself. She would find a way to search him out and she would appear before him saying, "Why, Jonas!" He would be working in the August tobacco at Barnet's place, far down the river past Goodlet's, past the bridge; she vaguely knew the place. She would find him where he walked along the rows in the tall tobacco, pulling a sucker here or breaking out a top there, and she would take off her hat and let the sun come down upon the shining coils of her hair. He had never seen the blue ribbon about her throat. Then she would say in surprise, "Why,

212

Jonas!" or she would say, "What's the use a-joken any longer? Ain't you been a-playen long enough?" and she would gather his head to her breast and he would be kissing her mouth.

She arose from the loom and slipped away from the house, walking down the shaded river road quickly, her mind set upon reaching the place before noon. An old man in a wagon gave her a ride for three miles or more, and then she asked him to let her down, for she wanted to come to Barnet's place in her own way. The road lifted up from the river and ran along a low ridge where the stones were hot in the open sun, and many turnings were passed, the road running mile after mile, farther than she had known. "Whose land is this-here?" she would ask a passing woman or a child, but none ever said "Barnet's." "Is it a far piece to Barnet's?" she would ask again, and the answers would vary, "Nigh three mile, I'd judge," or "Every lick of four mile yet, I calculate," or sometimes one would say, "Just a little piece on, around a couple of turns and down a hill." "Is there a boy named Jonas Prather that works at Barnet's place?" she asked, and the answer, "There is for a fact. I see him in the patch as I passed along, field back from the road behind a hay field. This very day it was, I believe, I see Prather." But later when she asked how far the answer came, "A right smart distance yet, better'n three mile, but there's a short cut across by the dirt road. You go on a mile, say, and then off to the right and it's no piece at all." She passed road-menders who were hauling crushed stone and forking it into place along the pike. They looked at her from over their shovels and forks as she passed but she asked them no questions. When they were out of sight she followed the road as it curved down into a cool thicket and there she bathed her face and hands in a little runlet that trickled over green moss, for she must be cool and sweet; the way was not far now to go. Beyond the shade of the thicket the dirt road appeared, and, following it, she wound down a hill into a stony flat where a great waste of washed-out land lay, white and brittle and salty in the hot sun of the mid-afternoon. A small house sat near the roadside, and as she approached it an old woman who was barefoot came to the door and looked stiffly out. Her grizzled hair hung in a short braid over her shoulder and her red swollen feet stood squarely below her dingy dress. When Ellen came opposite the door she stopped in the road and spoke, saying timidly, "Good evening, ma'am."

"Good evening," the woman said, and the tone of the greeting added, "And what do you want now?" to her words.

"Would this road take a body to Barnet's place?"

"It would and again it wouldn't. What you want at Barnet's?"

"I want to see a party on Barnet's."

"Would it be the young man, maybe, the tall young man with the brown filly for his nag?"

"Could I have a cup of water if it's not too much trouble to you?" Ellen asked.

Inside the house she drank from a dim can a sweetish water that was heavy and warm. "If you want fresh you could go to the spring and help yourself," the woman said, taking the cup away. "I got no call to be a-carryen water for big healthy trollops. Have you had bad luck with your sweethearten?"

Ellen thanked the woman for the water and said that she must hurry on.

"If it's bad luck that's your worry I can mix a charm to

bring your young man to your way right off, and he'll court you and nobody else. It's a powder to slip in his drink, water, coffee, anything. A dollar is what the price is. It's a sure charm, never fails. A dollar. Give me your dollar, now, and I'll give it in your hand right off."

"I don't want no powder. I got no dollar."

"It's a charm I make. For white gals I make it one way and for black wenches I make it another. I couldn't tell you how I mix it, not for money, no. All you do is sprinkle it in his drink. I'll let you have the charm for fifty cents. Just give me the money, four bits is all."

"I don't want no charm."

"Get out the money and I'll mix up the charm for a quarter. A quarter is all I ask from you. I see you're a poor sort and I've taken a downright fancy to you. Or maybe it's some other kind you want. I can tell." She drew near and whispered a rough old throaty whisper, her head forward, "Say, honey, I can mix something will help you out if it ain't gone far. A quarter I ask for them powders, same price for both."

"I don't want no powders. Is this-here a short way through to Barnet's place?"

"It might be. Is it some of the men there you aim to see, Prather maybe? He goes this road every day. You better let me get up the powders. Say, I'll give you both kinds for the quarter."

"Where would he be now, so late in the day? Would he go by here afore night, do you reckon?"

"Or maybe you'd like to have your fortune told. I can tell your fortune in no time, your true fortune, right outen your hand, and part of it outen the Bible with a door key, for ten cents. Or I'll tell you what; I'll tell your fortune and

215

give you both powders, all for the quarter's worth. I took a liken to you from the start. All for one quarter."

Ellen went toward the door, wanting to go but held by the voice which had spoken of Jonas, by the fact that Jonas passed that door and had perhaps spoken to the woman within a day. She shook her head to the woman's bargaining and moved toward the door, hesitating.

"Gals is queer," the woman said. "Do you know a gal named Sallie Brown?"

"Sallie Lou? I know her."

"Sallie comes here. She set in that-there very chair a many a time. I told her fortune yester. Umm-m, you ought to see what's in her hand! I says, when I see in her hand, 'There's a pretty gal that's got bright glossy hair all done up high and a blue ribbon around her neck. She'll beat your time,' I says. I says, 'You got no show, Sallie Brown.' Listen, I'll sell them powders, two kinds, for a quarter."

Ellen shook her head.

"Don't be so all-fired easy to give up. She's not pretty like you. Catfish mouth, she's got. Her hair ain't near so dark and her style ain't so handsome. A skinny little thing, runt-like. Buy the charm offen me and you'll never be sorry. A quarter is all."

"I don't want e'er charm."

"A quarter is all it takes, and she too close to spend it. Could have her man back for a quarter, and she too close. God knows!"

"I don't want e'er charm," Ellen said, "and I got no quarter." She held up empty hands.

"In your pocket you got it."

"I got no pocket in this-here dress."

"In your petticoat then."

"I got no pocket in my petticoat."

"Le's see. Got no pocket! Why ain't you got a pocket? Le's see."

Ellen suffered dirty hands to fumble at her skirts and she shuddered while they felt for all the folds of her clothing.

"Well, what you want then? What you come here for a-taken up my time?"

"I guess I'll go now," Ellen said.

"Was it Prather you aimed to see there?"

"Yes," Ellen said, speaking softly, looking at the woman's face. "It was Jonas I aimed to see. Just a short spell I wanted to see him."

"Well, I'll tell you, you couldn't see Prather now. You couldn't see him now and I'll tell you for why. He's gone two days back and he won't come this way no more. He's gone away to a place in the north, a long way past Cornishville. He went day afore yester. He married Sallie Brown and went off to live in a place far past Cornishville, away to the north."

"Do you know it?" Ellen whispered, leaning against the door.

"He left Sallie here while he went on to Barnet's to fetch his things and pack up to go. They married in town. Sallie, she didn't want to ride up to Barnet's while he got his traps and she waited here. It was the same body I see go by here a heap with Prather. Say, did you have bad luck with your sweethearten?"

"But maybe it's some other Prather," Ellen said, "some folks I don't even know."

"You feel fainty-sick, don't you now? Prather, when he come back, he had so much plunder and truck they had to sort it over and leave some behind. Mrs. Prather, she set in that-there chair and sorted out the truck and made up a bundle to leave behind till some of their folks is to pass and take it. It's that-there sack behind the door. I'll open it up and no harm to see inside. I'll open it up and you can see for your own self."

"No, no," Ellen said. She was unable to move as she leaned against the door. The woman dragged a sack from the corner.

"You see this-here coat, and this-here old hat? Them's Prather's, I judge. I see 'em go by on him many a time. This-here is Mrs. Prather's old petticoat, and here's her under-body, and here's her old blue dress. Here's his winter gloves. It's a right full bundle, but it's the quilts make it stand out. Help tie it up, will you? Tie a knot in the string. Are you satisfied now it's the parties I named to you?"

"I think I better go back now," Ellen said. "I'm right obliged to you for the rest and for the drink of water. I got a right far piece to go and I think I'll set out. I'll bid you good evening."

"How far you come, gal?"

"I come right far, five mile, maybe."

"You come better'n five mile. I know all the folks in five mile and I never set eyes on you afore. How far, now?"

"Better'n five mile, maybe. I guess I'll be a-goen. Good evening."

"Wait now. Did you come from up around the Robinson country?"

"On beyond that. I come from up around Wakefield's. Pappy crops on Wakefield's place."

"That's ten mile, now. You couldn't go a-walken back on foot this time of the day. Not a good looken gal like you. No. The country all full of road-menders and them that's

218

a-campen up the creek. No, no. Get in home away toward day or maybe not get in at all. It's ten mile, nohow. Wouldn't you be a sight by daylight!"

Ellen drew away from the door, putting on her hat.

"The road-menders is a feisty set and there's a fresh set a-campen on the river." The woman followed her out onto the road.

"I'll have to hurry on and so I'll be on my way. Good evening."

"You couldn't set out to walk ten mile now, and night right here at us. Dark would come afore you got two mile, now. Wait now, wench. Them road-menders is a feisty set. You better stay all night. I'll give you a quilt on the floor right alongside my bed, and you can pay me with your shoes, maybe, or your petticoat."

"No, no, I'd have to go. It's time I was gone now."

The woman followed Ellen a few steps from the door, her bare feet making stiff prints in the dust. All the while she was taunting Ellen with the distance and offering her a bed on the floor in return for her shoes or her hat, or she was leering at her in depicting the lusts of the road-menders. She would picture and prophesy the night on the lonely road or she would whimper that if Ellen would pay her with the shoes she would take her home in a cart, but since the girl had no money how could one expect a lonely old woman with hardly a cent to her name to be hauling a big lazy girl around, and then she would sniffle at her tears. In the end she hurled curses after Ellen, who was hurrying up the lane toward the highroad, who turned at the corner of the lane hearing the last curse, but no maledictions fell heavily upon her because she was drugged with her own sorrow and physical pain. She walked quickly down into the shadowed roadway and fell to weeping, her tears flowing down her quiet face as from some wells of grieving. She gave little heed to the road, but her feet followed the ways they had come although night soon fell.

Now and then a vehicle passed her, but she made no effort to be hailed by any passer nor did she shun these encounters, but rather she set herself to the business of the road and to her tears. She did not know when she passed the camps although the moon arose soon after sunset and she was well lighted along the way. How, her tears were continually questioning her, how did she, Ellen Chesser, ever come to such a state of need that a person outside herself, some other being, not herself, some person free to go and come and risk accidents far from herself, should hold the very key to her life and breath in his hand? Her tears flowed anew for pity of such a device among men and they flowed anew at each recognition of her own loss. Sometimes a low moaning came with her sighs, but she walked steadily forward. Once during the night a quick step sounded along the road behind her, but she did not look back nor did she in any manner change her pace nor take the sound of the coming footfalls into her thought. The ground and the air were as nothing to her, for all her life had been plucked out and there was nothing left but the knowledge that it had been taken away. The step came very near and a man fell in pace beside her, making some remark of greeting, but she was scarcely aware of his words. That a person outside herself, another being separate in flesh, should be a part of herself and, withdrawing, could break her—she wept afresh. The man announced his intention, laying his hand on her arm, but she walked steadily on and his words scarcely entered the outer porch of her ears. His hand still upon her arm they came out onto an open stretch of road where the moon shone brightly, and her face was revealed in all its sorrow and its flow of tears. The man dropped his hand from her and moved on beside her, talking, asking questions, but she changed no detail of her grieving. After a long interval a low moan would come with her sigh. Finally the man fell back from her way and she went forward alone.

In the road beyond Turpin's cabin she met one of the hounds, one of the large brown beasts from the Gowan farm that wandered masterless each night over the hills. It came toward her eagerly, licking her hands, and with the dog beside her she walked up through the lane. She could hear his stately tread on the road and feel now and then the rise and fall of his head as it brushed her hand. Thus they came into MacMurtrie's land where the fence was torn away and thus they walked through the wasted field where MacMurtrie's grain had once stood. They came down the pasture road, the dog making small half-circles about her, his step soft-padded and light, or he came back to walk beside her, licking her hand that was shed of its strength by the force of her grief. The hound stopped by the cherry clumps and she went unattended through the gate and onto the stoop of the cabin, walking softly, hushed more by her sorrow than by any wish to enter unheard. Her steps were softly plodding as she passed through the lower room, and in the same pace she took the stairs.

CALLED from her brief sleep, Ellen milked the cows and brought the wood for the cooking fire. After she had eaten she went away slowly across the plowed field toward the hill where the plant beds were set in the spring. The physical weariness which had followed the long walk had taken possession of her grief, and her thought was numbed, but the hills would ask her no questions, and a vague sense visited her that later she would know what to do. Now she must go from the cabin. Up in the hill where the Mac-Murtries had hunted the foxes she sat under the shade of some interlocking trees, and, as she sat among dry leaves looking down upon the hill of the plant beds where the cleared spots showed among the thick growth as rectangular patches, a faint dying wind seemed to blow over her and a faint phrase blow with it, dimly sensed with the fanning of the wind, " In the time of man, in the time of man."

She eased herself among the dry leaves, her folded arm for a pillow, and soon fell asleep although these winds blew over her laden with faint phrases and were all but lost, coming now and then into the confusion of a dream. She lay there all the day, falling out of her deep sleep into a hurt dream now and then but gathering back into nothingness and numbness in the end. The hot sun of the midday did not trouble this high glade, and into her sleep came a sense that she had been flung to some high and remote place from which she could look down upon the time of man, the world, squares and rectangles cut upon a virgin hill, and pity it with a great grief which she would assume all in her season.

Toward evening, waking, she saw the slanting rays of the sun and her habit somehow knew or sensed its duty toward the turkeys so that she arose at once and came back to the farm where she went stiffly through her task, knowing dimly what she did. She was walking across the pasture calling the hens, but when next she was aware she was carrying water from the old well, stepping through tangled masses of morning-glories that had overrun her path. As she awakened from her stupor of sleep a sense of her loss grew each moment more acute, and a sense of some act impending.

She was in the small meathouse behind the cabin cutting bacon for the breakfast while Nellie cleared away the supper. She was cutting with a butcher knife, the great blade making stabs through the meat, cutting quickly and deep. An awful strength came to her arm; she stabbed deeper, driving the knife to the handle. She would kill Jonas. She would stab him with her knife, thus and thus! She hated him. Deep in her body arose waves of hate, and a strength beyond any she had ever known drove the knife into the dried flesh. He was ugly. She remembered all his ugliness. His work clothes hung flat on his body, which was thin and tall. His work coat had a patch on the elbow and his shoulderblades stood out under his shirt. There were little white marks on his teeth. She hated him. There was a rough spot on his hand above the wrist. There were black hairs growing on his chin when he did not shave, growing away from his mouth, a white circle left around his lips. She could see his body through his clothes and she loathed it, despised it. When he was tired he limped a little on his left foot. "Slashed that-there foot wide open with a corn knife when I was a youngone, laid the raw meat back to the bone," he had said. She had seen his foot; once he had taken off his shoe to show it to her and she had trailed her finger over the long scar. She loathed him for his mutilations and she cringed away from the pain that had been his. She hated him for the pain and her hate drove the knife at each thrust.

"I'd kick him out. I'd kick him with my foot," she said.

Another wave arose out of her more inner passion, Jonas coming to her door at dusk after his day in the field. He would be sitting on the step when she came back from the milking lot, and his cigarette would make a little light in the dusk while he waited for her to come. His hands would be gentle upon her. She would sit beside him in the half-light and his shoulders would be drooping with weariness and his shoulder frame showing a little through the line of his shirt. His lips would curve around his cigarette and there would be the circle of white about his mouth before the dark began. His voice, wanting comfort, "Gosh! I'm monstrous tired tonight. Plowed and grubbed all day." And she, "If I could I'd like to cure all that-there outen you by just a-layen on of hands. I'd charm all the tiredness away in the twinkle of an eye if I could by just a-layen on of hands."

His hands would be gentle upon her. "You already done that-there, Elleen." It was autumn. "You didn't tell me to go outen your sight. . . . I been in torment ever since I knowed, downright hell . . . but I knowed you'd tell me what's right. . . ." She wept softly, hanging up the chain of the meathouse door and turning the key in the lock. She carried the meat into the house, going up the steep back steps. She threw the meat onto the kitchen table with the knife beside it and went up the stairs to her room, her feet striking hard blows upon the boards.

"I could kill Jonas with a knife," she said. "Jonas. I'll kill Jonas. I hate the look of him. I hate him last fall, a-comen every day for a spell."

An awful strength heaved up in her anger and hate. She jerked her bed before the window with one rough strong gesture and sat looking out into the dusk. Beyond the window there was nothing. Lines of fields were nothing and sky was nothing, less than foolishness. Strength pushed at her arms, unmeasured strength, closing her hand over a knife handle, and a great sickness arose in her abdomen and spread into her breast. There was nothing left but kill, kill, kill . . . Jonas bringing her the frostflowers gathered from MacMurtrie's field and the last goldenrod. Jonas bringing her the biggest hickory nut. Jonas telling her how many shocks he had cut that day, and telling her when old Mr. Chandler paid him off in the stripping room and called him trifling before all the other men and told him to get out. He almost cried when he told her. And then she was holding his head against her breast as they sat on the cabin step in the early cold, and telling him he was not trifling and that he would find another place. . . . His words, "Me and you, Elleen. Before summer, Elleen. . . ." A great sickness came to her breast. She hated the white about his mouth and she hated his limping foot. She would despise him. She would strangle him with her hand, and a great strength came to her that made her hands tremble under their grip. Then words that were printed into her memory long ago began to run forward, and this hour lost its identity before the force of another, long past, until she swam back into the past as if she were an apparition, without presence of its own. The voices spoke aloud, voices of men, filling the room with their terror, speaking sharply, speaking with authority or fright.

". . . how to get 'er down . . ."

"Cut the rope. . . ."

"No, don't cut no rope. She might be still a-liven."

"Bring up that lamp, Ellen."

One lamp, now, carried to the top of the hall. The stairs came up out of a dark hole and a long woman was hanging down into the hole, going down into the black.

She was running again through the night in a cold dark, slipping on the ice where it dipped down into the marsh place. The farm bell was ringing loud on MacMurtrie's hill and the hounds were baying and running in the fields and woods, the yelping of the hounds flowing up and down and lying under the quick steady beat of the farm bell. One light shone out from MacMurtrie's, from the hall door which was standing open. She was running up into the yard just as the woman came away from the bell rope, walking in uneven steps, her shoulder rising and falling with the limp. Then the light was coming out of the open door, falling on the lame woman and on herself, there present now, in the frost. Mr. Al was running up the drive on a horse and coming into the light, and then Henry came out of the dark, the path she had come. The men were going up the stairs in the hall. The woman on the stone doorsill was moaning, "Miss Cassie, child . . ."

"Bring up that-there lamp, Ellen."

Herself going up the bare stair, a long way to the level of the high ceiling. A long woman hanging down from the banister rail, hanging still.

"No, don't cut no rope, she might be still a-liven."

"Lift her up easy now."

"Get a hold under her arms. Take a hold there, Ellen."

"Lift her back over the banister rail."

"Easy now."

"Get water."

"Shut her eyes for her."

"Fan her in the face."

"Stand back. Open that window. Where's the brandy, now?"

226

"Oh, fix her mouth decent, fix it for her."

"Put the brandy in her mouth. Rub her. Rub her hands."

"Shut her eyes, I'd say."

"Try the brandy again, just a leetle more, try it once again, why don't you?"

"Fix her mouth decent. Take the rope offen her neck, there."

"Try the brandy again. Keep on a-tryen. Let's fan her. Where's the fan?"

"Oh, fold her hands crossways. Fold her hands and fix her decent. Quit a-worryen her, now. Poor soul!"

"What made her look so lax, spread on the floor and given away?" Ellen's own voice questioned the old event. "What made her look so lax? She was like a long rope spread on the floor. Miss Cassie MacMurtrie she used to be, a-riden on a horse or in her back yard to call her chickens. Now she was on a dusty floor with people a-taken hold of her to pull her this way and that. She was just some more of the rope that was tied to the banister, under foot."

The voices at the dialogue again: "Bring up that-there lamp, Ellen."

Herself going up the bare stairs, a long way to the level of the high upper floor. A long woman hanging down from the banister rail, hanging still.

Another voice, an old hard voice, from far off: "Let Cassie do hit. She'll drag Scott through fire and hell afore she's done. . . . Hit'll be like throwen a lame rabbit in a pack of fifty starved hound dogs. . . ." A low voice: "There won't be enough left of Scott MacMurtrie to wad a gun with. I know Cassie Beal. . . . She's made outen fire and hell. . . ."

"And while they were a-sayen it," Ellen spoke in her turn,

"she was even then a-thinken about a rope. . . . Had it in mind that Scott MacMurtrie had gone away with Mandy Cain."

Her own hour gathered with the old event, identified with it, standing over her. She could not be the same, could never go back and be the same she had been before Jonas. She would take him out of her mind. She would tear him out if she had to tear out her very entrails, if she had to gut herself and brain herself with her own hands.

She could never do it; he had run in very deep upon her life. She would kill him with her terrible hands. She would strangle him with one strong grip. He had run into her blood and into her very breath. She hated him. She would take him out of herself if she had to tear him out with a gun or with a knife. She would kill him where he stood when she saw him again.

She tried to be aware of the dark, to free herself of the specters, to push aside the old event and disentangle her own, to govern her own. She left the bed and sat on the floor before the window, placing her arms slowly along the narrow sill. She would go back very slowly and firmly and be what she was before. The return, she reflected, would come if she would be quiet. She would go after the turkeys and cut the wood and gather the beans and milk the cows, always looking for something that had not yet come, and be glad if a stranger passed and wonder who this one was and who that. She would go to bed thinking about a vague after-a-while or she would gather the blackberries for Miss Tod and be thinking that the money she would get would help buy her winter shoes. She would make her breath come quietly in and out, for she was still herself, Ellen Chesser.

"I'm Ellen Chesser. And I'm here, in myself," she said.

She turned her mind upon some happenings of her infancy. She had lived in a house under nut trees. The rinds of the nuts broke off in beautiful smooth segments and inside was the pale yellow hickory nut to be laid away to dry for the winter. One day she got a fish bone in her throat and Henry carried her a long way down the road, so far that she fell asleep in his arms as he walked. Then she was awake, in some strange house, and there a woman took out the bone with a bright tool.

She arose from the floor and sat on the bed again, flinging down hard. She could never be the same, could never go back. What had some withered, ancient past, tenderly remembered but dry, flat, apart, to do with this life she had now? Let it get out. Let it go. She could never be the same as before. Jonas had been in her thought too long so that her very breath had grown up around him. He was even then tearing a pain through her breast. She saw even more vividly the face on the floor, two men leaning over it, one preparing it for life and the other for death; and then the coroner, "Yes, she tied the rope herself, that's plain," and to herself, sworn to speak the truth, "Do you know any reason why Cassie MacMurtrie would hang herself?" Every human relation faded out and every physical tie. Up was no more than down and out undistinguished from in. Friends and possessions and relatives were gone, and hunger and need. She was leaning over Miss Cassie as she lay on the floor— Ellen and Miss Cassie and no other. She leaned over the dead face until she was merged with its likeness, looking into the bulging eyes, the blackened mouth, and the fallen jaw. She went down the stairs and out the door of the house, walking slowly, standing a little while in her tracks, going on. In her eyes, in the very core of her vision, was still the face. She was still merged with the face. Once she stopped by the pond and once she waited awhile by the mule barn. She wandered over the rise of the pasture hill; there was a turmoil in the fog of the earth, in the dew of the soil, in the sweat of the planet. Her feet wandered to the old barn and over into the edge of the marsh. Her tracks were seen the next day along the edge of the tobacco field and up the rise toward the old plant bed where the stone piles stood in the brambles.

ELLEN was sick for several days, unable to go to the field or the milking pen for her throat was swollen and her skin fevered and dry. Then Henry began to talk of going to another place, saying that he thought he would make a change before spring, fearing, as he said, that he had been at Wakefield's long enough, he not wanting to take root anywhere. He dropped hints of his intentions as the summer was passing.

"You're well enough off here," Nellie said. "You better stay one place awhile."

Returning from the tobacco field one evening Ellen knew by some disorder of the chairs in the cabin room and by some faint odor there, that Dorine had been to see Nellie. And while her mother prepared the supper, although she did not speak, from her hostile movements and rough gestures Ellen knew that Dorine had told her of Jonas and Sallie Lou. Ellen went to the table fearfully, but Nellie was quiet, eating little food as if she were sickened, and she spoke but once, to Henry, rebuking him with great bitterness for some slight comment upon the bread which he en-

acted by rejecting a burnt piece. She pushed aside her uneaten serving and stared at the lamplight. Afterward when
Ellen helped her to gather up the dishes she spoke, her voice
trailing half away under some enforced discipline.

"At the store, what kind of goods has he got for fall? I aim
for you to have a new fall dress if you are minded. A plaid
would be pretty for fall, I always think. A worsted or some
kind of wool goods, I'd get you, high price is no matter."

"I'll ride over some day to see," Ellen said, "or you could
go yourself." She cared nothing for the dress, cared only to
help Nellie pass the bitter moment.

Henry had already begun to search for another place and
Ellen dug the potatoes and put them into sacks ready for
hauling, two full sacks. Then Miss Tod gave her three geese,
two females and a gander. The stripping of the tobacco was
hurried so that Henry would be free to go, and all through
November this work went forward, John Bradshaw lending
a hand, or Mary his wife, or even Mr. Al Wakefield. Ellen
wore her hair drawn tight or let it hang in a braid, the high
coils neglected. She would sit listlessly in her dark dress, her
throat unribboned, or she would set herself to the tobacco
and work until twilight when the leaves were scarcely
visible in the dark stripping room. She would feel the gloom
of the barn and of her dingy dress and the limp weariness of
the tobacco, and if she continued to move in life it was as if
she were some vague memory in some careless mind. She
hated Jonas now as being unfit for her regret, as feeble, in
him a blending of weakness and appealing friendliness which
he had in part and which she had lent him. But working in
the stripping room she would often listen for his step in the
outer barn, for his voice there joking the men, coming
nearer to her, or inside the cabin she would imagine she

231

heard his voice calling to her from the pasture road, herself ready to go, listening intently for confirmation of her wish. Under this confusion she sank as under the dirt of the grave, and thus she sat endlessly stripping the leaves from the tobacco stems, but in her dreams in the night she often arose to a great quiet beauty. There a deep sense of eternal and changeless well-being suffused the dark, a great quiet structure reported of itself, and sometimes out of this wide edifice, harmonious and many-winged, floating back into blessed vapors, released from all need or obligation to visible form, a sweet quiet voice would arise, leisured and backward-floating, saying with all finality, "Here I am."

In December Henry said that he would go to a farm behind the St. Lucy country, to the southeast. It was a damp morning, the air mild and wet, the horizon standing close, when they were preparing to leave. Ellen was to start her cow on the way and then come back to help pack the things into the wagon, leaving the cow grazing along the road. She found the heifer unwilling to leave the herd, loath to pass through the gate and quit the pasture she had always known. Ellen could lay her hand on the animal's neck and lead her forward a short distance, but she would stand uncertain, gazing about at the road in bewilderment, and turn back toward the farm gate. Ellen was so occupied with getting the cow forward that she passed the farm with no thought of farewell and no sense of this as the last passing. There was no looking backward at the cabin, at the barns or pens, at the pond, and no pang at seeing acutely the pasture brow where she had last seen Jonas, and the paths and roads along which she had walked often with him in her mind. The little cow was a year and nine months old, delicately formed as yet, a mere heifer, but her calf would come before the summer. She had never known life except the life of the herd, she drifting across the pasture with the other cows, feeding on the pasture grass or on the fodder at the ricks, surrounded by the comfort of companions. Ellen passed beyond the reach of Wakefield's land and beyond Gowan's stone wall, intent upon the heifer. She thought that she would put the animal inside some small enclosure, some pasture she might pass, and go back for a rope to make a leading line, but before a convenient place appeared the wagon came, Henry driving and Nellie beside him on the seat, with all the furniture piled on the wagon frame and a coop holding the hens and geese tied on behind.

"I allowed to go back and help," Ellen said, surprised at the appearance, but the cow had given more trouble than they had expected and Henry had no word of blame for her. She had been cut free by the accident, and now, her attention upon the beast as before, she followed the slowly moving wagon and fell far behind it although it moved as a lodestar ahead of her, the shifting goal toward which she centered, for her thought could not go beyond it. She knew nothing of their destination, having been too listless to ask. "Over behind St. Lucy," Henry had said. The place was as remote to her as some uncharted land beyond unmeasured floes and lying out white on a map. Mile after mile she followed the slim heifer or led her gently along, letting her eat the dry winter grass by the road and drink as she pleased at any stream. The farms receded and strange roadsides closed about her, and she no longer knew the lay of the hills and meadows. There were herself and the cow, passing forward toward a moving destiny, the wagon, all moving down the turning roads and crossing lanes, going by some genius forward and on. She would watch the rise and fall of the cow's hips and the sway of her back, the slow undulations of her horns, until she was herself identified with the drifting beast. The heifer was a pale brown with darker shadings about her feet and darker clouds of brown lying over her face. She had no knowledge of the calf that was in her side. After the many turnings she had made no further resistance, but went slowly rising and falling, drifting along the roads, taking guidance from Ellen's hand on her hip.

They passed a wide road on which there were frequent travelers, drifting with this a short way along a valley beside a creek. When they left the great road they turned to the south and passed along a soft clay road that lifted up among rougher hills. The cow's feet made little two-toed tracks in the clay and her footfalls sounded less sharp. Henry stopped frequently to let Ellen rest, or he would offer to drive the cow and let her take his place on the wagon, but the beast knew Ellen's guidance best, and the journey soon moved forward as before, the wagon far ahead and dimly seen up a long vista or lost around a curve, but still the forward-drawing force, and she walked quietly on, bound in the immediate certainty of herself alive and of the little cow moving evenly before her.

They went by scattered farms, taking hill after hill and winding about along valleys, rising always a little higher. There was much uncultivated land grown over with brush that was now leafless, the color of these patches red and brown because of the December twigs and buds. A long hill lifted slowly from rise to rise, so gently that the cow scarcely slackened her gait, and Ellen came evenly after, her hand

now and then resting on the animal's back and herself rising and falling with the movements of the beast. Near the top of a hill Ellen lifted her eyes and, rising out of the near-lying road, far away against the sky, rolled a great land, space after space and hill floating after hill to the south where a chain of low mountains hung imbedded in the mesh of the air. A few steps farther and the whole landscape had lifted, a far rolling land but little marked by farms for there were few houses visible, although here and there the cleared places were green with winter wheat. The mountains grew more definite as she looked back to them, their shapes coming upon her mind as shapes dimly remembered and recognized, as contours burnt forever or carved forever into memory, into all memory. With the first recognition of their fixity came a faint recognition of those structures which seemed everlasting and undiminished within herself, recurring memories, feelings, responses, wonder, worship, all gathered into one final inner motion which might have been called spirit; this gathered with another, an acquired structure, fashioned out of her experience of the past years, out of her passions and the marks put upon her by the passions of others, this structure built up now to its high maturity. There was no name to come to her lips in this moment of faint recognition, a moment which dispersed itself in an emotion, for the word Jonas had been denied her, had been subtracted from the emotion it had caused and signified and with which it had been made one for many reasons. She stood very still on the top of the rise, the heifer standing beside her and biting at the low dry herbs.

The land lying out before her was rugged and brush-grown, sparsely inhabited and but little farmed. Here and there were stony rises and bluffs of torn stones, and while she looked up and down the expanse a gray tower appeared, rising out of the hills toward the east. The tower was of stone like the stone of the hills, an eight-sided tower with eight high indentures in its crown topped by eight stone crosses. The tower would be St. Lucy, for "Beyond St. Lucy" had been the legend by which she had walked all day through the roads and lanes. She would live, she reflected, somewhere down within that rugged stretch of land. She would sink down into the land, turning through the hills as the road went; she would go into the place. She laid her hand again on the heifer's side and together they walked down the sloping road. The near aspects of the land, hummocks and scrubby hills, stones and gullies, closed around them.

VII

THE farm Henry had rented was called the Orkeys place, a mere patch of land, twenty-five acres, small indeed beside Wakefield's two hundred or more, but here Henry was a renting tenant and full proprietor for the time. Many of the neighboring farms were small and poor and stony, and of the larger tracts much lay uncultivated and was used as rough pasturage. Off to the north stood St. Lucy, the abbey house and church, and the bell in the tower rang often during the day and the night. In still weather the notes came slowly and sweetly across the hills, beating on the stones and clods, each blow distinct, belonging to itself; but in high winds they came like a wailing horn, the beating falling into the midst of a continuous rising and sinking note. The house at the Orkeys place had once been a toll house. It stood at the roadside, a stoop reaching out

239

onto the road for the convenience of the toll-taker. Now few travelers passed, for this was a partly abandoned road, and no tolls were gathered. Ellen's room lay beside the family room, both extending along the road and both opening onto the stoop, and behind these two rooms lay the kitchen. The walls inside had been whitewashed the year before and the roof was tight so that there were no leaks. During the first rains of her stay there Ellen felt the snugness of the night, the dark outside, the falling wet, the dry security of the indoors, so that in her room, shut away from the elements, she felt the security to be within herself as if she were detached by the prison-like whiteness of the dry walls from her own memories, to begin her being anew; she had never before known this detachment from the immediacy of the weather. A small high shelf extended along one of her walls, and the print of a clock was shadowed above, a low rounded clock. She could even see the print of ghostly springs and a dial. This was the only mark which had meaning on the dull white walls.

The road came down a hill just before it reached the toll house and then turned away toward the south. Horses and vehicles coming from the east were unheard until they were almost at the door, making a great sudden clatter as if travelers were riding into the very walls inside. The sounds fell away slowly from the south road, and thus, if vehicles approached from that direction, the noise came at first faint and shallow. The hoofs would beat lightly on the distance and grow nearer under a running crescendo of wheels; the sound would arise to great clatter as it passed the door; then suddenly, like a clap of high thunder, it was gone, swallowed into the hill. Ellen found a delight in the snug dry room into which the rain could not come. She would go through the door with a keen rush of sense and, closing the door behind her, she would look about at the enclosing walls while a quiver of content would sweep over her nerves and gather deep in her mind. Her bed stood along one wall and a small wooden trunk which she had bought from the peddler stood along another. The key of the trunk lay on the shelf before the clock print. Names would play in her mind as she moved about in the tight little room in the midst of a stone-tight land surrounded by steep hills, the people speaking but little and that little in a close hard speech. " I wouldn't know what to be thinking," one had said, or another, "I think myself he was bragging. He's a bold one." The names, Regina Donahue, Pius Donahue, Pius, Pius, Regina, Old Mrs. Wingate, Leo Shuck, Mag Mudd, Kate Bannan, she would say them in mind, thinking nothing. It was a pleasure to lock the chest and slip the key onto the high shelf where it lay out of sight. She felt very young in her delight in the locked chest and the closed door although her shadow was tall on the white wall and her dress was a woman's dress, brushing the door as she passed. Sometimes in the field she felt the same, when she sang with a loud shout and remembered a little girl she had played with—it seemed only a little while ago—a girl named Fanny B., when she had lived beside a river. Fanny B. could climb any tree in the school yard, clinging with her little bare toes, going always a little higher and singing a song her granny had taught her.

Back in the farm there was a stone pit and an old quarry where the walls curved around in an irregular bow and rose to the top of the hill which had been sliced asunder. At the bottom of the wall a pool of water lay, a clear pool with a gray wall and a reach of sky reflected in it. Above the wall a stony pasture went toward the north and broke into crumbling bluffs at the northwest, but below the wall the land rolled down into a sloping field that rounded off to the ends of its confines and melted into the lifting fields of the next farm. Ellen's cow grazed in the high pasture; she would come slowly down the path beside the quarry each evening walking unevenly on the zigzag way. From the high pasture Ellen could see the Wingate house where the nearest neighbor lived. The rear walls, dull and weathered, stood distantly above the angles of two hills, the stone chimney with its frayed top leaning against a gable end. In one of the dark lower rooms old Mrs. Wingate sat all day tearing rags into strips and winding the strings into balls, rocking to and fro as she worked and muttering, "He's got to pay me for my skirt I ruined, nohow. . . . Meat and lard and flour. . . . I lay he held back part. You know calves is a-sellen dear now." Ellen had heard the mutterings one day while she waited for someone to answer her rap, but no one came. Inside the opened window an old voice muttered and the dusty odor of rags floated out when the tearing sound came. Another day Ellen had knocked at the door, wanting to know if the woman had three hens she would sell. The mutterings were flowing faster and a mocking old voice was simpering, "Better sell the mule colts, better sell . . . as if I don't know when to sell my own property. . . . I lay a dollar I'm robbed every day I live, robbed by my own hired help. . . . I ought to charge up for the sweet he wastes. I'll say 'fifty dollars for the victuals you wasted, a-leaven drips on your plate, Jasper Kent,' I'll say." Ellen had come away without making her knocking heard. When she saw the frayed chimney and the weathered roof from the top of the pasture she always thought of the mutterings at the window and the smell of dusty rags. The man, Kent, farmed Mrs. Wingate's land, the two sharing all profits equally. Ellen had seen him go along the road, walking or riding, a tall man, bent a little with his own height as if he stooped to meet the earth, or again she had seen him flinging down the fields—looking at him with her quick glance, as she looked at Pius Donahue or Kate Bannan's boy. Sitting in the dim room, admitted at last on the mission of hens, she had heard the voice of the mutterings now honeyed with praise. "There never was an honester man. 'Better sell the mules,' he says only today. I tell you he watches the market close, Jasper Kent does. He's a hearty eater but he don't waste, and I love to see a man eat hearty." When she had passed out at the door Ellen stayed a moment to hear the mutterings renewed, listening fearfully to her own voice as it was mocked inside the window. "Any hens to sell! As if I had a chicken farm. Any hens. 'Could you let Mammy have three hens?' I didn't ask but a quarter apiece. Well, if she comes again she'll find hens is advanced. Stick-out nose and flat belly, a slut, I'll lay a dollar on it. 'Any hens!' I never could fancy a wall-eyed wench." From the summit of the pasture the house would seem turned back upon itself to mutter and whine, the leaning chimney adhering to the end wall. "Any hens! A wall-eyed slut! I never could fancy." Regina had said that Mrs. Wingate was in a lasting quarrel with her son, Albert, because old Wingate when he died left all the property to his wife during her life, and because Albert tried to force his mother to give him a part. He was a great hearty man who stayed in the town roistering and working in turns, or he would come to the farm blustering. The bare old house stood blankly out of the hills and the trees, crouching under its debased chimney, and Ellen walked over the hill pasture looking for her heifer. The spring cold was clear in the sky.

243

ELLEN and Henry threw the stones into heaps on the hill field and Henry set the plow into the rough soil, making ready for corn. Later there would be a small tobacco crop in the lowest field where the farm tilted away from the stone pit. Henry's two beasts of burden were a mule and an old mare, its mother. They pulled unevenly together, the mule lagging until the weight dragged on the mare's tired old sinews. Ellen worked the garden without suggestion from Henry, selling eggs to the peddler and buying from him the garden seeds. The heifer bore a brown and tan calf in March and Ellen felt very calm and secure in her possessions, the two beasts her own. There were hens in the yard and two knotty sows walked about in the pen behind the hencoops to root the small stones out of the mud all day, but toward nightfall Ellen would pour them a mash of sour milk and meal. From the garden which lay beside the house and touched the road she could not see any neighbor's house nor any neighbor's field for the land was too poor to induce much clearing and there were many acres of scrubby woodland in which the hogs ran half wild. But up the road that lifted above the toll house and off a mile was the place of the Donahues, and as Ellen thumped at the clods she would think of the houses as they lay on the gentler rises, the Donahue yard pecked bare by geese, the Bannan house close along a road three miles away, a lonely house, always shut and still, or the Whelen cabin toward St. Lucy. Out of the upland pastures that were grown with scrub timber would come the slow uncertain crying of cattle bells.

As she gathered stones from Henry's plowing in the high

field she could see Regina Donahue at work with Pius in a far upland beyond a wasted ravine. Pius would be moving behind a plow, crawling worm-like along the lines of the corn, and Regina would be moving slowly after him, chopping weeds with a hoe perhaps, although she was too far away for her task to be discovered. Pius had very large round eyes that looked out staringly from behind long brown lashes. His cheeks were round and his lips were large and full and slow. He seemed never to understand what she said to him and he would look at her with still, questioning eyes, beseeching her. She hated his great foolish stare, but she was glad whenever he came to their house door on an errand, glad feeling her hate and contempt lightly flowing. At their house Regina would stump slowly and monotonously over the floor, cooking a supper, never changing her pace as she went up and down putting this or that on the stove to cook. Old Mrs. Donahue walked to St. Lucy every morning to pray in the church, striding up the road quickly, going to pray for the soul of her husband who was now in purgatory. When she returned from this duty she worked out all morning among the geese and hens. She would cry out: "Oh, Regina, come put this clucking hen under the barrel." Her words ticked and clucked as she hurried here and there, taking a living out of the hard earth. Once she had said to Ellen: "Ask your ma has she got a rooster to spare she wants to swap me. Sure my old rooster is the daddy to all them hens and that's not good." A high flare of the cries of the geese came over her words, the cold raw March and the damp odors of the henyard. "I seen a hard time since Joe Donahue he died on me."

Every day or so a woman went by the house door, a thin woman whose skimp dress hung flat against her limbs. She

245

would be carrying a small basket or a tin cup. Ellen, working in the garden or gathering greens along the roadside or sitting with Nellie in the stoop, would talk with the woman when she passed, although the interchange yielded little variety, for her look was vague out of fixed eyes, eyes stony as if they were made of bone. In her, life sank permanently back into the stones. She would lean against the garden fence and wait to be questioned if Ellen worked there among the seeds and the clods, and Ellen liked to give her whatever pleasure she might derive from these repeated dialogues.

"What you got in your cup?" Ellen would ask.

"Two eggs, I got."

"Where you a-goen with two eggs?"

"I'm a-goen to the store down at McGill."

"What all you think to buy with two eggs, now?"

"Chewen wax, that's what I aim. I taken two there again yester."

"Do you always buy chewen wax?"

"Might' near. Sometime I buy stick candy."

"What you do all day afore noon?"

"I set and waited for the hens to lay. Hit taken the red one a long time."

"Bill, that's my old man," she explained.

"Got any youngones?"

"Not e'er a one. I had one and hit died. Hit cried all time and then hit died. Bill said hit was a God's mercy hit did." She spoke without regret, faintly smiling, shaking her cup dreamily.

The woman would walk slowly off toward the crossroads store which was called McGill. Later in the day she would

246

return and pass up the rocky hill, three miles to go and three to come to get her bit of sweet. Ellen would think often of Fanny B. The spelling class was a game all the children played; two rows of words to learn and you had done enough. Walking home along the river road there would be men wading in the water to seine the fish, wading with their long white naked legs in sight, and Fanny B. would sing out a rhyme or a question. Fanny B. would know what her words meant but she knew in some young way; one could, being young, sing out words one minute and forget all about them the next, even forget whether the things the girls told were true, and forget things one had seen. Fanny B., going to the head of Miss Josie's spelling class, would look very little and young with her thin arms and legs and her little dark dress, knowing the words Miss Josie asked, knowing only the words that were in the book. That was what it was to be ten years old, all the secret things and the half-known put snugly away in the forgetting parts of the mind, and a fleeting identity with Fanny B., whom she had not remembered for many years, would come to her when she took the key from its hiding-place and unlocked her trunk in the whitewashed room or when she saw the secret security of the inside of the trunk revealed.

THERE was a spring boxed about with timbers across the road from the toll house door. Here Ellen dipped out the water for the house and here a traveler would sometimes stop for a drink. One day in April while Ellen hoed in the garden near the fence Bell Carrier, the woman who walked with the eggs each day to McGill, stopped. She carried the tin cup in her hand, and she waited beside the fence for a short while, looking knowingly from her vessel to Ellen.

While the questions were being asked and answered a man came down the road from the hill. His feet were bare and his shoes, which were tied together, were hung over his shoulder. When he came opposite Bell he stopped and spoke to her with a slight bow.

"I'd like to borrow the loan of your cup to get me a cup of water from that-there well, ma'am."

"You're right welcome," Bell said. She took the two eggs out of the cup and laid them carefully on the grass. The man reached for the cup eagerly and held it under the tiny stream that trickled from the rocks at the side of the road. When he had drunk he wiped his mouth on his cuff and looked about him.

"It's a right warm day for spring," he said.

"Hit is a warm day and that I know," Bell replied.

"I got a long piece to go against sundown," he said further, "but if night finds me on the road I'll stay at Colin Carico's. Colin will make me welcome at his table and give me a bed, or maybe Pius Edelen will or Terry Yocum. I'm on my way to a place a far piece off from here. Colin is a person of a kind turn now. He'll give me a bed maybe."

Ellen tapped the clods lightly with her hoe to hear the talk more easily, working toward the fence.

"You seem acquainted in these parts right well," Bell said. She had put the eggs back into her cup. "You seem acquainted like."

"I go this road once or twice a year and have now for near ten years. I'm on the lookout for a little piece of work that won't hold me fast, you know. I got to visit my brother over

248

on the Ridge for a spell. I thought I'd make it out to be over
there when cherries is ripe. Then I'll go over to Green and
stay a piece with my other brother. I got two brothers. He'll
be mighty proud to see me come walken up to his door some
day. I like to make a point to be down there in peach time.
Do you know anybody got a little piece of work to do?"

Bell looked at Ellen with bewildered eyes and Ellen
answered.

"Squire Stigall wants somebody enduren the set-out
season, I heared Pappy say. He wants a hand the worse kind
to help set out and plow."

"That would be too confinen. I allow to get some light
work to make me a dollar or so as I go along, pin money."

"I'd like, now, a new-laid egg for my supper, wherever
I happen on to be or to stay," he said, looking away from
Bell's cup, looking away from Bell altogether. "I often say
there's not another single one thing like a new-laid egg to
strengthen the stomach and make your supper set well, and
that's true too of a man that's walked more'n fourteen miles
since he had a bite. I wonder how much you'd take for one
of your eggs, ma'am, or maybe two. I might not reach
Colin's before a late supper."

"I aim to trade these-here at the store for chewen wax.
I'd get five cents worthen."

"Chewen wax is not a very nourishen food, and when a
man's walked twenty miles in round numbers he craves a
trifle of solid food, and Colin might not be at home. Come
to think on it I heared a man say a piece back on the road
he seen Colin go somewheres this evening about two o'clock.
I wouldn't go to his house to stay and him not there; I'm
a decent man, and maybe he might not get back till after
supper is all over and put away. Colin's wife is a fractious

woman and when a meal is over it's over in her way of thinken. She's not a good looken woman like you and not so even tempered. She's not got your shiny eyes. Her teeth, now, are not so well-favored and she herself is not so well-favored in no way or how and not so well set up."

"I'd be right glad to give you these-here eggs if you'd be so good as to have 'em."

"I'm much obliged to you, ma'am. They're fresh I know."

"My name's Bell Carrier," Bell said.

"How do you do, ma'am!"

"And who might this other lady be," he said, turning toward the garden.

"That's Ellen Chesser. She's a Miss."

"I'm right glad to get acquainted, right glad. My name is J. B. Tarbell. I'm a photographer when I'm at home, but sometimes I follow house-painten."

REGINA had tired colorless eyes of some dark sort, slightly out of focus. Ellen saw her moving evenly down the yard, taking the angry hen from her mother, saw her going up and down the field, fitting her every act to her monotonous passing. Susie Whelen's wide mouth broke easily into smiles and her good-natured oaths flowed as easily: "Before Hell! I never seen such a boy for kissing as you are, Pius Donahue." Martin Stigall lifted his hat when he passed along the road before the church. Sometimes if Bell had no eggs to take to the store she would take two from Nellie's basket that was hidden under the bed. She would hide them under her apron and slip dreamily out at the door when the talk lagged. "Bell taken two eggs," Ellen would say, without anger, and the basket remained in the same place. "She likes a little sweet," Nellie would say. The tower of St. Lucy stood up out of the hills, the crosses standing evenly, as fragile as air, stone turned fine and thin. From the hill above the quarry there was only the top of the tower to see, but near at hand the whole tower sloped downward like a delicately formed crystal of stone. Ellen had gone there one Sunday afternoon with Pius and Regina and Susie Whelen. A Dominican in a creamy white gown had come out of the door, his shawl collar blowing up in the wind and his long pair of beads clicking against his skirt as he walked, his shoes seeming large and heavy under the flowing white of his robe. One day, passing the toll house, Jasper Kent turned back and stopped a moment, speaking to Ellen, who was alone on the porch. "A little money I wish you would lay by for me. I got no safe place to keep e'er thing." She had taken the bills from his hand before she knew what he wished, had let him thrust them into her palm and close her hand over them. The sum, eight dollars, seemed very large as she counted the bills over. She put them into her locked trunk and laid the key safely on its shelf.

The bell at St. Lucy rang often during the day, for the Brothers were always busy, and when it rang they changed from one way of being busy to another. Ellen learned to relate the ringing of the bell to the shadows and thus to tell the time. When the mid-morning bell came she must leave the field and start toward the house to help finish the cooking. The late bell of the afternoon belonged with the milking and the time of feeding the hogs and geese and horses. The chickens would be plucking at the littered yard for the last of their corn and the little pigs would be crying at the trough where she had emptied their slop of refuse and bran. She would be carrying the milk pail down to the cow lot, and over the noise would come the sweet slow bell, elegant and tranquil and patient. There was no crowding at a trough in it, no pushing aside and no jealous complaining. It had enough. At the base of the stone tower lay the church-yard which undulated over the hills, the tombs set thickly and unevenly, crookedly about, massed and turned and mingled in confusion, but in the little enclosed yard behind the church and beside the priory, the Brothers that were dead lay in even rows, lying out straight one after another, in order, fenced off from the turning, cluttered graves out-side.

ONE evening late in May Henry failed to come home from the field. Nellie fretted over the uneaten supper and Ellen worked among the stock. When he had not come at night-fall, Nellie and Ellen went across the farm, calling with un-easy voices, and after a search through the lower field they heard his groan coming weakly from the direction of the quarry. They found him in one of the stone pits, fallen among the stones, and when they lifted him one of his legs fell limp from the thigh. Ellen went to Mrs. Donahue's house for help and Pius was soon hurrying to St. Lucy to telephone for a doctor. When Pius returned he brought the Carriers who remained all night. Bill and Pius helped the doctor set the bone and bind in the boards, and Bell sat near the bed for many hours, happy and kind, fervid because she knew someone who had broken a limb. Her blank face turned from the bed to Nellie and back again, but she was apart from the pain, feeling no twinge of it.

"It just seemed like the ground rose up in the air and hit me," Henry said. "I worked out till nigh dark and I was on my way in when all of a sudden the ground just rose up outen the earth and hit me a terrible lick. That's just how it seemed. The ground hit me one awful lick and then I found myself in the bottom of that-there hole and no idea how I got there. Like that, it was."

The doctor went through the small house gathering up the things he needed, or he would ask Ellen, and his assurance and his speed filled the house. When he had set the bone in place and bound on the splints, the limb lay very large and white and wooden and still on the bed, and Henry came sickly out from the sleep of the chloroform. He would have to lie in bed many days, the doctor said, and Ellen brought water in a basin and bathed away the dust of the fields, a new kindness in her mind. To be bathing her father who lay white and still under her hands, yielding easily to her gentle demands, she passed with quietness and dignity through the room, the world grown simpler and less significant.

Henry lay in his bed for two weeks and after that he learned to sit in a chair with his injured leg stretched out heavily upon some support, hobbling back to bed on the crutches the doctor loaned him. Ellen finished setting the tobacco without help when the rainy season came, the land having been prepared many weeks before. She went slowly along the rows, carrying the plants from the bed at the foot of the hill. The season lay before her as a vast unweighed burden, and all the stooping and dragging and hauling, felt in anticipation, rested on her shoulders, on her arms, on her thighs, on her mind. She wondered who would plow the corn, the next labor after the tobacco setting, and after that would be the cutting of the hay, and there would be the garden to hoe and the little wheat crop to reap. Half of everything would go to the man who owned the land, ten hills for the man who owned the soil and then ten for them, ten shocks for Orkeys before their ten. She came in from the field too tired to care for the garden. She ate her food too weary to listen to Henry's story of twinging bones and Nellie's report of the sow's litter and the disasters among the hens. She would eat her supper silently when Nellie piled it onto her plate and nod in her chair while the dishes were being cleared. But after she had set the tobacco, just when the need of the plowing grew actual, the man from Wingate's farm came offering to plow. "I'll put it in between my own and never miss the time," he said.

The next day Ellen saw a plow going up and down their rows and heard a voice speaking sharply to guide the horse. Jasper Kent had come to plow their fields. She could hear him gee and haw at the horse all morning, his voice speaking suddenly out of the hill, now and then hurling out an angry threat, oaths and threats and sharp commands a part of the business of getting the horse turned squarely in the furrow. She would stop her hoe in the garden to listen; she had long since ceased to heed Henry's more feeble plowing voice. In the late afternoon Kent stopped at the yard door to talk a little with Henry who sat there in a chair, to tell how the crops did and to offer help, and many afternoons later he would come. "I'll try to see my way to plow that-there patch out for you-all this week," he would say. As she went up and down the yard to feed the stock Ellen would catch the meanings of their voices. Sometimes both men talked at once, each trying to convince the other, but Henry was grateful and he would concede in the end, bought by his gratitude.

"Nohow I always taken notice if you plant potatoes in the dark moon of March you get a better crop," Kent said.

"Light moon," Henry said. "I always thought light moon."

"No, dark. Dark moon. That's science. Cabbage, now, in the light moon. Beans, corn, peas, all light. Beets, now, they go in in the dark of the moon. There's a science to that-there. You ought to set a post in the dark of the moon, did you ever hear? If you don't it'll rot under ground sure."

Passing down the yard with the feed for the hogs Ellen would catch the wonder of their talk. "I taken a look at the almanac and I see Venus was the morning star and forthwith I . . ." she would pass beyond the reach of their words. She never joined them at the kitchen door for Kent was felt to be Henry's friend. The thought that there should be a morning star, given to the morning, would haunt her sense of the pigs as she poured out their mash, and the beauty of the words lingered with her as she said them over and over. The morning star; she had never said these words before. The thought that men knew the morning star and had it in mind, calling it by name, other names—this reared a new wonder. Once as she returned to the house Kent arose suddenly and stood before her.

"Lock this-here away somewheres along with the other, will you, Ellen? I got no safe place to keep a trifle." He put some bills into her hand. "Sold the calves today and this-here is my share. Could you put it by for me for a spell?"

Albert Wingate came back from town any night, he said, and tormented his mother until she gave him whatever

255

money she had by her. When he came there were dark ways in the house, he and his mother quarreling all night and calling names. Sometimes he brought a band of revelers with him and there was a great noise with random pistol shots. When he was gone all the boxes and cupboards were turned out onto the floor, for he was never done searching the house for money and even robbed his mother if she slept.

"She lets him take all she's got and when he's gone she pukes up a pile of hard words after him for a spell. A Tuesday he drove off a heifer that was half mine. I let that go for the time, and whilst I'm a peaceful man I don't aim to let no low-trash like Albert run over me, and if he comes again and takes off the property he'll maybe see trouble and a lavish of it too."

Ellen put the money, twenty dollars, in the trunk and thought of it no more. The pressure of the planting was past and whenever the need for the plow became immediate Kent found a few spare hours to give. Ellen cut the hay, driving their old mare hitched to the cutting implement, and afterward she raked the hay by hand and built it into stacks. J. B. Tarbell would pass along the road every day, going and coming from his work; he was painting for Squire Stigall. He would stop for a drink at the spring by the roadside and in the sigh that followed his deep draught he would say:

"That-there's the best water anywheres this side of Muldraugh's Hill and I've tasted about all the wells in thirty mile around. That-there is rich cold water, I say."

Often he would sit all afternoon to chat. He would talk about tasty fruits and juicy mouth-watery berries until his own mouth dripped with its imagined sweet, or he would tell of clear springs and long ways to go, of the many times he had passed up and down. Often the Carriers came, and on Sunday afternoon Susie and Pius and Regina, and sometimes the Stigall youth would linger for a little about the door, or Kent would stop as he passed. J. B. Tarbell would have candy that was wrapped in bits of colored paper on which, folded inside, were lines of verse which expressed admiration and affection. He would pass the candy about with his own hand, taking the pieces out of the sack and presenting each with a bow, scraping his foot. He would hold back some choice bit, the largest piece or the piece wrapped in fringed paper, choosing another for Nellie, another for Bell or Regina, but when he came to Ellen he would kiss the chosen piece and give it to her with a deep bow, or he would say, "Here's a sweet for Sweetnen."

"I'm due over beyond the Ridge long afore now," he said. "I know they-all are a-wonderen why I don't show up. Well, they'll be powerful glad to see me walk in some day." He told long stories while all sat listening. "As soon as they seen it was J. B. Tarbell they called the dogs off. . . . They offered me a big salary to stay and work all year but I'd a heap rather be footloose and my own boss. There's only one man ever a-goen to boss old J. B. and that man is a woman. And so I says I'd a heap rather be my own boss, but no offense meant. That was when I followed picture-taken." His little string tie would sprangle under its faint blackness, always tied in a neat bow. Sometimes he would sing a song,

Oh, my poor Nellie Gray
They have taken her away,

or he would play a mouth harp. Often as he passed along the road he would leave a paper of the sweets for Ellen who would be in the field. Bell's hens were in a setting mood and she often came to sit with Henry to share in the taffy. Sometimes Ellen would pile her hair in its soft rolls and fasten a small blue ribbon at her throat, and then, if Tarbell came, she would sit apart smiling a little at the unveiled wooing, or she would laugh outright when she unrolled the bit of paper from the sweet drop he had kissed, and smile again as she passed into her hard white room and turned about from the clock shelf to the wooden chest. Jasper Kent's money lay on the bottom of the chest underneath her blue dress of thin muslin, the cloth for which Nellie had bought from the peddler. Ellen had taken the cloth quietly and had tried on the garment quietly when Nellie had sewed the seams, but her eyes liked to linger on the blue folds that were sweet-scented and crisp to touch. She had persuaded Nellie to buy herself a piece of bright cloth for a dress, and Nellie had chosen a gray with some small purple flower hanging in the mesh. They talked softly about the sewing of the seams and of whether there should be a bit of lace or a bow, for Ellen could not give delight or glee to a muslin or a frill now, her mind one with the wants of the fields, with the beasts and the plowed trenches. In the fields she wore the faded dresses of the summer before, and there, seen distantly, her figure blended evenly with the turned soil or sank into the corn rows, now waist high or more. In the dark blue dress, now turned to gray by the sun and the wind and the rain, she moved almost unseen through the windrows of the hay or came down the steep path among the stones beside the quarry. In the pale washed-out dress she drifted all morning up and down the lines of the tobacco, the tobacco flower come before its season, as the pale flower of the tobacco come to tend its young.

BUT the near way of the clods, as she knew them, as she leaned over them, were a strength to destroy her strength. There, present, the heaviness of the clods pulled at her arms and the field seemed to reach very far before it stopped at the pool by the quarry. The struggling grass, matted into the soil, clung about the plants here and there and scarcely yielded to the two or three blows of the tool. She felt the weight of the grass as she tore it away, and now and then a blow so sharp that it made her flanks ache was needed to turn the soil. The field had been neglected for the summer rains had lasted overlong. She ceased to think of any day before this day or of any task before this. Each plant freed of weeds was something liberated, but another stood trammeled, the same endlessly snared, the same, until she tramped a treadmill and her thought was clodded with earth. The sun was warm on her aching shoulders and her strong knees quivered with the strain. As she plied the hoe a quick image of a year, a season, from planting to cutting and stripping, stood forth as if it were in the soil, a design, all finished and set· apart. The design of the grass roots matted with the soil lay under her eyes, complete forever, varying in every detail but forever the same. The hoe came down over and over, no two blows exactly alike but no varying in the form. The year stood plainly designed, one with the grass and the dust, a certain year, formed with beginning and end, planting and cutting, gay laughing and places to go. She had said happy things and they had seemed to have meanings, and people had said things back to her, things she had kept in mind to smile at afterward. All now lay in the form of the year. A little nick in the bright edge of the hoe twinkled in and out of the brown of the earth. The hoe cut in half its depth or it cut in more, and the grains of earth fell airily against the dull upper part. The year began to turn, a form moving lightly upon itself, but she minded nothing of the year, for her body had changed, and the hoe and the soil now cut each other sharply, visible and near. "Jonas," she said, over and over. It was a name, that was all, a name for something that was gone.

Her feet were uncomfortable in Henry's old shoes, but her own were nearly out. The loose old plow shoes dragged heavily under her feet and rubbed at her bare ankles. She could say the word over and over, "Jonas, Jonas, Jonas." It was nothing but a word, gone out of her body, as gone as last year's breath. Clods had fallen into one of the shoes and she stopped an instant to shake the brogue free, then back to the hoe again. She felt the stride of her limbs as she moved to the next plant and her shoulders knew the power of the grass. "Jonas," she said, "Jonas." It was a word, less than a being, a bit of a design lost in a turning year. "Jonas," a flat sound without meaning. Suddenly a wave of pity and grief swept over her. She had played too long with the name and it had taken life. Lonely flesh beside her lonely flesh. She was standing by MacMurtrie's gate in the moonlight and the hounds were running down the field. She was sitting half the night seeing the logs burn low and renew. The year broke and fell out of its design, becoming real, becoming a stored-up part of herself, and emotion rolled over her to drown her. The dust was enlarged and the sharp edge of the hoe wavered, for tears were washing over her eyes.

But the dust was dust again and her vision was clear, the edge of the hoe standing straight and flashing keenly into the soil. "Not him," she said, "not him." She went endlessly down the row, plant after plant, the same, no thought of how long she would endure or of the end. Her body and

260

mind were of the earth, clodded with the clods; the strength of her arms and her back and her thighs arose out of the soil, the clods turned upon themselves to work back into their own substance endlessly. The bell at St. Lucy rang for the mid-morning but its tones beat upon the outside of the dust. A little while the bell flowed onto the outer faces of the clods but it could not pierce the inner part and it fell away, scarcely missed when it went. She turned the row end without thought, without liberation, treading a mill. Then she heard an echo of her blade falling, or a repetition of it, nearer than St. Lucy's bell and more resonant of the inner way of the soil, but she went steadily on. The echo became another hoe at work, drawing nearer, and then a shadow began to creep toward her down the row and she saw that Jasper Kent had come to the field. He worked toward her steadily and she stopped at the labor, aware now of the day and of the farm, and she rubbed her aching arms and smiled across the tobacco plants, aware now of the quarry. When he came up to her he stopped and looked at her and laughed a little, as if he knew that the conveyance of his arrival there had been the hoe.

"You could do some easy work if you'd rather," he said. "I can finish this in no time." Then he took some bills from his pocket and handed them to her, saying, "Another piece of money I wish you'd put away for me. Sold a little truck. Go do some easy work whilst I finish this-here."

She took the roll of bills from his hand and felt the coins wrapped inside it. Then she saw him move swiftly across the row, moving toward the end of the field with swift strokes of the hoe, three or four blows to each plant and it was finished. She went slowly away, startled and unprepared, hearing the withdrawing thud of the hoe as she went. Then she sat on

263

the stile beside the garden patch under a thin ash tree and shelled the peas for the dinner. She began to think of Susie Whelen and of how her mouth was full and wide and her eyes soft and blue, her dark hair in a roll over her forehead. If Jasper or if Tarbell should look at Susie Whelen it would be seen that she was pretty and they would want her in their arms, all the more if they should look at her mouth when she smiled. She was soft and warm and full of laughter, or sullen and short, easy with her curses. To look at her was to see how full she was with her woman-ness, and Tarbell would surely see. Beyond the fields rose the wall of the quarry and above this the crest of the high pasture ran in a rugged line against the sky, all faint now in the heat of the mid-morning. It would have taken her two days to finish the field, she reflected, but now it would be done that day. He had smiled when he had said "some easy work" and his eyes had been on her face and on her eyes. She thought that she might get another ribbon or a fan on a long chain of beads, and she could feel the fan softly opening in her hand. Perhaps Jasper would take it into his hand or touch it against his face as he talked, but Susie Whelen came as a menace to the edge of her vision of the fan against Jasper's face, or Tarbell's, her mouth breaking easily into a smile, careless of its smile or of its oath. Her curses broke on her smooth lips and her bright large teeth, and one could kiss her damp mouth with a deep kiss, pushing in on her lips, eating her oath back to its core and living on its life, knowing her soft bosom and her shoulders.

Now she dropped the peas into the basket and felt Jasper's money in the pocket of her skirt, lying against her thigh, and she remembered his words. She would hate Susie Whelen and she would watch her and she would not trust

264

her warm body and the warm breath of her laugh. After the sugar and coffee were bought she would have something for herself, and she reckoned the price of eggs against the number in the basket under Nellie's bed to test out the sum. The hens had fallen away from their laying with the mid-season and eggs were hard to find. The huckster refused any that were thin-shelled and old and often laid aside half she carried out to him. She remembered the huckster's drooping eyes and his serious mouth drawn in a little when he counted the eggs, his ways all intent upon his business. "Twelve cents," he would say, driving a hard bargain with Nellie, "I say twelve. If I let you women run my business I'll land in the poor farm." But for her his way was gentler, giving little kindnesses, reckoning the sum in her favor and giving her the odd unreckoned cents if she bought a ribbon or a pin, and he would let her try all the pins to see which looked best on her bosom. All this for her because she was young and because she had clear straight eyes, but he listened less to Regina because her looks were slow and her step plodding, her skin sewed crookedly onto her cheeks. But he laughed with Susie Whelen and let her have her time to choose a pin or a lace, easy and happy with her, walking briskly about the wagon, because she made him feel young himself.

There was something crooked about Jasper's skin as it was set to the contour of his face, but he was in no way like Regina. When he came up out of the pasture and out of the curve of the road she would see his face and its heavy skin, unevenly traced and deeply seamed, darkly stained with years of sun and wind, heavy with work. As he came bending toward her she would see his face, but after he came she would no longer see; his serious talk of plowing and seasons, of cures and signs and selling prices, and his suspicions and hates would surround him. She herself was a woman now, that she knew. She had seen her mouth that morning in the kitchen glass and again in the pool that lay at the foot of the quarry. Under his heavy skin with its uneven sewing and rugged marks of sun and wind, under his bent shoulders, he had been quietly bold, taking the field away from her with a few words and a smile, his hands strong on the hoe, the sinews working flat and strong, drawing directly, fast to their purpose. Some day Tarbell would look at Susie Whelen and he would see that her eyes were blue and bold and that she took the world easily, and that is what a man wants. Then he would give her the printed verses with the choicest sweets. Space between one and Susie Whelen melted down and away and she reached out all ways, her dark hair rolled up from her forehead. Jasper would be bound to look at Susie some time and then he would want her in his arms with her easy-going laugh and her careless curses. She herself, then, would hate Susie and she would watch her, and she would not trust the days or the accidents of the summer. She hated the house Susie lived in, back a little from the road with a few flowers struggling to bloom when the drouth had eased. A ragged shagbark tree grew across the road, in Susie's sight day after day, and the pigs in the pen beside the barn walked in and out of the sun, the gate tied up with a string, a rose bush over against the garden; she would hate all of it.

Jasper was visible as a distant spot on the even green of the field. His hoe would be tearing away the weeds to make the soil fresh and light, and his lips would hang loose as he worked, relaxed to the toil, his back bent deeply to the straight of the hoe, the sweat running into the furrows of his

266

uneven face. He was twenty-six years old. He gave her his money to hide away for him because she was near at hand and because he could trust her to be careful, but he would like Susie Whelen's carelessness and her easy mouth. He knew the wonder of the light moon and how it drew the herbs and grains, and how the dark moon settled things back into the earth, and he knew the name of the morning star. She gathered the shelled peas into her apron and carried the hulls to the pen for the pigs, her mouth shut upon its determination and anxiety. She would take more care. She would watch for the huckster when he came and buy the best he had, a fan on a long chain, perhaps. The land was hard and rough and she must take what she could out of the bitter soil, and she bent to lift the heavy pig trough, a hollowed log, to turn it over and set it to rights, ready for the mash she would bring after a little. The pigs ate the pods hurriedly and when the last one was gone there was not one green thing left in the brown trampled dirt of the pen. When they had eaten the pods the swine went back to lie in the shade of the barn, lying long and narrow side by side on the dried wallow.

On Sunday she put on the blue dress and brushed the soil from her shoes, making them neatly black. In the dusk when Susie Whelen and the Donahues were gone she continued to sit in the porch before the house, Tarbell sitting near with his mouth harp. He had given her all the sweets with fringed papers and printed avowals inside and some of the candy she had eaten but some she had tossed carelessly to Susie or Regina. He played tune after tune on the mouth harp, shaking his spittle from it from time to time. His chair was tilted against the railing and he named each piece as he played it, gravely intent upon his rendering. "This-here piece is the 'Arkansas Traveler.' Did you ever hear that on a French harp?" His feet were set high on the rung of the chair and his small black moustache kept clear of the musical instrument with difficulty. "Did you like that-there piece?" he asked when he had finished. "I recollect once I was on my way to Charlottetown and I met a man said he'd come from Tennessee. I recollect that man as well as if I see him today. I'm a master hand to recollect. He said down in Tennessee he knew a man had been all the way to Floridy and down there you sit under a orange palm same as you might sit under a peach tree here, and you'd reach up your hand and pluck a orange right without you'd bat your eye, he said. Would you like that-there, honey? Think about that-there and tell me would you like it or not. This piece I recollect I learned from a blind Negro down towards Campbellsville. It's called 'Sourwood Mountain.' Do you like it?" He set upon the piece with vigor, closing his eyes to turn his vision inward upon the tune. Now and then a buggy would pass, clattering out of the hill road and falling softly away toward the south. "Wherever I happen on to be they always like my way with a harp," he said. He played a slow dirge that finally frayed out into stiff arpeggios. "Wherever I happen on to be they say, 'Well, J. B., how's the music?' But if Miss Ellen Chesser don't like my music I'd throw this-here harp right over into the middle of Leo Whelen's weed patch and forget I ever owned it. I'm a plumb fool about you. Before I forget it I better tell you, I'm a plumb fool about you. Tell me now, how do you like this-here song?"

Ellen's chair was tilted back against the wall, her head against the white boards of the house, her dress, grown bluer in the dusk, turned to gray. The flavor of his travel and his carefree way emanated from his person and mingled with his music as he played tune after tune, "Black Joe," "Rosie O'Grady," "Nellie Was a Lady," naming each one and asking for praise; or he fell away from his singing to tell some tale of wonder. "Just where the road curved up past a sawmill I met a man on his way to Adair County to bury his aunt and heir her money, on a high bay mare. Says I, 'Do you know a man over in Adair owns a peach orchard half as big as the state of Kentucky?' I says. 'Well,' I says, 'I used to work right on that-there place, Gadley's place, near Willett's.' Well, he had to shake hands on it and said ain't the world little after all, that place not three miles from his aunt's property. Said old man Gadley was dead now and the peach orchard was all gone to rack and that was sad news to old J. B. because I'm partial to peaches. Did you get that point? As I came up from Greasy Creek once I met a parcel of travelers that owned a bear could read or tell fortunes—one, I forget which. Big brown bears and two little bears. They used to make good money on the bears before times got so hard. I recollect that bear had teeth long as my hand, and I recollect I wouldn't sleep out that night although it was away after dark before I found a place to stay. I recollected them bears' teeth. Say, while I don't forget it I'm plumb a fool over you. Here's a song gushes straight out of my heart.

> Her cheek is like some bloomen red rose
> All in the month of June;
> Her voice is like some sweet instrument
> That's just been put in tune.

Straight out of my heart. Say, when I go I lay off to kiss you goodnight tonight and no harm done and ne'er a thing bound by it. That's my aim when I go away. Her cheek is like some bloomen red rose. I aim to get a camera right off and then I'll take your picture first thing. I owned a first-rate camera before now. I used to take tintypes and cabinets, both. I'll tell you how I lost my camera; that's a story to please you. I was away down towards the Big Fork and I took up with a machine agent, but he never would let on he knowed me when he came to a house. 'You go here whilst I go there,' he'd whisper to me. He was afraid his trade would get ruined if he let on he went with a picture-taker, and I was afraid vicy versy, but we'd meet around the turn of the road and say, 'Any good?' He'd let old J. B. ride along for miles in his sewen machine wagon. He had a fancy to me, I see that. Well, one time we came to a ford, as we supposed, and we drove out and by the time we knew what was what the water was up in the wagon bed and the old horse off his feet. Them machines was so heavy they made the wagon want to stay down and that's how I lost my camera. I never laid eyes on that machine agent again after I see him climb up on the opposite bank, but I heard it said that when the water subsided, flood water, it was, he got his machines off a sand bar. That's how I lost my camera. Her cheek is like some bloomen red rose. And the horse, I'd hate to name what came to the horse, a big old roan. It was them heavy machines caused it and the old roan couldn't seem to kick clear of the harness. Her cheek is like some bloomen red rose. I couldn't name what happened to him. It's not decent to name. Anyway that-there horse drowned as dead as a door nail, neck stretched out and swelled up as big as a wagon wheel around the middle. Flood water, it was. Her cheek is like some bloomen red rose. I'll sing one more piece called 'Just as the Sun Went Down.' You ought to hear the tenor on that. I got to sing the treble because I got nobody to chord in, but sometime I'll show you how the tenor goes." He hitched his chair nearer and a little spasm passed over his shoulders. Some great star hung in the high point of the sky and the moon shone. Far away a lonely dog barked. Lonely crickets were crying in the grass beside the stones of the spring and the desolate voices of frogs cried. It seemed that a long while had passed as the moments moved from desolation to desolation.

She said that she would go in, that it was dark now, and she arose from her chair quickly. "I aim to do like I promised myself," he said, "and no harm done and ne'er a thing betokened," and standing in the moonlight she let him place his arm about her and kiss her many times. Then she went within the door although he called her to come back, and later she heard his step going the south way, beating unevenly on the road, passing on, pausing, returning and then going. She sat on the side of her cot, her mind pursuing some word that was unnamed and could not gather itself into form, the hands of her mind reaching and straining to shape the nebula. The steady flow of his talk still beat about her and warmed her body out of its loneliness. He was gone far on the road, past Wingate's, past Stigall's, on toward the place where he slept, and the uneven beat of his footfalls, stopping and going forward, melted into her own breathing when she lay to sleep, and into the picture of brightly sunlit field where the plow had lately rasped through the hard soil. Then a cry came from her lips and she was suddenly awake in the moonlight of the whitewashed room, raised to her elbow, hearing the word ring through the walls, hearing

271

still the cry that had lifted her, even jerked her back into the moonlit night. The word of her outcry receded from her, going in waves of remembered sound, throbbing on her ears as she searched from wall to wall to find some real and present token of it. The word, "Jasper," still throbbed in her own voice, still fitted itself into her throat, and beat at the stiff white walls.

HENRY went to the field now, limping unevenly, but little able to work. Ellen stayed near him to help and often brought him water to drink when he was weary. He was bitter for the time he had lost and jealous for every plan that had passed from his hands, speaking shortly to Nellie or to Ellen, but to Kent he gave only courtesy because his indebtedness to him was great. The tobacco was laid by now for the cutting, a scant crop. "A fool he is, to try to grow a crop there," one or two said. Ellen still took the burden of the farm.

The bell at St. Lucy rang each summer morning shortly after dawn, sounding across the cool dew of the fields, itself cool and clear with repose, and then, as Regina said, the Brothers put on their white robes and walked into the church to pray, all chanting together. The morning star was great and bright, shining down in the east near the place where the sun would rise, sometimes seen as if it were a little moon, plainly crescented. Ellen arose one morning before the first red of the dawn to see to a turmoil among the hens. Hurrying out into the yard she found a skunk among the chicken coops trying to force a way to the chickens, a great clatter arising. Off in the east a brilliant star burned, delicately crescent-formed, the morning star. She thought that it would be necessary to nail the chicken boxes securely before another night and she waited about in the cool dawn to see that the beast did not return. The morning star, whatever its name might be called, hung with softening brilliance as the dawn grew, and she thought of the dark of the moon and of the autumnal equinox, that strange saying. It was hard to bring the autumnal equinox into the same thought with the morning star, the last seen clearly in the sky while the other was something to remember, the days and the nights of equal length and the summer passing. A deep voice held the saying, Kent's voice as he sat beside the house door, "Autumnal equinox comes a Friday after next." A cool breeze sprang up from the low-lying space toward the corn-field and a shiver passed over her body. A deep voice held the saying or spoke again out of the hill, rolling out a great blast of oaths, admonishing the mules, bearing down the plowing team, getting the lazy mule along beside the tired old mother. The morning star stood high above the sunrise, pale now. The Brothers would put on their white robes and walk into the church in the morning quietness of the bell, in the fresh stillness of the new dawn, indifferent to the autumnal equinox and the days and nights grown even, and there would be no knowledge among them of the stubborn beasts upon which one cried with storms of words and oaths, and no knowledge of the crying hens, afraid of the skunk, of herself standing guard in the cool dawn. No knowledge of herself holding in mind a voice, "autumnal equinox," "morning star," and the great words rolled out upon the lagging beasts. The corn in the garden stood high and about it clung the beans, all inclined toward the wonder of the sun but belonging to their own hunger and to their labor in the furrows, all grown out of the soil and the rain and the seeds, but turned toward the wonder of the equinoxes, toward the light moon and toward the morning star.

WHERE the limestone came to an end the dolomite stones were hard like flint, the pebbles round and smooth. Sometimes these great stones were laid upon each other in even seams, and they stood, tall and brown, as cliffs topping the hills, the walls hanging straight downward, the stones great beyond all power of man to lift. Often as Ellen came and went among the hills the dignity of the great stones would pass into her being as she walked by them, and it added itself to her pride in being able to surmount them, to walk beyond them. Or, digging into the dust of the garden, bent over the herbs, she would remember the encroaching pebbles and flat rocks or the geese plucking at the thin grass. She would remember Regina's step on the stony road and Bell's two eggs in the tin cup. Two days after the skunk visited the chicken pens she worked in the garden toward the late afternoon, remembering the cedar shrubs that grew scantily over the slanting wastelands and pastures. The next year she would grow a large onion patch, she decided, and she rose from her hoe to look about on the garden, to scan its length, deciding then how great the onion bed should be. The huckster had told her that there was a good market for early onions, that he would buy all she could furnish. Into her decision about the onions came her dreaming half-knowledge, surging up from beneath, allied to the hoe in the clods, running with the slipping of the blade. Pius Donahue looked at her avidly with his watery eyes and

274

Leona Handrahan lay with Joe Lucas in a fence corner, it was said in whisper. The corn was scanty and thin and the tobacco stunted. If Jasper should look at Susie Whelen he would see that she had a kind of prettiness and he would want her in his house and in his arms. She would therefore hate Susie Whelen and she would hate the look of her eyes and the curves of her mouth, and hate the trees about her farm and the flowers in her yard. She would distrust her flowered dress and her bright pin on her bosom. The eggs in the basket were few and the nests, searched daily, were barren. Dreamily it came to her that she would take what there was out of the hard soil and out of the stones and she would have, in the end, something from the clattering rocks.

She dropped the hoe in the patch and went away across the two fields, set upon her path by her thought in the garden. She moved across the ground, more quick than any growing thing her feet passed or trampled, and when she had left the two fields behind she climbed the stony way beside the quarry cliff and went over the rim of the high pasture where her cow grazed. Jasper was at work in Wingate's field beyond the distant fence, and as she stood on the crest beside the cow, her hand along the animal's shoulder, the land seemed to reach endlessly away, pasture and thin woodland and stone-crowned hills, until the length and width of it cried back at her. The land surrounded her, lying away in all points, never to be measured in all its strength to surround and enclose and obliterate. Jasper knew that she had come to the crest of the hill for he had left his work and was coming out of his field, over the rail fence and up to the top of the pasture. St. Lucy's tower stood out of the land, the eight crosses evenly set on the eight-crowned turret, risen out of the earth, taken out of the rock of the ground, out of the hard lime, and after a little the bell would sing a tranquil psalm that would run unmoved above the beasts and above the clods, floating off quietly of itself to the sunset. Jasper's step was quick on the herbs and his shadow came quickly, the dark line of his form on the grass coming timed to the beating of her own life within her breast. As he drew near a smile brightened his face and a look passed between them, growing from tenderness to intimacy until she was merged with him in the deep moments of his last approaching steps. Then she was standing beside him, within his arms, and he began to kiss her and to lead her along the field's rise toward some thorn trees and off again beside the downward path or back to the summit of the brow. He would come that night and tell her the story of his life and then, if she was of a mind to have him, they would get married. He would come as soon as the night work was done.

SHE sat beside him on the porch while his story came to her, a story which leaped jerkily from between the quiet intervals when his speech praised her own beauty and goodness or fell away entirely before his fondling and caressing. Henry had stumbled away early to his bed, broken by his day in the field, and Nellie had moved aimlessly about inside the house, her bare steps falling stiffly on the boards before she settled to her sleep. Or Jasper lit his pipe afresh and saw to its drawing, his finger pressing down the tobacco, the light of the match burning for a moment against his face and lighting his eyes. Then she searched the massive planes of his skin for its beauty and searched his eyes, looking quickly

276

away and back. The story was of labor, of wandering from farm to farm, of good seasons and bad, of good luck or evil.

"I got in a dispute with Old Reed over the pay and up and quit that place. That was when I was twenty. Next year looked like there wasn't work enough at home for me and Pap both, and I left home and went over on the ridge for a spell. I got in a fight with Hank Beaver over a girl. She liked me best and was all set to marry but I couldn't marry no girl yet and she took Hank after all, and I went off to work up around Mayses Creek, and there was a girl up there too. Then Mammy died, and then Pappy, and I went back home to get what little was a-comen to me after the stock was sold, but it was a little trifle. By that time I didn't care so much about girls. Then I bought a monument stone for Mammy and Pappy. I recollect it took all that next year to pay off that."

At the memory of his mother he remembered Ellen again and drew her closer, looking at her through the dim light or brushing his hand over her hair. The story waited long while he searched again for her beauty and approved her with his broken endearments and his caressing hands. After a long interval his voice spoke again in questioning. He had been in jail; did she know that he had been in jail? Could she like a man who had been in the dirty lock-up and would she draw away from his arms? "I got in a fight with Ofatt's boy over a trifle—a grown man, he was, and his own master. I got in this-here fight with Dave Ofatt over some trifle, and Ofatt, the old man, made a remark to me in town one day, a remark I wouldn't countenance and I hauled off and knocked him over right on the street of the town, and for that I got locked up over night and tried next day in the court. On account of Ofatt being prominent, the Judge, he

277

fined me twenty dollars and ten days in jail. I borrowed the money to pay the fine offen Tobe Baily and worked, after I got outen jail, for Litsey a spell, long enough to pay Tobe back, I recollect. It was then I got to feelen my strength and I got set up over my powers to lift and pull. Ne'er other man at the blacksmith shop could lift equal to me, not even old Nathan though he was a strong man in his arms and neck."

He recounted tales of his power and his excellence at contests that were tried at the shop and his great strength in the harvest field, no other man quite his equal or mate, taking shock for shock at the cutting. His large hand closed and unclosed, feeling again its strength, and his arm muscles flexed in memory of their first hardy-brawn. Or he took up his story of wandering again, carelessly now, between interests in the pipe, lazily told between caresses.

"Then up around Tick Creek I worked for a man named Pike. A good clever fellow, and I stayed there two year. An old man, he was, that knew a heap about signs and farmed by tokens. His wife was young, thirty I reckon, and we-all made a jolly set till I see she had a fancy to me. In fact she was set to me more'n I liked and even got me so I couldn't seem to help, a big quick-eyed woman, a fine-looker. But I pulled loose and went off—good clever man, old Pike was, and I couldn't see my way to do him no dirt, so I pulled outen the country. I learned a heap from him about tokens. Then next year, over on Master's place, I went plumb a fool over a girl but she wouldn't marry me after all because the man she knew first come back from up around Clark County, and I got mad and quit the country. I was bad cut up over that and throwed away all the money ever I had saved up, every durn cent, on drink and one thing and another. Then I come up here in the St. Lucy country to

278

work for old Mrs. Wingate, sharen half and half. Are you tired of my long-winded yarn?"

Ellen said that she was not tired. She wanted to hear more of the old man, Pike, but she stilled the question on her lips because the thought of him filled her with pain, a pain borrowed from the greater pain that centered about the thought of the girl near Master's place. But she ruled her lips suddenly and asked the question she most wanted answered, whether the girl from near Master's place had married the man who came back from Clark, but the answer, "Yes, oh yes, they hitched up," held no stored regrets.

When he was gone she went into the house, moving dreamily through the moonlit rooms. To marry and go away, the idea came into her mind slowly, spreading unevenly through her sense of the half-lit kitchen and her own room which was bright with a square of white light on the floor. She fell asleep with no formed wish in her mind and no decision, but when Nellie called her out of sleep soon after dawn, while she dressed quickly in the faded blue garment, she heard a catbird singing clear fine phrases on a post near her window, clear phrases that were high and thin, decisive and final, and she knew at the instant that she would marry Jasper and go with him wherever he went, and her happiness made a mist that floated about her body as she carried the feedings to the hogs and opened the chicken boxes. She would remember every movement of his face, as it looked away, lost in its story, as it turned to her again, leaning nearer, and his name came often to her throat and lingered there, on the verge of utterance, the word her mind had been seeking, now grown fixed and eternal. She moved through the morning, while the name grew in her being, surrounded by her own renewed beauty which identified itself each moment with every lovely thing her eyes recognized, such as the pattern of black and white on a chicken's feather, as the figured undulations crisscrossed on the bark of the ash tree, the waves of the tall, full-grown corn. As the day passed, her need to see him grew, to rest her eyes upon his form and thus to quiet her longing. But the morning passed and her work did not take her to the fields and she did not once hear his voice admonishing the team in the upper fields or meadows. She remembered Albert Wingate and his treachery and thought with apprehension of old Mrs. Wingate, who was torn two ways by her maternal passion and her avarice. Toward nightfall a great rain came with thunder and lightning. Coming in at dark Henry said that Albert had come back to the farm, he himself had seen him riding pell-mell through the pasture, and all through the night the security of her snug, weather-tight room mocked at her as it shut her away from the storm.

On the following day while she helped Henry cut the small tobacco crop, while the warm sun undulated through the crisp rain-cooled air, Pius Donahue went through the farm, stopping a short while but bringing no evil news of the night, and she knew that Jasper was safe. A sense of finality came to her with the splendor of the sun and a certainty that Jasper's words had been real and were undiminished and that his want of her was actual. While she set the tobacco sticks evenly through the field, the physical pain that had bound her throat for a day grew less and went. Jasper came to the field late in the morning. Albert had come, he said, and had stripped his mother of her last earnings, making evil threats. He, Jasper, would not stay another year but he would go away out of the country and search for better land, and when he had found a place he would come back for her, if she were of a mind to go with him, and that was what he had come to ascertain. The sooner he left Wingate's place the better. She, Ellen, was the best favored girl he had ever set his mind on having and that surely was a token. He would leave as soon as he could be released without a total loss and they would go. He would take her to his mother's grave some day after they were gone. It was far past Stonebridge church and grown in weeds perhaps by this time, but they would make it smooth and decent before they came away, and she murmured that she would plant a flower beside it, a rose or a little clump of sweet-williams such as she had seen before the priory door at St. Lucy, for they were a fair sight with their round clusters of pink bloom that made a sweet smell all about. When Henry came back from the barn, where he had been to haul a load of the cut tobacco, Jasper said that he must go for he had much to do before nightfall.

"I aim to hunt out a hollow somewheres to use to fatten the hogs," he whispered to Ellen as they stood beside the fence. "Some well-hid place off on the back of the farm. A new-styled prodigal, Albert is. He drove off the fatted calf. I taken a heap of pains with that-there heifer, too. Let it suck three months and over. It was my aim to make a high-priced cow that time."

Ellen told Nellie that she was going away with Jasper when all the crops were housed, and Nellie and Henry were both well pleased. Nellie said that Ellen must save all the feathers from the geese and add to these all the plucked feathers laid away, for every girl should bring to her marriage a soft bed to lie in. When Tarbell stopped at the toll house door Ellen would seldom go outside. Instead she

281

would busy herself in the yard, and she would neither eat his fringe-papered taffy drops nor read the declarations printed within the wrapper. In the evening Jasper would come and Ellen would sit with him on the steps before the door. She would hear his high whistled phrase, a bit of some old song imperfectly remembered, penetrating every room of the cabin, and she would finish her task in gladness, knowing that he waited on the step before the door or on the stile under the ash tree. He would tell her of how things lay between him and Albert, of his fears and precautions. The autumn was approaching darkly in the house under the great poplars, old Mrs. Wingate tearing her rags and muttering her evil sayings. Jasper continued to bring Ellen each bit of cash he was paid as he had done since he had first made her his banker in the spring, and she hid the money deep in the locked chest, near two hundred dollars now. One dusk she brought it out for him to count and the sum pleased him very much, but he told her to put it back and he would be bringing more when the hogs were sold, and the whole sum would buy them their start in some better country, some fertile, well-watered land. He showed her his scars and told her how he had got each one, by what fights or accidents, and she drove her mind back into his experiences to try to merge with his sorrows and his pleasures and to share each one and to hold all in her thoughts. Or she would sit quietly on the step beside him, reposing in the quiet of his embrace, and they would speak to each other softly.

He had built a pen for the swine, far back among the hills where a little spring trickled out of the stones and made a damp place below in the soil. He had cut posts from the cedar glades and had hewed out knotty rails, enclosing a space about twenty feet wide which bent and turned with the flow of the hills. Over one end of the enclosure he had built a high platform and onto this he often loaded a great pile of fodder which was thus kept high, away from the hogs but always ready at feeding times. After he had brought the swine to the pen—eleven great shoats ready for fattening—he went down to the ravine twice each day to throw down fodder from the platform, but he was careful to make no paths as he went. The hogs churned the moistened soil into a cool wallow and there they lay all day, or they aroused themselves to crunch the corn he threw to them or returned to suck the wasted grains out of the mud. He told no one but Ellen where he had built the secret sty and how much labor had gone into hewing the rails and setting the platform.

They would speak to each other, gathering their thought gently about their common wish, or he would thunder out an imprecation upon his enemies until the massive angles of his face broke into new and harder lines and his shoulders twitched to be spending their strength. Then Ellen would gather herself into the heart of his brawn and feel herself at the core of his power while the waves of it sundered the air and beat on the cracked fragments of the night, or she would lay her fingers on his face and his throat and brush lightly away their hate while she gathered outward in his being, one now with his smile and his embrace. As September passed she would sit wrapped in her old long coat, for the nights were chilled as the season of the first frost drew near. The hogs were taking on their fat daily, he said, for their corn was never stinted, and when they were sold he would market the hay and then all would be done. They would be free to go, sooner than the first of the year, perhaps before December. They would speak softly, the one to the other.

"Hear the dogs howl," she said, "off toward Stigall's it is. It's a lonesome sound, like the end of the world. Are you afeared of the end of the world?"

"I feel like I could pick up a hill or I could break open a mountain with my fist, and what call have I got to be afeared of a lonesome sound tonight? But it's a lonesome one."

"Lonesome like doves a-callen in trees to each other. Did you ever in your time hear a dove call and then another one answers?"

"I could pick up a hill with my strength."

"One asks the question, the doves, and then the other comes right along with the next call."

"I could pick up a hill or I could break open a rock with my fist."

"It's the sorrowfulest sound there is, as if it knowed what would come. Fair and sorrowful all together. It calls to mind good times that are lost and bad sorrowful ones, both gone together somehow."

"I take notice of doves a heap in spring. A dove call denotes spring is come for sure, and it's safe then to plant corn."

"And a dove has got one drop of human blood in its body somewheres, they say."

"By spring I aim to find some fields worth a man's strength. I'm plumb tired trafficken about, good land and bad as it comes. I aim to go a long piece from here."

"Once when I was a youngone Pappy went to Tennessee and I saw cotton in bloom. We saw cotton grow."

"I'm plumb tired a-trafficken about."

"Saw cotton a-growen. The people gathered it after a while in big baskets, piled up white."

284

"We'll go to some pretty country where the fields lay out fair and smooth. A little clump of woodland. Just enough to shade the cows at noon."

"Smooth pasture is a pretty sight in a country, rollen up and cows dotted here and yon over it, red shorthorns and white and dun."

"And you won't say 'I know a prettier country in Adair or in Shelby or Tennessee.' Mountains or not."

"Smooth pastures, we'll have."

"Whatever I can do to pleasure you, Ellie. The house like the way you want."

"And the house fixed up, the shutters mended and the porch don't leak. To sit on a Saturday when the work is done. A vine up over the chimney. Once I saw a far piece from here . . ."

"The stumps all pulled and the roots grubbed out."

"A parlor to sit back in when the busy season is over."

"The stumps pulled and the roots grubbed out, the plow to slip easy through the field dirt. No root snags to tear your very guts outen you."

"A parlor to sit back in cool when the busy season is done. Stairs to go up and down maybe."

"A real tobacco patch, not some little acre bed. Some land to set your back to proper."

"And when you stand in the door of the house you could see the fields roll off, green, some of them, and some plowed, and far off the knob hills with blue . . . Birds in the trees in the spring of the year. Springbirds and redbreasts . . ."

"And in the winter drive the crop to town and sell for a fair price, prime good burley leaf, twelve cents a pound."

ONE day in October, while Ellen sat on the stoop to shell the corn for the hens, Bell came along the road, returning from the store, her loosely-hung mouth working noisily over the taffy she had bought. There had been no one but the storekeeper at the store that day, she said, but the day before there had been others.

"Well, there was several there yester," she answered, being idly asked. "There was J. B. Tarbell and Mr. Lucas and Pius. Then there was Albert Wingate and a town man. J. B. Tarbell he didn't buy e'er thing. Then Ambrose Mudd was there and I set a right smart while and listened. Tarbell he said he seen a sight today as he taken a short cut through Wingate's to the creek. He says that-there Kent ain't right in his mind, he reckoned. Got his hogs away back half a mile from the house to fatten. Down in a gully, he said, hard to get to, and there he's got a whole parcel of hogs fenced up in a pen. Everybody laughed. Said he'd taken trouble to make a pen, hewed right outen the scrub cedars, and all the time he's got a good pen right up alongside the barn. Said Jasper Kent ain't right in his head. Then Albert said which gully was it, and Ambrose said that reminds him he needs a few ten-penny nails and to give him a dime's worthen. I set and listened a right smart while."

Ellen watched for Jasper to return from the shop toward St. Lucy where she knew that he had gone, but when he did not pass she thought he might have walked through the fields above the quarry. After they had eaten supper Ellen and Henry went toward the back of the farm, climbing the fence into Wingate's scrubby woodland. They went into the ravines and Ellen found the place where the swine had been penned; but the enclosure was broken down and the hogs were gone. They went slowly back onto the high

286

pasture and walked along the crest of the ridge above the stone pit, uncertainly going. Henry thought that Jasper had probably moved the hogs to some other place, and they studied out the possibilities of this, uneasy and troubled. They climbed the fence into Wingate's field and took Jasper's path toward the barn. The night was dark because of a clouded moon and the old house loomed very great in the midst of its shadows. They could hear great cries and oaths and sounds of scuffling within the house, where one light burned dimly behind a back window. After a while a door was flung open and Jasper stood in the light of the doorframe, and then two, Jasper and another, lunged upon each other, their cries and curses sounding loud through the open door. Then Jasper sprang at another's throat and bent him down with his hand, holding him back upon the floor, and the door was closed. After that there was a long time of quiet.

Ellen and Henry went back to the barnyard and hid behind the tall fence. The noises inside the house had fallen away, but now and then an undetermined figure would move slowly through the door of the house or across the grass beyond the well path. A shape would loom under the trees and go bending away toward the road. A strange footstep came from the barn, and then, after a long stillness, a running step came from the garden. Henry whispered to Ellen that they would go farther back, that they would go to the tall brush at the side of the pasture, away from the house, and Ellen followed him there. After they were in the thicket beyond the yard, Ellen saw Jasper come out of the barn carrying a lighted lantern, but at the door of the barn he set the lantern down and went away for a short time. When he came back he was leading a plow horse, and this he took inside, fastening it into a stall. He was slow in his movements, plodding wearily. "He thinks Albert went off," she whispered to Henry; "He thinks they're all gone off somewheres," and she was afraid for him, remembering the step in the garden. A few drops of rain began to fall, hanging rather in the quiet heavy air. She moved down the grove, no longer able to see the front of the barn, but she thought she might draw nearer from the back and call out to Jasper to come away. Suddenly the light, which she now saw through the cracks in the barn, went out, and noises of scuffling feet came from the barn and the barnyard, or Jasper's voice came, or another voice called back to him, broken and angry. They were struggling behind the crib, lost in the shadows of the buildings, their cuffs and blows and oaths coming sharply out of the dark, or there would be a still moment following a deeply breathed cry. Then Jasper came alone out of the side of the corncrib and stood a short space, and Ellen called out his name. As he came toward the thicket she spoke again, and Henry came down from the upper part of the grove. Then they walked off through the trees, Jasper wiping the sweat and blood from his face, still breathing hard from his exhaustion, walking unevenly. He carried a pistol in his hand.

"I took this-here away from Albert in that last fight," he said. "He had it on me but I took it away outen his hand. He was right on me with this-here when I was inside the barn with the lantern. I thought he'd gone for good and in he comes with the gun on me. But I cut off his wind. He's up there alongside the barn now. 'Are you done?' I said. I had a strangle hold on his throat. Say 'I'm done,' I said, and he said it when I eased on his wind a trifle."

They waited in the thicket until they saw Albert leave the barnlot and go toward the house. He bent low as he walked and kept in the shadows, or he crawled over the ground when he passed the bare yard near the back door. Then they went down the thicket toward Henry's field, climbing the fence hurriedly, but Jasper hid the pistol deep in the brush before he left Wingate land. Albert had driven away the hogs and had sold them to a trader, had taken them swiftly away in a wagon. Jasper declared that he was ruined unless Mrs. Wingate chose to make amends for her son's thieving. It was said that Tarbell had spied out the hogs and had helped Albert off with them. Now Albert had come back with four of his set to drink all night in the kitchen, but he, Jasper, had given two of them the weight of his fist in the face and he had cut off Albert's wind until he was blue when they fought inside the house and had made him say "Enough" behind the corncrib. He would have the law on his side, Henry said, but at this Jasper swore an oath and said that he was his own law. He told and retold his grievance, piling up his wrath, crazed by his loss, or he walked about thumping the field with his harsh steps, or he would sit sullenly staring at the ground or lift his head to listen across the field or peer toward Wingate's expectantly.

"You still got the hay and your share of the corn," Henry said.

He muttered at the ground, recounting his losses. He cursed the corn. They sat on the hill above the quarry for a time, Jasper muttering of his fights with Albert and renewing his curse upon his loss. Then some cry of fire came through the air and other cries calling of fire replied. A light grew along the edge of the sky and a great blaze shot up

289

from Wingate's out-buildings and Wingate's barn was burning, the hill standing strange and high because of the flames that topped it.

They went back into the brush where Ellen and Henry had stood before, and by this time many had gathered to fight the flames. The clatter of hoofs was constant on the road.

"It was that-there lantern," Jasper said. "That-there lantern caused it."

"I see you throw down the lantern to take the gun outen his hand," Henry said.

"Is that how you see it? That must 'a' been how it was. I taken the lantern to get together my stuff. I allowed to go sometime tonight and let old Mrs. Wingate send the hay money after me. I threw down the lantern to take away the gun outen his hand."

Henry said that he would go to help but that Jasper had better stay in hiding. The fire rose to its greatest volume with the burning of the straw which had been stored in the loft, but after this blast of flame the wooden members continued to burn. Jasper sat on the ground in the heart of the thicket, sullen and dazed, staring at the flames as they sank slowly away. From her place of watching Ellen saw the people carrying water to save the other buildings, and she told Jasper who were there, the Stigalls, the Donahues, the Whelens, Tarbell, and people from farther away. The strange light made menacing shapes stand out of the tree shadows and out of the ragged cornfield, long arms and stooped shoulders, bent spines and lurching knees moved through the grove, and Jasper sat on the ground mingling his oaths with his breath. He sat staring at the ground, and

290

from time to time would declare that he was a ruined man. "I burned up that-there barn," he whispered, "but it was unknowen to me. I never planned on such. I never. That-there lantern burned up the stable. But Albert, he crowded on me with the gun and I flung down the light and it was unknowen to me what went with it."

They went away into Henry's field again and walked off toward the high place above the quarry, their heads bowed and their steps weary.

"You couldn't know," Ellen said.

"I burned that-there barn," he muttered, over and over. "I burned it." He went crookedly along the brow of the pasture. They waited at the top of the zigzag path Ellen's cow took to descend beside the cliff, and after a while Henry came, for the fire had died away to a pink glow on the sky low in the northwest. People were saying that Jasper burned the barn in spite; this was the story that was freely told at the fire; Henry brought word of it when he came.

"Albert says you put the lantern into the straw," Henry said. "He said you set off the straw for spite-work."

They stood in the deep shadows at the foot of the cliff and pondered the disaster, searching it for its right and wrong.

"They say you put the horse in the barn on purpose to burn it. You went to the pasture and fetched in the horse and fastened it in. The horse burned in the barn."

"Old Don burned up."

"He says you put up the horse on purpose to burn it, says you put up old Don. Said every time he tried to put out the blaze you fought him offen it."

Jasper walked up and down along the base of the quarry, stumbling over the rocks. Ellen tried to push her knowing

291

through his knowing to try to see as he had seen and to penetrate the interval when she had gone down the thicket. Whatever he had done was necessary and inevitable in her thought. The light had shone through the chinks and then it had gone. She tried to assume his chaos of anger and his confusion and to bring her more ordered knowing to it. She walked beside him as he paced along the stones or she stood beside him if he leaned against the wall, or if he sat on the ground she kept near, her shoulder touching his shoulder.

"I see you throw down the light to take the gun," Henry said. "I says to myself, 'If Albert ain't got a gun drawed!' I see you throw away the lantern myself but I never thought about it again nor see where it go."

"You see it like that?" Jasper said, again and again, "you could see?"

"Yes, I see you bring the old horse in outen the pasture and then I see Albert come up with the gun drawed. Then I see you throw down the light to take a hold on Albert. That's how I see what come to pass."

"Seems like I never planned on it nohow," Jasper whispered. "No matter how 'twas."

"How could you ever explain to the judge how-come it was you set fire to the barn?" Henry said.

"I never yet see the day I'd be afeared of white-trash like Albert. I already gave him a gash with my fist, drawen blood, and I had a strangle grip on his neck and cut off his wind a spell. He won't want e'er other fight with me with fists, but he'll sneak in behind the law. You're right. He'll sneak in behind the law and get me in trouble and when a man's in jail what show has he got! The law, it'll eat up all I saved, to pay lawyers nohow. I was a plumb fool to tie up with folks that's in a family ruction, the old woman cheaten Albert and Albert, him a-tryen to get even. When a man's in jail what show has he got!"

"You might maybe 'a' sued old Mrs. Wingate to settle if it hadn't been for the barn."

"I'm plumb ruined. The corn burned. If I stay I'll get in jail, maybe Frankfort."

"You better go," Henry said. "Away off for a spell. You better go, boy. There's a difference how things look if you're in jail. People look at things different and look at what you done in a different way."

"Yes, I better go. I'll go far away."

"Law is a good thing but how you look at it makes a difference, and which side you're on, and how people look at what you done. Law is fine if you get on the good side of it. It's all owen to which party gets the law on his side. But once you get it on the contrary side, why you might see a sight of worry from it."

"Yes, I'll go. I better go," Jasper said.

He would find another place to work, far off toward the north somewhere, or toward the east. Some night he would come back for Ellen. He would take a little of the money, enough to keep him until he found a place, and Ellen would take care of the rest. The wind changed and the sky began to clear, the smoke from the burning settling down into the hollows and scenting the air with a sickening heaviness. The midnight bell at St. Lucy rang as they came out of the stubble field and stood by the stile under the ash tree. Then Ellen went to the house to get the money, bringing all of it and pressing it into his hand, for he might need more than he thought, she said. They stood for a little in the stubble at the edge of the field, Henry having drifted away to the house unmissed, and they looked at each other dumbly, gathering together the sum of the disaster.

"I'll find a place and I'll come back," he said, shuffling uneasily in the dust. "You'll know when I come."

"I'll know, oh yes, I'll know," she said.

"You'll know when I come." He walked nearer and laid his hand on the trunk of the tree, uncertainly, leaning a moment on his outstretched hand. "I better go now," he said. "I'll go." Then he went away across the field, his footsteps growing heavier as he stumbled into the lower ground beyond the barn and becoming a hollow thin tap as he went along the edge of the tobacco field.

THE people who went along the road would stop at the toll house door to ask questions or to talk of the fire, and the peddler, when his day came, stopped to bargain slowly with Nellie, lenient in his trade. They would ask if it were true that Kent had run off, as was reported over the country, and was it true that he had been in a fight with Albert Wingate. He would never be seen again, hair nor hide, was the peddler's prediction. Albert Wingate was of no account on his side, but Kent had been in trouble before. The bright sun shone through the clear October air, the hills brightly green, the leaves beginning to burn to yellow and red. Regina said that there were bushels of hickory nuts on the roadside trees, away beyond Stigall's lane, and that they would go to gather their baskets full some day if Ellen was of a mind to have a share and would come too, but on the day set to go for the nuts Ellen forgot the plan and was not at the

294

house when Regina stopped for her. Reminded, she changed her dress from the one she had been wearing in the farm and went absently with Regina. Kent had gone, Regina said, and it was unlikely that he would ever come back. He had best stay away, she thought, for, present, he would be in endless trouble with Albert or with some other of that set. He would stay away until everything blew over and people forgot and by that time he would be settled somewhere else. She herself never hoped to see him again. Did Ellen think he would come back? Ellen wanted to turn upon Regina with an angry cry and to tell her to shut up her idleness, that Jasper would come. The hard words hammered at her throat as she bent over the fallen nuts, but she was cautious, for her wish to save Jasper was greater than her anger. Martin Stigall stopped at the nut tree and helped break away the hulls, or he climbed the trees to knock down the nuts, helping fill both baskets. He talked with Regina about the fire and told how it happened that he had been one of the first to discover it. He said that Albert was a mean loafer and that he himself would hate to have any sort of traffic with him and that one could never do any business with him in any square way, but to burn a man's barn down for spite was a right serious matter, even if Albert were the man. He did not know, he said, whether it had been spite-work or not, but Albert said it had and Mrs. Wingate said the same. If Kent kept away it might all blow over in time, he thought, and Kent surely had sense enough to stay out of the country. He would never come back. In a case of this kind it was better, he said, to stay away from trouble.

Or Susie Whelen stopped on her way from church on Sunday, lingering in the toll house door. Her eyes were blue, and her wide full mouth found its smiles easily, and her step was intimate on the cabin floor, at home anywhere. Ellen went away to the back of the farm and walked on the stony hill above the quarry. She climbed the fence to Wingate's woods and went down into the far ravine where the swine pen was broken down, and there she saw Jasper's large footprint in the mud, his rough shoe with its broken heel printed in the wallow. He would come back. She went about her tasks with a strain pulling at her face and at her eyes, drawing inwardly. She milked the cow each night and morning or slopped the hogs or gave them their fattening corn, or dug the potatoes in the garden, speaking little, waiting. He would come back. When a week had passed the air of expectation went out of the house, and Nellie turned to sewing at a shirt for Henry, leaving Ellen's dress half sewed. Henry went away to the barn to work in the tobacco without comment, and the fire and Jasper's going were not talked of any more. Jasper's probable whereabouts fell out of the talk in the kitchen before the second week had passed. The chest was no longer locked for it was empty of any treasure. Its key lay on the floor and its lid stood open, waiting, and as she passed into her room and closed the door behind her to sit for an hour or more, her waiting breath whispered, "He will come." Or one day, angered at some other mishap, Nellie said: "He's gone for good. You'll never see a sight of him again."

"He's gone for good," she flung out from above the hissing grease of the stove. "Ne'er another sight of him will you see."

"I will see a sight of him," Ellen said from the door. "He'll come back like he said he would." She had seen then that Nellie was weeping.

She went up to the pit below the quarry wall and sat

for a time among the stones. He would come back, her mind continued to affirm, but a great fear stood in her body, for there was nothing to bring him back except herself. She arose from the ground and walked among the herbs of the field or she wandered to the edge of the pool, her mother's words still hammering at her ears. There was nothing now to bring him back except herself. The water from the autumn rains lay clear and bright over the white rocks, and she found herself searching in the water, peering down into it, hole after hole, walking away and returning to look again, hoping now that he had gone far to some remote country and was moving there in life, half knowing as she searched in the pools that her fear to see some water-soaked body lying among the stones was ill devised.

VIII

THE month turned warm for the Indian summer, but
the leaves fell. Henry said that he looked for an early
cold spell and that he would kill the hogs during the first
hard freeze. He told Ellen to look for the jars and pails to
hold the lard and to have all ready by the next cold weather,
and to hunt among the rubbish in the shed for the missing
piece of the sausage mill. Nellie worked with the sewing for
the winter, mending a quilt for her bed, the dress she had
begun for Ellen lying untouched in the basket behind the
door. She told Ellen that the winter would be cold and they
had better save the potatoes now while there were turnips in
plenty, for three to feed all winter would lower the potato
hill fast. No thought and no plan turned upon her going or

the return of Jasper, and for this Ellen set to each task assigned her with detached and slavish diligence. She knew each night how the moon stood in the sky and how it waned from the full. The dogs at Stigall's place howled now and then all through the night, and once Tarbell tapped at her window in the hour when the moon was setting, whispering sweet words, but she cursed him in her breath as she lay in her bed, her body denying him even while it quivered in its loneliness. In the bright light of the early morning the farms seemed to touch hands to affirm that which they had decided. The fire had ceased to be a wonder; it was talked of but little; it was finished. She went about through the bright mornings protesting, her inner "no" wrought into her every task, opposing dumbly such casual phrases as "before Jasper Kent went off for good," until she felt herself to be some living denial, some *no* set opposite the farms and all the people, Mrs. Donahue, Bell, Squire Stigall, Nellie, Henry, Susie Whelen, Pius, Martin Stigall, Tarbell, Kate Bannan, the peddler, the children throwing stones into the walnut tree to knock down nuts.

The key still lay on the floor where she had dropped it and the trunk stood open, for she made nothing ready for any hour of her own, her hours hanging suspended upon the lasting *no* that lay under her breath like a cry. She found the pails for the lard and washed them clean and set them in the sun to sweeten, and she searched long for the missing cog of the sausage mill. The Indian summer lingered, mild on the hilltops, cool at night in the hollows. One evening while she helped clear the supper away she lifted her head suddenly from her task and looked across the kitchen to Nellie who was turning from a shelf, her arm outstretched.

They stood thus for a moment staring at each other, their arms stayed, and then Nellie said, her eyes wide, her bent shoulders lifted as she listened:

"Jasper! I heared his whistle!"

Ellen had not needed to hear, for the fact had spoken directly to her mind in the instant. She took her cloak from the nail behind the door and went quickly out to the roadside where he waited as his custom had been before he went, as if he had never been gone. When they had greeted each other he told her that he had a place to work far to the northwest of the town, the farm owned by a man named Phillips, that he had worked for the past week filling the silo.

"I got the papers for us to wed, got the papers here in my pocket," he said as they stood near the step together. He took the paper from his coat and gave it into her hand and she felt its crisp edges, turning it about in the dim light. But presently his hate and anger rose in great tide, for he remembered his ruin and his losses.

"There's one thing I aim to do afore I go from here," he said. "J. B. Tarbell made my trouble with his busybody ways. I got the rest about him in town today, and he told a tale and made me out a lie. I aim to thresh his hide afore I leave this-here land for good. I aim to wipe up the road with his dirty rags and I don't mind if I break a bone or so, but I have no aim to kill. I wouldn't feel like myself if I went without I tended to his dirty bones and if I hurt more than I aim why that's his bad luck. He'll remember this-here night all his life and that's my aim. He's at McGill store now, that I know, and I aim to go there or I'll meet him on the road. All fair and in the open and no ambush, is what I aim. 'Take your time and get ready,' I'll say, 'but you got to

300

fight or get busted.' I aim to go to McGill store now. It's a thing I got to do. My hands are in a twitchet to get fast on his neck."

Ellen stood in his embrace, gathered to the heart of his hate and the heart of his power, feeling his sinews taut about her, knowing the strength of his anger. "Jasper, I don't want you to do e'er hurt to J. B. Tarbell," she said. "Jasper, I don't want it."

Her pleading increased his anger, for why should she turn from him to defend a lazy tramp? He intended to thresh the scoundrel for his share in the disaster. "If you, Ellen, take up for his dirty carcass I'll crack his skull wide open and tear his heart plumb outen him."

"I don't want you to do e'er hurt toward him, Jasper," she pled. "I ask you now."

He walked away toward the garden fence where he stood, bewildered in his rage, but Ellen followed him there and stood beside him. He moved away along the road saying, "I aim to do as I said."

But she walked slowly beside him, calling him by name, and she took his hand and slowed his steps although he walked uneasily on the road as a man half blind might go. She kept beside him and after a little she drew her arm through his and his arm bent to meet her touch even while his words were still muttered oaths and threats of violent hurt. His arm yielded to her touch and his fingers bent over her hand, and presently she began to talk of other things, of the trouble the mule had given that day, jumping the fence and wandering down the road. Mrs. Donahue had passed and had stopped to talk for a while. She had said that Susie Whelen was a bold girl with her eyes on Pius. She herself had been three days looking for the cog from the sausage mill, and she had tumbled out all the rubbish from the shed and had picked it over, scrap by scrap, and where did he think she had found the cog in the end? On the top of the high fence post over beside the barn, laid up there some time in somebody's hurry. Then she began to talk of themselves, taking more entire possession of his sense and his thought. The time had been long when he was away, and why had he not written her a letter? She had cried in the night thinking that something might have harmed him, and once she had gone, past midnight, to the hill above the quarry, and she had been ready at any hour of the day or the night to go with him, for he had only to call to her. All the others had said, "He's gone for good. You'll never see a sight of him again," and she told him of those who had said this in one way or another, recounting what each had said.

Then he was telling her that he had had never a thought of anything else but to come. She had led him out of the road onto the lane that went toward the south, and the way was soft underfoot, dry with autumn dust, and thus they went far, winding among the hills, now upward and now down. The night was lit only by the stars. She talked from time to time, murmuring responses to his endearments, or murmuring the idle thoughts and surmises of her mind, keeping him far from his anger and his losses.

"The high bushes over there would be sassafras, red and maybe green, over there in clumps on the far side of the fence. Milkweed gone to seed is in the air today. . . . There's St. Lucy's bell. Can you hear it? It seems far off, hardly to sound at all. Can you hear? . . . The road comes here to a gate but I cannot tell what is beyond. . . . We will fasten the gate after us or their cattle might stray . . ."

The fences had fallen away from the lane and now the road drifted out into an open space that rose slowly as they walked, a mere beaten path which the cattle took as they went back into remote pasturage. They could no longer hear the dogs bark at Whelen's or at Stigall's, for they had walked far. The moon was rising down on the edge of the sky, and after a while they came out onto an upland and passed among a few scattered trees beyond which the land fell away suddenly, making a precipice below, stones rising on the left in great blocks, the hard dolomite, that made a cliff above, so that they stood on a shelf at the side of a wall that reached above and fell below them. Their feet were among fallen leaves, and below they could see the treetops, lit by the misty light of the rising moon, or they sat on the ledge, looking out over some great vale, their sentences falling, now one and now the other, or slipping over each other as their thoughts ran eagerly.

"I saw such a rock-cliff as this once," she said, "and I said I would . . ."

"We could go to Phillips's place, and if we don't like there we will go further until we find the land we want."

"And I said that sometimes I would climb to the top and see far out, mountains maybe, or cities. . . ."

"I will kiss you another time. I could sit here the whole of enduren life. If any man ever offered you any insult or any dirt just name his name to me and I'll give the nasty skunk my fist in his jaw."

"And now I am on the top of a rock-cliff and I can see the hickory trees down past the rock shoulder, scaly trees you can see there."

"We will not part any more. Some fair country is what we'll find, and never part, me and you."

"If it would be light I could see a far piece I know, but now it is dark but for the little way the moon goes."

"Rich soil, all cleared, land worth a man's sweat. And all my work will be for you all day."

"Or if it is mountains to see, blue they'll be, with trees over the top. Or cities. Could we see a city from this-here place by day, do you reckon?"

"Your mouth is sweet to taste and your hand against my skin, sweet. I can hear your heart beat inside your shoulder and I can feel it beat in your throat."

"I used to think when I was a youngone, Jasper, that all the things you read about or hear came to pass in some country, all in one country somewheres. 'Oh, Mary go and call the cattle home,' and 'Lady Nancy died like it might be today,' all in one country."

"I'll buy you whatever you want, just name it to me. And we'll not see any more trouble, e'er a bit. Whatever you so desire."

"All in one country somewheres, as 'Bangum rode to the wild boar's den,' and 'He married Virgin Mary the queen of Galilee.' A country a far piece off."

"If it so be that it's in my power."

"Off past Tennessee somewheres."

"God knows, I would, Ellie."

"All in one country somewheres."

"God knows."

"But now I know better and know how the world is, a little."

"The moon makes your eyes big and deep and your mouth, it's sweet like honey drips."

"If day came we could maybe see as far as Phillips's and

see the house we'd have, our house where we will live. To live together and we'll never be lonesome."

"Your fingers on my neck and on my throat, they are soft, Ellie, like feathers, and they rub gentle-like up and down. . . ."

"Or our own house sometime, that belongs to us and all our own stock in the pastures. Three quick taps on the farm bell to call you to dinner. A rose to grow up over the chimney. A row of little flowers down to the gate."

"Your skin is soft under the coat, and warm, and you are a fair sight to see. Your mouth is sweet to taste and your hair is sweet, and under the cloak is sweet. . . ."

"A strong house that the wind couldn't shake and the rain couldn't beat into."

"I will slip your arms outen the cloak and fold it around you. And me and you will sleep wrapped in the cloak."

"And I will never leave you, Jasper, forever, but I will stay with you all my enduren life and I will work for you all my days."

"It's sweet under the cloak . . ."

She began to dream. Jasper was in her own body and in her mind, was but more of herself. She sank slowly down to the stone and to the leaves lying upon the stone, and the great bulk of the rock arose to take her. Dolomite stones shut over her and she was folded deeply into the inner being of the rock and she was strong with a strength to hold up mountains. Far away, as if it were beyond the earth, she heard a dog bark, a strange voice, none she had ever heard before, and long after that the sour odor of a fox came up from below the cliff and a little step went off in the leaves. Then Jasper whispered something that was lost in the substance of her dream, but she remembered a little of the sweet odor of the fox and the barking of the dog, but after a while they were mingled with Jasper's unheard whisper and went when she sank more deeply into the stone. After a while the stones were still again, and when she waked from sleeping daylight had come over the small valley that lay beyond the cliff. They walked down into the pasture and found a spring to drink from and then walked hand in hand across an old meadow, avoiding a house or a cabin, until they had gone far toward the south. The dust of the road was red and brown, hard crumbled dolomite, and the herbs were tall and slender, growing out of the red hard soil. They walked along the way for a time, but later they were taken into a wagon where they sat beside the driver and floated along with the rise and fall of the horses. The land was very still in the quiet of the early morning, and her dream held. Then they left the wagon at a road turning and walked again, passing through a lane, and so came to a house set near the road. The man who lived in the house said that he had a brother living not far away and that the morning was fine and that they were welcome. Inside the house three tall women moved about, and the things they set here and there made low rich sounds as they were placed, a cup or a plate on the table. The dream widened to take in three tall women who came and went. Then all of them left the room but one, and the door was closed, and Ellen was given a basin and a towel. She removed her dress and bathed, and later she tended her hair while the woman handed her the things as she needed them, and her dream widened again to take in the darkened room with its quiet and privacy and the fall of the water into the basin, Jasper not far away, outside the door with the men talking softly,

306

the voices rising and falling. When she had pinned up her hair all the others came into the room, filing in quietly, and she and Jasper were set at a table where the food had been placed, the three women standing about to see that nothing was wanting, and one food after another was ceremoniously passed, bread and meat and sweet drips and coffee.

It was a quiet country, for there was no bell to ring to tell the time of day. The man's brother came, brought by a child who had been sent to fetch him, and the woman who stood beside the table poured Ellen a cup of sweet milk, fresh and good. The child was beautiful with dark hair and a soft clinging dress of dark cotton cloth. Her hair lay against the sides of her head in free waves that drifted softly when she moved and was gathered into a little braid below. Her brown legs moved quickly and her feet touched the floor with little taps of sound, her movements free and un-designed, unpredicted. She stood beside the door or she ran softly toward the window, toward the table, toward one of the women, or she fingered a cup or a spoon or knelt on a chair, moment by moment. Her smile was very open and sweet. Then they went, all, into the outer room and stood about the walls. Ellen's eyes followed the child as she slipped in unpremeditated motions from place to place or stood in unfixed quiet. The room became very still as Ellen and Jasper stood beside the man, the brother who had been brought; or the man faced them, and joining their hands, said ceremonial words. His face was thin and set with ceremony, his hands moving rigidly over the words or settling down in hard firm finality over the said word, fixed and done. Fixed forever, pronounced, finished, said and un-revoked, his words flowed through the great hardness of his voice, a groundwork on which to lean, a foundation beneath a foundation, the framework of the house set and fixed in timbers and pinned together with fine strong wedges of trimmed hard wood. His voice trembled a little with its own fixity and hardness, but it erected a strong tower. In the end he made a prayer for herself and Jasper, and he gave her a paper on which their names were written. The women shook her hand, and then the men came, their handshakes reserved and ceremonious. The child stood beside the wall, her gaze light and aloof, or she tapped her shoulder softly against the door or touched the latch, her look free and her way unhampered, and the beauty of her look came about Ellen as she gave her hand to the men.

Jasper talked with one of the women apart and later with one of the men, and he gave them money from that which he had. Ellen was sitting on one of the chairs beside the wall with the other women sitting near, while the voices of the men came through the open door. The women talked, but Ellen heard the up and down of their voices but faintly and forgot their sayings when they were said. The child walked nearer, fingering the wall with little nut-stained fingers, or she sat gravely on the chair beside the door, or she walked near to Ellen's chair, but Ellen's hands lay still in her lap. The child's little dress hung softly about her knees, its small sleeves a tender jest, a loving pretense, sleeves turned in their littleness to something precious and fine. Then Ellen asked her name and one of the women said that it was Melindy and that she was six years old. The sun flooded in at the window, having left the door, and after a little one of the women brought Ellen a hat which she put on over the coils of her hair, and another brought her cloak which she put on, Jasper standing beside her. There was a vehicle before the gate. Then Jasper wrote a letter to Henry and Nellie, and when he had sealed it, he climbed with Ellen into the rear seat of the wagon, one of the men sitting in the front to drive. One of the women had given them a package of sugar bread and this was set under the front seat, and they drove away.

SOME little pointed birds in a flock twitted from branch to branch in the sun, and the road went up a hilltop and lay along a ridge where a woman standing by a great gate stopped to watch them pass, her hand stayed on the latch pin. A woman sat before the door of her house among withering hollyhock stems where the road fell gently down to the valley again, and beside the bridge a kingfisher flew from a limb and darted behind the white of a plane tree, the departure of the bird standing out upon the air as something never seen before by man. Ellen looked at her hands as they lay before the folds of her cloak, her hands acutely recognized and the cloak, hardly her own, folded strangely about her, her body stilled and muffled under the strangeness of the old cloak and the kindness of Jasper whose hand touched her sleeve. The day lay outstretched laterally, no marks upon it, and she greeted herself intently. Sometimes Jasper held her hand and then the edge of her sleeve touched the worn edge of his and in that moment became more real. The strange road went over hills and through valleys, winding between farms or stretching along ridges, the dust red or sandy, or Jasper leaned nearer to kiss her as they passed before a grapevined tree and a great hawk flew over with wide frayed wings. A smoke lay along the sky in a long design, and then a band of color, gray and dull purple, gathered, and the town began to appear beneath the smoke. Many travelers were met in wagons or carriages. Then the old driver turned the horses down a long hill into the town, the white stones of the graves off to the right spreading about widely in the sun. The houses seemed very near together. The railroad was a black path leading straight away in a long strange line that turned outward from the hill, and beyond the railroad came the street with store windows, where wagons were drawn up to the curb or went quickly by. They passed through the court square without a stop, but Ellen saw the red wall of the courthouse and the gray wall of the jail. Then Jasper was pointing back to the jail and she saw its oblong windows set with one iron bar.

"That-there second window. I tried all night to get outen there, but the bar was fast. Then the next night the jailor he locked me inside a cage, and every night after."

The fear of the jail settled on Ellen for a space as they went quickly up the hill leading from the town, going north, and she wondered what stood in Jasper's mind as his eyes stared at the moving fencerow and what as they turned to the floor of the wagon or fixed upon the back of the driver. She noticed that the man on the seat before them was more than old, a being now the black of whose hair was thickly grizzled where it brushed against his coat collar and his neck was weathered and seamed, the thick skin burnt with age, and what did he have and what was his wish about the world? The road was stony beyond the town and a great flock of grackles were gathering above a thin wood, as if it were evening.

"The other place, Frankfort, is bigger," Jasper said. "A wall around it, they say. Striped clothes. I knowed a man got in trouble over a horse and got sent up for three year.

His own horse got its foot hung in a bridge that ought to 'a' been mended. It was the road overseer's fault the bridge was in a bad fix, or the magistrate's, one. Nohow his horse had to be killed. Then along came a stray that hung around a week and no owner, and he, the man that lost his horse in the bad bridge, he took the stray to pay himself back for the filly he lost. He said it was the magistrate's fault the bridge was all busted. The court gave him three year. A wall all around, he said. Striped clothes and you sleep in a cage made outen iron. Gray clothes after a while if you behave. He said he didn't mind so much after he got over the first, but right at first he thought he'd go outen his head, he said. I took notice that people never forgot he'd been there. Good careful man, after he got back—when I knowed the man— but I see people always remember. He said the man in the next cage to his'n killed his wife away back, fifteen or twenty year back. Was in for life. Said the man wouldn't talk about what he done. Said he was gentle as a lamb; looked like he wouldn't harm a flea, but it was true he'd killed her."

The road fell away toward the left, dipping into a valley, and the wheels of the wagon made a steady iron clatter on the gravel and the stones, and she thought of herself in the vague being she had formerly held, seen going through dim settled routines, going to the field, gathering in the hens, caring if there were four eggs or six in the nests. The old being rose woodenly in the morning and went evenly about through a set day, morning and night, heat and cold, going out and coming in, but this was now seen but dimly as something surpassed and rejected, and she gathered into a great mass that looked cunningly inward and spread outward in a vast determination: she would defend Jasper from every harm. A man had killed his wife long ago, and now he

311

seemed scarcely to remember it, as if he had never done the thing, for one went out of one life into another and the old life fell away. They moved along the road as it unwound to meet them, projecting themselves through rolling fields, and she entered the land far in advance of her recognition of its way, on the forefront of their going, but the land became real as it stretched out beside them and behind their wheels. She would defend Jasper. It was for this that she penetrated a strange land, for this her great strength arose and renewed itself at each instant.

They had eaten the sugar bread and night had come. The wagon moved slowly along in the unreality of the dark between faint rows of fence and trees, or it droned out upon a free upland or sank into cool hollows. Ellen knew the steps of the horses, the roan one from the black, and Jasper was a warmth beside her, gathering into a kindness that broke into endearments or rested in quiet. Or they left the highway and went unevenly through a lane and over a farm way, and Jasper walked ahead in the dark to lead the horses. Then she left the wagon and waited in the dark while Jasper said a few words to the driver and sent him back on his way.

They were inside the house, lighting a dim lamp that sat on a table. There were four things to be seen in the dim light of the lamp, a bed, a chair, a stove, and a table, but each moment of the room stood out sharp and intense. The man who owned the farm had promised to build another room to the house before spring, and Jasper took her to the door and pointed out the fields as they lay stretched forth in the dark, invisible, the tobacco barn on the hill, unseen, the way to the spring, the path to the stables, the silo, the thicket, all dark. Jasper built a fire in the stove and brought food to cook and cool water from the spring, walking quickly back and forth. He had bought some cups and plates at the store. They worked hurriedly to catch up with their own swift life and to overtake the intense moments that stood out luminously between the walls of the cabin. She put the flour into the tray and sifted it with the soda and the salt, or she stirred in the sour milk with her fingers and shaped the dough, or Jasper held her close to his body, and she felt the wide limits of her dream reach far into the dark to take up the fields, the silo, the barns, the spring, and the path.

THE days were hazy with smoke-filled air and the mornings cold with frost. Jasper worked at the barns where the to-bacco was housed or he plowed the land for rye and wheat, and when the food was cooked Ellen would stand in the door of the house to watch for him until he would gather into the path and come nearer, at first a spot moving in the path, a moving shape, a coming voice, and her beauty would grow with his coming until it would meet him full-blown as he stepped through the door; or two women would come to sit a short while through the afternoon, Hester and Marthy Shuck. Their talk would fall idly across the cool hours of the December days, purposeless but gathering weight and intent as it filled the time until Jasper came and as it filled the space about her with an idle neighborly kindness, and she thought often in the intervals of their talk, hearing some unfamiliar name spoken, that she would name her child Melissy. She made a little dress for it in the secret and quiet hours of the mid-morning, hiding the dress away in the trunk when she heard the women coming on the path. The farmer paid Jasper his wages every Saturday and with the money they bought their supplies at the store at the road crossing, two miles away, down the path to the barns and then out onto the highroad. They would walk there in the dusk and whisper at the counter over the spending of a coin; was there lard? was there soap in plenty? was there oil? or she would ask for a bit of flannel, two yards perhaps, or a bit of white print, whispering her want to the merchant, "A little something I needed," she would say to Jasper, "A small something I wanted for myself." But he knew at last why she bought these small bits of cloth and gave her five dollars into her hand, knew as they leaned together at the counter, and gave her five of the dollars although there was little left. They carried the packages home through the raw air of the early evening and cooked themselves a generous supper to reward their happiness.

Sometimes Bill Shuck and Marthy, his wife, would come to sit through the evening, Marthy a little sly, leading one to tell more than one had meant by undervaluing her own and bidding for sympathy. When they came the little house would seem about to split apart with their songs, Jasper's great voice playing over Bill's in a tussle of singing, a wrestle of rough-handled words and great thundering embellishments that grappled down in the bass notes and went scuffling off into their rumbling trebles, or Ellen and Marthy would sing and their song would come like a small plaintive crying after that of the men. The farmer said that he did not intend to build another room to the house; lumber was too high and work too dear; they could make out with what they had and if they did not like it they could go where they could do better. He cried out this decision in the stripping room one day where Jasper worked with the other men.

Then a letter came to their letterbox that cut into the inner fiber of Ellen's new life and made it more intense with purpose. She carried the letter across the field to Jasper where he worked at the fences and they read it together in the crisp cold. It was a summons from Squire Stigall for Jasper to appear before his court to be questioned in an incendiary investigation. Ellen put the white cloth she had been sewing deep in the trunk and they pondered the letter together even while their work lay apart, while Jasper mended the fences and she prepared their food in the cabin, or they pondered it while they slept or while they sat through the short evenings. The farmer came down to the cabin one morning angry over the straying of a pig which had escaped through a vent in the fence. He came without ceremony, thumping with his whip on the wall of the house, not troubling to knock at the door. The angry blow had seemed of a strength fit to burst the thin wall, and Ellen went out of the house to listen to his anger over the broken fence which he thought Jasper should have discovered. Ellen told him that Jasper's work lay on the distant side of the farm, a fact which he knew quite well, told him mildly because of her remoteness from his anger and because of the deep-running currents of her life which held him in but very little place. She folded her hands under her arms to warm them as she stood, indifferent, beside the small doorway. She looked at the blue of the sky or she let her gaze flow swiftly down the long path Jasper would take in coming, her look speeding swiftly to the end of it where it fell away among the barns. She felt the vigor of her being as she stood in the sharp cold of the morning where all tender living things were withered, herself in her richness and vigor the most living thing in the whole sight, her skin kindled by the cold, her eyes bright, the child within her hidden yet but alive, her throat, her step, her standing figure even and firm. She listened to the farmer's waning annoyance as he straightened the wires of the fence and laced in the pickets. She found two missing boards thrown aside among the brush and these she brought while he worked at the gap which he closed finally in easy good humor, eager to talk and to make a joke of the mishap, and his smile was intimate and kindly as if the broken fence were a bit of a secret they held together. He was middle-aged and full of life in his own kind, his hand firm on the fencewires, his face pink under his half-shaven scattered beard. Then he looked at the little house from all sides and said that he had laid off to build another room but that work was always pressing in another quarter, and she pointed out the spot where she and Jasper would like the addition built, and life ran higher and fuller in his being and poured out in a desire to assist life.

"You must have that room," he said. "You just point-blank need it, I know quite well."

Bill Shuck's sister, Hester Shuck, came and went from time to time, a black-eyed girl with wide shoulders and deep hips, drowsy-eyed and quick to laugh. She was free to come and go, uncommitted. Sometimes she stayed with Bill and Marthy for many weeks, or then she would go and work for some farmer's wife in hog-killing season or harvest time. She would ask Ellen questions of Jasper or of herself, questions that were their own answers, or she would have obscene stories to tell. Ellen kept her secret sewing locked in the trunk, safe from Hester's shifting eyes that drowsed easily and were amused at anything, and she kept Jasper's danger in secret likewise, setting her whole strength against it. She began to regather in mind bits of songs and stories, keeping them to sing and tell for the child, or when Nellie came or Henry she would ask about their mothers and fathers, as far back as they knew, which was only a little way. The farmer came again, knocking softly on the door. There would be a carpenter to begin building the room the following week, he said, and he lingered to ask her opinion of this plan or that. She could have a garden in the spring, he said; Jasper could fence off a little of the pasture, taking a day from the work of the farm any time he found convenient. Then Jasper borrowed a horse from him and rode away on the morning of the trial, going soon after daylight. In two hours or three he would be in the St. Lucy country, stopping at Squire Stigall's door, and she could see in her mind the Stigall gate, on the road beyond Wingate's, far down the long stretch of road where the wagons died away slowly, but she could not divine what would pass inside the house. Men would come, hitching their horses to the gate, and Henry would come to testify. He would hold up his right hand and swear that his words would be the truth, and she pondered a little at how a thing could be true and untrue, both at once, but this eluded her and she was left searching for Squire Stigall until he became clear in a picture, his high shoulders, his slow steps, his carefully spoken words that labored for exactness in any statement. "Did you or e'er one of yours see or hear a fifty pound shoat stray by today, shoat with a white band across its shoulder and a little white on its nose, fifty or fifty-five pound shoat?" He had asked this once at the toll house.

She watched the path toward the barn far into the

317

twilight and after the dusk had arisen, and then Jasper's step across the pasture stumping wearily on the uneven turf, the click of the gate, his foot at the door. He drank a long draught of water at the bucket and dropped his hat on the floor, his hand inert, or he sat at the table and ate hungrily, asking for more bread, calling shortly for more meat, his hunger sullen. He breathed heavily over his plate, sitting with his chest hanging over the table, leaning on the board, or if he dropped a crust to the floor he did not trouble to pick it up; tired to the core. "I'll take water," he said, and Ellen brought him the gourd full of the water and he drank deeply again. Squire Stigall had passed the matter on to the Grand Jury and that body would meet late in the spring. A dozen people had come to the trial to be questioned and they had remembered any little thing he had ever said and all that had happened was turned this way and that.

She set herself to save Jasper for it was her will that Jasper must not go. Whatever eggs were in the nest were for that purpose and the boiling of the pot over the fire was for that intent and the seeds she dropped in the garden row. Another letter came; the Grand Jury had found an indictment and Jasper would have to go to the court. He would have to give a bond and she thought of that and talked of it to the farmer. Then she asked the farmer to sign the bond. At the time of the May court Jasper went to the town and there he found that he must have a lawyer to defend him. Then the lawyer told the judge that Jasper was not ready with his defense and there was whispering to and fro. The judge saw that they were unready and he set the case for the October court. Hadn't he, Jasper Kent, known that he would have to have a lawyer? Unless he intended to defend himself, and a laugh went over the court at this. There was more whispering back and forth. "But Joe Phillips is on his bond," was said, "and Joe Phillips is a good man, his farm worth anyhow twenty thousand dollars." "Oh, yes, he's a good man." By the end of the week Jasper had told Ellen all that had happened in the court, a little now and a little then.

ONE night there came a call outside and a knock at the step, and, the door opened, a strange man stood beyond the doorframe, a tall man with heavy shoulders. Then Jasper called him by name, saying, "Well, Nathan, I vum!" and brought him over the threshold, and from their talk Ellen knew that he was a friend of Jasper's from up in the Pike country. Once in a lull in their conversation Jasper nodded his head toward her with dignity and said, "That's my wife," and the man replied, "I allowed so; I allowed she was your woman." "Well, Nathan, I vum!" Jasper would say, trying to hold afresh the idea of his friend's presence. "I came to see if I could be any help," Nathan had said soon after entering, "I heared you was maybe in for a little trouble." From time to time Ellen heard noises outside, footsteps muffled and a low voice, but she said nothing. Jasper told that the trial was set for October and told a little of what the lawyer advised, speaking with reticence but speaking straightforwardly, a clear story.

"Is somebody along with you?" Jasper asked.

"A couple of men I fetched along," Nathan said, "and Tom. You remember Tom."

They sat in silence after that until Ellen could hear the small clock on the shelf as it ticked. The man was older than Jasper by a few years and his dark hair was slightly touched with gray. His hands were large and strong and they hung idly folded between his knees.

"If you-all need any help, now," he said, "we wouldn't want, Tom and me, for you to think you lacked a friend or maybe two or three. Anything a strong man can do. Yes, we just said maybe we'd go."

After that they sat in silence for a while again, each man meditating the thought as it stood in his mind. Then Nathan arose and opened the door, waiting a moment as he leaned out into the dark. Two other shapes appeared rising on the steps, a large red-faced man and a strong gaunt boy of twenty or so. As they came into the room another followed and stood at the door, keeping back within the shadow. Jasper greeted the florid man as Tom and brought him to a seat, but the other stood by the door, twirling his hat about in his hand, some friend of Nathan's. Then they were all still for a time, or someone would make a question about some casual or seemingly trivial thing, but every speech counted in their communion. Jasper was moved that he had friends who had come. Ellen saw this in his stiff voice and his silence. She saw it in his question of the way.

"It's nigh twenty mile to where you come from. How far is it now from Pike's to where you turn off?"

"We taken the new road at Sidney's old place. About sixteen mile, it is to the road crossen. Eighteen in all I reckon."

"Around eighteen," Tom said. "I'd call hit eighteen."

"Is the road good now?" Jasper asked.

"Right good a piece of the way. New worked."

"You came a-horseback?" Jasper said. He was moved almost beyond speech by this expression of loyalty. "A-horseback I reckon."

"Yes, we rode our critters. Tom, he says to me, 'I reckon you heared Jasper Kent is in trouble.' We asked in town on court day where you live now and bye and bye Tom he finds a man that knows."

"Is the road worked all the way to Pike's now?" Jasper asked.

"All the way. A right fair road hit is in good weather."

They could feel Jasper's gratitude and it repaid them for the long journey they had taken. Acknowledged gratitude loosened Tom's speech so that he talked to great length of the roads, the ways to go, the short cuts one could make in a dry season. He disputed a little with Nathan as to which of two ways was shortest, but joined him heartily again in computing another distance. Their long dialogue made a solution in which Jasper's emotion could dissolve itself. When they were quiet again Jasper said:

"I'm right proud, right proud to know you-all thought to come."

"We thought you might maybe need a man or so," Tom said.

They sat a little while longer, stilled now for all had been said. Then Nathan said that they would go, and with a nod to her he went out at the doorway. Tom followed, nodding even more meagerly, and the young man inclined his head faintly in her direction as he went, looking at the ground. Jasper left the door open as long as their horses could be heard going back across the pasture.

ELLEN laid her infant in the cradle which Marthy Shuck loaned her. He was a serious creature, lying asleep nearly

321

all the day, a good baby, Marthy said, and Ellen left him to his solemn goodness while she churned the milk and swept the floors and planted the late garden. Marthy Shuck had helped her with the birth of the child. It, the infant, was a joke to Jasper, for its littleness brought from him great roars of mirth and subdued oaths, pledges of a joyous paternity. "Dadburn his little hide! Come to your Pappy. God knows! Look at it! God knows!"

They named the child Henry John. Jasper laid all his savings in Ellen's hand and told her to get the child everything he would need. He did not aim that his child should want some small thing and not have it, lawyer or no lawyer, for God knew he was a little thing, just look at him! Then Ellen said she would get Job Tucker to make a cradle, for Job could work in wood like a master hand, and they could send Marthy's cradle back. She sang to the child in the quiet of the cabin, morning and afternoon, song after song, from the first she had heard Nellie sing to the new songs Marthy Shuck had. Or she would stop as she held the child in her arms, dropping the song half-sung, and look at his flesh, at his eyes, his hair, his motions, another being that he was, apart from her and beyond her reach, and what did he want in life? What would Henry John want beyond what she wanted, and how could he want differently or more? She would try to lean down into his being and ask what did he want, to ask his soft neck and his crumpled legs, to ask his little round belly. She spent the money sparingly for the cradle, bargaining with Job Tucker until he lowered his price, saving the rest of the money for Jasper against the time of the trial. She tried to look beyond that time and to see them going about their ways, but every hour now pointed toward the week in October when the court would convene, and if Joe Phillips had signed to keep Jasper from having to lie in jail during the months before the trial, she had asked him to sign and he had done so after a day of thinking. If Jasper ran away the farmer would forfeit a thousand dollars, but Jasper would not run away without her, she thought, and it was she who had asked Phillips to sign. Sometimes she thought, turning about among the tasks in the cabin, that Jasper might think to run away as being the easiest course, or she would wonder if Jasper so thought, or she would look at him as he came in at the door with the stovewood in his arms, and the swift thought would arise. Then he would lean over the cradle and take Henry John, trundling out his great endearments, until the child knew him and beat his arms and legs in the air, quivering with delight because he was being taken. Henry would come, bringing Nellie, and then there would be a great noise in the cabin, for Henry would sing a loud song while he jolted Henry John in a chair, and Ellen would forget every other way but the way of that day and she would give them a basket filled with vegetables from her garden patch when they left or she would tell Nellie to keep the heifer but that she would take away her own little cow that Mr. Al gave her when it brought milk again. She was happy to be able to give gifts.

The time came when the trial was over and the anxious days past, but the lawyer was still to pay, fifty dollars in all, and Joe Phillips, the farmer, surety for the debt. Henry had been Jasper's witness, and what Henry had seen and sworn to became the way of what had been although Albert and three of his friends had told differently and Mrs. Wingate herself. But what Henry had seen was finally established as true. The trial had lasted two days, but on the second day

323

the farmer had come across the field to tell her that Jasper was cleared, for he had heard by the telephone soon after the verdict was given. Later Jasper came, noisy and merry at being released from suspicion, but reticent and unwilling to talk, as if he were weary of it.

Jasper was no longer in danger now of being taken away, and the prison where the men wore striped clothes and slept in cells of iron stood up clearly in her mind now as something one could look at without a sickening pang of fear. It grew sharper in line as her emotion withdrew from it, coldly pictured and apart, fading daily. The winter passed and spring came again, a spring of eager living in the pastures, in the cabin, eager living up in the plum thicket where the loud birds sang at early morning. There would be another child before the year was done. Slowly they were paying the lawyer, all that could be spared, Joe Phillips trusting them with the debt, giving them their time. Her body was strong now and the blood ran high in her cheeks and in her warm strong hands.

THE child was a girl and they named her Nannie because Jasper favored that name, his own mother having been called by it. The girl child lay more quietly than the boy had lain, and Jasper delighted in her even more and he softened his way to her as if he considered that she was of the woman kind, even as she lay in the cradle. Ellen would look on from the door, pleased to see his gallantry flowering anew, to see him become a wooer as he took her tiny body from the pillow, addressing her with chivalrous admiration. "God knows! Teach her old Pap to dance, she will. First four forward and the grand right and left! God knows! Miss Nannie Kent, could I have the compliments of this-here next dance? Miss Nannie? Could I have the pleasure of the compliments? Swing your partners! Stand around, you-all, stand aside. Here comes Miss Nannie. God knows! Look at it!"

He would take Hen to fish with him in the creek although Hen was but little over two years old and had to be carried. "The sign, she's right in the foot, Hen, and the fish is bound to bite, so come along." He would take Hen as if he were a half-grown boy or a man, giving him a fish pole of his own, finding a delight in his companionship. The lawyer was paid now and Joe Phillips no longer stood on Jasper's note for anything. Jasper stood clear in the sight of the law, but one or two remembered, perhaps, that he had been tried on a felonious charge, or one or two, here and there, in the St. Lucy country, still thought him guilty and Henry overheard him spoken of by some careless tongue as "the man who burned down Wingate's barn." Ellen had brought her cow from St. Lucy, Henry having driven it slowly across the country in midwinter, and by spring it had given them a heifer calf which, at weaning time, Ellen sold to the trader for twenty dollars, the last of the money needed to pay the lawyer's charge. The cow and a few hens were Ellen's property, and Joe Phillips gave her grape cuttings to plant and a little cherry tree. Nannie could walk now, and Hen could climb in the low trees of the plum thicket. The land about became more actual, hills and lowlands, trees and streams and hollows, yellow soil and dark, rocky roads and bushy paths. East to the crossroads and there was the little farm where Mrs. Sadley lived, three miles to go. North, and there was the farmhouse, big and white, where Joe Phillips and his wife and his two boys stayed. Beyond came the road going outward toward the schoolhouse and the cabin of Bill Shuck and Marthy and their two or three children. The land was real and their wants were real, bread and meat and clothing, sleep and firewood, the cow to milk and the chickens to tend. The wages Jasper had were scarcely enough, but real, money to earn and to spend, over and over. It came upon her one day when Nannie was two years old that the land was more real, more hard and actual, stone for stone and soil for soil, more than it had been when she first came there. Somewhere back a way it had become so, and somewhere likewise money had become money, twenty-five cents to make a quarter, and all buying little enough.

TWENTY-FIVE cents to make a quarter or ten cents to make a dime, and either buying little enough, and she slipped the coins through her fingers as they lay on the shelf. Jasper was clear of the law, but one or two had frankly thought him guilty, Henry had confided to her. She would sometimes glance at his great face as he came into the doorway and a quick thought would arise, and a question. Or she would see him lift some great weight, as a butchered hog, throwing it into a wagon, his sinews taut and his legs strong arched and groined, or see him stand relaxed after the feat, lighting his pipe to ease himself.

He said that he would go to another place, to a place where he could grow tobacco on a sharing plan, which was not the way Phillips used. He told Phillips that he would go and another man was hired in his place, but in the end he was forced to take work where he received mere hire, for there was a small crop to be grown that year and places of any sort were hard to find. Ellen pictured a place vaguely set among trees, the consummation of some deeply-lying dream, a house looking toward some wide valley. Jasper was free of the law now and it was time they began to be, to realize, to find the truth of their old wish in a physical fact, to find it set at their hand. Good land lying out smooth, a little clump of woodland, just enough to shade the cows at noon, a house fixed, the roof mended, a porch to sit on when the labor was done; these were her promise. When Jasper said that they would leave Phillips her mind leaped to the better land they would find, their farm sometime, perhaps, but at any rate some place nearer their need and wish. She made many vague pictures of a house on a green hill, a well with a bright new pump, the handle easy to lift, the water coolly flowing. Some vague better haunted her through the eagerness of her going preparations, and her fervor to be gone built cunningly about her imagined new abode.

They came to the place at mid-afternoon. The house was built starkly on the top of a stony hill in a waste place that would not serve for farming. The farmer, Byron Goddard, motioned them toward the cabin with a careless gesture, gave a few confused orders to Jasper, and rode away through the farm swiftly on his great horse. There were two rooms to the cabin. A few thin cedar trees grew on the hillside below the door.

Ellen carried the water from a spring in the valley below and often the way seemed so steep to climb that she would spare the water grudgingly and wash Hen and Nannie in the same pan. The stony earth in the garden behind the house yielded little in return for her work there. From the hilltop she could see the green fields of the farm roll away toward the creek and she envied them their growth and hated them that her own patch burnt in the sun. She wanted to ask Goddard for a bit of the valley, a mere strip at the foot of the hill, to use for a garden, but Jasper forbade her to. do this. "You stay up here on this-here hill," he said, "where we belong now." The contention became a permanent one and she was forbidden over and over. "Byron Goddard, he's got no time for you, now," Jasper said. "He'd ride right over you, Ellie, and never see. Byron Goddard, he's not Joe Phillips. Ask no favors, we will."

Jasper worked all day in the rich bottom fields where the crops teemed under the warm and abundant summer. From time to time his song would arise from the rich plowing or harvesting. The richness of Goddard's yields, his prancing blooded horses and quick trainers, his elegant barns and his training track, all made a show which captivated his men until they took all delight in the pageant, forgetting themselves. Ellen looked with hate upon the rich meadow that had taken Jasper's zeal until his pride was in telling over and over the abundance of its cuttings. Another child was born during the summer and this they named Joe in honor of Mr. Phillips.

Hen and Nannie wore their clothes to rags but Ellen kept them to the hillside and visitors seldom came there. Her garden burnt in the sun for the shallow soil quickly gave up its moisture, and Jasper laughed at her tomato vines and her withering beans. "We got to wait here a spell," he said, "whe'r we want to or not." Or he would say, "Afterwhile . . ." Goddard was slow to pay his hands, easy and light with their wages, gone from the farm on pay day as often as not and had no definite times for settlements. When

328

Jasper came from work he would bring the meat to cook, fetched from Goddard's smokehouse, or he would bring the flour or the meal or the sugar from the store, bought in small packages, scarcely more than a day's need supplied at a time. Sometimes Ellen had a few eggs to trade, so few that she would remember Bell as she walked along the highway and feel that Bell's stony gaze had come to her eyes.

One Sunday Jasper borrowed a wagon from one of the barns and took Ellen and the children riding over the field roads, even into neighboring land, up and down well-made ways that lay among fertile prospects, the harness streaming and jingling, beating lightly on the backs of the horses. Jasper pointed out the fields, taking a great pleasure and a pride in his labor, urging Ellen to look, showing Hen this and that. In the end they stopped at the stables to see the great show stallion which only the trainer was let ride. They looked at his sleek brown flesh that so throbbed with life that every morsel of it seemed a separate living thing. A stable man was leading him before the door, letting him drink at the smooth concrete watering trough where a jet of water fell, cool and leisured. Jasper stood before the great beast with pride and joy in his eyes, his feet wide apart, talking familiarly with the groom, and Ellen hated the neat boots on the horse's ankles and she hated Jasper's deep concern with the groom over the set of the horse's left fore shoe. Riding homeward they stopped at the creek where Hen caught a brightly-mottled red water animal, a brook salamander, a creature for which they had no name, but which filled Ellen and Hen with amazement and delight. Hen found a broken pail in the brook sand and, filling this with water, he made the creature a nest of fine moss at the bottom, and all the way homeward they watched the animal glide about in its small basin and they shouted and sang in their delight, or Ellen and Jasper sang, turn and turn about, each trying to remember a song the other had not heard.

THERE were other tenants living up and down the creek, some of the houses on the stony ridge where the creek bottom met the upland. Sometimes a woman would come up Ellen's hill to sit awhile, or Ellen would go to the church in the maple grove, taking Hen. Then she sat among the tenant women who gathered near the rear of the church, and she would listen to their murmur or speak a little herself. The wives of the farmers would sit at the front talking through the waiting hour. Ellen knew the names of those in her group and where each one lived. They would talk quietly as if half afraid of their own voices. Later when the service began all would sing and then the preacher would exhort the world to greater goodness and truth. Ellen would walk back in the dry after-hour, Hen running beside her. Once walking home from the church with Hen at her side, her feet weary of the road and her dull dress lying down skimply under her eyes, she remembered two years back and recalled that Joe Phillips had looked at her in ways that showed that he liked her and that he liked the sound of her voice, and that he listened to her words, whatever they were. He had liked to come to her house and his face had lightened when he looked at her as if he thought her pretty to see, and once he had said to Hen, "He's a pretty boy; he looks like his Mammy." Or, sitting waiting in the doorway, feeling a great weariness with her slow days, she would remember this again, and at the spring, before she dipped her bucket into the pool, she would lean over it to look at her face and search in the pool for any affirmation of her beauty.

When the cow was without milk Joe and Nannie became hollow-eyed and thin, their beings waiting upon the hazards of the seasons. The hazards of the seasons followed them into the cabin in long rainy periods, the leaking roof scarcely leaving them one dry corner for their play. "Nothing but a new roof will mend it," Jasper said. "There's ne'er a thing there to mend to." Ellen thought, when Joe was sick, that he might die, and she tried to build an indifference about her helplessness. She could not help it, the matter; she could not then care.

If she stirred their food or washed their bodies she sank into each occupation, buried in its momentary demand. One day as she mixed the dough in the pan, stirring around and around, mixing the soda well into the wet mash, she was haunted with some forgotten thing. The yellow of the egg gave the batter a faint glow and made it fall and rise in a rich oily lava, thick and pliable, but now and then the grains of the meal became visible, taking their granular form on the surface above the stiff pliability of the mass. Around and around, stirring, the oval ridge of the batter rising beside the spoon and sinking away into a lap of flowing mass, ring on ring, until there was nothing but the faint shape left as the ripple approached the outer rim of the pan. Circles flowing outward through thick oily dough, flowing outward through heavy pliant matter, rising and falling, nearer and farther, renewed and sinking back and renewed, over and over, in a perpetual orbit. She watched the flow as she stirred and stirred, looking at the motions and leaning a little nearer. Suddenly a soft whisper came to her lips as she looked, as she penetrated the moving mass, a whisper

331

scarcely breathed and scarcely articulated, as would say, "Here . . . I am . . . Ellen . . . I'm here." She went often to the church to be among the women and to feel the warmth of the singing and of the preacher's voice. She would sit in the hour before the service with the other quiet-spoken women at the rear of the church, and hear their talk, believing their words. They talked of good places where they had formerly lived, of the number of cows they were allowed to keep, or they would speak of their husbands, of their generosity and thought. One would tell a little of her childhood home, or of a sister or brother, or they would talk of sickness or death or grief. But they came back over and over to their men for they were young as yet. Ellen heard them as if she heard a fairy tale of life, believing, and it was comforting to be there, to sit among them before the time of the singing and the sterner comfort of the preacher.

"Lige, he gave me the money for a new dress, but law, I said, I'll wear the old a spell yet."

"Same with Charlie. And he gave me two dollars for shoes."

"Sam, he tells me to go to the store and buy whatsoever I fancy, no matter what hit comes to. But me, I don't like to spend."

Sometimes one wore a new garment, but usually they kept the same apparel all spring and summer, and their faded garments withered as the summer drew toward the autumn. Ellen could not go to the church many times more, for another child would come, a child she did not want. Autumn and it would come. All week she would sit in the doorway waiting. Jasper had spent the money that Goddard had owed him, his back pay, for a wild, unbroken horse; drunk he had become on horseflesh. She would sit in the door all week, idle, for there was nothing to sew. There was a small bit of coin in the tin can on the shelf, twenty cents, perhaps, and that would buy the next sugar or meal. One day she saw the children, the three born and the one unborn, as men and women, as they would be, and more beside them, all standing about the cabin door until they darkened the path with their shadows, all asking beyond what she had to give, always demanding, always wanting more of her and more of them always wanting to be. She took up the bucket and went down the hill to the spring, walking quickly as if she were pursued. "Out of me come people forever, forever," she said as she went down the hill-path.

Often she would meet one of the women at the store or see them trading there, offering a few eggs for a bit of sugar or some other food, or she would see them take a few small coins from the corner of a handkerchief and spend them carefully. Sunday she went to the church for the last time, for autumn was coming fast now. She sat among the women, speaking with them softly, saying but little; she had never spoken more than some acquiescence or some reply.

"Lige gave me money to get a new winter cloak," one said, "but I said to put hit in the bank. No need to waste, I say."

"He told me, Sam did, to get me a new hat, velvet maybe," another voice would murmur. "Said he was tired himself to see this-here old one again."

They were young like herself. The speaker would rock herself slowly as she spoke, speaking carelessly, often smiling in a shadowed way.

333

"Lige is a great hand to make," the first said. "And a great hand to spend on me. A new winter cloak he said for me to get."

"Abe laughed," one said, "laughed right out at my old shoes today and said, 'Land sake, Irie, where's the money I laid out for your shoes.'"

Then Ellen spoke, murmuring like the rest. She had never made so long a speech before. "Jasper, he said, 'Ellen, why don't you get yourself a new dress, a worsted, blue maybe? Here's the money,' he said, 'here on the shelf.' Jasper, he's partial to blue. 'Here's the money on the shelf,' he said. 'No use to stint or hoard up. And buy some pretty to trim it with, velvet maybe,' he says. 'Here's the money up here on the shelf any time you take it in head to buy.' But I'll wait awhile, I says. And Hen, he can go barefoot a spell yet, church or not. No need to waste money on shoes for young-ones in a summer time, I always say. Youngones don't need so much. 'The money is on the shelf nohow,' he says, 'whenever you take it in head to want the dress.'"

IX

JASPER had come back from town, where he had been to haul the tobacco crop for Goddard. He had been gone two nights, sleeping each night on a long bench in the waiting room of the warehouse. A great block of cold stood about him as he opened his overcoat and spread his hands to the fire. He had money in his pocket and he had something to tell.

"Stand offen me a spell yet," he said to Nannie. "I'd give a gal the pneumonia or a bad cold nohow, that wanted to hug me."

He stood up in the cabin, large and sure of himself, his shoulders drooping roundly in their accustomed stoop and his look free and high. He swaggered over the lighting of his tobacco. Ellen knew that he had something to tell although he had not yet spoken of it, for the money in his

335

pocket would scarcely have given him such a flowering. He knew a song to sing for Joe, he said, a song he'd learned the night before from a man from Taylor. It would be a good song for Joe to know. The man from Taylor said he had not sung it, he reckoned, for fifteen years, and a song that had lain away fifteen years to sweeten was a right proper song to have. As she tended the fire gaily, lending herself to the hour, Ellen thought contemptuously of his song and his leisured way of coming to the vital matter. "Make Pap sing his song then," she said to Joe, and Jasper sang over and over, each time better pleased with himself, a bit of an incident from the life of Joe Bowers, a native of Missouri, as was revealed by the verse.

> *My name it is Joe Bowers.*
> *I have a brother Ike.*
> *I came from old Missouri*
> *And all the way from Pike.*
>
> *I have a little gal there,*
> *Her name is Sallie Black.*
> *I asked her if she'd marry me,*
> *She said it was a whack.*
>
> *Says she to me, "Joe Bowers,*
> *Before we lock for life,*
> *You better get a little home*
> *To keep your little wife."*

"For God's sake!" Ellen thought, quoting Jasper's own usual comment. She stirred the fire gaily and took Jasper's kiss on her face. Then he began to tell his news, quieting now to his serious business. He had met Joe Phillips in town and Phillips had said that he intended to raise tobacco the next year and that he, Jasper Kent, could have the place cropping on shares. Then they asked Hen if he remembered

336

Phillips's farm and would he like to go back there to live, to the place where he was born, and Hen took a great advantage to himself, as if he had lent something to the house by being born in it, and Ellen cooked a feast of meat and bread and made an egg pie to be merry over while they talked of going back, herself yielded now to the happy event, so that the moment of Jasper's entering full of cold and full of his unsung song now seemed very remote.

The house at Phillips's place was vacant and they could take it at any time, and so they began at once to prepare for the journey. They had less goods than when they came, but two children more, Joe and Dick. Ellen rolled the clothing into bundles in a fever of joy because they were going. She would have a garden and some hens, and perhaps some turkeys, and the peddler would come to her house door to buy. There would be bright little dresses for Nannie and Dick, and Hen would go to school, perhaps, wearing a little duck suit from the store, and as she saw in her mind's eye his stout little body under the duck suit she melted to him afresh and trembled with pride and maternal feeling. The cherry tree would be bearing by this time and she was in a fidget to know what had come to the grapevines she had planted along the fence. Marthy Shuck would come with her youngones, glad she had come back, and as she gathered together the clothing it came to her, mingled with the pleasure of the return, that she would be planting the garden in six weeks, perhaps, with Joe Phillips in and out to give her seeds and plants and to show her ways and praise her skill. "I got to get my youngones packed and off," Jasper said. "Five youngones I got, all told, Hen the oldest, and then Nan, she's next, then Joe, then Ellie and then Dick, the least one. Five brats, I got. A house plumb full."

Ellen felt her eyes brighten as she leaned over the cooking pots to gather them together.

They quickly took to themselves the changes that had been made in the house while they were gone. Someone had built a bench under the locust tree, and a row of shelves had been fitted to the wall beyond the cookstove. A dugout had been made for a cellar; it stood on the north side of the house in the shade, stone steps, roughly set, going down inside. It would keep the milk cool and sweet in summer. Hen remembered the rooms and he told Nannie stories of how she used to run away to the pasture and how he would bring her back, but she shook her head and could not remember, wanting Hen to tell her just how she had looked then and what she had said, or she would turn to Ellen asking, "Did I, Mammy?" And once, as Hen said, she had lost her hippens over in the field, "stepped clean plumb outen her hippens and walked off."

"I reckon you want to know how you looked then," Hen said. "Right out in the plumb middle of the field."

But Nannie was angry and said she did not do anything of the kind, and at that Hen remembered other more embarrassing things to tell. Nannie fought and cried in turns.

"I could remember things about Hen," Ellen said, "that would match anything he knows on Nannie. Hen, he's done all the things Nannie she ever thought to do and more maybe. Poor Hen, he was the first and he had to make his own way. If Hen lost his hippens in the pasture why he didn't have no kind brother to pick it up for him and fetch it along home. I recall one time Hen lost his'n alongside the wheat field and the men at work in the field they picked it up and hung it on a pole against the fence, like it was a flag, it was. And it hung there a right smart while till I happened to see it and fetched it home."

When the cherry tree bloomed it was like a little plaything, shapely and white-feathered as it was seen against the rise of the pasture. The farmer gave Nannie a pig to raise. "You could buy yourself a fine present Christmas if you slop your hog proper," he said. He built another small room to the cabin toward the spring season, and there were henhouses. The milk house kept the cream sweet and cool and presently there were coins to jingle in Ellen's pocket, for the peddler, knowing she was there, came that way. She would save the egg money to buy a sewing machine, but the money from the butter she spent at once.

Marthy Shuck was the same she had been before, a little sly, a little round-about in her talk, but she was sure to come for a visit now and then and Ellen liked her. Sometimes she would bring one of her children to play with Dick or Joe.

"You must have a fine garden by now," Marthy said. "You always do have the earliest of anybody. I got no garden to speak of. Backward this time, everything is. I'm downright sick to go out and look how backward it is."

"Mine does right well," Ellen said. "I'm well enough pleased. It's forward enough to suit me. I'm right proud of my peas, ready to stick by a Tuesday of this week. I'm right proud on account of how early my peas are a-comen on."

"Are you?" said Marthy Shuck. "I got peas in bloom. They was stuck two weeks ago, I reckon."

Ellen would know when she had gone into Marthy Shuck's trap, and would know that Marthy had set her own low in order to set hers lower, but in spite of this she was pleasant company, always sure to come and sure to sit all afternoon. Hester Shuck was staying long with Marthy, all of a year she had stayed. She had grown taller since Ellen had first seen her and had gathered greater depth in her chest and hips. She gave no heed to the children, and presently Ellen knew that she heeded only Jasper. She would sit loosely in her chair when she came to sit for an evening and her eyes would gather at him.

Once, in the autumn, Marthy, sitting all afternoon, said in blame of Bill Shuck, calling him shiftless:

"Yes, we go on in the same old rut, year in, year out, in the same place. I tell Bill sometimes he ain't worth shucks. Same old go and come, that's Bill."

"Winter is the time to move," Ellen said, "on hand soon now. Some will be shiften about, I reckon."

"I reckon it was a heap of worry to you when Jasper was in court, now. That was something to upset a body, I lay that-there was."

"It was right worrysome whilst it lasted, but it's all done now and over, I reckon."

"I reckon so. I heared it said it was a right close call for Jasper Kent. They said so. Said there was three witnesses, one old man Chesser, that's your pap, and two men on Wingate's side, men that was hid in the garden and saw what come. Said these men swore Kent taken the horse to the barn on purpose to burn it up, horse had worked for him all summer in the plow. Said he had no call to take it in. There was a little mist of rain but not enough to bother a work horse used to stand out. Said a horse could go in by itself if it minded to. No, said Kent taken the critter in on

340

purpose to burn it to death. Kent had a close call, they said."

"If Jasper taken the horse in I reckon his aim was to hitch it to a buggy," Ellen said, speaking angrily. "His aim was to go that night, to get Pappy or Pius to drive with him to bring the critter back. He was in his rights to use any nag on the place any time, nohow. But it's over now," she said in a lower tone, knowing that her anger pleased Marthy too well, "It's all over and that's all there is to that-there."

"Yes. Jury said 'not guilty,' and I reckon that sounded good to Jasper. I was right glad he come off so easy. Glad, I am, sure and certain, mighty glad. I said to myself at the time, 'What,' I said, 'will become of poor Mrs. Kent and the youngone?' That's what I said. 'They could come over here and stay till they find a place to go,' I said."

Ellen knew that this was true, that Marthy had said this and that Marthy would have taken her in. "It's all past and over now, I reckon," she said.

"They said Jasper Kent he had a close shave that time, nohow," Marthy said, holding to the matter. "Said the lawyers traded cases, swapped. 'I let you win this-here and you let me have that-there.' That's how it was said it was. Some even said the lawyers played cards half the night before, and traded the cases back and forth all night, sometimes Kent was in the win and again the State—that's Wingate's side. That-there lawyer he ran for the legislature next election and that was what was told in the speeches. Said if they had quit the game, say, at ten o'clock Jasper Kent would 'a' been in the prison right now. That's what was told. But I reckon it wasn't so bad as that nohow. They

341

traded cases about, it was said, but maybe the card game might 'a' been campaign talk, election time. The other man won to the legislature, nohow. You never heared about all this, you gone from here, I reckon. It made a heap of talk up at the shop and all around."

"But I thought . . . I thought . . ." Ellen was greatly surprised, but she checked her speech before she had said what she thought, which was that the jury had found the right and had established it, finding it on Henry's statement. She had sold her calf to pay the lawyer. She had thought that the jury had set a certain way as right and had made every other way wrong. "But it's all over and done now, I reckon. All forgot. No call to bring it up and to hold it in mind. It was right worrysome whilst it was a-goen on, but it's over now," she said.

"Yes, it was worrysome, I reckon, and a right close shave for Jasper Kent, they said. I often say Bill he don't amount to shucks, but then he ain't never been in trouble yet in court, no way or how, and I reckon I got a right smart to be thankful about. Never yet in no sort of trouble to bring worry to a body."

"But it's all over now, I'd reckon, and no call to keep in mind about it, I say. Whatever it was and however it come, it's over, ain't it?"

"Maybe it is. I hope so, nohow. It wouldn't surprise me though if Jasper Kent, he saw trouble about it yet. I'd fear trouble about it all someway. I always said, Jasper Kent, he might maybe see a sight of trouble over that-there barn even yet and over that-there horse he burned up. It's a right serious thing. It was said the reason Jasper couldn't get a better place to work—Goddard's is no good place, every-body knows—was because of that-there trouble he was in.

342

Nobody wanted a man that was known to 'a' been in court that way, up for burnen a man's barn for spite. Folks is mean that way. Wish you no harm, but at the same time hire somebody else. That was why he had to stay to Goddard's, the worst place in the county, I reckon, treats his men like dirt. Bad place, everybody knows."

"But it's over now," Ellen murmured, "over and near forgotten, I reckon. Over, it is."

THE house had three rooms now, one standing forward on the side toward the farm. There were two outside doors, one looking toward the farm and the other toward the woods and the hill fields. The locust tree in the yard, down toward the fence, had a seat built beneath it, and a little way to the right beyond the farm-side door stood the dugout with rock steps going down, and beyond the path went on to the garden. The huckster would come through the pasture on the two wheel ruts along the fence and turn about at Ellen's gate, ready to trade. Hen, going to school, walking the mile he must go, carried about himself a new wonder, a hint and a sign of things unknown or long forgotten, for out of his mouth would come sayings she once had known. She would sometimes look from one child to another, searching them, bewildered. Nannie had a little pointed nose, like Nellie's. Her hair grew in soft waves over her ears, pale brown hair, soft and thin, and hung in a little braid at the back, tied with a tiny ribbon. Jasper said she looked like his mother, and between her and Jasper there was some close unspoken understanding. They would sometimes whisper together. Joe was a swaggerer, always ready for a fight, but Hen was

343

careful and old, his slightly staring eyes looking distrustfully upon the world. Ellen felt awed of him when he wore his new learning openly and gathered a new pride to herself from him.

After a while Jasper would own a place; they talked of it with a vague certainty. Jasper had a great joke to tell on Hen. Coming home from the creek where they had fished all afternoon, Jasper, Nannie and Hen, suddenly Hen had stopped in the path to look up into the trees, listening, and then he shouted:

"Mammy cooks for us-all."

Jasper told his joke over and over, roaring out his great laugh, and Hen joined him. He had heard the owl himself, Jasper said, up in the woods: "Whoo, whoo,—who-who-who-aw-y," but Hen had heard, "Who—cooks—for you—all? for you—all?"

Nannie was past five now, able to hold her own fish pole and to put on her own bait. Her little brown feet made small prints in the dust of the road as she ran along behind Jasper and Hen. Or all together they would come home through the dusk singing, Nannie's high shout unblended with the rest,

Ring around the raccoon's tail,
Possum's tail is bar,
Rabbit got no tail a-tall
But a little bunch of har.

Sometimes, hearing them come singing or talking toward the cabin, seeing them come down the fenceline through the field from the creek, all talking together of things they knew and shared, her heart would seem to stand in its measure and a question, "Oh, who are they?" would arise in her mind, pushing at her throat to be said.

Joe Phillips had brought her twenty or thirty raspberry cuttings from his garden, and in midsummer he had brought her sweet potato plants and had helped her to set them in rows. His own garden was a marvel of neatness and economy, and she tried to make hers the same. She dug in the garden during the growing season until dusk drove her to the house. Spring found her out with the first open days, spading for the onions. Later she cut sticks for the peas or she called Hen to drop the seeds when she had made the rows. Sun-stained and hearty, her body deep and broad, she tried to give each one the vegetable he liked best in ample profusion. Joe liked peas best; she would sow a plenty of peas, five rows. But Jasper was partial to beets, and she planted long rows of these, buying the finest seeds the peddler had. Or hoeing out the weeds after the rains she would smile to think of what Hen had said about a bird: "And the jaybirds have got longer tails 'n common this year. I took notice to that early in spring."

Phillips would come to work at the grindstone that stood under the locust tree, grinding his tool for an hour or more, or he would get Ellen to sew the torn pocket of his coat, offering to pay her but she would take nothing; he had given them much. "Mrs. Phillips, she won't do e'er thing for Phillips," Jasper had said once long ago. Sometimes he would talk of Lester, one of his boys. "If only he wouldn't lie to me, his pappy," he said. "Tells me he wants money to set up in business, and he's got no business. Boy nineteen. A-goen to the dogs fast."

He was a lonesome man. Sometimes he would come every day to linger about Ellen's yard, to watch her hands busy with the corn for the hens, busy with a garment she was sewing, busy with curds or cream. He would ask her advice.

345

"What would you think of me to buy the Neal place?" he asked. "Eighty-six acres, good corn land, fair at any rate, and for sale cheap. Would you think it too much for a man to take on?"

"It would be a heap of work, two places not touchen each other, to come and go."

"I'd have to get another tenant for over there. Maybe it wouldn't be a right good piece of business, like you say."

"A heap of corners to watch," she said. "Your hands already full. But I'm no trafficker to set up to know a heap."

Ellen had saved eighteen dollars toward her sewing machine, which was a very good sum, for she could buy one for twenty-seven or thirty dollars. Already the agent had come to her door, and he had said that he would come again in the summer. When the cherries ripened that year she sent a pail of them to Nellie along with a dozen early cabbage plants from her garden, proud she was to be able again to dispense gifts. It was late spring now, and Marthy Shuck came often, watching, curious, unable to find a way to say what was in her mind. Hester Shuck had ceased to come altogether, but now and then Ellen would meet her on the road.

At the time of the planting of the corn Ellen knew that a change had come to Jasper; she knew it as she mended the fence behind the hencoops or as she hoed at the garden, as she sewed in the cabin or cooked the food; her days were full of the knowledge and all her acts went with it. Hester had had her way with Jasper. Once Nannie had said that she had seen Hester in the crab thicket at dusk, and again

346

Ellen caught a glimpse of her there by the light of a newly risen moon. Jasper came from the field tired and sullen and if the children angered him he sent them early to bed. Often he went away after dark to return toward midnight, dull and silent, or he would cry out strange words in his sleep, lewd words and angered curses spoken out of some torment. He went often to the river with a man named Clark and there was another woman named Lena among them. When the knowledge had settled upon her, Ellen felt a curious hardness in her body, as if her life had grown solid and stiff within her flesh. She wondered why she cared who had Jasper, turning this thought over and over as she worked. When she thought of Hester in the crab thicket she wanted to go there and take her by the throat and choke the life back into her body until it turned hard and stiff like her own, until it hardened for death at last. At night, lying alone in her bed, she would want to go to the thicket with a knife in her hand, and her mind would keep remembering the knife in the kitchen beside the cups on the shelf. Joe Phillips had sharpened the knife at the grindstone. Then she would wonder why she cared who had Jasper and she would know that she would never so fall from her pride as to quarrel with Hester Shuck or to spy on the thicket or the river.

Jasper would laugh in his sleep, choking on his lewd words, drowned in his lewd dream, or he would blurt of Hester Shuck's bottle. All day Ellen would move from labor to labor, the garden, the kitchen, the cow, the milk house, her feet feeling the tug of the path toward the Shuck cabin and her throat aching with the words that would label Hester Shuck as a foul and bestial creature. The turmoil in her mind grew until she turned about in a maze, scarcely knowing whether the season were spring or fall, scarcely

347

knowing one day from another. Since May she had known herself to be carrying another child, but she told Jasper nothing of this. She baked Jasper's favorite cake but he ate it without noticing what he had. Then she dressed Nannie in her bright new dress and told her to take her father for a walk on Sunday, but he lay under the locust tree and slept. She wondered why she cared where Jasper went and why she contrived to try to bring him back, surprised at each plan she made, but the plans would arise suddenly out of her listless thought. She could not find that she cared whether he came or went and her days were full of her tasks as the summer came; he might go, what to her did it matter? She had saved twenty-two dollars for the sewing machine, and she thought that the agent would leave it for her if she made so large a payment as that. He would come later and collect the rest, as she would contrive to have it, and she would have the machine in the meanwhile, and her mind turned often toward it until she could clearly see the turning wheels and the throbbing needle carrying the thread, but through the thought of the machine lay the curious hardness felt in her body, a stiffness beneath her breath. Or sewing with her fingers, letting her mind dwell pleasantly upon the speed the machine would have and feeling the wheel at her finger tips and the anticipated flow of the treadle under her foot, she would come upon a swift image of her hand reaching for the knife that lay beside the cups, sharp now as a dagger since Joe Phillips had tooled it at the grindstone.

Then she fixed her hair in soft coils and wore her bright cotton dress all day, at work or for rest. She walked up to the field where the men were at work in the wheat harvest, taking Nannie and Dick, showing them the falling bundles and the clicking knives. She took off her bonnet and let the sun fall on her hair, and she knew that the coils shone brightly in the sunlight and that her dress was a bright spot moving over the dull green of the field and that her step was proud as she went through the stubble. The men, all but Jasper, looked at her, saying pleasant things, and Joe Phillips offered her a cup of the fresh cold water he had just brought to the field in a large bucket. Then all the men came for water and she dipped the cups for them while they eagerly crowded about her, making pleasant jokes, but Jasper drank his draught and was away without pleasantry. When she came back from the field, leading Dick through the pasture and talking with Nannie, she knew that Joe Phillips had seen the sheen on her hair and had seen the strong lift of her bosom as she had walked through the cut grain, and had felt the vigor of her being. There was a pleasure to her in this in spite of the woodenness that gathered back into her body as she came down from the field, while she wondered why she had gone there and why she cared, even for one moment, to seem lovely before Jasper. He might play with his company along the river any night; she would never care again, she reflected, but her reflection became a determination and died of its own force, leaving a chaos which lasted until her pleasure in her own loveliness as reflected in Phillips arose again.

Hen and Joe were waiting at the yard gate, expecting her, for they had climbed to the gate to peer out over the pasture. They had missed her and had found the yard unbearable without her there, unwilling to play until she was found again, and a great joy surged through her. There were stains of tears on Joe's face; he had lost her with bitterness and fear, and she stopped at the gate a moment with all her children standing close about her feet. But passing through the yard her mind turned toward the crab thicket with a great hate and she sickened with hate as she neared the milk house and grew dizzy with pain and evil-wishing as she passed over the doorsill.

PHILLIPS was grinding a tool at the stone when she came from the garden one mid-afternoon, the wheat being cut now and the labor slack. She had pinned Nannie's blue metal brooch on her breast and her hair was well coiled on her head. She set her basket in the shade beside the door of the house and carried the squashes to the milk house to keep them fresh. Jasper was coming across the pasture with a sack of meal across the plow horse he was riding. She walked past the grindstone and spoke to Phillips as she tarried under the locust tree.

"Where's Hen to pour the water for you?" she asked.

"I squirt the water outen my mouth sometimes, when I've got nobody to pour," he said.

She offered to pour the water this time. "I got little to do for a spell now. As well as not pour the water, I might."

"Your advice about the Neal place was prime good advice, as it turned out," he said, speaking softly as if continuing a confidence. "I got my hands full as 'tis."

"I don't set up to be a first-rate trafficker. I only guessed it, seems like."

"You are a first-rate guesser, Miss Ellen, you are. Prime."

She poured the water when he called for it, a little at a time. Jasper was carrying the meal across the yard and busying himself about the house door. He would wash himself in the kitchen, as he always did on Saturday, surly and indifferent, or jocularly indifferent, and then he would go away across the field to join Clark at the river. "I don't countenance Hester's way," Marthy had said the day before. "Hester, she don't get but blame from me, now. If I had my way she'd go off afore sunset and take all her duds along to stay gone a spell." Marthy had said this to offer consolation and to shed all blame from herself.

"That's a pretty dress you got," Phillips said. "I noticed it one day when you came up the field. I saw you make it yourself, too, one day when you sewed, a-sitten on the bench all day. You are a master hand to make things, I see that long ago."

"I don't set up as a prime trafficker in no way nor how," she said, but she was pleased at the praise of her skill.

"I wish there was another one just like you, exactly like, you understand."

"She'd be a right smart way off from perfect, now."

"Exactly like and free, you understand."

"I don't set up in no way to be perfect and I expect I aggravate a body a good deal."

"If ever you need, you understand, you just let me know, just send. If ever you want a friend or any help. As I just said I wish there was another just like you, exactly like, and don't you forget what I say."

"You'd be tormented plumb outen your life inside a week," she said, beginning to laugh. Jasper was coming out of the house door, dressed now in the clean work clothes he would wear the next week. She talked brightly, laughing, wanting Jasper to see as he walked across the yard. "A stone that turns by a treadle, that would be the way to have it. Then a man would have a free hand to pour the water. Turns like a spinnen wheel."

"I had my eyes on you a right smart while," he said, whispering, "and I know you don't laugh at a man that's in earnest like I am."

"I don't know why I laugh," she said. "I want to laugh all the time, maybe. I got to go now to get supper ready. Here's Hen in the pasture now with the things I sent for at the store. I got to call Nannie to get the little chickens in and to see after the geese. I got a heap to do afore dark. Laugh I do. I reckon I haven't cried for three year, no not for three, and I don't aim to cry. A body that waits for me to cry will wait a long spell. A grindstone with a treadle to go by your foot-power is what ought to be. Maybe I've seen one in my time somewheres and that's how it comes to mind now, and I can't tell whe'r I made it up myself or not."

Jasper was going away across the pasture and she would not see him until the next day sometime or the day after. He had looked back from the gate just as she had laughed about the grindstone. Her thought followed Phillips home after he had gone and clung about him when she heard him calling his hogs at the barn. Later she saw his lantern light going about the stables. The children were hungry, clamoring endlessly, and Dick cried for Jasper when he had finished eating; his crying put a weariness upon the house as if the whimperings came out of the boards and out of the floor. She remembered Phillips and saw his firm hand turning the blade on the stone. Hen and Joe quarreled and fought and Dick broke into tears over one thing and another. Nannie wandered a little way into the yard but returned to sit beside Ellen at the doorsill. "What's the

matter with tonight?" she said once. "What's so bad about
the air? It pushes down on my breath."

THROUGH the weeks she would hear Joe Phillips calling to
the men in the fields or hammering at the barn where he
was mending a roof. The weeds grew fast after the midsummer rains, but Ellen cared less to work at the garden,
grown listless and weary. Nannie was going to school now,
and Ellen would see the two of them, Nannie and Hen,
running along the path or along the road, far past two farms,
Hen with the dinner bucket and Nannie carrying the book;
as she sat in the house she would see them. She would hear
Phillips as he hammered at the barn, and hear the two
small children humming at their play, their words lost under
the purr of their voices, and her listlessness would give her
each picture as something remote and unrelated to her own
being, as felt through a veil, until the little children would
float in an unreality so entire that they seemed to be any
children, belonging to some other woman in some remote
house. Or suddenly, under this withdrawing mist in which
each sense had sunk and each obligation had drowned,
would appear, more vivid than lightning, Hester Shuck's
way, gathering into sound, into words, and she would know
all that Hester did and all Hester's slobbering talk. The fact
of Hester, in her face and in her acts and in her body,
gathered into an oblique thought, blighted and throttled,
shrinking back of half-said words: "When it comes knock
it in the head with a stick of stovewood and bury it in the
ashpile out behind the henhouse": this was Hester. "A little

353

red stringy brat, looks like a rabbit new skinned, God knows! Look at it": this was Hester. Ellen's hand would feel for the knife as she sat limply in her chair, and her left hand would catch at Hester's throat to still her vile breath. Or she would sink again into a half sleep and remember some task undone, hearing Dick and Joe as they talked at their play, floating back again into the unreality of their voices and the remoteness of every obligation. If she heard Phillips in the yard she would not stir from her place, and when he had talked a little with the children or when he had ground his tool, he would go away again. The sounds of one day blurred against those of another. The quiet of the morning would enhance the quality of her drowsing being and thus she would sit, idle and weak, until, to penetrate the fog, she would gather the ashes of some spent thought, torn snarls of knowing, and she would sometimes moan softly under the confusion. Hester Shuck, her way of crawling about in the thicket, turning herself into a sow; her dark hair; her wide jaws and deep hips: "a little red stringy brat, look at it!" this was Hester. She knew the whole of Hester's way; she could gather her together; she knew her in her own mind, saw her in bestial postures in a swift picture, as sharp as a lightning flash on a dark sky: "a sharp crack on the head with a stick of stovewood and bury it along with the chicken guts and feathers out behind the ash hopper."

THE threshers had come to work in the wheat and the oats, the season being well spent now, and Ellen was to provide food for three of the hands while the others would eat at the farmer's table. She was carrying water from the spring at the foot of the hill, hurrying to be ready for the heavy meal when the noon hour should come. Hester Shuck was gone from the country now; she and Lena had gone away together to the town, but later, Marthy said, they had gone to the city. Ellen could not find that she felt glad; she could not find that she felt anything. Nannie was glad and so also were the boys, although they did not know why, perhaps, except that Jasper had begun to take them with him to fish in the creek again. When Hester had been gone two weeks or more he said, carelessly, to Joe and Hen, "How are the fish poles? Busy season about over, we might fish a little, buddie." He would sit quietly on Sundays under the bench by the tree, speaking with latent hilarity to Nannie or the boys, or he would stare with a gentle gaze, turning from one thing to another, as if he looked upon his acts with surprise and forgiveness. Ellen could not find that she cared. The sense of hardness lingered in her body, stiffening her limbs and her mind. It was all one. Hester was gone. She was glad, no doubt; Nannie went with Jasper again to the creek and their song would come up from the hollow as they returned at dusk. Her own body was stiff and tired and she could see that her hands were thin. Except when she went to the spring to get water or when she went to the garden to get the dinner, she kept inside the house now almost all day. "We'll have to feed three thresher hands," Jasper had said, standing uncertainly in the doorway. As she returned from the spring she moved dully across the yard, one with the dull load of the water as it drew upon her arm and shoulder. Jasper was coming across the pasture, walking rapidly, as if he came on some mission of great importance, bearing some news.

He sent Dick and Joe outside and closed the kitchen door,

355

turning to Ellen as she set the water pail on the table. He walked near her and said a few low words, accusing and threatening, and when he was gone, she continued to plod dully through her tasks, fitting his words slowly together and making for them a meaning. He had become aware of the unborn child and of the farmer's liking for her at one time and he had held the two ideas together in his mind. His fist had tightened when he spoke to her. His words had gathered meaning slowly as she cooked the food, piling up force as she turned them over in mind, but his hate and his threat were immediately seen. She grew more frightened as the hour passed and her knees tottered as she went down the steps to the milk house. After a little the men came for dinner and she walked back and forth, serving their plates over and over. Jasper talked with the threshers during the meal, but afterward he went back to the field without speaking to her. That night she spoke to him in spite of her fear.

"What's that you say to me?"

"No brat of Joe Phillips can be borned in my house."

"Who's thought to born a brat of Joe Phillips in your house?"

"You ask it!"

"You got little call to talk to me, you!"

"I say what I mean, now. Not in my house."

After that they did not speak for many days. Jasper called upon Nannie for his wants and spent but little time about the cabin. Sometimes he would take the boys to fish. Ellen sickened often and lay on her bed, scarcely knowing that she breathed. The entire bitterness and hate of the summer gathered into each moment and into each brief interchange with Jasper. After many days in which he had not spoken to her, he turned upon her one evening as they passed in the yard.

"Joe Phillips, why don't he support you? Cheap, he is. Has he made his plans to bring up his brat?"

The cold of the autumn found the children unprepared, their garments thin and ragged. Ellen would rouse herself from her bed to guide Hen or Nannie in preparing the food and lie stiffly down again. She would answer dully if Marthy Shuck came, giving her ready-made replies. Jasper left money on the shelf as he always had, but he spoke but little and she never addressed him.

"I was a cock-eyed fool," he said. "Not sense enough to see my hand afore my eyes."

"You think you see a far piece now, don't you?"

"Right afore my eyes, and me not sense enough."

"I reckon you got your good eyesight from Hester Shuck. Her eyes are good, God knows."

Each tried to hurt the other more, thrust after thrust, and they haggled over the unborn.

"I don't aim to stay on Joe Phillips's place e'er other year," Jasper said one night to Hen and Joe. "I'll be off against spring comes."

The cold of January bit through the thin boards of the house and made frost on the windows and latches. Ellen never went to the woodpile now. She trusted Hen and Nannie to bring the wood Jasper had cut. "February, and I'll be gone from here," Jasper said over and over, speaking always to Nannie or Hen. Ellen lay on her bed almost continually, scarcely knowing that she continued in life.

"I reckon you think you'll run off," she spoke once out of a long silence. "I reckon you think you'll run. I see you a-goen! You'll not run off, Jasper Kent. I know you too well. You'll not run off from your youngones. You're tied down with a whole bale of rope."

There were cold days when Jasper stayed in the cabin to cook the food. Once when the children were in the kitchen at the table he came to the sleeping room for some coat and said tauntingly to her, "I reckon Joe Phillips he fetches down fine victuals when I'm gone to work. I see you got no appetite now."

"I got victuals you don't know e'er thing about," she said. And then she added out of some dreaming state, as if she forgot her anger, "I reckon you'd think I was a-lyen if I said I haven't seen Phillips in four months or over, not even laid eyes on Phillips."

"Well, you can see the fine rich man all you want after a little spell. I aim to go right soon. I reckon he's afeared of me."

"You'll never get off, Jasper Kent. You're tied a heap tighter'n you know for. You are wedded up tight, Jasper Kent."

"I already told Phillips I aim to be off."

"All right, but you won't go unwedded. You'll see."

"I'll go. And I'll take the four youngones, my youngones. You can keep the balance for yourself."

She laughed at him. "You think you can ever get Hen and Nannie and Dick and Joe away from me? God knows, you're simple, Jasper Kent. And you yourself are wedded deep. Not even Hester Shuck could unwed you."

"Hester she's got ne'er thing to do about this."

"How you know Joe is your youngone?" She could not let him be.

"Nohow, you'll find me gone some day soon. I aim to be gone afore March. I already got a place to go to. And afore

358

I go I aim to make Joe Phillips feel the whole weight of my strength in his face. I'll gouge his heart outen his chest and more, afore I go. I aim to wait till I get ready to leave here. That's my aim, but I might not hold out to wait. Let me get a hold on his entrails, for God's sake."

"What a fool he is. In the law again, he'll be, in the jail, maybe. I'll sell my cow maybe to pay you out."

"But I'll keep my hands offen you. I'm no brute nohow. I'll not touch you, but I ought."

"I'll sell my cow Wakefield gave me and put alongside the money my trifle I saved for the machine. To bail you outen jail, Jasper."

"I'll gouge his heart outen his body and empty out his body of his guts. My whole strength in his face."

"And Joe Phillips, he'll go on your bond. Sign your paper that you won't run off. God knows."

"God knows!"

"Wedded deep, you are."

"I'll tear his brains outen his skull. Afore I go. Any day now."

ONE bright morning in early February Ellen fastened the small children into the kitchen, tying the latch with a string. Then she bore her child alone, being finally delivered toward the noon of the day. When Jasper came he broke the string with a blow on the door and went in where she lay, the child beside her rolled in a piece of an old blanket. The child was a thin wizened creature, the skin pulled gauntly over its bony face. With its long protruding skull and its wrinkled brow it looked like a dwarfed image of an old man,

359

as Jasper would look if he lived to be a hundred years old. When it began to cry a strange wail, the thin cry of the new-born, seemed to be coming from Jasper as an old withered man, and Ellen covered the child with her arms and hid it in her bosom.

It was March before they moved away although Phillips told Jasper he need not hurry, he might take his time about finding a place for his family to live, but Jasper said that he had as well go now as later. He would work that year on Robinson's farm and the house there was vacant; he would go as soon as the winter broke. The infant was soon very much endeared to the other children, who began to call him Chick as they played about him, and after a little that name was established and the child seemed much too precious to be encumbered with any name less light. "After a while I will name him, Thomas maybe, or Albert," Ellen said, or she would say that Jasper might choose the name. "Thomas Albert," Jasper said, "afterwhile, when he's bigger we'll call him Tom or Al." Then he had Job Tucker make a new cradle, stinting nothing in the wood or the work, and Job took seasoned cherry boards which he had saved for some fine task and rubbed the finished pieces with oil until they shone darkly red, the finest cradle he had ever made, he said. Chick was so little and thin that one scarcely knew that one held him in arms. He gained a few pounds in weight as the months passed but he kept his look of great age, his bulging forehead and his long unfleshed jaws.

At Robinson's place the house stood close beside the road, but a few feet back from the fenceline. Wagons rumbling along the way would wake the infant from his sleep. Ellen mended the rude coops and cleared them of vermin and set her hens on fresh straw which Jasper brought. The money she had saved for the machine went, a little here and a little there, and it was gone, blankets for Chick, medicine and infant foods. The child often fell into paroxysms or lay half asleep. Ellen and Jasper went softly about the house, or they spoke softly to each other from room to room. At the end of the year they went to McKnight's farm, three miles farther on the road. It mattered much less to her now what country she lived in, here or there, or whether there was a tree in the yard or a spring or a well for water, a stove for heat or a fireplace. A year on Robinson's place, a year on McKnight's, it was all one, or if there was a hoe to dig the garden or a mattock, a fork or a spade. If there were vermin in the hencoops her labor was doubled; it was all one. Hen and Nannie and Joe would read their small books by the fire after supper or they would rouse little Chick to play with them, but the light in his eyes was faint. Ellen set her strength to work all the harder because of Chick, planting more because of him, and when he lay wanly uncommitted to life she would work over the bean rows with the mattock. She must work in the garden and so her work there became a fervor of service to the child.

"But he looks old," Joe said, "like old men. What makes him look so funny, Mammy?"

"How?"

"He feels hard, but crumbly when you take him up. And he smells sour, or bitter. That's it. He smells bitter and tastes bitter."

Her work in the garden was a fervor of service to the child. Jasper would go out of the house softly in the morning so that Chick need not wake, but at noon, while he waited for the horses to rest and have their feed, he would play with the child and sing a great rousing song, and Chick would leap in his arms with the whole of his small strength and flush faintly pink under his blue-veined skin. Jasper and Chick had many understandings which hung about great raucous words that grew up, syllable by syllable, out of vast associations of past mirth and present wonder. Jasper would clap his hands, catch Chick's eye and hold it for an instant, and then out would come the great nonsense word, thundered out of his stubby beard and poured over Chick's small laughter. Ellen would watch them with a curious joy she could not bring into any relation with her pain.

Breaking the soil her mind would penetrate the crumbling clod with a question that searched each new-turned lump of earth and pushed always more and more inwardly upon the ground, a lasting question that gathered around some unspoken word such as "why" or "how." Thus until her act of breaking open the clay was itself a search, as if she were digging carefully to find some buried morsel, some reply. Working among the hens or the swine, in the broad light of day, a wind tearing at her garments would awaken in her some sense of another time and another wish, another longing now forgotten and unknown but keeping some faint being in a half-known phrase said at some time long past on some wind-blown hill where stones were piled in a mound. And her lasting inquiry, her questioning anguish, would gather about this remote image, this phrase, and ask it, and beg it for redress, for remission, for pity. Or once, looking quickly up into the sky where the sun shone brightly, she remembered with a sudden flash of bright, pictured light a hill grave where the sun had poured over a white marble shaft and where she had sung of life with a great shout, and she turned upon that picture the whole of her questioning pain and begged of it for life for her child, as if she would pray that hour to take from herself half, even all, she had and give it to him. Or, in the yard, cutting the wood for the dinner fire, she would remember Chick's spasm of the night before, his muscles tight and stiff and his face blue, his eyes half closed, and then his writhing body and his wild cries, and she would hate the pain that held the child and hate his withered limbs and his bent spine, until hate and pain would distort her own face and numb her mind. How she hated, but not the sleepless nights for herself till her limbs were like wood and her throat rasped with dry grief, nor Jasper, never complaining and never weary in his compassion, walking the floor with the child half the night after he had driven the plow all day. It was not this she hated, but the pain in the child, bending his spine and twisting his limbs, until she could not separate the pain from the suffering infant and she would hate Chick himself as she slashed at the firewood. Then she would throw down the axe and hurry to the house to lean over his pillow and settle his comforter nearer, or if he were awake she would take him to her bosom and hold him in a fervor of tenderness and kiss his sad little face and hold his hands to warm them.

But Chick died. In the midst of his spasm one morning he grew limp in Ellen's arms and she saw that he had changed. It was mid-morning and she was alone in the cabin, but her call brought Jasper. He knelt beside her chair while she held Chick, stroking his cold hands. They were both weeping.

"He's gone now," Ellen said. "Jasper honey, don't cry."

"Poorly all his enduren days, and never a well hour, ne'er one."

Ellen stroked gently downward on the child's eyelids and

closed them, and settled his limbs. "Gone," she whispered.

"I'll take him to the bed now," Jasper said. "I'll take him . . ."

"No, no, not yet. I had him in arms so long. I couldn't nohow put him by yet. No. Jasper honey, no, not yet, to take him away, not yet."

"Not one well day in three year, almost three, God knows!"

"He never in all his time seen any ease or comfort outen the earth."

"God knows!"

"Bright too, ready to laugh whenever he could."

"He knowed us, all to the last one, and always wanted to play when he could notice."

"He knowed you best, Jasper, and liked you. I see him pick up his head when you'd come."

"I best take him, Ellie, take him to the bed. I'll lay him out on . . ."

"No, no, not yet."

"I'd best take him, Ellie."

"Always looked like you, Jasper, from the first, and look, he looks like you now."

"Always from the start, but hair like your'n, Ellie."

"And now he looks like you more. Now. He looks like you'll look. When you're dead, Jasper."

"God knows! Maybe he does."

They were both weeping, speaking between their sobs. Jasper knelt beside Ellen's chair, his hands at his face.

"He knowed you best, Jasper, best of all. He knowed Hen and Nannie and Joe and Dick, but he knowed you the best and liked you first."

"I'll take him now, to put him on the bed. . . ."

"No, no, not awhile yet. A little spell longer I'll have him. . . . See, he looks like you, Jasper, like you, more and more."

"God Almighty! He does!"

"Like you dead. . . ."

"I better take him now. To put him by. . . ."

"No. He's my baby I had all by myself with nobody to help. Hands offen him. Hands offen him."

"I best take him, Ellen, best . . ."

"Hands offen him. He's my baby I had without any to lift a hand's stir for me. Stand offen him, Jasper Kent. And before he came. . . . No help."

"You best let me lay him down now, Ellen, and rest yourself a spell."

"Get back a way, Jasper Kent. I maybe marked him with the way I took on afore he came. I couldn't see to help. But he's mine. He knowed you best and liked you, and I was glad for it. I was glad he liked you. But he's mine and always was. I earned him all for myself. Get back offen him, Jasper Kent."

"God knows, you're beside yourself, Ellen, and you best let me take him now, to rest you. . . ."

"And now he looks like you. Like you some time hence."

"Oh, God Almighty!"

They wept a long while now, each in his place, Jasper calling aloud and Ellen bending over the still child. They wept thus until they were spent and quiet, and then for a while they were still.

"You could take him now, Jasper," Ellen whispered at last. "You could take him and lay him out on the bed. Now you could."

"I'll get Job Tucker to make a little box to be his coffin.

Three miles will not be far to go," Jasper said while they stood beside the cot.

"I'll wrap him in a piece of fair cloth I got to make aprons for myself and Nannie. A fair piece, white it is, I bought from the store. Never a bit of ease outen the earth he had, in all his enduren life. Knowed you best and liked you first," she whispered.

X

THE wind blew almost always on this hilltop. It shook
the old boards of the house and raveled the stones from
the chimney; it swayed the bough of the poplar tree beside
the door and it turned the shade of the locust tree before the
gate to quivering powdered shadows. Little Melissy could
not remember beyond the Powers country, for she had been
born here. The hills undulated freely under the cultivated
fields and reached in rough sheer bluffs up to the ridge that
divided these farms from the north country. The house
stood on the crest of an upland that dipped to rise again to
a hill where open timber grew and where the unmilked
cattle were pastured. It had, in the early days of the country,
been the farmhouse, the center of all its acres, and for this
it was larger than tenant houses usually are, having four
rooms and a loft. Hen was a tall boy now, becoming great

in stature, like Jasper, his great gaunt arms strong to lift and haul. He had begun to chew tobacco. Some rumor of this had reached the fireside a year before, a hushed rumor, unconfirmed, but one day when Ellen sewed buttons on his garment a piece of the stuff rolled out onto the floor, spilled from his pocket.

"For land's sake, Hen," Ellen said, "a man grown already!"

After that no one questioned Hen's coming and going. He worked for Jasper all day or he milked the cow for Ellen, a heifer from the first cow, which was gone now, a brown and tan beast that still bore the marks of the great Wakefield herd, and the last tie which bound Ellen to a past that was remembered perhaps infrequently, but held with constancy as a finished picture, complete and set apart, dimly shadowed but done, scarcely belonging to herself more than to another. The huckster came to her door to trade for butter, chickens, eggs, whatever she had. She hung the butter down in the well to keep it fresh and cool, the pail standing on a shelf halfway down the stone wall, to be drawn up with a rope. She went busily from day to day, eager with Nannie, making plans.

"Here's how Granny looks," Melissy said, sucking in her lips to look toothless. "Here's Granny."

"Shame to you," Ellen said. "I'll whip you and whip hard if I hear you make fun of your granny. Don't let me hear e'er one of you make fun of your granny or your grandpap either. Granny, she's old. It's a shame to make fun of old folks. You'll be old yourself some day."

"I won't be old," Melissy said. "I don't aim to let it come, not that-there. I'll grow up but that's all I aim."

An old man lived down the road beyond the schoolhouse,

living with some woman, his niece or granddaughter who was always seen plodding through the work or sitting barefoot in the doorway. The old man walked with a bent spine, throwing out his twisted legs, carrying a basket and searching the herbs of the roadside for something. The schoolboys called him Old Live-forever. They would shout to him as they passed him on the road or as he searched the grass. "Hi, there, Old Live-forever!" And then, out of his high thin voice, bursting from his crumpled old throat, "God-almighty!" Searching the roadside for some greens or something to eat. The boys: "Hello, Old Live-forever!" and the reply, "A little piece of greens for my dinner, a little mess." Sometimes he would laugh with the boys and call out, "Good-day, young men!" waving his twisted hand spirally under his shoulder. "Oh, God knows! A little piece of greens for my pot." Ellen often saw old Sansbury as she passed along the road going to the store down beyond the creek. One day she saw him eating a piece of something he had picked up from the road, a bit of some child's school lunch thrown away.

"Nor old Sansbury," Ellen said. "Don't ever let me hear a one of you youngones call out to old Mr. Sansbury and call him names. No matter if he can't hear."

"I don't aim to get old," Melissy said. "I'll grow up but that's all I aim to do. Wrinkledy face! Crooked back! You reckon I'd be like that? Grow up is all I aim."

NANNIE was pretty now, thirteen years old. She watched how the other girls had their dresses made and was eager for a bit of ribbon or a lace or a scallop or a ruffle. A woman, she was, come early to her flowering, like the women of

369

Jasper's people. In the heat of the summer she would put her hair in a little twist on the top of her head and bits of it would fall in tiny curls over her forehead. She would bring a girl home with her named Cordie Peters and they would gather the berries from the pasture briars and make them into a conserve, or they would wash their hands afterward in sour milk to whiten their fingers. A boy from a neighboring farm, Lige Newton, would sometimes come on an errand or pass over the hill going to the creek to seine, and he would stop to talk to Hen or to them where they rested under the poplar tree, and after he was gone they would tell over all that he had said, laughing and calling his name, pursuing his words with repetitions and laughter and contriving sayings that would bring back his name to their talk. With Dick and Joe, Nannie went away to the school in the early morning, during late summer and autumn when the school kept, trudging off through the dust of the wagon track to the dustier road and then out of sight beyond the turn, or they came home late in the day, having stopped at the wild crab tree, soiled and tired, often carrying their dusty shoes in their hands.

"I aim to read books," Dick said. "There's more than a million books in the world and I've not read e'er one yet. I aim to know everything. I aim to read a heap of books. It's in books is found the wisdom of the world, they say."

"You!" Hen said. "What books?"

"More than a million, maybe two million. I lay off to read all the books on the earth, or nohow all the good ones. But I ain't read e'er a one yet."

A MAN, Luke Wimble, came into the country to sell fruit trees to the farmers, the trees to be delivered to the farms and set in the ground in late autumn. He came to the tenant house on the hill many times, always eager to talk, always sitting down in the house or in the doorway. Then he asked Ellen and Jasper to board him, saying that he would be glad to sleep in the loft with the boys. All day he went up and down the roads and lanes, selling fruit trees and vines and shrubs to the farm owners, but at supper time he was back at Ellen's table where he liked to talk with any who gave him replies. His face bore a perpetual smile imbedded in the way of its muscles, and everyone liked him. He said that he was twenty-eight years old. He would lean near her to hear what little Melissy whispered, his round boyish face in a faint smile of anxiety and concern, and then, having replied to her, he would beam a great smile upon the whole table and pass his hand over his hair in delight. He would tell of the wonders of plants and trees and he never knew or noticed if the boys teased.

"And onions, they belong to the lily family, would you suppose it? And garlic," he said. "But apples now, they belong to the rose."

"Pass the lilies, please," Hen said, speaking very softly, "please pass the lilies o' the valley."

"I'm plumb a fool about my lilies," Joe said. "But they do strong me, seem like. They strong my breath."

"When Hen lays off to kiss Cordie Peters, that day he don't eat his lilies," Joe said again. "You just watch Hen."

"I eat whatsoever I want to," Hen said, "and if Cordie she don't like it she can lump it."

"But the best peaches are the Mayflower, and that's a white cling, white meat and a good pie peach or eater,'

Luke said. "And there's the Carmen, white in the meat and part cling and part free, or if you want a yellow meat, why there's the Elberta or maybe there's the J. H. Hale, both yellow meat and free stone, or the Crawford Late and that's a prime peach for sure."

Or he would lean aside to catch little Melissy's whisper and to help her plate, or he would ask for another noggin of milk, beaming over his words. He ate his food heartily, never knowing one kind from another nor caring which he ate, for all were happily taken.

"And apples, there's the Hawkseye, Greening, a big apple from a seedlen, or take the Secor and that's a cross between Salome and Jonathan. It's medium red, very good it is, fine. Stores away better than old Jonathan, too. A cross between old Jonathan and Salome."

"For God's sake!" Jasper said.

"But the J. H. Hale peach, it don't bear fruit when it's planted by itself. It has to be planted near a Banner or, say, a Elberta. And the reason for that-there, it's simple. It has to get the pollen offen one or the other. And the Sharon, that's a cross-bred apple. But the American Beauty, that's my favorite to eat in hand. I'll be back to set out along in late fall."

"October light moon be about right for that-there," Jasper said.

"I wouldn't set any great store by the moon to tell me when to plant. The moon has got some properties, that I'd say, but I never set out by the moon."

JOE had been in a fight again with Lin Wallace and Ellen knew what the fight had been about. Lin had called out to

Joe at playtime, called out before all the school, "Jasper Kent, he's a barn burner. He burned up a man's barn over around St. Lucy and almost got in the pen. I'd be afeared to let old Jasper Kent come on my place. Joe Barn-Burner is that boy's name."

"What did you do to Lin?" Ellen asked. "In your turn what did you do?" Her head was lifted and her bosom high.

"I gouged his head but he pinned me down. He's bigger. I fought back but he pinned me down and I couldn't get my hand loose. He's bigger."

"I'll get him along the road a Monday," Hen said. "You just wait."

"He's bigger'n you even," Joe said. "He's got a knife to stab with, too."

"I saw that knife, Lin's knife. It's plumb five inches long, the blade is," Dick said. "I saw it today."

"For God's sake," Ellen muttered to Jasper as they stood together beside the door. "A knife to cut my boy with. To let your boys get cut to pieces in a fight over what you done or didn't do. Did you burn up that-there barn or not, Jasper Kent? A knife to stab with! For God's sake!"

Jasper went out to the well and drew up a bucket of water, slow with the winch. Then he carried the bucket in at the door, a great man that filled up the doorway, and strode across the floor with it to the place where it always stood on the table. The lamp quivered in its own light and settled back to a nucleus of light on the shelf above the fireplace, and Ellen left the corner by the door and moved through the atmosphere that had suddenly grown real—half comprehended and half vague—as the menace of the knife was less keenly realized. Clearing away the food and the dishes while Nannie put Melissy to bed and Hen

373

mended a tool under the light she heard them all, going, ordering, calling, hurrying in and out, quarreling, snarling back, defending each other, laughing, making jokes she could never have thought to make, and it came to her that these were of her, these people, but that they owned her somehow more than she owned them. Luke Wimble had said before he went that words came out of his mouth sometimes so fast that he hardly knew himself that he had said them or how he came to think them at all. They were his own words, he said, but they somehow stood outside himself as if they talked to him and made him wonder.

Jasper went plodding over the fields, laboring without end, a great man, tall in a doorway, bent a little forward when he walked. He was always busy, making off to work as soon as he had eaten, falling asleep at night as soon as he became quiet, even while he sat in his chair. As he came from the autumn plowing, stooped by the furrows, he would stalk over the stones that lay behind the kitchen door. He seemed old and weary, effaced, as if he withdrew and left no reckoning. Or inside the house one day she heard Nannie and Joe and Dick as they came from school, stopping to drink, each one, a deep draught from the bucket at the well, continuing a conversation they had been holding as they came, weary and dry after the long walk home in the heat of the day, contemplative and final:

"Nohow, my pap, he's an upright man. I heared a man say one time while I waited inside the shop, the time Collie Childs fixed the singletree, I heared a man say, a man I never knowed, 'Jasper Kent, he's a good upright man and you can lay your last copper on that.'"

"My pap is honest," Nannie said. "Wouldn't steal a pin, Pap wouldn't. I heared a man talk once to Mr. Enzer . . ."

374

"I did too," Joe said. " 'Jasper Kent you could trust to the end of the world,' he said. Said, 'You could take Jasper Kent's reckonen and never count the change.' "

JASPER and Hen were cutting the tobacco crop now, early autumn, all day long, working slowly and stooping again and again over the field. Jasper would split the stalk from the top downward and then sever it near the ground, handing it then to Hen who hung the inverted plant on the long lath that stood by, later loading these onto the wagon to haul them to the barn, and the field grew more and more ragged as the labor passed over it and its yield was taken away. Or, moonlight, and Cordie and Nannie and Hen and Joe and Lige Newton—they romped under the locust tree, and played Lay Low Sheep and Wheel and Turn, or ran down to the persimmon tree to hunt for the ripened fruit. All the other tobacco fields were despoiled now, ragged, cut-over as they lay, in the valleys and onto the hill-slopes, and all the barns from farm to farm were filled with the limp plants, the shutters opened to the air, and an odor of burning hung in the winds, or hazes lay inert against the sky and against the sloping hills. Then Joe tracked an opossum home to his den in a hollow tree, and on the next night all the dogs were out and all the boys, over the pastures and hills to the bluffs along the river, whooping and barking, the boys and the dogs, until the beast took shelter in a tall tree that even Hen could not climb and crouched there looking down upon them, glistening white in the moonlight.

Then Luke Wimble came back to set his trees into the soil, came across the fields one twilight with his spade on his shoulder, and that night there was playing again under the locust tree until the roystering surged out into the pasture beyond any shadows, beyond the mockernut tree, Hen and Cordie and Nan and Joe dancing, until Luke was begged to join in the play and he said that he would if Ellen would come. Then Ellen danced with them and her feet were light and her steps quick, as eager as Hen's or as light as Nannie's, even more eager and light. She saw her shadow on the ground as she danced and she could scarcely take her eyes from it, for it was the shadow of a girl with slim ankles and straight round thighs and supple shoulders. She danced with Luke Wimble or with Hen, and then with Luke again, and the moonlight made the blood run like cold liquid silver in her veins, and when Luke came back for her at the second turn his face was open like the moonlight.

"I'll shake you down a mockernut ball and that is the fruit of the mockernut tree, like a split golden apple. I'll get you one and one for Nannie and one for Cordie, to dance with them in your hair."

Those autumn mornings Ellen went from one labor to the next, her feet light and her lips softly singing some tune Nannie sang, and she remembered the odor of the mockernut hulls and remembered the soft feel of the turf underfoot, her eye seeing inwardly her slim shadow as it danced, a shadow taller than Nannie's but as slim and light moving, or she walked proudly erect through her rooms and onto the platform behind the house, carrying this or that task forward, feeling that she had forgotten something but caring little for any lost recollections, living lightly and freely with the passing days, identified with Nannie, merged with her in the lightness of limb and in the vague, misty outward-

376

flowing thought of her mind. Then Luke Wimble brought her an apple tree, a gift to her, and he set it out in a sunny, wind-sheltered place one noon of day. It was a Kentucky Bell, he said, a great red apple to ripen in the fall, delicious to eat in the hand and to store away for the winter. While he cut away the sod he talked of a red mulberry tree he had seen at the edge of a field, the leaves fallen now, but a glory it would be in the early summer, the leaves yellow-green then. He stopped then to take out his order book and read the names of the trees the farmers had bought.

"J. B. Brown, six apple trees, Sweet Delicious and Early Harvest. I can see the Sweet Delicious where I set out in a row, like little girls a-waiten to bloom. Arland Booker, he took peaches, Sharons and Elbertas, a dozen trees. He'll be right glad he took Elbertas when they come on to ripen, two or three years from now. A big ripe peach is like a promise in a wilderness and like the sweet breath of Jehovah in the early day." He would dig a little at the hole for the gift tree, spading with care. "Apple blossoms are a shy flower, did you ever notice? Pale white and close to the branch, up and down. I set out two Solways and ten Elbertas and four Carmens and a Mayflower today, a white cling that is, white meat and good any way you take it, juicy and full of sweet, and when I see you dance under the mockernut tree I says to myself, 'She's like a flower in bloom.'"

"You ought to be a-sayen such to some girl, Nannie maybe. You ought to be a-sayen the likes of that to Nan or Cordie, not me," Ellen said.

He would spade a little and talk again. "And when I dig the hole for the Sweet Delicious I says to myself, 'She's like a apple ripe on the tree.'"

"You ought to be a-sayen it to some girl. That's what you want."

"And if I could kiss you once, Ellen Kent. I says today when I planted out the Elbertas, pink on one side and free of the stone, luscious and sweet, I says, 'Could I kiss her once . . .' And that night under the mockernut I wanted."

"Haven't you got a girl somewheres to say it to, some girl eighteen or twenty maybe?"

"You're a bright shiny woman, Ellen Kent, and it's all I can do to keep my eyes offen you. The apple tree, it blooms with a little pink in the white and the peach is all pink. The dogwood is like a star in the forest and the redbud is a sunset against a hillside. Then there's honey and that's the fruit of the bee, the flower of the bee-gum, you might say, and there's kinds of that, bee honey and ant honey, did you ever hear it said?" He fitted the little tree to the place but took it away and spaded again. "They take the sweet outen the grass even, and even outen the mud. Some of it dark, the wild honey, and some strong and bitter, but all of it sweet, and it's the fruit of the bee." He fitted the tree into place for the last time and began to set the earth about it. "Did you ever walk in spring in the woods and find these-here little white flowers, rare they are, under a layer of old leaves, little white flowers just out of the ground? Hepaticas they are. Did you ever? God bless you! And in the hill country, arbutus and laurel. Windflowers are little white sheep on a mountain pasture, and all the time you're as shiny as a dogwood tree in spring, Ellen Kent."

"You ought to be a-sayen it to Nan, or to Cordie," Ellen said. "Nan, she's a little woman, grown she is, but young, all a grown woman's ways sometimes. And Cordie is pretty, I see that. Sharp teeth in a smooth row and a little dimple

378

on her face. Nan with her hair up in a knot, particular about her dress and whe'r there's lace or not."

"If I could kiss you one time I'd chance the rest in life, Ellen Kent."

"You never noticed yet how Nan has got a pretty dimple aside her eye or how quick Cordie is to get angry, a frown on her face and her mouth to say sharp things, sharp talk, bite in it. 'You needn't be so smart, Luke Wimble,' she'd say, 'so stuck on your own self and so sure you're wanted.' Hear her say it? 'So sure you're wanted.' In another year a dozen will be after Cordie. You'll see. Or some other girl, the same as Cordie but away from here, where you live maybe. Her mouth gives up its mad and smiles again, and you there close. Your own girl and ne'er a thing to hinder."

Luke pressed the earth close around the apple tree, treading it with his foot and smiling at the toe of his shoe, his head bent and his brows drawn, smiling in his perplexity. "You're worth all the balance put alongside each other," he said. He pressed the soil firmly down and laid the sods in place, pressing them carefully. "You're worth all the balance and to spare. You got the very honey of life in your heart. Today I says to myself while I dug the holes for the Sharons and the Elbertas in Arland Booker's orchard, 1 says, 'She's got the honey of life in her heart.' "

NELLIE went about habitual tasks, doing each one in the ways her hands had long ago learned, glad she no longer cared, eased from caring now, and forgetful whether there were six eggs in the basket or ten, but hoarding the basket under the bed from a long habit, even if there were none.

It seemed that for her it was over, and no matter, whatever it had been, this passage, this life, this strange long curious thing without alternative. Ellen prepared clothing for Nellie and Henry and sent Hen to them often, for he could make the long journey on horseback in half a day and return a day or two later; or sometimes she went herself, driving with Hen or Joe. Henry became sick, lying in a stupor on his bed or fretting. He wanted to leave St. Lucy, he said. He was afraid he would take root there and he was not of a mind to take root in that poor place. When he died he seemed alone in his dying. To Ellen, as she straightened Nellie's house, preparing for it, he seemed to have taken an arbitrary course, bent upon it, while she and Nellie left him to his chosen way, abandoned him to it, though she could find no other mood or feeling within herself and no approach to him, no help. She set Nellie's house to rights while he lay in his long stupor, distraught by the universal feeling which one has for the dying; pain, vexation, weariness, sorrow.

Ellen and Jasper took all the money they had, with Hen helping with his savings, to buy Henry a simple burial. Nellie went to live with Bell Carrier. She had feared emotion as a visitation from without herself, and Bell, having none, gave her ease. "I'm here now and I'll stay," she said. Going about the small rough farm in the Rock Creek country, her home now, Ellen would remember Nellie, from first to last, a structure which she knew almost entirely in her senses, her deep inner knowledge which lay behind memory. She would gather Nellie to an entity, remembering her youth, her ways, her history, her look; Nellie had had yellow curls when she was a child, but her hair had turned to dun-brown before it had become streaked with gray; when she was a little child she had once climbed to

380

the top of a tall gate to watch some people pass, and she had sung out, "Mr. Man, your pipe made some smoke get in my eyes," and the passer had given her a dime, had folded the coin tight into her little fist. She screamed all night when she lost her first children, all then being dead, but when she lost all again she had gone about in a hard quiet or had sat still in her house.

Going about the rough barnlot of the farm above Rock Creek, calling in the hens, breaking them corn, Ellen would merge with Nellie in the long memory she had of her from the time when she had called from the fence with so much prettiness, through the numberless places she had lived or stayed and the pain she had known, until her mother's life merged into her own and she could scarcely divide the one from the other, both flowing continuously and mounting. Or hearing Hen's foxhorn, a hoarse note without music, a rough throaty call, she would wonder that the swift cry of a horn had once gone into her like a glad spear, and she would penetrate her own history, into memories long habitually forgotten. It had seemed forever that she had traveled up and down roads, having no claim upon the fields but that which was snatched as she passed. Back of that somewhere in a dim darkened dream like a prenatal vision, she saw a house under some nut trees, a place where she lived, but as clearly seen as this she could see her brother Davie and the others, the more shadowy forms of the older children although all of them were dead before she was born. So that this house with the odor about it of nut shells was all imbedded now in the one dream that extended bedimmed into some region where it merged with Nellie's memories. Life began somewhere on the roads, traveling after the wagons where she had claim upon all the land and no claim, all at once, and where what she knew of the world and what she wanted of it sparkled and glittered and ran forward quickly as if it would always find something better. Down one road and up another and down again, and the woman she called Tessie West always went ahead, but at each journey's end she herself would run to Tessie's wagon where it was hitched beside the road. She tried to think then what might have come to Tessie in all the years that had passed and how she would seem now and how look, but there was no way to think of her except as something brightly shining and diffused through the years of the roads and through the roads themselves. She could not clearly see how Tessie looked although she remembered her sitting beside her log fire one night and remembered her dull coat and her red and blue head scarf. "If I met Tessie on the road," she thought, "I'd maybe not know it. Even if I met her as she was then without e'er change in her look," and she thought of this sadly for a little while. "Or maybe if I knowed her now I'd say what a durned fool woman that is, to talk eternally about tom-foolery, God knows!" But this thought she denied any place although it lasted in spite. "She might come in that-there door or she might already 'a' come, any day, and I, maybe, said, 'What a no-account wearisome woman, God knows!' It might be that way."

As she sewed at some garment, rocking softly to and fro with the sway of her needle, she stopped, the seam stayed and the thread taut in her hand, stopped and remembered life. Life and herself, one, comprehensible and entire, without flaw, with beginning and end, and on the instant she herself was imaged in the lucid thought. A sense of happiness surged over her and engulfed her thinking until she floated in a tide of sense and could not divide herself from the flood and could not now restore the memory of the clear fine image, gone in its own accompanying joy. The joy exhausted, she sat lax in an apathy, unthinking and unfeeling, staring at the wall without sight, but her hands remembered their habit of the needle and the stitches fell again, over and over, her body swaying softly to and fro. It was early spring now, the lean time of the year, the cold spring. There was little to eat but bread and bacon. Some farm bell rang, far off over the hard hills, a faint sound beating thin against the air. It was after eleven o'clock, then, time to prepare the food. Jasper would come across the meadow, bent, stiff. She could feel the noon reaching over the entire country, valley and stony hills, the farm bell leaving faint echoes in the mind together with hunger, a feel of the approach of food, bacon and bread and grease.

She felt the noon on her skin, and she heard it in her ears and tasted it in her mouth. It lay on her seam like a load and dragged at her needle. It was imperative; it could not be set aside.

She carried the slop to the pigs while the kitchen fire kindled. They were running in the lot behind the barn, and while they lapped at the greasy water and nosed out the choice morsels she looked after the hens. When the pigs had eaten she could feel their soft round noses on her ankles as they followed her down the lot grumbling, squealing, wanting more, the white-nosed one at her right heel, the runt at her left.

"I couldn't fill you-all if I tried," she said. "It's a hog's way to be empty." A sudden thought of them in November, wallowing in corn and mud, knocked in the head, their

383

throats cut, hung up to bleed, scalded in the big pot. Then cut into sides and hams and shoulders. She herself would render the lard; she would trim the little pieces of gut fat off the chitterlings and stew it down in a kettle by the well. She would give some of the offal to the dogs and bury some of it in the garden, offal from the little white-footed runt now at her right ankle. This was his measure of life. "I'd like to know how you'd live in winter," she said to herself. "The only way is not to make any pet out of stock. How you'd live in winter without you had your sowbelly to eat and your lard to fry in and the hams to trade at the store for sugar and coffee?"

The farms about were poor and rough, the land selling for small sums by the acre. Jasper had thought that in a year or two he might begin to buy the place he now farmed.

The people met at the store or at the smith-shop in the hamlet or at the church a few miles away. Many of their men were outspoken in anger and many of them carried weapons, even to the church. On preaching days the great voice of the preacher rolled over their scuffling feet as they came and went during the service, as he admonished their hates and their too-ready angers. The men stood together to oppose some marketing measure which had been initiated outside their neighborhood, resenting it. "It's a poor country," Ellen said. "That I see. Hard, it is. But some of the folks are right nice. Mrs. Shepherd to send us milk when little Melissy was sick. And Mrs. Scruggs so glad to get the flower seeds Nan had to swap her for another kind. But a hard country, no matter." "But I could buy this farm cheap, and easy terms," Jasper said. The cold spring had begun, winter lingering. Jasper and Hen had burned their plant bed to prepare for the sowing of the seeds, and Nannie and Dick cut greens from the pasture. One day as they worked together in the barn Hen told Ellen of a mishap at the shop the day before. Jasper had had words with Lobe Baker. Lobe had stopped his wagon before Jasper's team and when Jasper had asked Lobe to draw aside he had been given a curt reply and an oath. He would drive off when he pleased, Lobe had said, and not sooner, sitting swaggering on his lead horse.

"He and Pap had words," Hen said.

"Pap, he's not afeared of Lobe Baker," Ellen said after a little.

"Then Lobe, he made Pap wait a right smart while and all the rest stood around to see if there'd be a fight, but Pap sat still on his seat. I see he was out-done and ready to fight, he was that mad. But Pap didn't want e'er fight, not that day nohow. Seems as if Pap had it in head he wouldn't fight that-there time. He just sat still and waited till Lobe Baker drove off, a right long while it was too."

Ellen mended the coops, with Hen to help, preparing for the summer broods when they should come. She would grow many chickens, she decided, to have something for Nan to trade at the store, for Nan would be wanting a fresh new dress or more with the summer. Perhaps she would make a little parlor for Nan in the room beyond the chimney, or so she thought, a place where her children's young friends could come for their play-parties, and she thought of what she would do to freshen the room and make it fair, the roof mended and the window panes set in the sashes and the walls newly whitewashed some good bright day in late spring. Nannie and Joe would do the work gladly, and later she would buy some chairs and then carpeting when she could. She told Nannie of her plan one day when the spring was still cold and wet, bleak with the overlate winter, and Nannie and Joe worked over the coops and cleaned the pens eagerly, hurrying the spring.

They were sitting about the open fire in the short evening, Ellen, Hen, Nannie, Joe, and Dick. Jasper had gone to his bed in the rear of the cabin room and slept, his face turned away from the firelight.

"The light in the sky last night was Lobe Baker's stable," Hen said. "Baker's stable went up last night. Lum Crouch passed along the lane just afore dark. He told me."

"Nohow my Pap didn't burn it," Joe said. "Pap wasn't offen the place for two days back."

"I wouldn't let e'er other boy even say what you said. Of course Pap didn't," Hen said.

"Pap wasn't off this place for two days, three, was he Mammy? I'd swear to that in court."

"Nobody thinks Pap burned it," Ellen said. "Don't talk about any such. Pap was right here with us and nohow he never. Don't even say it in a joke."

"A fire at night against the sky is a sight to see," Nannie said. "Last night it was. Like the end of the world. Like the song, 'Cast on Water.' Scotland to burn, all Scotland in the song."

"I aim to know songs and about the things in songs," Dick said, speaking softly. "I aim to know more than I can now think about or tell."

"Mammy can sing you a heap of songs herself," Hen said. "You could learn a heap from Mammy."

"I already know all Mammy knows. And I want better.

386

And more. I want more than songs. And I want better than 'Bangum and the Boar' and 'Mary Go and Call' and 'Lady Nancy Belle.' Better than any you'd name."

"'Nancy Belle' is a good piece," Nannie said, "and 'Sweet William' too."

"I want better. It's a good piece enough but I want songs I never yet heard. There must be better songs, a hundred maybe, songs to tell you all you want to know about the world."

"'Sweet William' is like a story book. Sing 'Sweet William,' Mammy."

"I want better songs," Dick said. "I already know 'Sweet William.' And I want books to know and read over and over. I aim to have some of the wisdom of the world, or as much as ever I can get a hold on. There's a heap of wisdom in books, it's said, all the learnen of the world, and that's what I want to have, or as much as ever I can. I couldn't bear not to. I couldn't bear to settle down in life and not."

The strangeness of Dick's want bewildered Ellen and saddened her until her contemplation passed into a remote rapture. This strange want rendered her speechless while the children sat on by the fire or stole away one by one to their beds, for she felt her own being, in Dick, pushed outward against the great over-lying barrier, the enveloping dark. His want startled her with its determination and its reach, coming upon her as something she knew already, had always known, now enhanced and magnified, unappeased. She continued to sit beside the fire long after they were gone, trying to penetrate the thought, her eyes on the embers. Finally she went to her bed, lying down beyond Jasper, with the curious sadness still about her.

ELLEN awakened to hear a great burst of voices beating upon the cabin and cutting the air of the room where she lay. The cold of the night streamed in at the opened door, and many great hooded shapes, men, had dragged Jasper from the bed. The creatures wore black cloths over their faces. They had carried Jasper out at the door, and "The Barn-Burner!" was in the chaos of their yells and cries, rose out of their tramping clamor. "Bring out that Barn-Burner! Hang to this-here limb! No, whips this time. Get back offen the road! Let the whips!" Their feet sopped incessantly in the mud and churned the soft dooryard to a wallow. Then the lashes fell like a swift hail, a lash and then another hard upon it. She was standing in the shadow of the door, her body shivering with the cold and her breath stilled except where it leaped and jerked with the spasmodic leap of her heart where life would not quit her. Jasper was down where he had been flung, a white shape in the dark of the mud, and the black creatures with the whips were standing and turning about, a circle of cleared ground left about the white of the mud in which the whips could play. The clamor and the scene moved swiftly; "The Barn-Burner! Give fifty more!"

She walked out of the house, her bare feet sinking into the cold mud, her night garment limp against her body as she went swiftly through the damp air. She walked into the circle of the men and stood in the bare space left for the whips, and her coming was so headlong that blows fell upon her shoulders and on her breast before she was seen. She

388

came with hard words and a deep malediction, laying curse on curse, speaking into the black rag faces without fear, careless of what came to her for it. "You get offen him," she said. "You white-trash! Rags on your faces! Take off your whips. You dirty low skunks! You hit him again now if you dare. Get back. I know you. I know the last one. I could call out your names. Lay your whips on me; you already hit me. Hit more. You skulken low-down trash!"

She cursed them with a blasting prediction that they would never forget this night, that they would remember it in dying, and she called out their names. But they went quickly. The lashes that had fallen upon her were the last, for while she was speaking they leaped to their horses and rode away in a hard gallop. She did not wait for their going nor give them one moment of watching as they leaped down the lane, but she turned to Jasper, who lay still on the ground, as one dead or deeply swooned. She unbound the rope that held fast his arms and roused him a little and lifted him to his feet so that he walked or was dragged to the house, leaning upon her and not knowing what he did. Inside the house he fell to the floor before the fireplace and she turned quickly back to the door, which she fastened securely with a chair, wedging the chair tightly under the rail, for the mob had broken the latch. Then she hung a comforter over the window, working swiftly in an agony of fear and caution and pride in her own. When she had secured the door from attack and the window from prying eyes she turned to Jasper, who lay filthy with mud and blood, lying across the floor before the fireplace. It seemed to her that this was her own matter, hers and Jasper's, and that she would not call Hen or Nannie. She would not want them to see Jasper lying naked and bleeding in a welter of mud. It was her own matter. She kindled the fire quickly and brought water to heat and a basin and cloths. Then she bathed Jasper's wounds, weeping over them, and she washed all the mud from his body and put warm clothing upon him, rubbing his feet to warm them, and after a while he came to consciousness and turned to his side with a great shuddering sob of humiliation.

On the next day rain fell without ceasing, and if anyone came to the lane Ellen did not know of it. Jasper sat all day before the fire in the darkened room. "Pap must be sick," Joe said. The boys worked all day in the barn, mending the harness, embarrassed by the subdued house, or if they entered they walked on tiptoe. Once Nannie stood beside Jasper's chair, her arm across his shoulder, and they whispered a little together. Often he slept in his chair as one broken with weariness. Toward nightfall the rain ceased and the air grew crisp for a frost.

Ellen prepared supper early, the children having gathered to the kitchen. From some look of trouble in his face she knew that Hen had learned of what had happened. All day she had seen the distant houses, cabins like their own, as they stood remotely set in the mist of the rain and in their menacing withdrawals, as if a great circle had been drawn about their cabin to exclude it from the countryside.

"Pap he's sick today," Joe said. "I see that. He's dauncy all day."

"He's got some trifle on his mind," Nannie said, "and it's unknowen how much a trifle can worry a body, when you study it over."

"Pap's not much to talk, but he studies out a heap in his head."

"If all the people in a country turned against you why that would be a thing to study over," Hen said. He spoke bitterly, biting at his twitching lips.

The young went early to their beds, repelled by the strangeness of the night. When they were gone Jasper called Ellen with a dry toneless voice and when she came near the fireplace he said that he would have to go away, that he could not stay longer in that country.

"I'll go somewheres far out of hearen of this place. I've done little that's amiss here, but still I'd have to go. I couldn't see my way to stay here and that's what I studied out all day. I aim to go far, so far that word from this place can't come there or is not likely. The strongest man in the place, I was, vigrous to lift above the rest, but they sneaked in on me when I was asleep and tied me with a rope. If I could 'a' got one hand free. It wouldn't be in reason to ask a man to stay on here now, and I aim to start when the moon rises, although I done little amiss here, God knows. I'll be a long piece off by sunup. Walk, I will, and leave you the horses, and you and Hen can make out right well. After-while I'll send for you-all if you're of a mind to come where I am, but I got to go now. You and the rest better stay where you got a roof over your heads and no man can take it away from you. I paid the rent ahead as you know. Don't let any man tell you different, but they won't trouble you, Ellie. If they do there's men up around Pike's will take your part, and I'll come back, God knows, and come fixed to fight with the law on my side or maybe a weapon. But I'll be gone at moonrise. I can't see e'er other way, every man's arm raised against me."

Ellen was sitting in her stiff little chair across the hearth rocks, receiving his words, staring at the floor where the footmarks of the mob still stained the boards although she had swept them. Then she said:

"No, I'd go with you, Jasper, wherever you see fitten to go. I couldn't nohow see my way to stay behind. I'd go where you go and live where you live, all my enduren life. If you need to go afore sunup, why then I need to go afore sunup too. I couldn't make out to live on here with you gone. I'd have to go where you go and when."

They sat in silence for a time, repeating their decisions, approaching each other. He would go far, to the Beechgrove country or perhaps farther.

"Whatever this country feels to you, why it feels the same to me," Ellen murmured. "I'd have to go."

Then they held the thought together in mind, altering it and repeating it until it became a plan. They would load all onto the wagon, as long as it would hold, and leave the rest behind. "I'd want my plow and my axe, Jasper said, "but the balance of the wagon room could be for the house plunder. The team is strong and we can load on as long as e'er thing more can stick. We'd take the pigs and the chickens. It wouldn't be right nohow to leave them here to starve." The plan lost its strangeness as they talked of it, mellowed it, and presently it became inevitable. They would lie down awhile to sleep but when the moon rose they would awaken and prepare to go quickly.

Jasper awakened when, at midnight, the moonlight began to pale the air outside. He brought the wagon near the door, hitched for the departure, and Ellen called Hen and Nannie and Joe to help. Then the furniture was loaded onto the wagon, set snugly together, and as many of the utensils as could be taken, but the rest were left behind. Joe put the hens and the pigs into a coop together and this was secured.

Then Ellen gathered all the food that she had and all the foodstuffs, murmuring, "They did me harm, those men with the black rags on their faces," for the food was in no great quantity and there were seven to feed. Jasper made a warm seat of the feather beds and quilts near the front of the wagon, a place for the smaller children and Nannie to ride, but Hen and Joe sat near. By the time the moon was well above the trees they were on the road, the horses stepping briskly, for they must be far from the reach of this country before the night was done. They hurried down hillroads and over mire, or they turned at crossings without waiting to dispute of ways or to talk of destinations. The damp of the frost arose from the plowed fields that had been set in readiness before the spring. The stony fields and the rough hills lying around Rock Creek began to recede but they did not slacken the pace of their journey.

"Where are we a-goen, Mammy?" Nan said.

"I don't know. Somewheres. . . ."

"Some better place," Hen said. "Rock Creek is a poor country to settle in."

"A hard country, not gentle like you'd want," Ellen said.

Then Nannie began to talk about the sky, looking out upon the stars. "They are wide apart tonight, the stars, and they're a few, only bright ones."

"It's the moon sets the stars off and away like that, if you ever noticed," another said.

"I heared it said one time that all the stars have names. Wouldn't it be a thing to do now, to walk out of a night and to say, 'there's this one and there's that,' a-callen by name?"

"You could learn that in books," Dick said, "and that I'm sure. You could learn the names of all the stars maybe."

393

"Where are any books? We got no books," Hen said.

"And all the sky and how deep it goes, and whe'r it's got an end or not?"

"You could learn that too in books, it's said. I got a heap of books to read and ne'er a one have I read yet but two or maybe three. You could never read all the books in the world, I reckon, if you read all your days until you're old."

"I don't aim to get old. I wouldn't. Grow up is all I aim."

"But the wisdom of the world is the dearest thing in life, learnen is, and it's my wish to get a hold onto some of that-there. It's found in books, is said, and that's what I know. I couldn't bear to settle down in life withouten I had it. It means as much as all the balance of life, seems like. Books is what I want. In books, it's said, you'd find the wisdom of all the ages."

"Another year and I aim to have a crop all my own, share and share on some good land. I'm big enough to set out for my own self by now."

"Where do we think we'll go now, Mammy, and where will we stay tonight?" one asked.

"I don't know. A far piece from here."

"God knows!"

"Some better country. Our own place maybe. Our trees in the orchard. Our own land sometime. Our place to keep. . . ."

"In them you'd find the answers to all the questions you'd ever ask and why it's so. . . ."

"I wonder how deep it goes and whe'r it's got an end and what the end is like. . . ."

"And nohow I couldn't bear to settle down and not . . ."

"How blue it is, even of a night, and a little whiter round the moon, but deep in, as far as you can see. . . ."

394

They went a long way while the moon was still high above the trees, stopping only at some creek to water the beasts. They asked no questions of the way but took their own turnings.